Throne of Nyte

The castle housed far more secrets
than either had ever expected

BOOK TWO *of the* NYTE SERIES

ALEXANDRIA CAINLOCKE

Throne of Nyte

The castle housed far more secrets
than either had ever expected

BOOK TWO *of the* NYTE SERIES

Cover Design: Enchanted Ink Publishing
Book Design and Typesetting: Enchanted Ink Publishing

ISBN: 978-1-7352704-3-2 (ebook)
ISBN: 978-1-7352704-4-9 (Paperback)
ISBN: 978-1-7352704-5-6 (Hardcover)

Printed in the United States of America

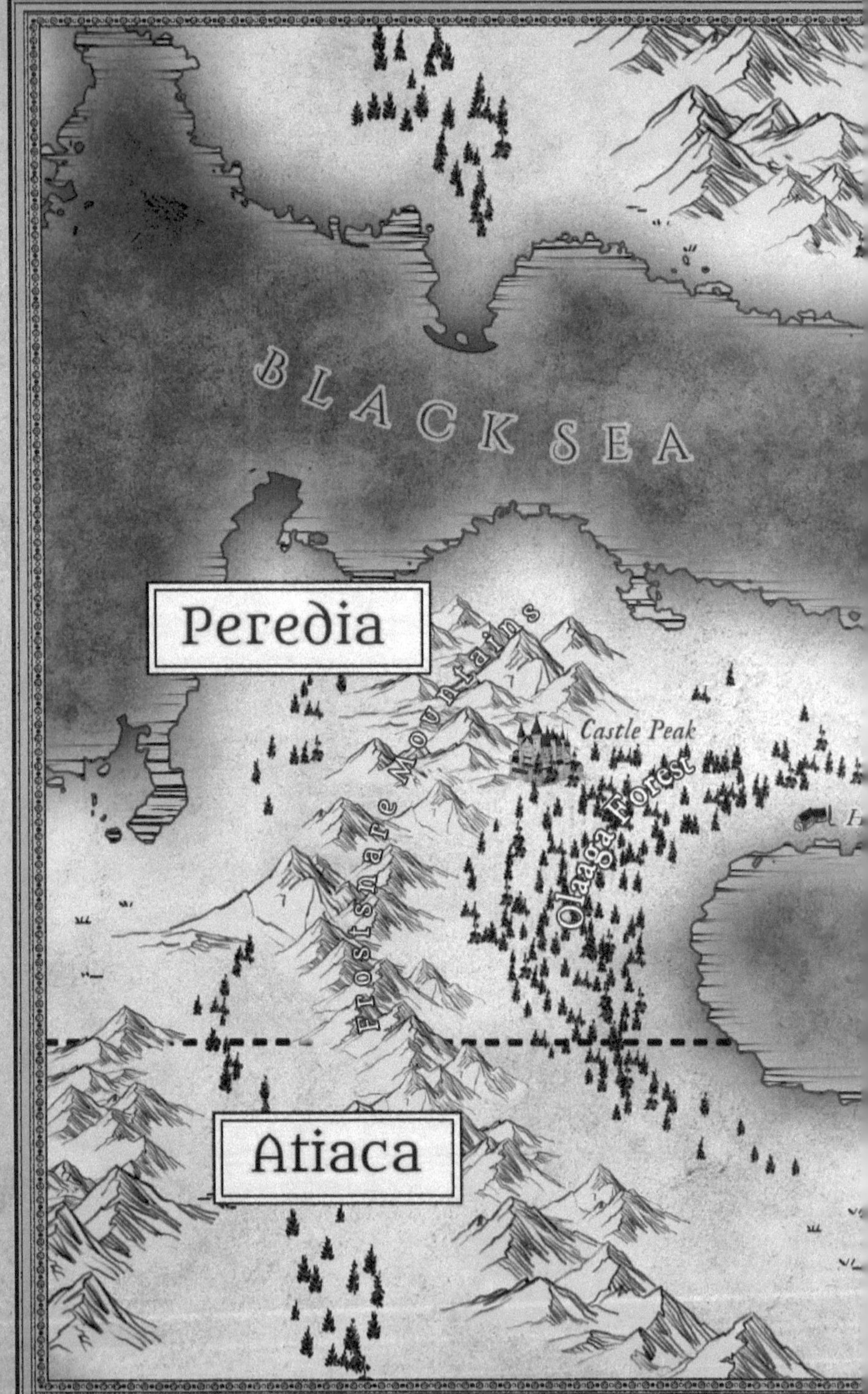

BLACK SEA
Peredia
Atiaca
Frostsnare Mountains
Castle Peak
Olaaga Forest

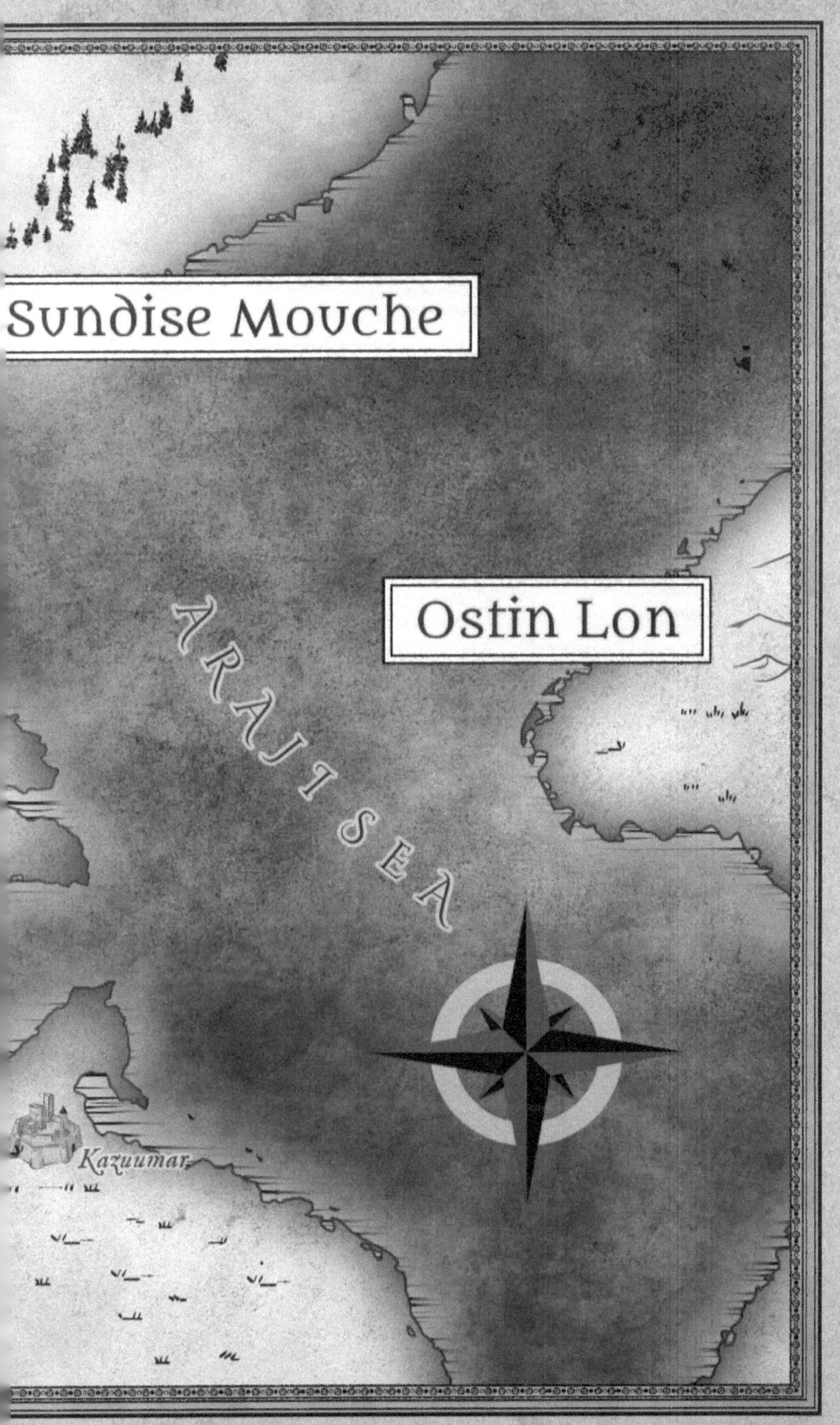

Sundise Mouche
Ostin Lon
ARAJI SEA
Kazuumar

PART I

THE MONSTERS THAT LIVE IN THE DARK

CHAPTER 1

Sweat beaded down the small of her back as Evangeline made quick work of ripping out the strands of her hair she had twirled too tightly around her fingers.

"I'm going to die, aren't I?" she said, more to herself, as she turned to stare at Raiythlen.

The Caster man leaned against the stone wall of her friend Lani's room. If it could be called that. A single bed, chest, and fireplace cramped the tight space. Trapped moisture saturated the air along with the rest of the underground slave quarters, but at least it was hundreds of steps away from the castle. And from those who would be searching for her.

Raiythlen's blue eyes gazed at her beneath hooded lashes. Thick black hair curled in ringlets around his face and hid the shaved horns on his head. A long-sleeved black uniform, worn by all slaves in the castle, covered the swirl of tattoos that splayed across his arms and chest. To anyone else, he looked human. Harmless. But she knew better. Had *seen* better. Casters, and all other species of Nyte, were far from harmless.

He didn't respond, not that she expected him to. She was worrying out loud. But judging by his expression, she had probably insulted his ability to protect her from whatever dangers were inside the cursed west wing they were about to enter. *He doesn't even know what's inside. What if the king's men are there? What if they drag me away? Execute me? I'm sure he wouldn't risk revealing his presence here to save my neck.* She closed her eyes, trying not to think about her dead foster father. The way his face had contorted in pain, how his hands had clawed at his throat as he'd gulped his last breath. *I'm going to die.*

The Caster leaned down and, from underneath the iron cot, picked up a large cloth bag. He thrust it her way, and she almost didn't catch it. "Change into these. There will also be some perfume in there. Use it."

Her cheeks warmed. "I didn't realize smelling nice was going to help protect me."

"It's to keep the Rathan guards from tracking you."

Evangeline formed an 'O' with her mouth. *Of course, I hadn't even thought of a Rathan's heightened sense of smell. They could track my scent.* Her blood went cold. Even if she left Raiythlen and fled Peredia on her own—not that she would ever leave Lani behind—the Peredian army would hunt her down and drag her back to be executed. Tortured. Whatever the king deemed a worthy death for the murder of his own personal advisor.

Evangeline mentally shrugged away those thoughts. "Where did you get all of this?"

"You're about to find out."

He took off his shirt, and she glimpsed blue and black Castanian symbols grazing his defined chest before she spun around. *I swear this Caster has no morals.* She scowled. *Not that I should be surprised anymore.* She peeked into the bag and pulled out a pair of dark leather slacks and a torso piece with small circles embroidered on the front. Instead of silver, they were the color of dark onyx. Peering over her shoulder, she found Raiythlen already dressed.

He caught her staring and raised an eyebrow. "Do you need help?" His lips curled. "I must admit, I'm better at undressing women, but—"

"Turn around, blast you!"

With an arrogant grin in place, he turned to give her some privacy. She quickly changed. The slacks and torso were loose, but fit more snugly than the other pair of breeches she had worn when she first escaped Castle Peak weeks ago. When she had attempted to prepare an escape route for herself and Lani and wound up saving this Caster. And Gods, had it been one of her worst mistakes.

Raiythlen continued to stare at the wall, missing Evangeline's heated glare in his direction. If it hadn't been for him, Evangeline wouldn't have been tricked into killing Ryker Ardonis, the Aerian who had protected her for most of her childhood—though he'd been less of an adopted father and more her abusive keeper. Beating her and even locking her up with Vane, Peredia's notorious torturer and Evangeline's personal nightmare. Who now had Lani in his clutches all the way in the forbidden west wing of the castle.

If it hadn't been for Raiythlen, Lani could've been safe. If the Caster hadn't threatened her and Lani's life, the two of them could've been far away by now.

But a thread of doubt curled around her mind, the same one always reminding her who she was—all her faults, flaws, and weaknesses. Would she and Lani, two helpless humans in a world of Nytes, even have made it very far on their own?

She didn't want to think too closely about that.

Evangeline pulled her long hair back into a rough braid. She knew she looked as haggard as she felt, with bags underneath her green eyes, her dirty blond hair sticking out in places and a thin body that looked more unstable than the bare trees of the Olaaga forest that surrounded the castle and its towering walls. Raiythlen dressed in the same attire but, while it made Evangeline look paler than a ghost, on him it looked natural. Made him appear more dangerous, like the predator that he was.

Curse this puss-filled Caster. If only he wasn't her best option for saving Lani. Her childhood friend, Ceven, would say otherwise. She imagined him running his hands through his cropped brown hair, sighing at her. His magnificent blue-and-gold wings twitching with irritation. But she wouldn't risk the king targeting him as an accomplice in her plans. He was an Aerian prince, destined for better things; he didn't deserve to be dragged into her mess.

Raiythlen handed her two daggers. She hesitated.

"Trust me, they don't bite," he quipped, and a cold smile settled across his lips. "And it's not like Ryker can punish you anymore."

Her nostrils flared, and she snatched the sheathed blades from him. *Spitting, puss-filled Caster.* She had only ever practiced with a sword—as a child in secret and during her private sessions with Prince Ceven and his Rathan friend, Barto—but the blades felt natural. Like they belonged in her hands.

"I enchanted them to strike true. No matter who your target is, if the intent is there and your hands are touching the runes, you'll hit them."

She lifted the handle and several Castanian letters were etched into the hilt, though she couldn't read them.

"You know that the west wing is huge, right? It could be days before we find Lani." Knowing her friend was somewhere in that crumbling building made Evangeline's jaw clench.

"Changed your mind?"

She scowled at him. "Of course not. I'm just being realistic."

After the welcome ball for Prince Ceven and Sehn, Evangeline had discovered her worst fear come to life: that her friend had been taken, like the other humans that had gone missing inside the castle for months, by a letter left by Vane. Her heart still rammed against her ribcage at the thought of Lani, the closest thing she had to a mother, to any parent, being in the hands of that sadist. She had spent the latter part of the night debating if going along with Raiythlen's plan was the best thing to do. But it was hard to weigh the pros and cons when the man wouldn't even share all the details of said plan.

She squeezed the handle of her blades, ignoring the fact that her hands were shaking. The thought of going to the west wing, of facing Vane . . . Images of herself trapped in the dark cell, his knife digging into her skin, the utter hopelessness she'd felt, sent icicles down her throat. She tightened her grip. Even if she was a human going up against a Nyte like Vane, she refused to fail. Not just to save Lani, but to put an end to that Rathan for the good of all humans.

Raiythlen glanced at her daggers. "You are not to leave my side while we're in there. I enchanted those to last ten swings, but I don't expect you to actually use them."

She bristled. "I'm well aware of my human shortcomings, but that doesn't mean I can't wield a weapon." But the hand she placed on the hilt of her dagger shook. "How are we going to get inside the west wing? There are guards crawling all over the castle."

He smirked. "I have a way, but you're not going to like it."

Frigid wind smacked at Evangeline's face as she climbed out of Lani's window—the better alternative than using the front entrance leading into the shared communal above them—behind Raiythlen. The sun had set, leaving the night colder and more desolate than its daytime counterpart. A hundred and four steps up the lit and winding mountainside was all that separated them from the castle, its white towers spearing into the inky sky.

Evangeline raised one leg at a time, trudging through the thick snow, the wind howling in her ears. Her clothes kept her surprisingly warm. Though she wished she had a coat to block some of the chilled air that pecked her exposed neck. They stopped a few paces away from Lani's window, the frosted pane set into a stone building, plain and unassuming. The complete opposite of the opulence that spilled from the castle.

Raiythlen stared into the distance with his arm outstretched and muttered something, but she couldn't hear over the wind.

"What are you doing?" she yelled over a particularly powerful gust.

"Look."

Evangeline squinted. She looked around expectantly, but aside from a few barren trees and shrubbery, she saw nothing. She said as much.

"Look again. Closely."

She was cold, tired, and had lost all her patience with the

Caster weeks ago when he'd first threatened her and Lani, which was why she cursed at him—then she felt it. It was electric. She peered out again, and this time, the space near Raiythlen looked distorted. The trees rippled like drops of rain falling into a bucket of stagnant water.

"What is that? What's happening?" Evangeline took a few steps back.

"It's a Shadow Door."

A Shadow Door. She remembered seeing something similar with Avana back at the cave (where she was first found as a child before her life inside the castle) just days ago.

"Or in other terms: a rift in space," he continued, as if he expected her to ask for an explanation. "It's connected to others like it all around the world. It used to be a popular form of transportation until somebody tampered with their balance." Raiythlen looked at her and narrowed his eyes. "You don't seem surprised."

She avoided his gaze, glancing at her hand instead. Underneath the black glove lay a mark emboldened with runes in the shape of a circle that took up the top expanse of her hand. It was the reason his sister, Avana, was so interested in her, why they had gone to the ruin in the first place. Before the Caster showed her true colors. "After the past few days, it's hard to be surprised about much anymore." Which was partly true.

He saw right through her lie. "Avana." His lip curled in disgust. "What other secrets did she tell you, I wonder?" His eyes seared hers, as if waiting for an answer.

Evangeline ignored his question. "So, this will be our way inside the west wing?"

"Yes."

"Is this safe?" She stared at the shimmering surface. The one she'd encountered in the ruin was nowhere near safe, the pressure around it enough to crush a person. Even Avana had said as much.

"Shadow Doors don't just teleport an individual; they temporarily make them cease to exist before reforming them on the other side. If not used properly, it could lead to potential death. So, no." Raiythlen smiled. "But don't worry, with me you'll be just fine."

That didn't reassure her in the slightest.

"When we get there, I won't know exactly where we will arrive. If we encounter any Nytes, let me take care of it."

Evangeline nodded and grimaced at the portal. *Well, if I die, at least it will be a quicker death than the alternative.* She chuckled a bit hysterically.

He held out his hand, and she stared at it a moment, reevaluating the decisions that had brought her here, before clasping it. He pulled her in close—too close. Her nose smashed into his chest, and his arms shackled around her hips. She tensed.

"There better be a good reason why you're crushing my face into your chest," Evangeline grumbled into said chest.

Raiythlen laughed, tickling her cheek. "Of course there is, my dear."

"Just get on with it," she barked.

"Take off your glove." He removed his own and drew something onto his skin.

She removed hers too and he enclosed his hand around hers while chanting in Castanian. His words echoed around them, and Evangeline felt like another layer of skin was being wrapped around her, her entire body sensitive—ticklish, almost.

Raiythlen touched the center of the rift. "Hold on tight." She gripped his plated shirt as if her life depended on it, and they entered the Shadow Door.

CHAPTER 2

CEVEN

Ceven ran a hand through his hair, tousling the knotted brown strands. He needed a shower after running around the castle all night. "There's no way that this is a coincidence."

Sprawled across the white loveseat with his arms crossed behind his head was Ceven's friend Barto. His gold pants and unbuttoned tunic shimmered in the light of the fire, making even more of a statement here, inside Ceven's single bedroom suite, than it had at the welcome ball that ended mere hours ago. Barto flicked his black furred ears sideways, but kept his eyes closed. His slender tail twitched back and forth and told Ceven that his friend was far from sleep. That made two of them.

"If you say that one more time, I'll start to think you're going crazy," Barto murmured from the couch, eyes still closed.

Ceven shot the Rathan a furious look, and Rasha, Barto's bodyguard, shifted closer to her charge. His own bodyguards, Xilo and Tarry, had split up. Xilo kept watch outside the suite, while Tarry was out looking for any sign of Evangeline. Or Lord Ryker. Both had been missing since the ball.

It can't be a coincidence.

The suite was quiet aside from the crackling fire, Rasha's leather padded steps not even registering as she glided across the marble. One sharp, furred ear prodded out from a set of tight braids. Ceven had always wondered if she had been born without a tail or if it had met a fate like her left ear, which had been removed in the line of battle, but he didn't dare ask. During his two-year stay in Atiaca with Barto, he'd quickly learned his friend got himself into more trouble than he knew what to do with, and Rasha was one of the few people who could handle him—and the tough situations that came with accompanying Atiaca's emissary. One of those situations being now.

"I figured you'd be more concerned, considering she's currently of interest to you as well." Ceven scowled into the fire, the flames licking and devouring the wood with the occasional ember escaping the granite fireplace.

His jab struck a chord, and Barto sat up, matching his scowl. "You know it's not like that. I don't wish the girl any ill-will, but this is beyond my control. Beyond yours."

When his friend had first told him that their empress wanted custody of Evangeline, Ceven had dismissed it. There was no way Evangeline was guilty of anything, let alone the missing persons in both of their countries. But what hurt him more was that Barto wasn't on his side for this—no, if Ceven was being honest with himself, it was the devotion Barto had towards his empress and country. All Ceven ever did was hate the king and this kingdom that he would never inherit, that his older brother, Sehn, was bound to rule in the next few years.

"I never took you for a coward," he said. It was cheap, and the farthest thing from the fierce warrior that lounged in front of him, but Ceven didn't know what else to say, what else to do. All he could envision in his head was Evangeline's shy smile. Her beautiful blue-and-green eyes squinting up at him whenever he teased her, before they widened in terror, her lips contorting into a scream as she was—

Gods, if anyone hurt her, he swore he was going to *kill* them.

The Rathan's yellow eyes dilated, his sharp words echoing Ceven's previous ire. "It's called loyalty. And at least I have more concern about Peredia going into a full-blown war than its own prince." Rasha moved closer to the couch, and Ceven didn't miss the look in her dark gaze. It said to be careful. As if he wasn't two steps away from begging them to just call this whole thing off and return home—and he might've done just that, but his stubbornness, the only thing he had in common with the rest of his royal family, prevented him from saying the words.

Ceven crossed his arms, wrinkling the black material of his shirt. "You're being dramatic. She's just a girl. This wouldn't cause the empress to do anything against us. Besides, Lord Ryker won't give Evangeline up." In fact, Ryker would be the only one to care besides himself. Nobody here would bat an eye if Empress Zelene decided to steal Evangeline away to Atiaca, as she was only one human girl. The king would even be glad—or maybe disappointed he wasn't the one to dismiss her. Ceven knew how much Evangeline's presence, the first human amongst the Aerian court (at Ryker's behest), dug beneath the king's skin. "The man keeps a sharper eye on her than you when you're with your sisters." And no one knew why the king's advisor had such an interest in an ordinary human. Granted, Ceven's thoughts on Evangeline were far from ordinary.

"Evangeline is the closest thing we have to clues on this, Ceven."

"So she shares a mark with the other missing persons. That doesn't mean she's behind everything."

"I'm not saying that—"

"No, you just mean to take her to be tried as a suspect, with no other evidence."

Barto growled. "Look, I'm not here to argue with you. You know I will have to go to the king with this information soon, and even he will see the importance of this, Ryker or not. As your friend, I told you first, but I won't betray my empress, Ceven."

They stared at each other, and a dangerous undercurrent shifted in the air.

Barto was the first to break eye contact, sighing as he sank back into the couch. Ceven's gaze returned to the fire, the only source of warmth in the room. The cold, overly formal room that he hardly used.

Do you ever get tired of staring at all this purple? Evangeline had said to him one night in this suite. Ceven had never thought much of it, only caring about what sat behind the display glass he had hanging on the walls or in shelves throughout the suite. Some encrusted swords with gems only found in the northern hemisphere, others bows with attached scopes made from refined glass imported from Ostin Lon.

My mother had this room designed for me, he'd told her. Beatrix's favorite color was purple, and while the room served as a comforting reminder of his mother, with the embroidered curtains, frilled bed linens, and purple-trimmed table coverings, it told nothing of who the true owner was. As if this had never been his home at all.

Ceven massaged his eyes, exhausted. All night he and Barto had searched the castle top to bottom, and there was no sign of Evangeline or Lord Ryker anywhere. The king didn't seem concerned that his advisor had disappeared, which only worried Ceven more. It made him think the king knew where Lord Ryker was, despite his nonchalance when he'd asked him earlier in the night.

When he glanced up, Barto was looking at him, a crease burrowing between his bushy brows.

"I promise no harm will come to her. If she's not found guilty, I will personally make sure she returns to Peredia safely," he said, the crease deepening.

Ceven sighed. He was tired of fighting, especially with a man who had always been on his side for the past two years. "We both know you can't guarantee that. The empress will have her put on trial. The decision is up to the people, and if they deem her guilty, no one can save her. Even if she's innocent, and I know she is."

Barto was quiet for a moment before he whispered, "Do you?"

Ceven's jaw clenched. "You can't seriously think some small, defenseless girl is capable of kidnapping hundreds of people. Come on, I know you're not that stupid."

"She isn't defenseless if she's walking around with glamours and working with Casters." Rasha's words were soft like the brush of metal. The fire reflected off the chains of the necklace nestled against her midnight skin, the frostlite stone a creamy white, showing the absence of magic. Her brown eyes held a predatory gaze.

Barto cast her a look, as if in warning. Ceven wasn't aware of how deep their suspicions had gone until now.

"I like Evangeline, I really do," he added when Ceven gave him a pointed look. "But you have to admit that her actions haven't screamed innocence."

Ceven pushed off the wall to prowl the room, his hands tucked into the pockets of his brown trousers. After the ball, he had stripped off the ill-fitting three-piece suit and traded it for his normal casual wear—loose-fitting trousers tucked into boots with a single buttoned top. His hand instinctually rested at his hip, inches away from his sword forged of Atiacan steel.

Barto gave him a sympathetic look. "I'm not blaming you. I know you were just as surprised to find her in a glamour in the middle of an Aerian ball. But she has been awfully close with that Caster, Avana, even going against Ryker and traveling with her beyond the wall. It seems she has more determination and guts than you give her credit for. Which isn't a bad thing, but we don't know the reasons behind it."

To say Ceven had been surprised to find Evangeline in a glamour looking like a red-headed Caster, was a severe under-statement. If her fake dress hadn't gone through his leg when she had run into him, he never would have known she was in a disguise—at least not right away. Still . . . "Evangeline's not like that."

Barto stared at him. "You haven't seen her in two years. People change, Ceven."

A knock at the door interrupted them, and the tension in the room rose another notch.

"Come in," Ceven said, his hand tightening on the sword strapped to his side.

Tarry strode through the front foyer, his black ringed armor meshed around a broad frame, the golden wings seared over his breast encased in stars, indicating the presence of a Royal Guard.

He paused before Ceven, standing just to his shoulders. His lips pressed into a thin line. "I saw no sign of either of them, Your Highness."

Ceven slammed his fist into the back of the sofa. There was a crack, and the fabric strained.

"But there is someone who knows where Evangeline is," Tarry finished, his eyes flicking to Barto and Rasha, whose heads whipped around to the room's entryway. Ceven frowned and followed their gazes to the doorway. A silent shadow stood in its frame.

"Hello again, brother," Prince Sehn LuRogue purred.

CHAPTER 3

An invisible force squeezed Evangeline from all sides. It stole her breath from her lungs, and the heavy weight compressing her chest made it impossible for her to take in air. She panicked and tried to claw at her throat, but Raiythlen's grip tightened. The world around them shuddered and blurred, then went black. A small bead of light grew in the distance, drawing closer—right before her face smacked into a bank of snow.

Evangeline coughed and sucked in big heaps of air. Raiythlen crouched beside her, his hand on her back. "It's okay, steady your breathing. In. Out. In and out."

She closed her eyes, inhaling and exhaling to the sound of his voice. At least she could breathe again. He helped her up, but the world spun too fast. He moved out of the way just in time for her to lose her dinner.

Holding her stomach, she groaned, "Never again." She wiped her mouth with her sleeve. "Ever."

He smiled, but it was gentle. "The first time using the Shadow Doors was an unpleasant experience for me, too. You handled yourself very well."

She frowned. She trusted him less when he was nice to her.

They weren't inside the west wing but behind it, in the courtyard that originally had been a garden. The building not only looked condemned, but foreboding. Withered vines overtook the gray pavement, and matching stone statues and benches lay tarnished and crumbling. The entire west wing showed no signs of life. No light and no sound. Even the wind had died.

Before she lost her nerve, Evangeline took a step, her hand on her dagger.

"*Wait*," Raiythlen snapped, jerking her back. "I told you to stay close to me. Do you want to die?"

Heat rushed to her cheeks. "Nothing's here," she fired back. "The danger is supposed to be inside the building. Not around it."

His expression didn't change. "You want to test that theory?" She crossed her arms. She wasn't that much of a fool. "There is something wrong inside that building," he said with an edge to his voice. "If we get closer, I may be able to find the source of the problem, but be careful."

She let him go first. Rumor had it that everyone who entered the west wing after the attack on the castle had never come back out. She chewed on her lip. *Please don't let us be its next victims.*

They approached what was once the back entrance, but rocks and hunks of stone blocked it. Raiythlen tapped her shoulder and gestured at a broken window on the second-floor balcony. He climbed an old lattice attached to the brick building with the deftness a Caster assassin should have. She followed suit up the lattice, its once-green vines now brown and decayed, crawling up the side of the wall. She wasn't as graceful as Raiythlen and stumbled onto the balcony. He gripped her shoulder to steady her on the uneven stone. It looked like it was going to cave at any minute.

"This way." Raiythlen helped her through the broken window, careful to avoid the jagged glass along its sides.

Their landing echoed throughout the vast room. It was pitch-black, and the sound of rats—or what she hoped was rats—and other unwanted rodents scurrying away bounced off high ceilings and a stretched space before an uncomfortable silence descended.

"Something is definitely wrong here . . ." Raiythlen trailed off, and Evangeline's gut tightened. She didn't want to hear that things could be worse than they already were. Before she could ask him about it, he said, "You were here for the ambush, I assume? I've only collected a bit of information on it. Is it true they never found out who the attackers were?" Raiythlen whispered, but it still seemed too loud.

"There are rumors, of course, but no one knows for certain." She carefully reached into the darkness in hopes her hand would graze a wall to help guide her. "The king claims it was a group of rebellious humans. But there had been no whispers of rebellion amongst the slaves. It seemed to happen out of nowhere."

Evangeline had been young but still remembered that day. She had just ended her morning tutoring session with Prince Ceven and Lord Ryker when the marble floor shook beneath her heeled boots. She flattened against the wall as waves of

Peredian soldiers poured past her into the west wing, their silver-and-black plated armor rattling like sirens. An explosion had corroded most of the hallways connecting the massive wing to the rest of the castle. When other soldiers, slaves, and Nytes went to investigate, none of them had returned, and since then the king had the entire wing severed from the castle. It now served as the last resting place of Queen Beatrix and as a giant thorn in the king's side.

"Here." His gloved fingers were smooth against hers as he pressed something into her palm. "Shake it."

She did, and the faintest bit of blue grew brighter from her hand. Flecks of yellow dust flitted inside a small vial, reflecting off its own light and casting shadows along the walls. At least she could vaguely see where she was going now.

"Most of the levels above us have collapsed or are highly un-stable. If Lani is going to be anywhere, it will be underground. There should be a staircase leading down around here." He paused. "Be careful. I don't know what I'm sensing, but none of this feels right." Raiythlen didn't wait for a reply, taking off and leaving her to catch up.

The corridor was dank, its coldness settling right into Evangeline's bones. The dull blue light bounced off torn, garish, green wallpaper. Her boots padded across cracked tile, trying to avoid the chunks of upturned floor, destroyed paintings, and folded rugs. She didn't see anyone else, not that she expected to, but it would still be more reassuring if she wasn't the only human this deep in the west wing.

Evangeline lurked along the sides, eyes wide. She was blind beyond the small glow of her vial, and the way her shadow flickered against the wall made her stomach flip. They encoun-tered an opening where the upper floors caved in.

"It doesn't look like we'll be able to get through. We'll have to find another way," Evangeline said.

A high-pitched squeal ricocheted down the hall from where they stood, swallowing Raiythlen's reply.

Evangeline jumped. The vial flew from her hand and shattered against the tiled floor. The squealing continued to echo off the walls, this time closer and louder. She flattened her hands against her ears, her heart pounding in her chest. *What in the mighty Gods is that horrible sound?*

A gentle touch on her arm jerked her out of her own frantic thoughts. Raiythlen was here. She wasn't alone.

As he pulled her farther away from the sounds, she asked, "What was that?" She heard the fear in her own voice but pushed it down. He didn't respond, and she had no choice but to continue following him. Their pace rushed.

"Raiythlen, I can't see a thing," she whispered, stumbling through the darkness.

His response was only to grip her hand tighter, keeping a brisk walk. His silence was scaring her more than the screams.

Another loud wail reverberated around them. It couldn't be human or any Nyte that she knew of. It sounded like the cries of a beast.

The next scream was right behind them, and they broke into a sprint.

Evangeline's heart pounded with pure adrenaline. She knocked into piles of broken stone and pain radiated up her legs, but she didn't dare slow down. Raiythlen yanked on her hand, and they whipped to the left. She tripped but regained her footing, trying to keep up with his long stride.

Suddenly, something cold and slimy wrapped around her leg. It jerked her backwards, her feet flying out from under her.

"Raiythlen!" she screamed. Her nails scrapped against the floor as something sucked her into the blackness behind her. She fumbled for her daggers as she kicked into the darkness. Her boot met something thick and squishy, and a horrible stench eroded the air.

Footsteps thundered to her right before she felt a *swoosh* as something flew past her face and into the monster behind her. The screech it released was almost unbearable, but the hold on her leg loosened. Evangeline scrambled to her feet and ran.

"This way!" Raiythlen yelled and grabbed her arm, shoving her into a room. He slammed the door shut, a lock sliding into place. Evangeline took a moment to catch her breath. Her throat burned, and her legs wouldn't stop shaking. *All that time training and I still can barely run for my life.* A disgusting, cold wetness lingered on her calf where the monster had grabbed her.

"Raiythlen?" she asked, scanning the room as much as she could. She cursed herself for losing the only light she'd had in this forsaken place. The outline of objects formed in her vision. Judging by the sound of her voice, they were in a smaller room. The screeching stopped.

"Raiythlen?" she called again, her voice still a whisper.

"Are you okay?" he said, inches away from her.

Evangeline flinched before collecting herself. "What . . . what was that thing?"

"Wretched."

Her brows furrowed. She had heard of the Wretched in her lessons with Ryker, but never in her entire life had she imagined she would encounter them.

"The Wretched are supposed to live only in the deserts of

Ostin Lon. How can they be here?" Her voice sounded shrill even to her ears.

"I don't know."

"Are you sure?"

"Avana and I used to take trips with our parents to Ostin Lon growing up. The Council had a research facility planted over there. Trust me, what we're dealing with here are Wretched."

"But aren't they supposed to be docile? Why are they attacking us?"

"I don't know, Evangeline. None of this makes sense."

Was he scared too? She stopped talking.

"Someone has to be controlling them," Raiythlen murmured. "That explains why..."

Evangeline waited for him to finish, but when he didn't, she prompted him instead. "Explains what?"

"It explains why I had felt something off before. There isn't just one Shadow Door here, but enough that I could sense a severe distortion in space."

Evangeline tilted her head. "Is that bad?"

She couldn't see him, but she imagined him giving her a condescending look. "When I use the Shadow Doors, I only use rifts that were created centuries ago. But these rifts . . . They're recent, at least within the past decade."

She rubbed her arms and squinted into the dark. Honestly, she couldn't care less. Right now, she just wanted to be somewhere far away from the Wretched. "So?"

"So, someone is opening these rifts for the Wretched to use," he said.

A dull thud came from outside the door, and Evangeline froze. They both sat in the silence as rocks crunched and skittered came from paces beyond the room they were stood in. Her nostrils flared, and her breath tangled in her throat. The shifting then echoed from farther away, but her heart didn't stop racing. She fingered the hilt of her daggers, but they wouldn't be enough to kill the things that crept in the dark around them. At least she didn't think so. "It isn't safe here."

"Obviously," he said.

"Well, you're just standing there talking about magical rifts," she snapped, "when we should be moving."

She let out a small yelp when he grabbed the front of her shirt. Her eyes widened, and the shape of his face appeared close to hers. "You don't understand," he hissed. "Creating a rift requires an enormous amount of magic and skill. And we're not talking about just one rift, but *hundreds*." He released her, and she stepped back, putting her hand across her chest. "Do you understand now?"

Evangeline nodded. "We're screwed."

"Pretty close to it," he said, and she jerked, not expecting this near-invincible Caster to agree with her. "There has to be an entire herd of enraged Wretched here. And whoever is behind them, they know about the Shadow Doors and, I'm assuming, the power behind your mark, both ancient, hidden magic. Whoever we're dealing with is far beyond my abilities. I just wish I knew how many are behind this, what their goal is."

This doesn't sound good. "How are we going to get Lani out of here?" The task had seemed impossible before, and now she was experiencing firsthand that it actually was.

"There should be a set of stairs farther into this chamber. If my calculations are correct, Lani is right below us."

Evangeline's mouth opened. She looked at the floor and, for the first time since they'd entered this dreaded place, hope sprouted. "Are you sure?"

"No."

Her smile vanished.

"But based on the layout, it is likely. It seems the castle had a private dungeon beneath the west wing, with tunnels connecting all over. They were made after the castle was built."

It still amazed her, the amount of information this man could gather. "How do you know?"

"I have eyes and ears everywhere. Remember?"

She knew he was smirking judging by the tone of his voice. She remembered Avana with her pet raven and Raiythlen with his mouse. Must be convenient having another set of ears and eyes.

A soft breeze told her he had walked past her, and she followed, making sure to match her footsteps with his. Every crunch and step sounded too loud, like the Wretched would come bursting through the door at any moment. Where was this blasted stairwell?

"You should know . . ." he said after a moment of silence. "The dungeon and tunnels, Casters formed them," he said. "This place was crawling in magic well before the attack."

She frowned, trying to focus on any sound over her pounding heartbeat. "But how? The king rarely worked with Casters." He didn't reply, and she caught on. "Are you saying Casters attacked the west wing?" She gave him an incredulous look. "That would be a declaration of war."

"Or they were working together in secret."

The weight of that knowledge lingered between them.

"Raiythlen, I can't see a blasted thing. How am I supposed to know where the stairwell is?" She hissed beneath her breath. She knew from experience he could use his magic to see in the dark. Would've been nice to have that again now.

He didn't answer.

"Raiythlen…?" She didn't finish when the floor beneath them rumbled. Right before the doors to their small room flew off their hinges.

CHAPTER 4

The air felt static, everyone's hair on end as Prince Sehn LuRogue glided into the chamber. He passed all of them and propped himself in the armchair by the fire. He pressed the collar of his beige shirt, which was unfashionably buttoned all the way to the top.

"I shouldn't be surprised." Ceven's tone dropped to almost a growl. "Of course you would be involved."

Sehn brushed his hair over one shoulder, away from the mass of his burgundy wings. Auburn strands of it illuminated like fiery tendrils in the light. "Please, Ceven. Not every conversation we have has to be unpleasant."

"With you, it's inevitable," he retorted.

Sehn met his gaze. Ceven had their mother's emerald eyes, but Sehn had the king's eerie gray. The only proof they had different fathers.

"I would like some privacy," his brother said.

Everyone's eyes shifted from Sehn to Ceven. Ceven had always hated to be alone with his brother, especially when they were children, but he was stronger now. He could defend himself. And he was sure the only way to find Evangeline was to entertain him. "Very well."

He didn't need to say anything as Barto and Rasha got up, Rasha stalking behind his friend, half her body still exposed as they left. Tarry remained expressionless, but Ceven could judge the reluctance in him by the shifting of his neck muscles.

"You can go, Tarry," he reassured him.

Tarry's lips pursed for a fraction of a second, but he bowed and left the two of them alone. Sehn crossed his legs and smiled. "My, how loyal he is. I wonder, when I become king, if he would show me the same loyalty."

"Where is she?" Ceven demanded.

Sehn gestured to the spot where Barto had been. "Won't you sit with me? You're making me nervous, standing like that. As if I'm going to attack you." Ceven didn't move, and Sehn sighed. "For a prince, you certainly lack manners. Very well, I'll indulge you, but I'm sure you're aware I won't be giving this information freely."

Ceven's gut clenched. "I wouldn't expect anything less from you."

Sehn folded his hands on his lap, and Ceven already knew what he was going to say. "I'm sure you'll recall our previous conversation."

"How could I forget?" His smile was callous as a roaring rage rumbled inside his chest.

"I'd like to revisit that subject. Mayhap this time you will have a change of heart, especially now that your . . . special friend's life is on the line."

Ceven flared his nostrils and reigned in the temper that tried to claw out of him. "Don't you think your price is a little steep?" His brother had been clear in his intentions. He wanted the king removed, but Ceven wouldn't play a hand in treason, unless he had a good enough reason to. One he wanted to make. On his own terms.

Sehn wasn't ruffled. "Depends. How much do you think Evangeline's life is worth?"

Her name on his lips unchained Ceven, and he was across the room in three quick strides, his arms planted on either side of his brother. "Don't test me, Sehn. I'm not beyond ripping the information out of you by force."

Sehn raised his brows. "Are you threatening your future king?"

"If you continue with this game, there will be no future king." His nails dug into the upholstery of the chair.

Sehn leaned back, twirling a long strand of his hair between two pale digits. "How adorable that you think you could beat me." His face hardened. "Remember, it was always up to me to put you in your place. Don't make me have to embarrass you again."

Ceven repressed a shiver. Ignored the buried instinct to shield his face as Sehn pounded his fists into him. Choked him. Held him down and snapped the tender bone and muscle in his wings. He snarled, "Where is she?"

Sehn's haughty expression didn't waver. "I'll tell you . . . after you do something for me first."

Ceven entertained the idea of wrapping his hands around Sehn's throat but took a deep breath and stepped back.

After his years of training with the Royal Guard and his time in Atiaca, he was confident he could take on the older brother who had tormented him throughout his childhood if push came to shove, but time was of the essence. "Depends on what it is."

Sehn fixed his collar. "During my time in Sundise Mouche, I've acquired quite a library of knowledge. Magic, technology, so many things that we've been missing out on."

"The point?" Ceven snapped.

Sehn's eyes narrowed. "Do you know what a blood oath is, brother?"

Ceven should have known Sehn wouldn't be quick about this. Evangeline could be in dire danger, and here he was talking in circles with a sadist. "So, you want to make a promise bound in blood. What's the blasted promise?"

Sehn sighed, as if he had the right to be impatient in this situation. "Not in the traditional sense. Clasping your bloody hand to mine will achieve nothing but disappointment. No, I want to make absolutely sure you follow through on your promise." He reached into the pocket of his pants, and Ceven steeled himself, but all he pulled out was a red vial. "With a few drops of Caster blood, I can ensure you won't betray me." His smile was sharper than the sword at Ceven's side.

Ceven, like most Peredians, wasn't well versed in Caster magic. Peredia wasn't fond of Casters or anything regarding them, but in this instance, Ceven wished he knew more. "And how can you be so sure?"

His brother's smile remained. "In exchange for Evangeline's whereabouts, I want you to make me a blood oath."

"I'm not doing anything I don't know about. Especially from you."

Sehn leaned back, his crossed leg dangling, his eyes illuminated. "Evangeline has been gone for quite some time. I know where she is, but that doesn't guarantee she'll still be alive. It's in your best interest to take my offer. In a timely manner."

Ceven's hands curled, his teeth bared, but Sehn was right. Time was of the essence. His deep-seated hatred toward his brother and the ground he walked on would wait another day. He needed to save Evangeline. "Very well. What are your terms?"

CHAPTER 5

Evangeline scrambled into a defensive crouch. Her eyes had adjusted, but she would've felt a lot more confident if she could see more than shadows.

In the broken doorway stood the outline of a creature. It was taller than the doorframe and double its width. The creature squeezed through the entrance, like black liquid pouring into another container, and slithered toward them, the sickening sound of wetness suctioning against the floor as it moved. In place of arms and legs were slimy tentacles, and though she couldn't see the small feelers at the end of each, she knew they were there from her studies with Ryker. One of its tentacles extended, its length stretching almost half the room, flicking about hastily.

Raiythlen and Evangeline remained frozen as the tentacle slid across the floor, missing them by just a few feet. The

Wretched were blind, and their ability to process information was no better than livestock except for a handful of Wretched that could speak, but all of them had superb hearing and killer instincts.

The walls rumbled, and it took Evangeline a moment to realize it was caused by the creature. It morphed into a cacophonous roar. Evangeline screamed when the tentacle lashed out, splitting the table next to her in two.

She fumbled with the blades at her sides, holding them in front of her. The Wretched moved fast, a whirl of black coming at her. She thrust out her dagger, keeping a firm grip on the hilt, her legs bent into the attack, like she had done countless times in her training. The Wretched's tentacle slammed into steel. The force of it pushed her backwards, and something warm splattered across her face. A tight ball uncurled in the pit of her stomach, an unfamiliar sensation unraveling inside her as the smell of the Wretched's blood hit her. The scent reminded her of a dead carcass and mildewed clothes combined, making her want to hurl, but after the wave of foulness washed away, an underlying smell, like seasoned meat, remained . . . and it tempted her to lick her lips for a taste.

A roar jolted her from that disturbing thought. She had hit her mark, but the creature didn't seem affected at all.

Raiythlen's figure swept past her, rolling out of the way of another tentacle. "Distract it!"

What? She didn't have a choice when more tentacles emerged from the creature's shadow, another screech piercing her eardrums. Raiythlen was on the ground, but she didn't have time to see if he was okay when she dodged a tentacle from swiping her off her feet. She panted, but kept a firm grip on her blades. Pushing everything from her mind, she focused on her target, on surviving. She widened her stance. Her eyes locked on its moving tentacles, watching them recoil and wind up to strike once more. *Come on, you big, stupid monster, attack me!* Her blood rushed in her ears as she waited, but they were no longer aiming for her.

"Hey! Over here!" she yelled.

The Wretched growled and Evangeline instantly regretted her decision. It darted at her, faster than Evangeline would have thought possible.

"*Aiiieeeeeaaaa!*" Her own battle cry mingled with the Wretched's screeches as she struck with her daggers. They found purchase, slicing a tentacle into bits, but her newfound confidence didn't last long when two more tentacles wriggled toward her. She lashed out again, her blade cutting through the Wretched's skin with ease, but one escaped her aim and knocked into her chest, the air rushing from her lungs.

"Eva . . . nge . . . line . . . ?" The sound came from the creature.

Three more tentacles emerged from its body. Searching and feeling over the floors, walls, and furniture. One crawled closer to her, and she started to move away when Raiythlen pressed a firm hand on her shoulder. She hadn't even seen him move from his crouched position on the floor.

"This one seems to have some intelligence," Raiythlen murmured. "Let it feel you. I want to gather some information from it."

"Easy for you to say. It wasn't just trying to kill you a moment ago!" Evangeline spat.

The tentacle squirmed toward her. It wrapped around her arm, cold and slimy and raising every hair on her body. With each flick of its feelers, Evangeline's heart slammed against her ribs. The dizzying, conflicting smell of decayed flesh and warm stew entering her nose, combined with the coolness of its feelers as they ran over her skin painstakingly slowly, made her shake. She dared not breathe.

Its feelers continued down her arms, to her legs, and over her feet—where it tangled around her ankles. Other tentacles around them lunged, but Raiythlen intervened, removing two small blades from his belt and severing them. The remains flopped against the ground like beached fish. Evangeline shoved her daggers into the flesh wrapped around her ankles. The Wretched bellowed in pain and released its grip.

"Brilliant plan." Evangeline scrambled backwards, desperate to get out of the Wretched's reach.

"We . . . not . . . harm . . . Evan . . . geline. Leave . . . here . . ." the creature spat.

"How do you know Evangeline?"

She gave him an incredulous look. *He's still trying to converse with it?*

"He . . . order . . . nnn . . . Wretched. Order . . . all of . . . mmmm . . . us." It gurgled up liquid from what she assumed was its mouth. "Protect . . . Eve . . . an . . . geline . . . nnn . . . our . . . queen."

"Queen? This Evangeline?" Raiythlen inquired.

Evangeline clenched her teeth. *Is he trying to antagonize it to kill me? Did he plan on killing me this entire time?* She lifted her weapon, prepared for anything. She couldn't die here. Not yet.

Its enormous shadow seemed to fixate on her. "Her . . . nnn . . . scent . . . nnn . . . the same. He . . . mmm . . . order. Leave . . . here."

Needles pricked the pit of her stomach. She understood what the creature was saying, but it made little sense to her. How did the Wretched know who she was? Who was the mysterious man pulling the strings behind them? And what did they want with her?

"Who is this man that orders you?" Raiythlen echoed. "What are you protecting here?"

The Wretched made another sound that was oddly similar to a laugh. "He . . . strong enough. He . . . take . . . back . . . nnn . . . world!" A high-pitched scream erupted from it. "We don't . . . nnn . . . answer . . . to you!" it screamed.

Raiythlen didn't move, but Evangeline didn't wait around to see what would happen. The heady mix of survival instincts and adrenaline compelled her, and she ran at the creature, using her momentum to shove her dagger into its chest. Something warm hit her face and body, but the slimy mass still moved beneath her.

"Watch out!" Raiythlen yanked her behind him and shouted in Castanian. Evangeline recognized the words "fire" and "embrace," but he spoke too fast for her to decipher the rest. The floor burst to life. Runes around the beast pulsated with a blinding light, tendrils of it rising from the ground to envelop the Wretched in a deadly embrace. Raiythlen had been drawing runes around it this whole time.

His shout commanded the runes to burst into a fiery blue flame, disintegrating the creature into an indescribable mass of flesh. Evangeline gaped at the dancing flames. With glamours and charmed daggers, she'd experienced only a taste of Caster magic. Being so close to something this destructive...Her eyes flicked to Raiythlen's figure. Now she knew why so many Nytes distrusted Casters. The power they held was terrifying.

Raiythlen's voice startled her. "Something you want to tell me, Evangeline?"

Her mouth was still open when she stared at him. "What do you mean? If I knew something, I would tell you."

"Would you?"

"Unlike you, I don't make it a point to deceive others." Ceven popped into her mind, all the lies she had fed him since he had returned to the kingdom, but she pushed it away. *That was different,* she convinced herself.

Their victory was short-lived, however, when the ground vibrated once more. An uncomfortable pressure entered the air, electrifying it. It was undoubtedly a Shadow Door, but it felt different from the one by Lani's quarters. This one was more prominent. Stronger.

"Go. The staircase shouldn't be much father in this chamber," he said.

"What about you?" Evangeline knew he could handle himself, but a single Wretched was one thing. A horde of them was another.

"I won't be too far behind you."

The leftover flames from Raiythlen's spell lit her path as she ran farther into the chamber, the walls coming together to form a hallway leading to a stairwell. He was right.

"Found it!" She gripped the railing of the staircase. It was made of iron, and some steps were missing, but it was accessible. Evangeline whipped around as the roar of several Wretched shredded through the room. As much as she itched to leave, she couldn't abandon Raiythlen. She needed him. Needed his magic.

"Come on!" she yelled. The dim blue runes illuminated the mass of monsters swarming in and Raiythlen's blood-covered figure running at her. She took a step, and the staircase groaned and rattled. *This is so not safe.*

Raiythlen shouted over another chorus of screeches, "When you find Lani, stay there! I'll come to you!"

"You don't seriously expect to fight all of those, do you? Let's just go, now!"

Tentacles emerged from the horde of Wretched, spilling into the room like tidal water. Searching.

Evangeline reached to grab Raiythlen, but he had other plans. "Watch your step," was all he said before pushing her down the stairwell.

She tumbled headfirst into the dark pit. Her hip slammed into something hard, and she bounced into an iron rail, broken bits scraping through leather into skin. Air rushed past as her shoulder and head knocked into more iron. Creaks, groans, and screaming Wretched drowned out her muffled cries. She finally stopped moving, pulsing fire radiating throughout her limbs, head, shoulders—blast it, she spitting hurt everywhere. She wiped the dust and grime from her face. The whole stairwell had collapsed.

"Raiythlen! Blast you!" she screamed when a series of sharp coughs cut her short. "I swear that Caster is trying to kill me!" She rolled onto her side, her body thrumming with pain. Nothing felt broken, the armored clothing having taken the brunt of the fall. She patted her sides but only felt one of the two daggers. *You fool, you left the other one sticking inside the Wretched.* She grimaced, but at least she still had one.

A burning aching didn't begin to describe how she felt as she got back on her feet. Between the endless bruises she now had and the blood and dust coating her entire body, she didn't know what was worse. She wasn't religious; she had stopped believing in the Gods long ago. The final tipping point was watching Nytes step over the body of a dead human girl who had collapsed from exhaustion. No remorse. Not even a second glance from the poshly dressed nobles and uniformed soldiers who strutted down the halls to their multi-room suites and warm beds. All while humans, like the dead girl, were picked up by an Overseer and chucked into a pit to be burned along with other humans who had perished under the weight of the Aerian rule.

Nobody cared, least of all the Gods, but still Evangeline prayed to whoever was out there to make sure Raiythlen made it out safe.

So she could kill him herself.

Darkness shrouded her again, the blackness swallowing her up. She couldn't even see her hand in front of her. The cold was damp, something she was used to from Lani's quarters, and her throat and eyes burned from the trapped dust. She ignored a burning desire to sink into a hot bath, like the one in Ryker's suite, and walked in what she hoped was the direction out of here. Her fingers grazed the wall for guidance, her footsteps crunching against broken rocks. The passage seemed to go on forever, and her patience was wearing thin. Sweat stung her eyes, but she couldn't wipe it away for fear of getting black ooze and Gods-know-what-else all over her face. And her hip was still protesting in pain.

Farther down, the inky pit was disrupted by a white light. No, wait, they weren't lights, but vents. There was a room right above her, but she needed to get closer to see.

Discarded furniture lay scattered about, and Evangeline brushed off a few broken pieces of wood and glass from a chair before dragging it beneath the vent. She climbed and peered through the cracks, squinting at the bright light. The room was open, with stacks of cells lining both walls. White light cascaded down from the ceiling, so high that it almost looked like the sun, but it couldn't be if they were underground.

Evangeline shifted on the decrepit chair to get a better view. Dark blurs moaned and twisted behind the iron cages. Footsteps pattered against cracked tile. The sounds combining into one low grumble against the uneven walls that were carved out of rock. *Raiythlen was right; there is something going on here.*

A shadow passed overhead, and she ducked.

"He's late. Again." The voice was low and gruff, but the words carried clearly. They were right next to her.

"What do you expect? That Rathan does whatever he wants. I don't know how he got promoted to officer," another replied.

The smell of cigar smoke wafted through the vents, and her face puckered.

"Probably because he scares everyone to death. The man's a spitting sadist. Just shut up and do what you're told and you won't end up like them."

There was a pause, then a drawn-out sigh. "I hate doing his dirty work."

Evangeline risked standing and glimpsed the two Aerians slipping away. They were fitted in silver mesh armor, but the lack of the golden wings emblazed in stars on their breasts told her they were only regular guards and not Royal Guards. Her brows scrunched together. *There are guards here? How are they alive with all the Wretched in this place?* She thought back to the speaking Wretched. If they were working together, how? Who was their leader? Was it the king?

She thumbed her dagger, but it didn't melt away how vulnerable she felt. Raiythlen said this was big, bigger than she could imagine, and here, alone, she knew she was getting in way over her head. *But I don't have a choice. Not if I want to save Lani.*

The guards didn't leave the room, instead migrating to each cell, rattling against them, yelling at the occupants. "Not her," the guard with pink-and-red wings said.

Their boots clacked further into the cavernous room, and Evangeline made her move. She pushed up on the vent, crawling through, her hips brushing the sides. This place was even more vast than she'd originally thought. She had to crane her neck to see all the cages stretching upward several floors. She covered her mouth in horror. Humans, all in their slave attire, curled up in cells, in pain. Marked, just like Lani.

And there had to be *hundreds* of cells.

How could they do this? But it wasn't surprising. Again and again, Nytes had proven they had no morals, no remorse. Then Ceven's green-and-brown eyes, crinkled into a smile, flitted inside her mind. *Not all,* she amended.

Evangeline was grateful for the sleek, black outfit Raiythlen had given her as she danced in and out of the darker parts of the room, shadows caused by structural beams connecting the floor to the ceiling of the cavernous dungeon. With nothing to hide behind, her only hope was for the guards to keep walking in their current direction, her sounds covered by their own chattering and the rattling of the cell doors as they passed. Though it was hard to tell if she was being quiet enough over the screaming inside her own ears, a side effect of imagining the guards or the king finding her and dragging her to her death.

Why is there a dungeon of this size beneath the west wing? The only one that she knew about (and had experienced firsthand) was below the east wing, where Ryker had locked her away for days and where Vane had tortured her. She'd felt like she was the only one down there at the time, but she knew the king had others locked away there, whether it be a human for stealing a plate of food or something equally petty, or a Nyte for insulting the nobles in the castle or getting tangled in love affair gone awry. So why would there be another dungeon? Especially beneath the formerly residential part of the castle?

Her clammy palms brushed the rock walls, and with every step the guards took, her heart thudded with such force she thought she would collapse. Raiythlen had overestimated her ability to defend herself against a Nyte.

The guards paused, then circled back. Right towards her.

Panic. *There's nowhere to hide, nowhere to go!* She whirled around—there. An empty cell beckoned her like a godsend.

The metal gate was ajar, and she swept in, closing the iron bars enough to make it appear shut but not lock herself in. It would be her luck to do just that. She plastered herself to the back corner, curling into a ball. If they passed by quickly enough, hopefully they wouldn't notice her presence. It was risky, but she had no other options aside from running.

They didn't notice, too busy mumbling to each other. But she caught the dark lines curling up their necks like their heads were a snake's afternoon meal. The skin beneath pulsed in different colors as if plagued by sickness, but they stood with a height that spoke of power, not disease. Those marks . . . she'd seen the same ones on Lani before she was taken. Why were they on these guards, too? What was going on?

When they were a comfortable distance away, Evangeline slipped from her cell. Moans and pained whispers still wrapped around her, but nobody paid her any attention. They all were curled on the floor like dehydrated corpses, and she shivered at the thought that this could be Lani, could've been her, when a light shining beneath the crack of a door caught her attention. And a woman's cry for help came from the other side.

Lani!

Evangeline kept to the pads of her feet, being as silent as possible even as her friend's cries pushed her to run, to yell back, to reassure Lani that she was here. But if those guards caught her, this would all lead to nothing. They both would die here.

So, with every scream, Evangeline bit her cheek and took another step. With every cry, her nails bit into her black leather gloves. One step at a time until she was face-to-face with a metal door, an opening engraved on top, perfect for her eyes to peer through. She reared back in horror.

Lani was wrapped in chains, a Rathan's claws sinking into her shoulders, forcing her to the floor. Another Nyte, an Aerian, stood on the other side, not dressed in armor but in a dark coat. His fingers grabbed a needle from the metal plate beside him, but instead of reaching for Lani, the needle pierced the pasty flesh of the Rathan, the sleeve on his forearm rolled up. Its sharp edge danced across his skin, red and black, adhering to the fleshy canvas. And all the time Lani whimpered, as if the needle were attacking her own skin.

Evangeline's hand wavered on the door, her teeth mashed together, her hands curled so tightly she thought she might break them. She wanted to storm in there. To shove them away. To protect Lani.

You're still a human. No matter how hard you train, you'll never be able to outmatch a Nyte. Ceven's words taunted her. A part of her knew he was right, but the other part wanted so badly to prove him wrong. To prove herself wrong.

Her fingers ached where she clenched her enchanted dagger. She didn't know how many lucky hits she had left, but she only needed two. With magic and the element of surprise on her side, she'd target the Rathan's throat, since he looked the more deadly of the two, and then stab the other Nyte in the heart.

Evangeline smiled and, for a moment, felt powerful.

She squeezed the hilt of her weapon, her palm resting on the doorknob, when bits of gravel shuffled behind her. Before she could turn, a firm hand on her shoulder whipped her around.

Her smile and bravado plummeted as she locked eyes with the King of Peredia.

CHAPTER 6

King Calais towered over Evangeline, his golden wings tucked tight against his sides, feathers dripping to the floor. He leaned down and graced her with his usual sneer, his white, braided hair falling over his shoulder and cascading down his black shirt and practical trousers. An outfit she would find on Ceven, but never the king.

"What an unpleasant surprise." His eyes, like cold steel, pegged her to the spot.

I'm going to die.

He snatched her arm before flinging open the metal door and dragging her into the room. The two Nytes bowed, their brows rising when their gazes met Evangeline's. Lani lay crumpled and defeated on the floor. She didn't lift her head.

"Leave." King Calais flicked his hand, and the two left, dragging Lani behind them.

Evangeline jerked out of the king's hold, reaching for her friend, but Calais shoved her back. She snarled at him, fury burning hotter and stronger than the logic warring insider her brain.

The king retaliated with a swift blow. Pain erupted in her cheek, and she stumbled into the wall. Her fury dissipated, replaced with a shot of fear.

"It seems Ryker hadn't trained you at all. Such disrespect." He surveyed her from head to toe, but it wasn't full of disgust, like his usual assessment of her. It was as if he were searching for something. "My, my, what an outfit." He inspected the caked blood on her face and clothes. His nose wrinkled, and she knew she reeked. "Certainly not something befitting your station. Or maybe it is. A sneaky, dirty spy." He snapped his fingers, and she flinched. "Tell me, why did Ryker send you of all people to spy on our little operation?"

Evangeline gaped at him. She'd been wondering all the different ways the king was going to kill her for murdering Ryker Ardonis. She'd imagined being hanged, burned alive, or having her head removed from her shoulders. And here he was, suspecting her of *spying* for a dead man. Did he not know? If he didn't, he would soon enough.

He raised a brow. "Or maybe he did it in hopes I would find you. And dispose of you myself."

She swallowed.

He laughed, and the feathers of his wings shook, the bright light overhead shimmering off the golden pieces. "Such a model display of terror." His lips thinned. "What little trinkets did he give you? Any defenseless human wouldn't have lasted a second in this place."

Trinkets? Avana had mentioned magicked jewelry that some Nytes wore to protect themselves against Caster spells.

Maybe they also used some for offensive measures, like Raiythlen's daggers.

I can't let him take away my dagger. It's my only chance of getting out of this mess. "Another accompanied me," she said. It wasn't a lie. "But I don't know what happened to him. I don't think he made it."

His eyes grazed her dagger, and she resisted the urge to shield it with her arm. *Please, let the king still be the arrogant tyrant he's always been.* If he took away her dagger, that would be him admitting she and her small knife cowed him, and his pride wouldn't allow that. Right?

"Describe him."

"B-black hair, about two heads shorter than you, with blue eyes," she stammered. Her fear had choked the truth out of her before she could think. To redeem herself, she fibbed, "He was a Rathan with gray ears and a white tail."

He didn't question her any further on that matter but asked about a new dilemma. "My advisor was supposed to meet me here tonight, so tell me, human. Why has he sent you instead? Surely that is why your pathetic self is here and not him."

It's because your precious right-hand man is dead. Killed by me. She inhaled through her nostrils. *I can do this. I can say a believable lie to the King of Peredia. I can survive this.*

Could she?

"He said he was meeting someone tonight," she started, keeping her tone level. Maybe she could throw him off her trail. Cast their eyes on other suspects. "He wouldn't tell me who." And knowing Ryker, he wouldn't have. He never answered her truthfully on anything—even when it came to her own past and the mysterious marking branding the top of her hand.

The king clenched his fists, and it was enough to stir acid in the pit of her bowels.

"Why am I not surprised he's with him again? Makes me think he's no longer loyal to his crown but another, regardless of how valuable he has been to our cause."

Evangeline kept her face placid, but her mind was working through the sludge of fear, calculating his words. Ryker had been working with someone else? Was it the same person behind the Shadow Doors and the Wretched in the west wing?

She was tempted to ask when the door creaked open and the same guard whose claws had been digging into Lani's shoulder poked his head in. "Another tribute is here."

The king's smile was wicked. Gray irises flicked to her, his lips twisting, as if debating whether to kill a roach that had entered his quarters. "Take this one to a cell. If Ryker so desires, he can pick her up himself." Evangeline blanched but didn't protest or move when the Rathan came in, seizing her forearm. "And I want you to track down a spy." He repeated her fake description of Raiythlen, and she hoped it was enough to not put him in any real danger. If he was still alive.

The guard nodded and pulled her out of the room. *I can walk by myself,* she wanted to spit at him, but she kept her chin down. As the door shut, the king pulled a necklace out of his pant sleeve, his thumb caressing the silver locket. She thought she heard him whisper, "Soon, my love," but then the door slammed shut.

To Evangeline's dismay, the Rathan had a friend, one guard from earlier, leaning against an empty cell. The pink-and-red-winged Aerian didn't bother looking at her or addressing her as the Rathan yanked her along. Being human was like being invisible. No, it was worse. She was vermin to them. Like rats in cages.

Her arm hurt where the Rathan's fingers bit into her skin. He laughed at something the Aerian said as they passed withering, dying humans in cages next to them. Her brain spun, thinking of ways to weasel out of this situation.

She still had her lucky dagger. Like the king, the guards thought themselves powerful enough not to be fazed by one measly human with a blade the size of her hand. And they were right. But this time she had Caster magic on her side and the element of surprise. They wouldn't be expecting an attack from someone like her—they hadn't even glanced her way. Their own arrogance would be their downfall.

Someone moaned when they passed another cell. A husk of a human withering away in the corner. Their footsteps were the only thing breaking up the cries of pain.

There were two of them. She'd only have the element of surprise for one, and she may be too slow to land a hit on the other. And what if the dagger didn't hit its mark? How many lucky swings did she have left?

They stopped in front of an empty cell. A white static clouded her thoughts.

"Move, human." The Rathan shoved her forward, and his friend hovered close to the cell.

Now!

Evangeline used her own momentum and pressed her palms squarely on the Aerian's chest. He stumbled back as she unsheathed her dagger, chucking it at the Rathan behind her. She just needed one lucky hit.

Before the pink-and-red-winged Aerian could push to his feet, Evangeline slammed the cell door shut on him at the same time the Rathan behind her yelled in agony. She twisted on her heel and sprinted. But not fast enough. The guard—now with a dagger sticking out of his chest—grabbed her. Like Barto and Ceven had taught her, Evangeline brought up her knee, knocking away his hand before she pounded the hilt of the blade deeper into his chest. The Rathan pulsated in pain, his claws lashing at her face as he collapsed to the floor. The Aerian guard shouted at her, but she couldn't hear over the white static in her head.

She needed to get out of there, fast.

Blood trickled down her cheek, the air burning the claw marks on her face as her boots stamped into the ground. She didn't know where she was going, but she didn't care; she just needed as much distance as possible.

Smaller hallways branched off, and she turned, hoping it wouldn't be a dead end. She was weaponless, with no definite way to escape, and Raiythlen was surely dead or incapacitated. Gods, she was so screwed.

The hallways were narrow, the rock on the sides less refined. Her fear of a dead end didn't happen, but the hallway stretched on, branching out again.

I'm going to get nowhere at this rate!

She didn't have time to waste; she had to think. Where would Lani be?

The cells in the large room were a possibility, but there had to be a way around, maybe a path up to another level? One where she could have a better perspective of the room and avoid the calamity she had caused with the guards.

She went with her instinct, taking a left on what she thought would lead to the opposite end of the cavernous room. Luck had to be on her side when she stumbled on a staircase. This time brick and tile made up each step, with a mosaic inlay. As if this wasn't recently added on, but an original piece of the west wing, mayhap even older, since she had seen nothing like it throughout the rest of the castle.

Her padded feet climbed the stairway, but instead of opening up into the cavernous room, it spiraled up another level. Of course, it wouldn't be that easy, but she couldn't turn back now. She just had to hope there was something useful up these stairs. Maybe it was a way out of the west wing for her and Lani to use. Or a room conveniently full of weapons.

She snorted.

Her hand grazed the wall, the steps winding, and winding, and winding . . . A familiar ache formed, and her head felt heavy. *No . . .*

Evangeline snapped her eyes shut and pinched herself, but the pull on her mind was too strong. She knew what was going to happen but couldn't stop it as she fell over and sank into the darkness.

CHAPTER 7

The stairway and uneven walls faded from Evangeline's existence, morphing into another room where rock and stone floors still enclosed her. The cool dampness of it seeped into her bare arms; she wore only a short-sleeved blue top, untucked into tailored pants with fine beading along the cuffs. Both were soft against her skin as she followed a familiar-looking face.

"I discovered this beauty not too long after we stormed the castle," Jaden said, his black shoulder-length hair pulled into a tight bun. Green eyes set into a tanned, handsome face met hers as he pulled something from the wall.

Evangeline recognized the dark bottle he held, and then looked around at others just like it, resting in row after row, spanning a few heads taller than herself. Her lips pulled into a smile. "Your greatest discovery yet. This has to be the best aged wine in all the land."

"I say we celebrate our findings—and our victory."

She let Jaden pull her along up the spiral stairwell next to the cellar. Blue, yellow, and white mosaic tiles decorated each step as they made their way to the top. A door greeted them at the end of the hallway, a part of the castle Evangeline hadn't seen yet.

Multiple rugs, each with a unique pattern, littered the floor between couches that hung low. Maroon and gold designs fashioned the walls, and hanging lamps trimmed with dangling beads dimly lit the space—which was unusually small and cozy compared to the rest of the castle.

"A private room for our private celebration. How quaint." Evangeline raised a brow at Jaden, who had let go of her hand to present her a small bow.

"It looks like the Council had used this room for wine tastings. Judging by the decor, they wanted to pretend they were far, far away from Peredia." He placed the bottle on the knee-length table that sat between the sofas and procured two wineglasses from the shelves fixated to the wall. "And now it is ours."

Jaden poured them both a glass, and Evangeline took it, raising it for a toast before taking a sip.

"Too bad we don't have any guests to share it with." Evangeline swirled the red contents, its liquid burning all the way down her throat, along with a hint of remorse and something close to guilt. The sacrifices it took to claw her way to the top of this world . . . were they worth it?

Jaden raised his glass, oblivious to her thoughts. "Soon, we will. The entire world will recognize us for who we are, and when they feel the echo of our power, they will come."

Evangeline sat down on the sofa and crossed her legs. She peered up at the man she had laid down her life for and loved with a burning passion that she held for no other. And as if a veil had been lifted for the first time, she suddenly looked at him more closely. Differently. Had the man she'd grown up with—fallen in love with—changed?

Or was it she who had changed?

Evangeline came to, her head resting on the floor. She brought a hand up to her temple, where a dull throb remained. At least she had made it up the stairs. She didn't know if she could handle falling down another flight today.

She gripped the wall, hefting herself to her feet. Her surroundings looked eerily similar. At the end of the hallway a door greeted her, the same one from her hallucination.

The taste of blood didn't linger in her mouth, not like it had in the past when she'd experienced these hallucinations, dreams, or, as Avana had said, memories.

Memories of what? And from when?

Her nails scraped along the jagged edges of the wall, her brows shoved together. Not only did she have to deal with being a human facing a horde of Nytes, but she was also fighting against herself. Her own growing sickness, increased hallucinations, loss of appetite, and changing body.

Shaking off the pain that thrummed in her head along with her previous scrapes, bruises, and aches, she stretched toward the door. Her cheek still burned, and she was sure her face was a mess. If what was behind that door was the same room as the one she had seen, she could, at the very least, take those wine glasses, shatter them, and use the stems as makeshift knives.

Better than nothing.

She crouched beside the door, taking a breather. Gods, she so badly wanted to lie down and rest. Adrenaline had gotten her this far, but her energy was dwindling. She'd love nothing more than to close her eyes and not have to worry about anything for a while. But right now, she couldn't afford that luxury—not with Lani's life on the line.

Steadying her breath, she closed her eyes and listened. Far away shuffling reverberated off the rock walls, whether from guards or the humans moving about in the cages, she didn't know. A low hum echoed across the rocky underground, but she couldn't decipher what it was. It could've been her own mind, still humming in pain, for all she knew. She pressed her ear against the wood frame to get a better sense of anyone on the other side. No footsteps, or the mumblings of another person. Nothing that hinted at a Nyte waiting to kill her.

Her fingers grazed the knob of the door, her heart thundering. This could very well be the end of the road for her, but she had to do something.

The door was quieter than expected as she slid it open. The maroon-and-gold patterned walls didn't surprise her, but the state of them did. The wallpaper hung off them in curled chunks, like worms she would sweep away in Lani's room. Her boots padded across pockets of carpet sprawled across the concrete floor. No rugs. A single overhead chandelier illuminated a pair of sofas—one of them occupied.

Evangeline froze.

Fortunately, the Aerian looked to be sleeping, his chest rising and falling in a slow rhythm. His wings stayed tucked to his sides, the pink, red, and purple feathers looking softer than the dull sofa they rested on. He didn't look to be a guard, donning a black coat instead of plated armor, and upon closer inspection, she recognized him as the same Aerian who had been in the room with Lani. While that Rathan had forced her friend to the floor, this man had woven a needle into that Nyte's flesh, inking him like those guards. Except, she didn't see a single marking on this Aerian.

Her skin prickled with bumps, her teeth slamming against one another. She wanted to make him pay, to suffer like all those humans rotting away in those cells. Her eyes shifted from his sleeping form to the half empty bottle next to him. She wetted her lips as if she could still taste the wine from that memory.

The bottle was uncorked, with no glass beside it. But to her luck, a shelf of glasses sat on the other side of the room. Red cloths now covered the wood shelves she'd seen in her memory and looked to have a hefty layer of dust, but it held several glasses all the same.

She knew what she had to do.

Her knees stayed bent as she shifted her weight to make no sound as she crept across the room. Every snore, every shift of his body, made her pause, waiting for a few stammering heartbeats before continuing.

Glass in hand, she now hovered over the sleeping Aerian. His nose was slanted, his lips as thin as the silver chain necklaces hanging between the unbuttoned coat that hung down past his waist. Her nostrils flared as she pictured Lani whimpering in pain while this Nyte stood there and accepted it. As if it were any other day. She couldn't take away the suffering this Aerian had caused countless humans, but she could avenge them. She could make sure this Aerian felt the same pain.

Her finger curled around the stem of the wine glass. She would only have a fraction of time to smash it against the concrete floor before angling the broken stem at this Aerian's throat. Or, on second thought . . .

Crash!

The glass smashed into smithereens at the same time the Aerian jolted straight up—and stilled. Evangeline applied just enough pressure against the tender crevice between his thigh and groin.

"Make one move and I'll shove this glass so deep you'll never be able to piss again," she said, mustering as much venom as she could into her voice. She felt alive, like every joint in her body was wound tight and prepped to fling into motion at any second. Her gaze fixated on the man's brown ones, his face oddly plain for an Aerian possessing wings with all the colors of a sunset.

"What . . . what's going on?" His words sounded heavy, and his lips were stained red, like the ladies of the Aerian court.

"My friend, Delani Thompson, she was in the room with you and that Rathan before the king came. I want you to tell me where she is. Give me a spitting poor answer and I'll cut you to pieces." She pressed harder, and the man squirmed, eyes widening as his drunken stupor faded.

"Now, calm down. You got this all wrong—"

"Not the answer I'm looking for." She prodded the tip of the glass stem deeper.

"Okay, okay! Stop! I'll tell you, please, just . . . please stop?" He raised his hands in a gesture of surrender. Evangeline wondered how many humans had cried for mercy and if he had ever shown them any. She didn't let the pressure up.

"Start talking."

"Look, I'm not the enemy, though it may look like it—" Her hand moved, and he spit out, "She was taken to the isolated holding cells! I don't know why. That was just the orders we were given. I was told to look after her wounds, to make sure she didn't die. I'm a healer."

"Didn't look like you were healing anybody the last time I checked."

"If you let me explain—"

Her makeshift glass needle cut his words off as she shifted her palm. "Where are these holding cells?"

"It's pointless! She'll be locked up, and only Officer Vane has the keys. You wouldn't be able to get her out anyway!"

Nausea crept up her throat at the thought of Vane. But of course, it was his note that had brought her here. She had known she was potentially going to face him. "I'll be the judge of that. I won't ask again, where are the blasted holding cells?"

He shook his head but complied. "They're down these stairs and across the hall, adjacent to the main dungeon. It'll be a room with a metal door. You'll know it when you see four claw marks gouged into its frame—don't ask how they got there, you don't want to know."

She did want to know, especially if it was where Lani was, but more importantly . . . "You better not be lying."

"I'm not!" His face darkened. "Despite what you think, I want to help you. I want to help all these blasted humans."

"Sure you do. And while my knife is pressed against your crotch, I'm sure you'd promise to behead the king and save all the humans of Peredia while you're at it."

"Look, you seem capable of handling yourself"—he glanced up and down her person—"and even if you don't believe me now, if you ever change your mind, I think you'd be a great addition to our cause."

Evangeline frowned. Well, this was unexpected. Her plan of shoving her makeshift knife through this man, watching him holler and bleed out right before she stabbed his neck withered away. What if by some chance this Aerian was telling the truth? After all, she'd risked her life on a rumor about Nytes who smuggled humans out of Peredia in the nearby town, Helgard, when she'd first trekked beyond the city walls.

But even if she were foolish enough to consider the possibility that he may be telling the truth, she wasn't stupid enough to remove the knife altogether. "And just how do you plan to save these humans? There must be hundreds here, and even more in the rest of the castle. You don't seriously expect me to believe you could save everyone."

His brows knitted together, a pained expression crossing his features. "No . . . of course not. Many lives have been taken, and many more will follow. But I vow to save as many as I can. There are many of us, hidden throughout the castle, and more in the city. I can't tell you what we have planned. There's not enough time."

"Maybe, but if you mean to help us humans, you can start by saving my friend Lani." It was dangerous, trusting this Nyte even a bit, but going alone across unknown territory was also an enormous risk.

"I can't." He glanced at the bottle of wine, his face twisting into a grimace. "I have to go back and continue the king's work. To gain leverage—and information."

Evangeline now wondered if he had been drinking to ease the guilt he felt. For continuing the suffering, even if it meant it was all for a bigger cause—supposedly.

She sighed and removed the makeshift knife, sliding the glass pick into the band of her waist. "As much as I would love to save everyone here, it's a lost cause. The king and the Peredian army are unstoppable. Even if managed to get these people out of here, more would take their place." The only way to put an end would be to chop off the head of the operation. To kill

King Calais. And there was no way she'd be capable of doing that.

The Aerian stood and backed away from her, as if she may try to stab him despite her words. "But we still have to try. If you ever change your mind, look for the cut of an ear, four marks of freckles that linger beneath the eye, or a scar above the mouth. Those marks will show who is for our cause." She noted he had none of these marks. Then again, she assumed some members would need to be discreet. If everyone was identifiable, they would be sniffed out and killed.

She shrugged and half-turned toward the door, still keeping an eye on him. "Maybe. I won't promise anything."

"The name's Petri, by the way."

"Evangeline. Though, if you've been in the castle long enough, I'm sure you knew that."

He nodded. "I hope you find your friend, Evangeline, and may the Gods watch over you. You're going to need it."

CHAPTER 8

Ceven wiped the Wretched's black blood from his sword onto his black pant leg before sheathing it. After his unpleasant encounter with his brother, Sehn had told him Eve's location. And that she was responsible for Lord Ryker's recent disappearance. His mood had darkened. At first, he'd thought it was some trick of his brother's. There was no way Eve was in the west wing. But they hadn't been able to find her anywhere else, and his brother was right about one thing: If she was in danger, their time was running out.

For tonight's endeavor, he opted for his plated bracers and woven chain mail to encase his body. The metal was stained, allowing him to blend in more with the low-lit surroundings while giving him protection and the ability to move more freely. He also plated the arch of his wings to protect the tender muscle there.

"What in sea watery hells are the Wretched doing here?" Barto said behind him, dressed similarly, trading his gold attire for hardened leather, molding to his body like a second skin.

Ceven would have felt better leaving his friend and his two bodyguards, Rasha and Quan, behind in his suite. But years of strategy and training with the Royal Guard as a child had taught him it would be wiser to keep him close. To make sure his friend didn't go behind his back and kidnap Eve—or involve the king in this matter. Just the mere thought made him frown, and he couldn't meet Barto's eyes.

"I don't know. None of this makes sense." And it didn't. He didn't know why Evangeline was here, or why the Wretched— which belonged on the other side of the world—now resided in the west wing. They'd first encountered the disgusting creatures on their way to the detached wing using the maze of tunnels beneath the castle. Only Ceven and a few other members of the royal family knew of these escape routes that had been used centuries ago, when Peredia was last at war. Trusted guards maintained and guarded these tunnels, sworn to secrecy and protecting the castle, but most had already been dispatched. Either by Wretched or whoever else was down here, Ceven didn't know.

"I have something here," Quan said, another Rathan companion who had traveled from Atiaca with both Barto and Rasha. He served as Barto's second protector, though where the sleek and powerful Rasha stayed close to their charge's side, the bald Rathan was often a distance away, watching and collecting information from afar.

The Rathan warrior crouched near one of the Wretched, his thin leather armor encasing only parts of his body. Ceven could make the outline of his russet arm as he smudged the ground with his gloved hand. "A Caster was here, not too long ago. Judging by the language and the style of writing, this was done by an expert."

Although Ceven was physically stronger than his Rathan companions, he envied their eyesight and keen sense of smell. While he could only make out the basics of what once had been a sitting chamber, he could hardly see these Caster symbols.

Xilo hovered over Quan's shoulder, his long black hair streaked with gray, braided back to nestle between purple wings. His slanted eyes narrowed at the ground, his deceivingly calm demeanor not giving away the tension that hung in every muscle in his body. Much like Ceven's other bodyguard, Tarry, the two Royal Guards were similar and very different. Having grown up all his life with both, Ceven had learned how to read them, and also when to sense a dire situation. Though Ceven didn't need to look to Xilo to know their situation was dire right now.

He couldn't see, but he was sure the frostlite rings on his bodyguard's fingers were whirling with a dark blue, much like his own frostlite necklace he kept tucked in his shirt. Unlike the rest of the Aerians in the castle, he hated the feel of jewelry on his skin, much preferring to admire it from afar. But he needed whatever protection he could get, especially if he was going up against Casters.

Barto pursed his lips. "If a Caster is here, that doesn't bode well." His carefree friend was more serious than Ceven had ever seen him these past couple of days.

"I hope the other two didn't encounter any problems," he said. Rasha and Tarry had left to explore the wing further, left with explicit instructions to keep quiet and not engage in any battles. It was why Ceven accepted his limited eyesight. He didn't want to draw any unwanted attention with a torch or lantern. "Let's keep moving."

The four of them ventured farther into the room. They had entered the west wing while the moon was high, and with how long it took them to get this far deep, it had to be almost dawn. Though it was hard to tell, since the entire wing seemed to hang in a cloud of black smoke. The air was thick, with every corner of the room shrouded in darkness and no chance of light coming in. The chilliness in this place even transcended the usual winter coldness.

As the two Rathans ventured farther, Ceven tugged on Xilo's armor-meshed shoulder. Blue eyes found his.

"Keep an eye on them. I don't know if they're planning something, but I don't want it to be a surprise if it happens." The words were a soft blow to his gut, but he had to stay aware of his situation. Ceven didn't want to think his good friend would betray him, but to believe that would never be an option would be foolish. Xilo nodded.

They all approached a crumbled mess of rock at the back of the room. The warped iron railing was the only indicator that this used to be a set of stairs.

"Dead end." Barto swept his hand over a tarnished chunk of flooring and brought it to his fingers. "It reeks of Caster. I can smell the blood and charcoal."

"But no scent of Eve or Delani?" Prior to entering the wing, Ceven had swung by Lani's room, which was smaller than his closet, and picked up a few things belonging to her and Eve. He didn't need any reminders of Eve's scent. It was one he had grown up with. Whenever he smelled lilac and vanilla, he always thought of her, but it helped the others in trying to find them in this desolate labyrinth.

Barto shook his head. "I'm not sure, but it's a possibility. There's a mix of smells, but it's too fragrant, too fresh. Almost like perfume." Something clicked in his expression at the same time Ceven's did. "Either she or someone else is covering their scent."

Quan's furless ear flicked, the only giveaway to any emotion in his character. "It's clear a Caster was here, and if the human is hiding her scent, she doesn't want to be found. She's picked her side."

"Her name's Evangeline," Ceven growled.

Barto held up his hand but also shot Quan a look of distaste. "Now is not the time to share your prejudice, comrade. She may be working with a Caster, or it could be someone else entirely. Let's not jump to hasty conclusions."

Barto's words triggered the last bit of Ceven's conversation with his brother. When Sehn had said, *you say my price is too steep, but you don't realize how much of a bargain I'm giving you. Not only will I tell you where Evangeline is, but also the means to protect her. After all, it won't be long before the king finds out she was behind his advisor's death. And nobody, not even you, can protect her from the wrath of the Peredian army and its bloodthirsty king.*

That detail would've been like a blade to the gut. If he had believed him. Now, faced with the fact that Evangeline could be working with a powerful Caster like she had in the past, he felt the blow of those words hours later. And what Sehn had meant. The last time his brother had asked him to help murder the king, he'd refused, but if Eve was behind Lord Ryker's death, eliminating the king would save her from certain execution.

I'm not the same girl you used to know, Eve had said to him. She was right. She wasn't the same person, and he continued to underestimate her.

They surveyed the room, but it seemed they were at a dead end. The smell of blood and magic was promising at first and had led them this far, but now there was nothing left to show for it. He clawed through debris and the flesh of Wretched to see for himself if any sign of Evangeline was here. It was dark, and only seeing the outline of what he was searching for irritated him, but his determination paid off when he spotted something small and round. It was a ring.

He rubbed off the caked blood, and even with his Aerian eyesight, he could tell how much it was worth. The band was thin, but the jewels encrusting it were not cheap. In fact, out of all the artifacts in his collections, from ruby-encrusted swords, gold-laced bows, and ancient crowns made from diamonds, this small ring out-valued all of those. Ceven stared in awe at the rare gemstones, reminding him of opals with the way so many colors refracted in the low light, but they were more transparent, like glass. Despite the surrounding destruction, the stones remained unmarred, unaffected by heat or abrasion with a cut that was specific and hard to tailor for a ring of this size. Even the name of these stones eluded him; he had only heard about the rarity of such a gem from craftsmen.

On the inside, something was etched. "Will you be my queen?" Ceven frowned, and his first thought was of his mother, Queen Beatrix, but he had never seen her wear this before. He certainly would have noticed.

"What's that?" Barto weighed one hand on Ceven's shoulder, and he was tempted to hide the ring, as if his friend would know the worth of his find.

"Just a ring." He shrugged.

Barto wasn't buying it. "Judging by your smile, I'm thinking it's more than that. Let me guess: you're going to add it to that weird collection of yours."

"It's not weird," he mumbled to himself as his friend peered behind him.

It was then the stirring of rock or debris, revealed footsteps, but they padded lightly as if they were trying to disguise their presence. Even a spy would have trouble navigating discretely through all the ruined furniture, bodies, and crumbling structure with little to no light.

Save maybe a Caster, he thought, with no small amount of jealousy. He withdrew his sword, and his companions followed suit: Barto flexing his hands, which had nails as sharp as the spear Quan pulled from his back and the small blades Xilo twirled with dexterous skill.

The ruse was up, and whoever had tried to hide their presence stopped bothering as two figures stood in the doorway.

Ceven narrowed his eyes. It was two Rathans, judging by the outline of their pointed ears and small tails. The gold-encrusted wings on their plated armor told him they were guards, but not Royal Guards, who displayed a band of stars with theirs, like Xilo's. Ceven almost pitied them. A Royal Guard was a formidable foe, Ceven knew. He used to train with them, and he'd seen Xilo and Tarry fight, but a regular guard didn't have the same training and determination. These Rathans were no match for him, let alone all four of them.

"Didn't expect to find you here, *Your Highness,*" one said with a bite of snark.

Ceven was taken aback, not by this guard's tone but the implication of it. Even if he was a bastard prince, he *was* still a prince.

"Likewise," he replied evenly. "I was unaware the west wing had a new clean-up crew."

Ceven couldn't make out their expressions, but judging by Barto's snicker, he could tell they weren't happy.

"If you meant we're here to discard trash like you, then I can't disagree," he said, reaching for his side.

Ceven was disturbed. He was used to the dirty looks and rumors, but never had another outright slandered him. To do so was blasphemy, and punishment was swift. Either they weren't guards from Peredia, or something had changed to where his demise was no longer punishable—or maybe they just had a death wish.

"Those who betray their loyalty to the crown and his kin have no morals. And that makes you something far, far worse." Barto's accent thickened as the last sentence was a half-growl.

"I didn't swear my loyalty to a queen's love child," was all he said before the Rathan leaped.

Everyone sprang into action.

Xilo's knives soared through the air, finding their mark in the upper abdomen of one guard. The Rathan caught the remaining knife before it landed in his throat as Quan swept his spear across his legs. Too fast, the guard jumped in time, landing on the black metal rod and striking Quan in the face.

Ceven lunged forward with his sword at the other guard while Barto crouched, aiming for the Rathan's side. The guard caught Ceven's sword and snapped it like it was a chair leg and not a weapon forged of the strongest Atiacan metal. His other hand deflected Barto's blow at a speed that was fast. *Abnormally* fast. Ceven ditched the broken sword, but before he could land an upper-cut, the Rathan was already swiping a dagger at his face. Ceven leaned back in time as the blade came an inch from slicing his temple open.

The guard lashed out again, and Ceven caught one wrist, the other digging into his side, his nails finding purchase between the metal mesh armor. This close, the Rathan had a buzz cut, his ears large and furred with eyes that were strained. Sunken into a skull that was littered with pulsing dark ink.

That's not normal.

He hissed as the nails twisted in his side and Xilo slid on the ground behind the Rathan, digging two knives into the tender part of the back leg, slicing up. The inked guard growled but didn't seem hindered and whipped around in a blur and snapped out at his bodyguard's wings, scarlet soaking his feathers into a matted, dark purple. Barto and Quan weren't faring well either, the other guard moving at a speed that was faster than his two friends, who excelled in swiftness and precision, earning the right to fight at their empress's side in Atiaca.

In a matter of seconds, the two guards had all four of them on the defensive.

Just then, black braids and blue-and-white feathers flashed by him, sweeping up dust and rocks, as Rasha and Tarry flew into the room. It took everyone by surprise—including the guards, who tried turning around, but weren't quick enough. Tarry's axe slammed into the back of one of the unsuspecting Rathans, pounding him to the ground. Rasha whipped out and stabbed the other guard with her short sword, slowing him down enough for Xilo to lurch forward and slit the man's throat with his knives. Judging by Xilo's scary expression, it was payback for his wing, which was still bleeding.

"What the hell was that?" Ceven gripped his side, testing the severity of his wound. "I've never seen a Nyte move that fast."

"So, it wasn't just me," Barto said. "For a moment there, I thought I had lost my touch."

Rasha sheathed her blades at her side. "We encountered others in the hall. We found out the hard way."

When Ceven narrowed his eyes. Tarry was favoring his right arm.

"What happened?" Xilo asked, seeing his partner's injury.

"Nothing we couldn't handle. Just caught us by surprise. Much like they did you guys." Tarry's expression was hard-set, not showing any pain. "We didn't catch Evangeline's scent, but we caught Lani's. She's further below us."

Ceven's lips peeled open. In truth, he hadn't expected Lani to still be alive. He didn't dare think about Evangeline; she was alive, because he wouldn't have it otherwise.

One guard squirmed, and Rasha bent down, gripping the shaggy head of the Rathan with Tarry's gaping axe wound. No normal Nyte would have been able to survive that blow.

"What's wrong with your face?" Rasha demanded, gripping the man's jaw so tight, his skin bulged around her sharpened nails. The dark swirls danced across his white, freckled skin, traveling farther down beneath his armor.

As if reading his mind, Quan turned to the dead guard and ripped open the chest plate. They all stared in disgust at the littered flesh, not a clean slate of skin left as tattoos covered his entire torso and face.

The guard in Rasha's grip laughed, blood dribbling from his lips.

Without lessening her hold, she withdrew her sword and punctured below his ribs. "I used to work as the empress's First Lady. Sometimes that meant brushing her hair and helping her pick out a dress, but most of the time it was torturing assassins who thought getting close to the empress was a good idea. I was very good at it." Ceven couldn't see what she was doing, but the pained yowl reminded him why Rasha always made him uncomfortable.

He mumbled something that Ceven couldn't hear, but Rasha did. "You know exactly what I want to hear." Her nails bit into his cheeks, and the Rathan whimpered. "What are those marks on your face, what are you doing here, who are you working for?"

Everyone drew closer, curiosity tying them together like the finely woven tapestries that had once covered these halls.

"These marks . . . They're to make us stronger . . ."

"We figured out that much," Barto murmured.

"They're marking as many . . . as they . . . can." He tried to move, but Rasha held him firm, and he grimaced.

"Who? And why?"

He smiled, and his eyes slid to meet Ceven's. "To get ready for the war."

CHAPTER 9

At least Petri hadn't lied to her, as Evangeline approached the metal door in a semi-hallway off the cavernous room.

A few guards had slunk by, but too far ahead to notice her. In fact, after stabbing that Rathan and imprisoning his friend, it surprised her that more guards weren't storming the dungeon looking for her. It made her wary. Did the Wretched take care of them? Maybe Raiythlen had survived and they were too busy looking for him? Either way, she wouldn't waste this opportunity by standing around. She just prayed she would have the same luck in getting Lani out of here.

But deep in her core, she had a feeling this wouldn't end well.

Silencing those doubts, she faced what could only be the entrance to the room with the isolated holding cells. Four lines dug across the frame's exterior, at least an inch wide and two feet across. She cursed, realizing she had never asked Petri about these claw marks.

Gripping her makeshift knife, she opened the door, prepared for the worst.

The room was plain, made up of concrete floors, rock walls, and overhead lighting she had never seen throughout the rest of the castle, its whiteness almost blinding her, much like the light that had illuminated the room with the hundreds of cells. A simple desk and chair were shoved into the corner of the room, and two cells made of iron bars (much like the other cages) encased small, thin cots, like those found in the slave quarters. The room was empty aside from one person.

Lani!

Her friend sat on the cot in the right holding cell, her shoulders slumped over, her hair in clumps of brown and gray hanging in knots around her face. Her wrinkled black uniform covered the series of markings carved into her skin.

Tears pricked the back of Evangeline's eyes. *I'm going to get you out of here. I swear it.*

The room may have been empty, but that didn't mean there weren't Nytes lurking nearby, or that the owner of those claw marks didn't plan on returning soon. The thought of Vane opening that door, his twisted smile and brown eyes beaming at her . . . Evangeline's hands shook, and if Lani weren't standing in front of her, she would've turned around and run. Run as far away from this place as she could. But it was too late for that now, and she needed to get a move-on.

Because time was of the essence.

Evangeline pulled on her friend's cell door, but as expected, it was firmly locked. "Lani!" she whispered urgently.

Her friend didn't look up. She cradled her head in her hands, murmuring something Evangeline didn't understand. The top of her uniform was unbuttoned, revealing a little of her chest and neck. Her skin was better than the last time Evangeline had seen it, when Lani had been bleeding out in the slave quarters. The marred, bloody runes were now a matted black, the surrounding flesh rosy.

Evangeline frowned. The Aerian had said only Vane had the keys, but there had to be a spare somewhere . . . right? "Lani, it's me, Eve. Please . . . I need to know where the keys are."

Her friend dragged her gaze away from her hands. Her eyes were wide and blurry. Unfocused. Her skin was so thin that it wrapped around her cheekbones in a deadly embrace. She smiled, and teeth were missing. It was like looking at an animated skeleton.

Evangeline trembled. Lani didn't deserve this. After everything she had done for Evangeline . . . offering her guidance and companionship when Evangeline was first thrown into life as a Peredian slave with no warning. Sneaking sweet rolls at the risk of her own life just to see her smile. Evangeline had been a child then, before Ryker adopted her into Aerian society, and in return, all Lani'd ever received from her was suffering.

"Lani . . . I'm sorry. I'm so, so sorry. I'll make this right, I promise you."

Her words unraveled the spell holding her friend, and she shuffled to the cell bars. Her frail, withered hands curled around the iron. "Eve . . . is that you? Your face . . ."

Evangeline rubbed her cheek, her sleeve coming back stained with blood. The pain was nothing compared to seeing Lani in this state. "It's me. I've come to get you out of this mess." Evangeline squeezed her hand around Lani's, relishing in the simple connection.

Lani yanked away. "No! You must leave at once! Quick,

before they catch you!"

"They?"

"You don't understand. . . . They've done horrible things. . . ." Lani covered her face. "Please, I can't bear to watch anyone get hurt. No more."

Evangeline's nostrils flared. Raw, primal rage flooded her. She curled her hands into fists to the point her knuckles bled white. "Where are the keys? Is there another set in here, anywhere?"

Her friend didn't reply, her shoulders quivering, locked in her own nightmare. Evangeline's nails bit further into her skin. *I'll make them pay for this.* But how? She possessed the strength of a gazelle facing a lion, with only her measly glass knife for a weapon. She paused and glanced down at the broken glass stem.

Gripping the sturdy end, she shoved the tip of the glass into the palm-sized lock cradling the cell door. She had never lockpicked anything in her entire life, but why not try her hand at it now? How hard could it be?

Very hard, she realized as she twisted, turned and rotated the blasted glass stem with no luck. When her only weapon snapped in half, leaving the broken bit jammed inside the lock, she gave up on the idea that she would magically learn lockpicking.

Time for Plan B.

There had to be a spitting spare somewhere in this blasted room. She tore through the desk, pulling out drawers and upturning the entire thing. Nothing. She splintered the wood against the concrete floor, ripping into the old worn chair, but she found no secret compartments. She knocked on the torn wallpaper, hoping to find a safe, anything that could be of value, but she found nothing.

The keys weren't here.

Evangeline gritted her teeth. No, this wasn't the end. She broke off the limb of the desk and banged it against the metal bars. *If Raiythlen wants to show up, now would be the time!*

The banging woke Lani from her nightmare. "Stop it, Evangeline."

She swung harder.

"You're acting a fool! This will get you nowhere. Do you want to die?"

"There she is." Evangeline wiped her brow. "I thought I lost you."

"This isn't the time." Lani's eyes lit up like Raiythlen's fiery caster magic, dissolving any previous despair. "You've always been a naïve, foolish girl, and this tops it. You can't fix everything!"

"Watch me!" she snarled and slammed the wooden peg into the bar. It split in two.

"Dying with me will accomplish nothing. The moment they brought me to this blasted place, I accepted my fate. We're humans. Slaves. I'm going to die, Evangeline. You need to let me go and save yourself." She lowered her head, a shadow grazing her features. "If our roles were reversed, I would've never come for you."

"Maybe not, but you would tear yourself up about it every night. Call me what you want, but I'm not leaving you." She tossed the useless piece of wood and slammed herself against the iron bars. "You don't deserve this." *You were the only one who treated me like a normal human being. Showed me the kindness a mother would give to her child. I love you, Lani, and you deserve the world.* She didn't say it aloud, because it sounded like goodbye.

Her friend didn't raise her head. Evangeline kept slamming into the bars, as if the sheer strength of her hope could crack metal.

"You know a way out of this city. You have supplies in those woods. Leave. Leave here, and this time don't make the mistake of coming back," she whispered.

"There's no point if you're not with me." Evangeline's shoulder ached, and she stopped, sliding down the bars. The cuts on her face stung, and when she swiped at them, she realized it was because she was crying.

Lani joined her on the dusty ground. "Please go, Eve."

The click of a lock sliced off Evangeline's reply. The doorknob turned, the squeaking like razors down her back, before it swung open.

If Evangeline wasn't already on the ground, she would've sunk to her knees.

Vane, Peredia's notorious torturer—one with a personal vendetta against her—stood in the doorway, his twisted smile and dark eyes beaming at her.

CHAPTER 10

"Well, well, if it isn't my favorite pet!" Vane's grin was like a stab to Evangeline's gut. She imagined each sharpened tooth digging into her tender flesh. "We have so much to catch up on, you and I."

Evangeline almost didn't recognize the gangly Rathan. His appearance had never been intimidating—rather, it was his reputation. But now…it was beyond a doubt the man was more monstrous than any Wretched in this place. Maybe even more so than the Olaaga that prowled Peredia's woods.

Vane wore a full-length black robe, his head now shaven, revealing the same twining Castanian runes along his scalp that the guards sported. His eyes were dark to the point you couldn't see his pupils. The Rathan pinned Evangeline and Lani with a gaze dripping with sadistic intent.

He narrowed in on Lani. "Did you miss me, sweet Delani? Don't worry, after I deal with your friend, we'll pick up where we left off."

Lani's whimper was soft, but it triggered a fire inside Evangeline. The room dulled to a red hue, and her blood boiled, flames pumping in her veins. Vane stared at her friend, and Lani shrank in on herself. It was all the kindling she needed.

Evangeline lunged at him.

Vane sidestepped her and pushed her back, but it didn't hinder Evangeline. She spun around and aimed her knuckles at his face. Vane caught the blow and chuckled. Evangeline's chest heaved, Lani's sobs ringing through her head like a siren, screaming for retribution.

With a guttural cry, Evangeline swung again and again, writhing, kicking, anything to land a hit—when her nails tore at his cheek, blood welling up. His face darkened, and he shoved a fist into her stomach.

Crack!

Evangeline gripped her side, pain piercing her with every inhale. Vane reached into his robe to reveal a set of knives. Paralyzing fear struck her harder than his blow. Flashbacks of him shoving a knife into her mouth, the helplessness locking her in place as he cut her over and over again. The fire was gone.

"We had little time together per our last encounter." He sneered. "If he wasn't so spitting important, I'd love to teach your *father* a lesson as well."

Evangeline sucked in a breath through clenched teeth. *Why?* she couldn't say. Was it because Ryker had denied Vane the right to continue her punishment the first time he'd found Evangeline escaping the city's walls? Then she remembered Vane's crumpled form on the dungeon floor, when Ryker had taken her out of the cell. She had wondered what had happened.

"Ryker beat you," she guessed. But why? Was it because Ryker felt protective over what he considered his property? But then, why have her punished by Vane in the first place?

"He's a *pathetic coward*!" As if to calm himself, Vane closed his eyes, laughing. "He has gone soft. To think a lowly human had changed him." He smiled, revealing the wickedness of his thoughts. "But now I'm the one in control. And you"—He charged her, and his black nails seared into her skull with a painful sharpness—"are going to die a slow, painful death in honor of your father."

A hysterical laugh bubbled in her throat. Evangeline had already done Vane the honor of killing her father, but the threat of his claws ripping open her temples had her swallowing the urge.

Vane wrinkled his nose in disgust. "You reek of Wretched. My dear, how did you make it this far?" His black eyes widened. "Did that bastard prince of yours help you?" He licked his lips. "Now, this is the excitement I have been waiting for."

He released her, and she doubled over, ribs screaming in agony. Vane's black robe slid open, and the markings continued down the entire length of his leg. Evangeline stared in horror. He grinned at her, slipping his robe farther down to reveal his bare torso. Nausea pegged her stomach. His entire body was an ink-ridden canvas.

"Welcome to the future," Vane said, pleased with himself.

"What. . .?" She couldn't finish her sentence. Her mouth went dry, her lips sealed together like bricks. *Lani and the other humans, the guards, and now Vane. What's going on? Why are they doing this?* But what really hurt her: *How could Ryker have done this to Lani?*

It was the reason she didn't mourn his death.

"A language, lost in time. A language of power. This is

only the beginning." Vane walked behind her and rested his hands on her shoulders, each finger digging into her skin. Evangeline bit her lip to hold back a yelp of pain. "You and Lani should consider yourselves honored to take part in this evolution. This is going to change Peredia. It's going to change everything."

She felt as if she had swallowed a lump of stone, the pit weighing in her stomach. *This is a cult, and I'm about to be its next victim.*

"But don't worry, I will make sure your death won't be in vain." He tilted his head. "Don't you want to change the world? Lani understood her role. You would do well to follow her lead." Vane pulled out a set of keys, unlocking Lani's cell. Lani screamed, and it brought Evangeline to her feet. She squeezed between him and the cell door, but he kicked her square in the chest, too fast for her to dodge, and she slammed into the ground.

He yanked her friend out of the cell and tossed her to the floor. He ripped her shirt right down her back to reveal her markings, the symbols red around the edges, the color stark against her white, thin skin. Her bones protruded outward along her lower back and left shoulder blade, her skin turning black, almost as if it was decaying right before Evangeline's very eyes.

You're killing her! Evangeline wanted to scream, but the pain in her chest encumbered her, stealing her breath. She clutched her beating heart, wishing it didn't pound so hard against her broken ribs.

"I made her a part of something greater. I will show you the potential of what just one life can do."

Vane transformed.

His bones cracked and moved beneath his skin, his eyes rolling into the back of his head. Hair grew all over his body at an alarming rate, a dark coarse fur taking the place of his flesh. The black robe tore at the seams from where Vane's muscles enlarged and morphed, the discarded fabric falling to the floor. His face contorted to reveal two rows of sharp canine teeth, and when his eyes rolled back, two narrow pupils focused on her. He crouched back on two legs and howled.

Beast . . . Vane had become a beast.

The pain in her body was nothing now. Evangeline was already dead. No one was coming to save her. Raiythlen was dead, and she was going to be torn to bits by this beast.

"Imagine just how much more power I can get from you," the monster said, creeping closer. It yanked her head back and wrapped a hand around her throat. "I might have pitied you, if I didn't have the urge to tear your—"

The door splintered apart, and a cluster of fur and wings rammed into Vane's beastly form.

With a sharp tug, Evangeline fell backwards. Blue-and-gold wings crowded her view. It was Ceven, but the usual playful, stubborn friend she had grown up with wasn't here. Instead, it was an Aerian who had trained for years as a soldier to strike with lethal precision, a prince with the confidence to command an army. Under other circumstances, the look in his eyes would have terrified her.

"Get her and Lani out of here!" Ceven barked at Tarry.

The Royal Guard looked like the last thing he wanted to do was leave his prince's side, but he reached for her when the beast barreled into him and Ceven. The bald Rathan, Quan, latched onto the beast's back with Barto hooked to his side, but it didn't stop Vane from swiping out. Tarry shielded Ceven in time, the sharpened nails ripping into his wings. Chunks of feathers tore away, blood spattering the floor. The usually stoic Aerian howled in pain, and Evangeline felt the hit as if it was her own.

Barto's other companion, Rasha, dug her sword into the beast's side as Xilo leaped, spreading his wings before sliding them closed, using his momentum to strike the monster's unprotected head. Evangeline didn't look to see if he hit his mark as she scrambled to Lani, who looked more shaken than she was. She threw her arms around her friend as a cacophony of growls and yells filled the room.

It didn't last long. Something hot and wet smacked into her back. She turned and a trail of dark blood, almost black, covered herself, the walls, and the splintered door as Vane ran out of the room. Nobody moved to follow him.

"In all my years, never have I witnessed something like that." Xilo was beside Tarry, ripping his trousers and tying them around his companion's waist. Tarry's wings were a mangled mess, but less serious than the heavy blood flowing from his side.

"A *Monkobo Loopa.* Beast Walker." Barto's furred hands trembled as he helped Rasha hold Quan up, his face appearing like it had been pummeled by a club. They shared a look of mutual horror. "I never thought I'd see one here."

Ceven crouched beside Evangeline and Lani. Slash wounds covered his neck but didn't seem as serious as his friend's injuries. "Whatever it was, we don't have the power to fight it if it comes back. We need to move."

He helped Lani up, although her limbs were shaking, her eyes wide. If Evangeline didn't have Lani to focus on, she feared she would've looked much the same. Maybe she did. He stretched out his hand to her when arcing fire ripped down her side. She doubled over.

"Eve!" Ceven gripped her shoulder.

"My chest," she bit out. "I'll be fine." She didn't feel like it, but with everyone else's injuries, she almost considered herself lucky. Ceven carefully pulled her to her feet. A crease formed between his eyes, but she shrugged off his hand and gestured to his bodyguard, who struggled to hold up Tarry.

"Can you walk?" Evangeline turned to Lani, mentally asking herself the same question. Lani nodded but kept her arm around Evangeline's shoulder, her body still trembling. "Do you have a way out?" she asked Ceven.

Ceven helped Xilo hold up Tarry, whose eyes were closing. He didn't look good. "Yes, there's a set of tunnels that connect this wing to the rest of the castle. We can make for my suite or any empty one that's closest."

"I think it would be wiser if we left the castle," Rasha said. "Those soldiers attacked you, regardless of your title. Who's to say there won't be more of them to follow?"

"There isn't a guarantee we would be safer in the city, and we need immediate medical attention. There are doctors in the castle that can help us," Ceven countered, frowning at Tarry.

"Who are loyal to the king and could give away our location," Barto pointed out.

Ceven's shoulders squared, and Evangeline sensed his impatience. "He's dying, Barto. We don't have a choice."

"We could go to my son's house," said Xilo. "It's on the outskirts of the city, close enough that we could use the tunnels to avoid detection, and far enough away to give us some breathing room from what's happening here."

Evangeline blinked at him. Most Royal Guards didn't have family. Not because the king didn't allow it, but because they didn't have time for that lifestyle. Their lives belonged to the royal family, protecting them at all hours.

"He used to be a traveling surgeon," Xilo continued. "There are medical supplies there and, most importantly, privacy."

Ceven glanced at Tarry and Quan. Time was running out. "Very well, let's go."

PART 2

HEARTS DIVIDED

CHAPTER 11

Ceven gritted his teeth. Not from the weight of Tarry as he and Xilo carried him through the dark, damp underground tunnels, but at his inability to do more for his friend. *Blast it, I won't have him die like this.*

Evangeline huddled beside Lani, both decked head-to-toe in black, making their faces appear like they were floating in the darkness. He'd seen Evangeline dressed in slacks before, in training, or whenever they had ridden together as kids, but he had never seen her—or anyone in the castle—dressed in such odd armor. Where had she gotten it?

She wrapped her arm around her friend's shoulder while clenching her side. If Tarry weren't so bad off, the first thing he would've done was make sure she was okay, despite her false assurances otherwise. The two of them had to be terrified. Delani looked like her soul was ready to leave her body at any point. Behind them, Rasha and Barto held Quan in a similar fashion, dark blood trailing behind them. They needed to hurry and get to their destination. Fast.

Xilo was the only one with a lantern, guiding their path. The yellow flame shifted off the occasional body on the ground, mixed with red and black blood. Reflecting what everyone was covered in. The tunnels were narrower than Ceven remembered, but then again, it had been some time since he'd traversed them.

As a kid, his brother would lead him down here, only to leave him in the dark, forcing Ceven to find his own way out. Knowing Sehn, he had hoped Ceven would starve to death or get trapped in an underground earthquake, even though quakes in this area of Peredia were rare. If it hadn't been for the king's intense teachings of all the escape routes and his survival instincts, Ceven would have died. These tunnels were purposefully long, complicated, and confusing. Even if someone found the secret entrances, traversing the labyrinth required either luck or knowledge.

The stretch of darkness and cold extended for a grueling amount of time. Each clambering of steps was met with a pained moan.

"Up ahead, should lead us to a barn, near the east wall in the outer district." Xilo lifted the lamp. Tarry's blood drenched his side.

True to his word, they met a sharp incline, then came across a glimmer of light.

"Are we going to crawl through?" Evangeline frowned at the opening.

"No," Xilo said. Tarry's weight doubled, his friend's head swiveling toward Ceven as Xilo left his side. Tarry said nothing.

A snap echoed off the rock walls, a sudden cool breeze teasing his nose. Xilo had kicked a large hole in the wood panel covering the entrance.

Ceven and Tarry were first to enter the barn, morning light creeping through the cracks of wood and shining on the broken stall door from which they'd just exited. A horse occupying the stall next to him reared back and whinnied. Rasha brushed past Ceven, stroking the brown and white mare, calming her. The rest of the crew walked through one by one, blood splattering like drops of rain against hay and dirt.

Xilo slid open the barn doors, and a gust of ice-cold air seized Ceven's muscles. Lani sidled closer to Evangeline, who had wrapped her arms around her, even as she herself shivered. Ceven hoped this place wasn't much farther. The sooner everyone was warm and healed and not bleeding out on the snow, the better.

"Not much father," Xilo said, echoing his thoughts. "We'll cut through the wheat fields. It'll be the house with the screen porch facing the east wall."

The wheat fields were less wheat and more just fields of snow. The dead stocks, whimpering under the dust of white pellets. A couple blocks away, the east wall soared into the air, its long shadow straining to touch them. The sun was waking up, and soon the rest of the city would come alive—and look for Evangeline.

You don't know that; Sehn could have been lying. There's no way she could have murdered Lord Ryker. Right? In the past, he would've taken Evangeline's side, but now he wasn't sure.

He thought back to the guards in the west wing, markings covering their faces and bodies, how his people had turned on him, attempting to murder their prince. Ceven wished they had gotten more out of that guard, but he had lost too much blood, dying before they could gather any information. And now there was a strange beast on the loose, one he had never seen before.

It seemed he wasn't sure about a lot of things these days.

A smattering of houses came into focus. Square, tall structures built from stone and lumber from the Olaaga forest. Beiges, grays, and muted whites were the popular color choices of the outer district's houses, except for one. A deep green, two-story farmhouse—with a screened porch. Ceven sighed in relief.

Everyone's sodden boots thumped onto the porch, shaking snow on the slicked wood steps. The house itself was not as warm as Ceven had hoped and looked like it'd been abandoned. Cracks of light filtered through closed curtains, shining on clothes strewn on the floor. A small, circular table crammed against the violet and mahogany wall had a mug and a plate of food covered in what had to be mold. Ceven frowned but pushed those thoughts from his mind, focusing on helping Xilo drag Tarry through the kitchen and into the living room.

Rasha and Barto placed Quan, whose face scrunched in pain, on the black leather couch. Xilo pulled out blankets from the wood chest next to it, forming a makeshift bed for Tarry as they laid him on his stomach, his bloody wings stretched.

Xilo bent next to the white-bricked fireplace, whispering life into it, as Evangeline helped Lani into the matching armchair next to Quan. Ceven looked around and spotted a folded blanket on a stack of books and balls of yarn. He tossed it to Evangeline, and she gave him a grateful look, tucking Lani in, who murmured a thanks before her eyes drifted closed.

"Here, these should help." Xilo came down the creaking stairwell, hands full. Ceven hadn't even seen him leave. Xilo placed pillows and more blankets on the floor, along with a dark suitcase.

Tarry's makeshift bandages had opened up, staining the blankets cushioned beneath him.

Quan was sprawled across the couch. His eyes were still open, unlike Tarry's. "Help him first. He's worse off."

Xilo opened the suitcase. Inside were needles, bandages, and alcohol. He handed some tools to Barto, who looked at his friend. Quan's expression soured.

"Oh, don't act like such a martyr." Barto smiled, but with the sharp needle in his hand, it wasn't reassuring. "I'll patch you up just fine. Remember that one time you lost a chunk of skin to that weasel at the tavern? Who called you a half-breed? I mean, we sure showed him, but—"

The Rathan's furless ears flicked back as he groaned. "Barto."

Barto waved his needle hand dismissively, and Quan's face pinched even more.

Ceven unhinged and dismantled Tarry's steel meshed armor to give Xilo better room to work. He weaved the sutures in and out of Tarry's skin with ease. He was a master with a needle, having patched up Ceven more times than he could count, more so during his excursions into the jungles of Atiaca than when he was a kid. Tarry would walk away from this with a small scar. If he lived.

Evangeline glanced away, looking ill. Ceven didn't blame her.

The flames ate at the stack of wood, its warmth lapping at Ceven's side as he crouched beside Tarry, brows shoved together. Nobody spoke. Barto concentrated on stitching while Rasha cleaned the wounds. Intervals of hisses and pained murmurs broke the silence.

Evangeline came over with two large bowls of water, placing them next to Xilo and Rasha. The purple-winged Aerian nodded at her, cleaning his tools and Tarry's cut, while Rasha's one ear twitched in acknowledgement, her eyes still fixed on Quan. She was far more nervous about the situation than she was letting on.

"I'll see if I can grab more towels." Evangeline got up, her expression taut. She was trying her best to hide the pain, but Ceven knew better.

He attempted a smile, but he was sure it looked forced. "We have everything under control." His eyes trailed down her frame, searching for any wounds he may have missed. He knew his friend made a habit of putting others before herself. If she was injured, it was unlikely she'd say anything. "I want you to lie down and rest. After Tarry and Quan, you're next."

Thankfully, she didn't argue.

Lani shifted on the chair, and Xilo glanced up for a moment before returning to his stitching, which was almost done and a lot neater than Barto's work. But Ceven would break that news to Quan later.

"There's a few bedrooms upstairs. Nobody's home, so you can choose whichever one. A bed will be much nicer for your friend," Xilo offered. "There's also a bathing room, if you'd like a shower, with spare clothes in the dresser."

Evangeline's face lit up, while Ceven was more preoccupied with a question: where was Xilo's son? Ceven knew Eyvan had to have been in the city recently. Xilo had just been with him the night Ceven met with Sehn, after his first dinner back with the king. The same night his brother had suggested he help him murder his father, as if they were cohorts in the same scheme and not brothers who hated one another. Not to mention they hadn't spoken more than a few words to each other in two years.

Evangeline rubbed Lani awake. She coerced her with the promise of a comfortable bed, and the two shuffled upstairs, the wood creaking as they climbed the staircase. Relief swelled in Ceven's chest.

If Tarry died, he didn't want Evangeline to see him cry.

CHAPTER 12

Someone had closed all the curtains in the house at one point. It could've been evening or night. Ceven didn't know, but either way he was beyond exhausted, only having stolen a couple hours here and there of some much-needed shut-eye. Tarry's blood covered him, his back and legs aching from hunching over his friend for so long. But they'd managed to patch Tarry up, and he was on his way to recovery.

After dozing off for a bit, Ceven woke to Quan's snore droning from the couch and the clattering of utensils from the kitchen as Xilo cooked. Barto and Rasha were nowhere to be found. He sat up, and over the stirring of pots and pans, he could make out the faintest creaking and whispers from upstairs. His lip curled, and his thoughts turned sour. Were the two of them discussing a way to kidnap Eve? To bring her back to the empress to be killed for crimes she didn't commit? Rasha's loyalty to the empress matched Barto's, if not more so. It was only a matter of time before his friend betrayed him.

Eager to find out for sure, Ceven rubbed his hands on the red-stained towel beside him and crept up the stairs. He wasn't as agile as his Atiacan companions, but it was enough to pick up the tail end of their conversation.

". . . her mark may be the key to figuring it out. It'd be best for us to leave now." They were in the bedroom, closest to the stairwell.

"With everything going on? It's better to figure out what the king is up to and—" Barto's sentence cut off.

A moment later, his friend opened the bedroom door.

Ceven flashed him a chilling smile. "Maybe we can all have an open discussion together downstairs. We're all friends, after all, right?"

Barto's lips curled, showing a row of sharp canines. "Friends don't eavesdrop on each other." He shoved past him downstairs.

Rasha folded her arms, her gaze across the hall where Lani and Evangeline slept. Ceven stepped in front of her. She narrowed her eyes but shrugged and followed Barto. Ceven watched her leave, his stomach feeling as if he had guzzled a bed of nails.

The bathing room was nowhere near the size of Ceven's in his suite, but the water was just as hot and cleansed him of the blood that coated his hands and parts of his neck where the exposed skin was in his armor. The black-and-gray cotton slacks and shirt were a lot easier to move around in than his plated metal.

If he had to find a bright side to his current situation, it was at least he didn't have to uphold the mask of formality he wore for the king and nobles inside the castle. *I need to return soon, before the king wonders about my whereabouts.* But first he needed to figure out a plan, and what the blazes Evangeline had been up to.

He gently rapped on the door before peeking in. Evangeline was curled up next to Lani, both sound asleep on the four-post bed, wrapped in a colorful quilt. Xilo had checked on both of them after attending Tarry.

"Miss Evangeline may have fractured one or more ribs, but if she rests and takes it easy, she will be fine," Xilo had told him. "Delani, on the other hand . . ." The two of them had shared a look, and the Royal Guard didn't have to say anything more. It was going to be a hard truth for Eve to swallow.

For a moment, all of Ceven's frustration and worry melted at the sight of Evangeline's sleeping form. She looked better, at least. Her cheeks rosy and clean of blood, her hair falling messily across her face. It reminded him of the times they would nap together as children after their tutoring sessions with Ryker. Before he got to the age where he wanted to do more than just sleep beside her.

Ceven brushed back her hair, and she stirred awake. "There's food downstairs."

She rubbed her eyes and glanced at Lani.

"Let her sleep for a little while longer." He turned his gaze away, knowing she would see the resurfacing anger in it. "Besides, we have much to discuss." He left her to change into whatever clothes Xilo's son had lying around and went downstairs.

The living room reeked of blood and alcohol, but it was worth it to see Tarry conscious. His Aerian bodyguard was leaning against the couch, chatting with Quan, who was shoveling down the contents of his bowl. Tarry looked pretty nonchalant for having more bandages on him than clothing.

Xilo offered Ceven a steaming bowl of roasted beans and rice with a slice of bread, but he declined. His stomach seemed to have an appetite for knots. Rasha and Barto were at the table, discussing Barto's sisters. Something regarding the letters they had been sending to Barto, asking about the castle, and if the Aerian royalty was as stuffy as Barto made them out to be. At least it wasn't about Evangeline.

The creaking of the stairwell alerted him to Evangeline's presence. She clearly had struggled to tie the simple shirt and loose brown breeches into a somewhat presentable attire. Everyone stared at her, and if Ceven didn't know better, he would've thought he was in the city's plaza, about to witness an execution.

Barto stood up. "We need to talk."

Ceven scowled at him. "At least let her eat first."

Barto's black-furred ears flicked back. "Of course, I didn't mean to sound so harsh."

To his childhood friend's credit, Evangeline kept her head high even as she walked through the invisible thickness that lingered in the air. She sat across from Rasha at the round table, the worn wooden chair shifting as she slid in. At least Xilo had cleaned up the spoiled food that had been sitting out upon their arrival. Ceven had never gotten around to asking Xilo where his son was.

Evangeline no longer favored her right side, and in the overhead light, her skin was chalky white, her eyes more vibrant than he remembered them ever being.

Xilo set down what would've been Ceven's bowl in front of her.

"What is this?" She leaned in to smell it.

"Food, and that's what should be important." Rasha crossed her arms, leaning away, as if she were diseased. Ceven wanted to tell the she-beast off but knew it would only stir more tension.

Evangeline looked insulted but didn't hesitate to take a spoonful, as if to prove a point.

"Did you sleep well?" Ceven asked, breaking the hanging silence.

She nodded. "How is everyone?" She looked at Tarry, then Quan, but when she met the Rathan's brown eyes, he turned away. "And how did you find us?"

"We're better, though if you asked Quan, you'd think I'd butchered him." Barto glared pointedly at his friend. Quan shrugged.

Ceven smirked despite himself. "Admit it, you have much to learn from Xilo's needlework."

Barto threw up his hands. "What do you expect? I'm a warrior, not a seamstress." His cheeks darkened, and he gave Xilo a small smile. "Not that that's a bad thing, mind you."

Xilo raised a brow but didn't reply, turning and scrubbing down everyone's plates and bowls. It was odd seeing his bodyguard, an Aerian whom he had watched take down countless enemies without his expression wavering from its intense focus whenever in battle and with a bloody history of something far from mundane or holy, in such a relaxed setting. Ceven had to admit, seeing the older, quiet Aerian surrounded by beige tile and hovering over the wide-set copper sink was disconcerting. As if he were dreaming.

He grimaced. After everything that had happened, with Evangeline potentially wanted for murder, his bodyguard almost dying today, and his friend planning to go behind his back and kidnap the woman he loved, he really wished that he was.

Ceven pressed his lips together. "Sehn told us where you were. If he hadn't, you'd be dead."

Evangeline frowned and looked at the extra bowl on the table, still hot.

"I should take this to Lani." Evangeline went to stand, but Ceven placed a hand on her shoulder. She wasn't going anywhere yet.

"I'll take it," Xilo said, drying his hands before taking the bowl from the table. "It'll give me a chance to check on her wounds again." He looked Evangeline over. "I'll need to check yours later on."

Evangeline smiled at him, and he left. Ceven sat next to her. He didn't have to say anything; she knew him well enough to recognize his expression.

She sighed. "I'll tell you everything. And before you ask, I had good reason not to come to you."

Ceven leaned back, crossing his arms. "Do you?"

"You lied to me first, remember?" she retorted, then glanced around the room, pink blooming in her face. "We should speak privately."

Ceven had lied to her about Lani's well-being that day in Ryker's suite, but it was to protect her from running off and putting herself in danger. Like escaping to the west wing and almost being a beast's meal.

Before he could speak, Barto interrupted, "We're all in this together now. We need to clear the air, figure out what's going on." The sun-kissed wrinkles around Barto's eyes softened, and for a moment, Ceven believed his friend cared about Eve. But if he did, he wouldn't be wanting to drag her off to be killed in Atiaca.

"You're right," she started. "Let's clear everything up."

She explained about a letter she'd found in Lani's room that said Vane had kidnapped her friend and how, after the ball, she'd discovered Lani was in the west wing.

"Who was the Caster helping you?" Rasha said, but it was more of a demand.

Evangeline flinched. It was a guess, but judging by her reaction, it was now confirmed. Ceven would've felt bad for her being put on the spot—if she hadn't lied to him about everything.

"I can't say their name." Her hand tightened on her spoon. "If I did, it would put mine and Lani's life in danger."

Rasha glared, and Evangeline stared at her bowl.

"Where are they now?" Ceven asked, surprised by the curtness in his voice. He'd thought he was doing a decent job of keeping his emotions in check. Apparently not.

"Dead, maybe, I don't know. We got separated, and that's when I ran into the king—"

Ceven slammed his hands on the table, and she jumped. "You ran into the *king*!"

"Well, it wasn't on purpose," she spat, her face as red as the shirt that kept sliding off her shoulders.

"Well, I'd certainly hope not." Barto put a hand on his hip. "I'm sure the old man wasn't happy to see you."

It won't be long before the king finds out she was behind his advisor's death. And nobody, not even you, can protect her from the wrath of the Peredian army and its bloodthirsty king. Sehn's words rang inside his skull. "Maybe we do need to speak in private."

Rasha directed her glare at him. "What happened to clearing the air? Something you'd like to add, Your Highness?"

Rasha's jab dug under his skin. Since arriving in Peredia two weeks ago, she had been mostly quiet, probably adjusting to her new surroundings and calculating all possible threats. Very different from the woman he had first met in Atiaca's capital city, Kazummar, whose tongue fired off faster than one of Xilo's throwing knives. At the time, he'd respected her bluntness and ability to get straight to the point. But right now, it ticked him off.

"Stop acting like I didn't catch you two whispering alone upstairs. Maybe there's something you'd like to share?" Ceven cocked his head, pointedly daring her to say anything else.

She didn't respond, and he couldn't help but feel smug.

Evangeline shook her head. "She's right. Having secrets isn't going to help."

Rasha raised her brows but kept her focus on Ceven.

His hands curled into fists, which he kept tucked into the folds of his arms. He wanted to keep it a secret from Barto and his friends. Who knew what they would tell their empress—maybe even King Calais. But he already had plans to get Eve far away from the Atiacan warriors. Sooner rather than later.

He kept his stare even and released the blow. "Did you kill Ryker?"

The room turned deadly quiet.

Evangeline's head dropped, but Ceven witnessed the truth in her horrified expression. Her unsaid admission ended up throwing a punch to his gut instead of hers.

"It was an accident. . . ." Her voice was small, but it caused him to explode.

"Gods *blast* it, Eve! What . . ." Ceven stood, the floorboards straining as he paced the room. "Anything else you'd like to share?" he snarled.

"I was tricked!" she exclaimed, color rising throughout her face. "He was supposed to fall asleep, so we could find out more about the missing people!"

Rasha's expression didn't change, but her brown eyes roved over Evangeline, re-assessing her. "I'm assuming your Caster friend put you up to this. And that is how you found out your friend was in the west wing?"

Evangeline nodded but added, "I wouldn't say 'friend.'"

Ceven paused and demanded, "And did the king know?"

Barto snorted. "If she's alive, I'd say not, unless she's more silver-tongued than we thought." Quan made a noise that sounded insulting.

Evangeline crossed her arms, but her shoulders trembled, and some of his anger dissipated. "The king doesn't know . . . yet. But I've learned what they're doing, what's happening inside Castle Peak. The point of kidnapping all those humans."

She showed off her mark, the bold lines and runes reminding Ceven that, as much as he didn't like to admit it, she was somehow involved—whether it be as a victim or something more sinister. She continued to explain what her mark meant, that it was ancient Caster magic, used to open a channel between two people. Soul to soul. Ceven shook his head, the others looked skeptical as well, but Evangeline argued that what they had all seen in the west wing was proof of it. That her mark was being manipulated and used on these humans to drain them. Peredia was empowering itself off the backs of Caster magic and human lives.

He asked her how she knew all of this, but judging by her expression, he assumed the information came from her Caster.

Tarry sat up, and only the slight furrow of his brow indicated the pain he was probably in. "I saw those cells. They didn't look human anymore," he said. "It's something I believe my old employer would do, but not the king."

Ceven was surprised Tarry would bring up his past. He and Xilo rarely talked about it.

"We all saw that monster, the markings on those soldiers with more strength than a small army. What the blazes does the king want with that kind of power? To go to war? To have the ability to say he's the strongest country in the world?" Barto shook his head. "Why can't he just be satisfied with winning an arm-wrestling match or something instead?"

Quan's lips twitched. "All he would have to do is play you once to feel all-powerful." Barto was close in taking out the Rathan's furless ears, which bent back in the nick of time.

"Well, Your Highness, what now? After all, you are the prince of this kingdom." Rasha raised her brows, the comment also acting as a jab. She knew his weight as a bastard prince was only a little better than one of the drunk nobles pawing at Rasha and every other female at the Aerian ball. He grimaced. If only he could do more.

Ceven forced a smile. "Your favorite, Rasha. It's time to come up with a plan."

CHAPTER 13

Sehn walked into the gaudy, outdated suite that this prince was forced to live in. Their muscles cramped in pain, their head pounding. It was like they were carrying an entire body on their shoulders.

"Curse these wings," they griped.

It had been a long day of keeping up pretenses. The spell they wore peeled at the edges, with spikes of blue prodded out of Sehn's long brown locks, where their real hair tried to escape. The prince's burgundy wings had stiffened, painfully so, to where they couldn't maneuver them. If it wasn't for the bloody king rambling on for another four hours, they wouldn't be in this mess.

They stumbled to Sehn's white ornate vanity, happy that he had some taste in furniture. Yanking open the drawer, they fumbled around inside before pulling out a vial and downing its contents. Their skin tightened and readjusted, every muscle shifting. They glanced at the mirror, brushing Sehn's pale, fair skin, making sure everything looked the way it was supposed to. *He didn't have any freckles, did he?*

A knock at the door wrought a sigh from them.

"Who is it?" Their tone deepened, following the low, sultry voice Sehn had awed the Council with two years ago.

The door creaked open. A Caster dressed in dark leather, with two purple, curved horns, peered at her from under their hood. The Caster bowed low, their head almost touching the floor.

"I'm sorry, ma'am, but Raiythlen remains elusive. He was last seen in the west wing, but all traces of him have disappeared," the Caster said in Castanian.

They took a seat on the armchair, sighing in reprieve. "I told you to call me Your Highness," they said, switching to Castanian as well, the words rolling off the roof of their mouth. They pinched their nose in pain. They hated this spell and couldn't wait to be back in their own skin.

"Of course, Your Highness."

He's one of our best spies. Of course, he wouldn't be captured easily. They sighed. *Why did you have to stick your nose into this, Raiythlen?* "How many are inside the castle?"

"We got most of our troops inside. Enough to provide you the opportunity you need."

They stretched, their brow crinkling as they felt the fake wing pop into place. It'd taken awhile to adjust to the weight and size. If they hadn't calculated the length of them and evaluated their routes and the people and objects they'd be near while practicing for hours in front of a mirror, a novice would have blown the disguise by now. But they were no novice. "Lovely. Inform the Council and be ready at my signal."

"Yes, M—Your Highness." The Caster bowed again, leaving the chamber.

Their lips twitched. *Now to set the stage.*

They snapped their fingers. Coarse fur brushed their leg, and they smiled at the gray wolf sitting patiently at their feet. They rubbed the top of the wolf's head.

"Find me Evangeline," they told their familiar, their smile widening. "It's time for a new king."

CHAPTER 14

CEVEN

The frigid air settled into Ceven's bones as his boots plowed through the snow. If he had been born human, it would've sapped all his warmth even between the layer of his brown fur coat and dark slacks. The outer district of the city was quiet tonight aside from the squeak of a single carriage and the frantic steps of someone who was out way later than they should be. Smoke billowed from the tops of tin and plated roofs that were more spread out than the ones closer to the castle. He was still within the walls, but at least he felt he could breathe a little easier here. If only for a moment.

Xilo walked beside him, his long strides keeping up with his. Ceven was tall, even for an Aerian, but Xilo met his height. Mayhap was even a little taller, but his lithe frame could've given more of that impression. Tarry had stayed behind at the house to heal—and to keep watch in case his friends from Atiaca suddenly made their own move as well.

Up ahead, a structure, slightly crooked if Ceven stared at it for too long, emerged between the light flurries of snow. It was the moon's light that helped him see the worn barn house, the street lamps a hundred paces in the opposite direction, past Xilo's son's house. Two figures emerged from between its doors, and Ceven's hand tightened on the letter rolled in his coat pocket.

After what he had witnessed in the west wing, he had to warn his other comrades back at the castle. They were young guards, eager to butter up to him to win favor, but since his return to Castle Peak, they had grown on him. Literally. He remembered them coming up to his waist before he'd left for Atiaca. Now the same Rathans and Aerians stood almost at his height with the same determination Ceven'd had in his youth.

Ceven snorted and knew what Tarry and Xilo would say: *you're still young, and you have much to learn.* Maybe he did, but he didn't like to be reminded of it, nor of the fact that he felt he could think more clearly on matters than his own king, at over a hundred years old. If only he hadn't been born a bastard, if only Sehn hadn't come back from Sundise Mouche. Ceven could've become a great king.

"Your Highness," the broad-framed soldier said when they got closer, fisting his right hand over his breast. His companion, whose braids outnumbered Rasha's, did the same. Both were Aerians, their snow-dusted wings tucked tightly behind them.

Ceven had seen the two of them occasionally from afar but never caught their names. They weren't in uniform and matched closely in physique. According to Xilo, one was a guard of twenty years, the other a Royal Guard much longer than that. They were here only because of their respect for Xilo, him and Tarry earning their positions within the Royal Guard rather than being born into it like most Aerians.

They weren't here for a bastard prince.

Ceven pulled out his letter, the parchment rolled into a palm-size note. "Thanks for coming out here tonight. We have a serious problem on our hands." They both nodded, but their eyes darted to Xilo's. Ceven frowned and shrugged it off.

"We'll make sure it gets into the right hands," braids said.

The letter contained what he had seen in the west wing, the potential war Peredia was about to face, and the Caster disease that was plaguing its soldiers.

Ceven pinched his brows. He wished they had gotten more out of that soldier in the west wing, but he had lost too much blood, becoming incoherent before bleeding to death on the ground. *It doesn't make sense. We just signed the treaty with Sundise Mouche, and we have strong relations with Atiaca. There's no way the king would create a treaty just to break another,* had been his current thought ever since they'd encountered that marked soldier. *Unless it was a false sense of protection to give way for an attack? No, I don't think so. Sign a treaty, only to turn around and stab them in the back? Still an unwise move. The king is smarter than that.*

When the question of war was brought up last night, Evangeline had asked if the king may have another incentive. Ceven didn't know, but if anyone would, it would be his brother. Sehn had said killing the king would solve all their problems, and Ceven was inclined to agree. Removing King Calais would save Evangeline and prevent a war—that was, if Sehn wasn't in on what the king had planned. But Ceven was going to figure that out.

"I plan on returning to the castle soon," Ceven said, tempted to step in front of Xilo so they would look only at him. "But I need you to get word to Xilo here, for our . . . later plan."

The 'plan' from last night wasn't so much a plan as it was a compromise. Ceven needed to return to the castle to figure out what Sehn and the king were up to, but he couldn't bring Eve with him, and like hell was he going to leave her with the Atiacan warriors.

So, in the meantime, when Tarry has healed a bit more, the two of them would make their way to the castle, along with Barto and Rasha. He would leave Quan and Xilo at Eyvan's house with Evangeline and Lani until they returned. What Ceven neglected to say that night was his plan to get Eve and Lani beyond the walls without the Rathans finding out. Hence, tonight's meeting.

"It's for that human girl, isn't it?" the broad-shouldered soldier said, catching Ceven off guard. "Xilo said you planned to smuggle a few people beyond the walls. One of them has to be her." He kept his face still, expressionless, but Ceven sensed his dissatisfaction. The disrespect. And while it shouldn't bother him, it did.

Before Ceven could stop himself, he said, "You got a problem with that?" He shook his head. "I know what you're thinking, and you're wrong. Just plain wrong. This whole blasted kingdom is wrong. Humans aren't animals and shouldn't be treated as such simply because they're weaker." The two had shifted their gazes away from him, but Ceven stared them down. "Would you beat, torture, and force a Nyte child to do the things these humans do in the castle? They're weaker than us, after all."

The two men didn't answer. Ceven knew they wanted to

argue, to bite back and say, *but a Nyte child isn't a human*, as if that were the answer and not the problem.

A hand gripped his shoulder, and he turned to face Xilo.

Ceven sighed, biting back the words he wanted to say to these two guards. "Thank you for coming out here tonight. I hope our letter gets into safe hands, and for your information, this is more than just smuggling a couple of humans beyond the walls. This concerns the safety of our kingdom and its future."

He turned before the two could reply, storming past Xilo back to Eyvan's house.

Ceven's hands stayed curled into fists, his back straight as he stepped across the missing, broken floorboards on the porch. When he entered the house, he was as quiet as he could be, though with Rathans sharing the residence, it was likely they'd already heard.

Barto and the others were upstairs, with Tarry lying on the couch in the living room, his shirtless torso covered in bandages that matched his left wing. The fire sizzled and cracked, showcasing the worn leather couch Tarry sat on, seams unraveling at the edges, along with the faded green and brown rug that was still covered with bloody sheets and pillows since they'd patched up Tarry and Quan.

Tarry wobbled to his feet upon Ceven's arrival, and Ceven recognized his expression.

"I don't want to talk," he said, raising his hand to dissuade Tarry from standing and opening his wounds. Ceven had a feeling he knew what it would be about, considering they've had little time to chat since last night's discussion. Whatever Xilo had given the Aerian had knocked him out a whole day.

Tarry ignored him, standing to his full height, holding his side. His wings had seen better days.

Xilo was close behind him, eyeing Tarry's bandages before giving him a similar look. "It would be wise to listen to us, Your Highness."

Ceven frowned. Great, now he was being tag-teamed. He buckled underneath their combined stares and nodded. Xilo gestured for Ceven and Tarry to follow him.

Rather than going back outside for privacy, Xilo guided them into the basement of the house that Eyvan had remodeled into a study. Bookshelves covered the walls, which looked to be painted burgundy to hide the concrete beneath. Papers lay neatly stacked next to a cup of pens on a white desk, revealing a meticulous owner. Labeled bottles lined the shelves, but Ceven didn't observe further when the two Aerians cornered him, their arms folded.

Tarry cut straight to the point. "With the threat of war coming, and Nytes turning into monsters, we have more important things to focus on than aiding Miss Evangeline and Delani." The Aerian stood heads shorter than Ceven but still made him feel small. "We know you care for the girl, but she's becoming a liability."

Ceven's eyes narrowed. "I get plenty of that from Barto and the others. I don't need it from you two."

They didn't budge. He wondered if they had always been this way, stoic and expressionless, or if it was a prerequisite for joining the Royal Guard. Or a product of their shared past.

"Barto and his guards . . . they also pose an issue. They know too much, can use this situation to their advantage," Xilo said. "We risk them turning you over to the king for sheltering Ryker's murderer to gain sway for their empress."

Ceven flinched. After Evangeline's admission last night of killing a Nyte, of killing Ryker Ardonis, he hadn't been able to look at her the same way. As if he still couldn't believe it.

Tarry nodded. "Evangeline has admitted to it. If you continue to associate with her, the king—"

"The king will what?" Ceven barked. "Belittle me? Beat me? Cast me out?" He snorted. "At least it'd be better than being forced into a political cage for his own gain."

"You'll be executed," Tarry finished.

Ceven waved his hand. "He wouldn't. He hates me, but he hates taboo even more. Killing a prince, bastard or not, would tarnish his name." But the thought sobered him. Maybe they were right. Maybe he was underestimating how much King Calais hated his presence, hated what he was. Proof that Queen Beatrix, whom the king had adored, had loved another. "Either way, it doesn't matter. I don't plan on staying."

Xilo raised his brows, and Ceven would argue he looked almost haughtier than the king himself. "And where would you go? Back to Atiaca?"

He didn't like this pointed observation.

"Your life and men are here. I know you don't believe it, but your presence amongst the Peredian army is highly respected," Tarry said.

Ceven bite back a laugh. "Only you two think that. Like a parent boasting that their kid is the best swordsmen in the world when he can't even pick up a proper blade." Calais had said a similar sentiment about him, before he stopped loving him, and before Ceven started taking his training more seriously.

Tarry continued as if he hadn't spoken. "You once told us you wanted to change Peredia. For the better. How are you going to do that if you're not here?"

Ceven flung out his hands at an invisible opponent. "Don't throw that at me. Those were the words of a child. And I'm just barely respected amongst the rookies, because they think I can somehow promote them or put a good word in for them.

Anyone with enough rank knows I don't amount to anything in the kingdom."

There was a knock, and the door to the basement opened. It was Barto.

"What?" Ceven said harshly. Tarry and Xilo's advice never got easier to swallow, even as he was nearing twenty.

"We need to talk."

Everyone needed to talk. It sounded like a broken record around here.

Barto was alone, his black tuft of hair looking tousled as if he had been running his hands through it. His face had no hint of a smile. It didn't surprise Ceven that the Rathan was awake at this hour, knowing the man always slept with one eye open.

"If this is about Evangeline, I'll only listen if you can swear to me you won't take her to Atiaca," Ceven started.

Barto scoffed, crossing his arms. His green coat rolled up to show the thickened black fur underneath. "I won't take her without telling you. And if you imply that I'm going to backstab you one more time, I'm going to deck you in the face, like you rightly deserve."

Tarry and Xilo shared a look of agreement. Ceven bristled. Whose side were they on?

"Why would I think otherwise? We've never had to go against each other like this before. You expect me to think you'd disobey your empress, whom you're *loyal* to? I'm not stupid enough to believe friendship is going to make everything okay."

Barto growled and unsheathed his claws. "I'm *loyal* to my empress *and* my friends. I didn't think I'd have to prove it to you. Again. Remember, it was me who saved your ass more times than I can count back in Atiaca. It was me who convinced the empress to send me as an emissary to Peredia, because I wanted to show the king how great of a son you could be to him." He paused and then glanced at the ground. "But mostly it was because I couldn't bear the thought of not seeing you again."

Ceven frowned at the admission. Out of the corner of his eye, Tarry nodded at Xilo and, before Ceven caught on to what they were planning, it was too late.

From the speed with which Tarry had his ax unchained and in his hand, Ceven would think he'd never been injured at all. Xilo moved a tad faster as they rushed Barto, who whirled around just in time.

Everyone froze.

Tarry's ax hovered above Barto's throat while Xilo's knife pressed against his heart. Barto had one dagger to Xilo's neck, the other held backwards, jabbing into Tarry's existing wound.

"What the spitting blazes are you two doing?" Ceven had drawn his sword as well.

"A reminder." Tarry's side bled where Barto's dagger re-opened the stitching. "That if Sir Nu'yuen decides to do something that isn't in His Highness's best interests, there would be no hesitation."

"Killing me will only create more problems for you. I'm not someone you can make disappear that easily," Barto said. "And trust me, you don't want to deal with Rasha and Quan when they find out what you've done."

"Enough. No one's killing anyone. Let me make my own decisions; I'm not a child anymore." Ceven's voice was sharp. "Unless you plan to break your oath."

The three men warily stepped away from each other before silently agreeing to a temporary truce.

"I pledged my loyalty to you nineteen years ago. Again, when you turned eighteen. That hasn't changed," Tarry said.

"And I as well, Your Highness." Xilo clenched a fist over his heart in a sign of respect. "We chose this path. We just want to see you survive it."

Barto remained silent, but his face said it all. It was an expression Ceven had seen on him once when he'd shared how he was the one to find his eldest sister's body. Erika hadn't believed in violence, had spent most of her time foraging for food for their small tribe. A group of passing bandits killed her, all because she had tried to talk them out of stealing their season's harvest.

"Barto . . ." Ceven's words felt heavy on his tongue.

He held up his hand. "I came to patch things up, but it's clear to see where you" —he gave Xilo and Tarry a nasty look— "and your men stand. I just hope it doesn't come back to haunt you later." He turned and left.

CHAPTER 15

Evangeline stared at her disguise in the floor-length mirror inside her and Lani's temporary bedroom. She had to wipe the dust off to get a good look at herself. Her dark brown coat covered her arms and legs, its thick hood swooping up to cover her head and ears. Taking the soil from the flowerpots that sat dead outside their bedroom window, she marked her skin, giving herself a dirty appearance. But, more importantly, it helped hide her in plain sight.

It's not a glamour, but it'll do.

It'd been two days since arriving at this house and a full day since they'd discussed their plans moving forward—which didn't involve her at all. Ceven and the others were to return to the castle to find out what Sehn and the king were up to while they left here her with Xilo and a moody, hairless Rathan who hadn't spoken a word to her. Ceven would make arrangements to get them all beyond the wall when the time was right. Not only did that not tell her anything about when and how they would escape, but it left her with nothing to do but slowly watch her friend dying before her eyes.

Her palm caressed her right side. Xilo had bandaged her ribs, telling her she should take care until she was healed, but the pain had already subsided—which was unusually fast. She remembered another instance, a morning when she had stayed in Ryker's suite, and her bruised cheek from Ryker's slap the previous night had vanished—and a familiar voice had woken her from her sleep. What it meant, she had no idea, nor did she want to think of that right now when more pressing matters swarmed her thoughts.

Evangeline frowned and looked at Lani, who was rolled up in bed. Her skin was still without color, her breathing ragged. Xilo had checked on her several times, giving her medicine to help ease the pain. She now slept most of the day away, only waking to eat and pass a few words.

An image of Vane throwing her friend to the floor, watching her crumple in fear, interrupted her thoughts. She clenched her fists, stretching her leather gloves as something indescribable took hold of her. Not panic or fear this time, but a deep, burning rage that had been churning beneath the surface since they'd left the west wing. Blazes, it could've been her entire life.

She wanted Vane and the king—all those bloody Nytes—to pay. To suffer.

To die.

Evangeline slowly unclenched her fists, staring at Lani. Her priority was to get her friend to safety. She gave her a light peck on her wrinkled cheek and tucked her in tighter before gently closing the door. The living room was empty, everyone either in the kitchen or scattered about doing Gods-knows-what. It seemed a permanent tension always hung in the air when everyone was around now.

"There has to be a way to stop this. To help her. To help all of those humans," said Ceven as she turned the corner into the kitchen. He sat at the small round table, drinking a steaming cup of coffee, next to Xilo, who was reading.

Evangeline had said something similar the other night.

"We have to help them. There has to be a way to get them out of there," she had said.

"And while we're at it, maybe hope for world peace and a fat coin purse." Rasha had sneered at her, her intense gaze remaining on her most of the night. The Rathan had made it clear she thought her the enemy when Evangeline had barely spoken two words to the woman.

Evangeline's eyes narrowed, and she swallowed the choice words she really wanted to hurl the she-beast's way. "I didn't say it was going to be easy. I'm just making a suggestion—"

"That wasn't a suggestion. It was a wish. What we need is a plan, resources, and information. Hoping and wishing won't save anyone."

Barto had placed a hand on Rasha's shoulder, but she shrugged it off.

"I know you're worried about the empress, Rasha, what this could mean for Atiaca, but don't take it out on Eve. We do need to make a plan, however." Barto smiled at Evangeline. "And get you and Lani to safety, especially now that we know the truth."

Evangeline didn't miss Ceven stiffening. Xilo had shifted, and Tarry propped a leg up. Quan and Rasha reacted in turn. Like the silent swing of a blade, a thread of violence pierced the air. One wrong move and things would get nasty. Evangeline had thought it was because of her admission about Ryker, that she had killed a Nyte, and the king's advisor, but it looked like she hadn't been the only one keeping secrets.

Jaw tight, Ceven had stared at Barto. "She's not going to Atiaca."

Barto raised his hands, his tail twitching back and forth. "Calm down, prince. You're acting like I just suggested we kill her."

"Isn't it? Sending her there, to go on trial, is the same thing. I won't have her trade one death sentence for another."

She hated them talking about her as if she wasn't there. "What do you mean?"

They both looked at her.

Barto's face suffused with heat. "Well, it's nothing to be worried about, just—"

"The empress has found you to be an accomplice in kidnapping hundreds of humans." Ceven cocked his head at Barto, as if to say otherwise, but Quan did in his stead.

"Nobody was found of anything. That's what the trial is for."

"Trial? For what?" She had thrown her hands up. "I haven't done anything!"

Ceven laughed humorlessly. "Except murder an important advisor, work behind my back with a Caster, and risk your own life against Wretched and Nytes in the west wing."

"For once, we agree," Rasha chimed.

"Your mark, it's the same as the ones on Lani, as I'm sure you figured out. The empress wants to question you and see if you're involved at all." Barto shot Ceven a disgruntled look. "You'll be on trial, asked lots of questions, but death is the farthest thing you'll have to worry about. Unlike here."

Evangeline had wanted to laugh. Of course, more problems would arise for her because of this blasted mark. All it had ever done was cause her issues. It was the reason Ryker had adopted her and abused her for so many years, why Avana was so obsessed with her, and now it was the reason so many humans were going missing in the castle.

It was the reason Lani was now dying.

"By the Gods, why are you dressed like that, Eve? Is that . . . is that dirt on your face?"

Ceven's words and puzzled look pulled her from her thoughts.

She smirked. "Oh, haven't you heard? It's just the latest fashion—all the rage back in the castle."

She sensed he was suppressing an eye roll, but he crossed his arms and remained silent. His way of saying she better tell him the truth. And just to annoy him, she didn't, sliding by him to snag a piece of bread from the table.

"Eve . . ."

She sighed. "I'm going into the city."

"No, you're not."

"There's an apothecary a few streets from the main plaza I used to visit with Ryker for his special tea. Maybe there's something there that can help Lani."

"Absolutely not."

She'd expected this. Ceven had always been overprotective of her, even as kids, but it didn't bother her any less. "I don't remember asking you for permission, unless you planned on taking Ryker's place?"

He stood, raising at least three heads taller than her, with his blue-and-gold wings fanning out on either side of her. She took a step back, and he frowned.

"You know well it's not like that." His frown deepened. "You're a wanted criminal now, Eve. They'll kill you for sure."

He had been trying to talk to her since they'd arrived here, but she kept avoiding him and the subject. She knew she would have to face him, and all his questions, eventually. But not now.

"I'm human; it's like being invisible. Dressed like this, they'll assume I'm a slave. Nobody important."

"Then I'm going with you."

She raised a brow, gesturing at him, from the buckled brown tunic and dark slacks that showed off his athletic form to his firm jaw prickling with aftergrowth and hazel eyes that had a way of making her heart stutter every time she met them. "You're a Nyte, a prince." *And a wickedly handsome one at that,* she thought. "Even with a coat, your unique wings would stick out. No, I'm going alone."

He didn't argue, because she was right.

She read his expression, how his body tightened, and before he could respond, she released the final blow: "Are you going to lock me up in a cage like Ryker did?"

He stayed silent, like she'd expected, and she turned and walked out the front door.

The smell of smoke and horse dung was the first thing that bombarded her before the storm of hooves, carriage wheels, and scattered conversations surrounded her. Bundled Nytes walked by on the snow-covered streets, tracks from wagons and carriages revealing the bricked paving beneath it. She tucked her coat tighter around her, forcing her legs to move even as they locked up—and it wasn't from cold. But blazes if she was going to admit this might be a bad idea.

You're just going to the store and back. Keep your head down and no one will notice you. It's the one thing you've been good at for most of your life.

The air needled through her coat and long-sleeve shirt, tickling her skin. She eyed a couple of Rathan women to her left, wearing thin dresses, the hems not even warm material but made of lace, their coats carried by the human woman behind them with a coat worse off than Evangeline's. It was a shame the puss-filled Rathans wouldn't freeze to death because of their blood, but a girl could dream.

Evangeline recognized the cluster of slanted and pitched roofs, the wooden structures morphing into brick with wide windows to showcase the goods on the inside. She was familiar with the area, having made regular trips into the city, mapping and planning out her escape route ever since Ryker had adopted her. It had taken years and luck to spot the loose stone, and a couple of Aerian kids flying around. One had crash-landed into the giant stone when she noticed the shift. It'd been her saving grace, while it had been just another day for those kids, not a care in the world. After all, they had been born Nytes.

It was likely other escapees had used the weakness in the wall in the past, or to bring illegal goods into the castle. She was too far from it now, but it wasn't a bad idea to check it again soon—the more possible ways to get herself and Lani out of here, the better.

The sun warmed her skin and the sky was clear, but Evangeline felt as if someone were wringing out her intestines. The streets became denser, Rathans, Aerians, and other humans bumping her shoulder, stepping on her foot, and elbowing her side without so much as an apology. She tightened her hood around her face, invisible hands wrapping around her throat as she imagined the Nytes and humans surrounding her discovering who she was.

Murderer, criminal, filthy pet!

She brushed off the imaginary hands that clawed at her and focused on not tripping and being stampeded by the crowd.

Just across the plaza was the apothecary shop. She was almost there. Her fingers squeezed the gold and silver coins she'd found in the bedroom's drawer. She felt a tinge of guilt at stealing it from Xilo, but if it would help Lani, that was all that mattered.

She knew she had made it to the city's center when a variety of smells hit her—fresh fish, fried sweets, and spicy delicacies, all making her mouth water. It beat the beans and bread she'd been eating the past couple of days. The streets throughout the city all met here, pouring red and gray bricked paths into a giant arena, bordered by tall buildings and stalls of all different shapes and patterns—the only color in these dull streets. It was the city's plaza that morphed into a bustling marketplace at noon.

Evangeline ducked and maneuvered through the crowd. Coming here, when the sun was at its highest, was no accident. If anyone caught her, she needed to make a quick escape into the crowds. Still, the overwhelming amount of bodies made her temples pulse and her hands itch to shove everyone away from her, but she controlled herself. After all, if she didn't, the execution block was only a few steps away, the looming wooden beam at the center of the bricked circle, reminding her of the Nytes' favorite pastime—the occasional hanging.

She'd been almost out of the crowd, just steps from taking the side street where the white-bricked shop lay on the corner, when someone gripped her arm and yanked. Evangeline whipped around and met the gaze of a hooded figured in dark blue.

Squinting, she peered into the shadow of the person's cowl, but when she spotted the black mask and the same slanted eyes she had stared at in terror in the Olaaga forest, she jerked away. At the same time, the fingers tightened around her forearm, pulling her back into the crowd.

A Caster. One of the same Casters who had attacked her and Avana days ago. She had been expecting Peredian guards, blast it, even the king, but not this.

They took out their index finger, the tip covered in blood, and Evangeline knew if they got a single mark on her, she was done for. "Let me go," she seethed, pulling away with all her might. The person was heads shorter than her, but their might was twice her own, even as she kicked, yanked, and pulled, doing whatever it took to make sure they couldn't mark her.

No one in the crowd noticed them, all fixated on something else. It wasn't as if she could call them for help anyway. Her heart sank. She should have listened to Ceven and just stayed at the house. What good was she to Lani, to anyone, if she let herself get kidnapped, or worse, killed right here, right now?

"Ladies and gentlemen! My fair folk, gather around and witness something so horrible, treacherous, it's beyond belief!"

Without hesitating, Evangeline dug her feet into the ground, hurtling herself at the voice that had to be only a couple of rows of people ahead of her. She knew exactly what was about to happen, and while guards would storm the area in mere seconds, she had a feeling this Caster didn't want their presence here known as well.

The crowd shifted, expanding and condensing like a sea, if the sea also had giant tails and wings smacking her in the face. But she embraced the crowd, delving deeper into it as the Caster lost their grip, both of them being pressed in by the crowd, the air turning heavy as the familiar tinge of anger and bloodthirstiness rippled through the Nytes and humans alike. Conversations became maddening howls, indifferent smiles became ravenous ones, and the flurry of arms, wings, and tails wailed about.

Without a doubt, an execution was about to take place.

Chains rang out from the cacophonous crown, chiming in tune to the guard's plated metal, even if Evangeline could only catch glimpses through pockets of moving limbs. Nails bit into her flesh, and something wet touched her skin, but she refused to give up, pulling and throwing her body at the sound of the chains and the announcer whose voice was swallowed by the hungry crowd. Closer and closer, until she catapulted to the ground.

Pain splintered in her back and left shoulder as multiple people stepped on her, and she clawed and elbowed her way back to her feet. The Caster had disappeared into the crowd, but when she turned, she came face-to-face with a row of metal that beamed in the afternoon sun.

And behind the guards, a familiar Aerian stood, thick chains tied around his neck, his sunset wings shifting like flames against the backdrop of clear blue skies.

CHAPTER 16

It's a shame Petri is going to die on such a beautiful day, was Evangeline's first thought as she gazed up at the Aerian whose focus was beyond the crowd.

She had delved back into the sea of people, just enough the guards wouldn't recognize her, but not too far away in case that Caster came back. They had disappeared from her sight, but she was sure they were lingering close by, waiting to catch her alone.

Spitting blazes, she felt foolish. She refused to admit Ceven was right. After all, it was his fault for not telling her a blasted thing about his plan to get her and Lani beyond the wall. Did he expect her to just sit by and wait around for something to happen—or for Lani to get worse?

The announcer's voice rose over the crowd once more, and the Nytes and humans around her came to a dull hum of conversation. ". . . in aiding slaves out of Castle Peak and betraying the trust of our king, Petri Dianonos is hereby sentenced to death."

Evangeline scrounged for some pity, some emotion, but she couldn't muster anything. Except maybe an ounce of regret. For not getting more information out of him when she had the chance.

Petri didn't respond, his words muffled by a black cloth stuffed in his mouth. Usually the guards allowed those to be executed a few last words, but it looked like they'd made an exception for Petri. Most likely to keep him from revealing how the king was using forbidden Caster magic to steal the lives of humans for his own power. To go to war, based on what Ceven had said.

Her nails bit into her skin, her teeth slamming together at the thought of the king, Vane, and all those other guards marking and destroying her kind in the worst way.

She'd almost turned around—she had no desire to watch an Aerian hang as everyone cheered and hollered at his limp body—when her gaze caught on something. A man, a human, with four dots under his left eye.

Petri's words rattled inside her skull. *If you ever change your mind, look for the cut of an ear, four marks of freckles that linger beneath the eye, or a scar above the mouth. Those marks will show who is for our cause.*

Without thinking about what she was doing, she sucked in a breath and squeezed through the crowd at the same time the man moved away. Nytes and humans pressed against her, screams and cheers vibrating her body as she was stuck amid a bloodthirsty mob. She imagined the guards finding her, anyone finding her and discovering what she did, and her taking Petri's place. Everyone screaming at her, cheering for her death. She clamped down on her hood, shoving more forcefully until she exited the crowd and took a deep breath of the cold air.

The man was fast, already slipping past the brick walls between two shops, a narrow alley normally crowded by traveling humans taking the backstreets to get to their given destinations faster. After all, the carefree Nytes who strolled the streets didn't have to worry about being punished if they returned to their masters later than expected.

Shadows doused her as the tall brick walls encased her on both sides. The man was running now, but she was faster—and determined.

Evangeline slammed into his back at full speed, knocking them both to the hard ground. She landed on top of him, his thin coat soaking in the melted snow. He looked to be twice her age, with thin lips and eyes that were round in fear.

"Get away from me! I've done nothing!" He squirmed, but Evangeline held on tight.

"I need help."

The man stopped moving and turned his head to look at her, just now noticing she didn't have wings, horns, or a tail. His eyes narrowed, and he yanked back her cowl.

"No, no, and no. Gods, no, I want nothing to do with you." The man began squirming again, but she refused to let him leave.

"Please, this isn't for me. It's for my friend Delani."

"Why don't you go ask your *father* for help, Pet," he spat, emphasizing the slur he and other humans at the castle had used for her. She frowned at him. He hadn't heard the news about Ryker? Why was the king keeping it secret—he surely had to know by now? Her brows pinched. Were they hiding it for another purpose?

"Look, we don't have time to fight." Though she wanted nothing more than to slam him harder against the ground. She hated that blasted slur. "I know you were working with Petri and others. I want in. I want to help my friend."

"I don't know what you're talking about."

Evangeline's grip tightened, her face pressing closer to his. His heart pounded beneath her fingers, fear lingering beneath the angry scowl he wore. "I've been to the west wing. I've seen what these Nytes have done to us humans, what they've done to my friend. Please, I want to help."

His scowl wavered, but then his eyes flickered over her shoulder, to the screams and shouts in the distance as Petri took his last breaths.

"No."

She was going to throttle this man. "Aren't you a little far from home right now?" Though she hadn't seen him in the castle halls, if he knew who she was and her hated nickname, then he no doubt was far from where he was supposed to be. "I could just as easily tell my *father* that there's a human not following orders. Or better yet, that there's a group of humans conspiring against the king. You being at the top of the list."

"You don't even know my name."

"Don't have to. You have four marks below your eye, and I'm sure there are others with the same marks as well."

"How do you . . .?" He shook his head, eyes shifting to her mark. "And how do I know you're not working for them? You're the only human who's been marked and survived."

"I was found like this well before all of this started happening in the castle." He tried to move away from her, or maybe just to put more space between them, but she dug her nails deeper into his arms. "I don't know how I got this marking, but maybe we can use it to find a cure or help the others. I just want to save Delani. *Please.*"

He sighed, closing his eyes. "I don't know who told you, but they're a blasted fool."

Evangeline omitted the fact that said fool was about to meet his end. She tried to summon more empathy for the Aerian, but nothing came.

"Fine, fine. But don't expect any five-course meals or fancy dresses." She prepped for a retort when he continued, "Meet at the Flighted Inn, on the west part of the city, past sundown. If you don't know where that is, not my problem."

He shoved her off, and this time Evangeline let him. Flighted Inn. She had no idea where that was.

She went to ask when an explosion ricocheted behind her, making her cover her ears. The earlier bloodthirsty screams turned into ones of panic as smoke filled the alleyway. The ground vibrated as feet stampeded, and she was grateful she was far away from the crowd, but it wouldn't be long until Nytes and humans started cramming this alleyway, running from whatever had just happened. Curiosity gripped her, but she wasn't a fool. She needed to get the blazes out of there, too.

Black smoke poured into the alleyway as Evangeline scrambled to her feet. She turned and swore she saw the man smirk right before he disappeared into the fog.

CHAPTER 17

EVANGELINE

Evangeline returned to Eyvan's house, only finding Barto, who was reading on the couch in front of the fire. Everyone else was upstairs or out.

"Ceven's been worried about you," Barto said as she passed him. "But I told him you'd be fine."

She gave the Rathan, whose gaze hadn't left his book, a small smile. The worn binding of his novel read, "Warrior Lover," and her smile grew. "Skip to chapter eight, trust me." She didn't wait for Barto's reply but liked to think she heard a low gasp as she climbed the stairs.

The upper floor of the house was dark and quiet, only the floorboards shifting beneath her feet. Her legs ached from running all the way back, expecting to see a hooded individual pop from the panicked crowd and grab her. The curtains hadn't been closed in her and Lani's temporary bedroom; an orange glow spilled onto the room from the setting sun, catching flits of trapped dust.

Lani was awake, the patterned quilt bunched around her frame as she sat upright in bed. Her silhouette in the window's outline looked like a reanimated corpse out of a horror novel, but since this was real life, Evangeline was less horrified and more heartbroken. What had Lani done to deserve this? Did the Gods—or anyone out there—not care at all?

Evangeline plastered on a smile. "I'm glad you're awake. How are you feeling?" A bowl of beans someone had brought up earlier sat on the bedside table next to her friend. It was still full.

Lani's head wobbled to her. Evangeline's smile wavered, then disappeared.

Her eyes sank into her cheeks, her skin dripping off her head. Seeing the harsh, bold lines of those tattoos—Evangeline's own mark—on her skin was worse than watching Xilo weave a needle through Tarry like cloth. Worse than even fighting off that Caster assassin in the crowd today.

Evangeline crept onto the bed and embraced her, sinking her head into her friend's shoulder. If anyone should be crying, it was Lani, but Evangeline couldn't help it. Couldn't help the disgusting self-pity she felt at not being there for her. At not being able to protect her.

Lani patted her back, like she often had when Evangeline was a kid. "I'll be fine, Eve."

"Don't lie to me."

She didn't reply and dropped her hand. "Then the truth: I feel like my bones are cracking every time I breathe. My skin weighs about a ton, and all I want to do is sleep and not wake up."

Evangeline looked at the bed, unable to face the reality of

what her friend was saying. She scoffed at herself. *You wanted the truth.* "I'm going to look for a cure. And then I'm going to save those people and put a stop to this."

For a blink, Lani's face twisted, then fell as if even that took too much energy. "It's too late for me, for all those people. We're already dead." Her pale eyes found hers, and Evangeline recoiled at the bitter truth in them—and the familiar glare of jealousy. Evangeline had gotten lucky in life, unlike her friend. And much like when Ryker had adopted her and taken her away from the life of a slave, Lani had always secretly damned her for it. She'd never say that, but Evangeline knew. She knew it in the way Lani slowly traded her smiles for insults, her back pats for the cold shoulder.

Lani loved her but also hated her.

At first, Evangeline hadn't blamed her. Lani was right: Evangeline had gotten lucky, and she may not know the horrors her friend went through daily in the castle, or what she had experienced in the west wing. But it wasn't fair of her to discount everything Evangeline had done for her. The risks she took. She'd faced the king, Wretched, even stabbed a Nyte and almost died to save her. She may not have always lived the life Lani had, endured the pain she had, but she'd had her fair share of horror. Ryker's dead eyes still haunted her, as much as the blade of Vane's knife cutting her skin over and over again. And how she'd almost met her fate at the end of his teeth.

"I'm starting to wonder if you'd be happier if this was happening to me." Evangeline regretted saying it the moment it left her mouth. Regretted it when Lani's shoulders shook and she cried. And still Evangeline couldn't help wondering: was she crying because Evangeline thought of her like that? Or because it was the truth?

The room felt heavy, suffocating. She had to get out.

Without a backwards glance, Evangeline left the room—and came face-to-face with a chest.

"Ceven?" She craned her head up. He looked as happy as she did.

"Can I steal you for a moment?" His expression told her it wouldn't be their usual playful banter. She almost preferred the west wing. Running for her life was far less complicated than navigating all these emotions.

They walked into the bedroom across the hall, one with two twin beds and a wood dresser shoved in opposite corners. Similar to the rest of the house, it was plain and simple. Like a blank canvas ready to take on whatever new artist it gained.

Ceven ran his hand through his brown waves. Evangeline mused how many times he was going to do that throughout this conversation. Maybe he'd have a standing mohawk by the end. She smiled, pushing away all thoughts of Lani.

"So many things, you don't know where to start?" Evangeline raised a brow.

Ceven scowled. "It seems you had an eventful time at the market. Who was the man you were talking to in the alley?"

She narrowed her eyes. "None of your concern." Actually, she had wanted to talk to Ceven about the movement, about finding others who could help Lani and the other humans, but the fact he'd spied on her, didn't trust her, riled up her temper and kept her lips sealed. "Who did you send to spy on me?"

"It was to make sure you were safe, Eve. Not to spy on you."

She thought of the Caster, a hand snatching her from the crowd out of nowhere. A sliver of guilt formed in her stomach. She hated that he was right, but she wouldn't admit it. Then again, if he'd witnessed the Caster attack, he would surely be more upset. Tarry was too injured to leave just yet, and Ceven stood out way too much, not to mention his birth defect left him unable to fly. He most likely had sent Xilo out, flying over-head—maybe he had lost sight of her in the crowd when the assault happened.

"Could've fooled me." She shrugged.

He threw up his hands. "How can you be so casual about all this? You're a wanted criminal. You *killed* Ryker. And you went into the west wing, a *human*—"

"As you so often like to point out."

"—went against Wretched and the king! And now you're working with some Caster?" Both his hands dove through his hair.

A bubble of laughter tickled Evangeline's throat. Was this her coping mechanism? Laughing hysterically at every foul thing in her life?

"You're not even taking this seriously," he snapped.

The laughter evaporated. "Tell me this: Why did you lie and say Lani was fine when I asked you in Ryker's suite the other day? Why would you keep from me the fact that she had *already been kidnapped?*" The words exploded from her, along with all her previous ire. If he was going to chastise her for her choices, she sure as spitting blazes was going to give him what she thought of his.

"You know why!" His hand swept the room, as if all of this were her fault. "Because you like to think you're invincible! You do everything on your own, without caring how others would feel if you, oh, I don't know, *died*."

"I didn't act on my own."

"Oh, that's right, because you had your *Caster friend* to help you."

"He's not a friend!"

"He?" Ceven's face darkened. "Any other descriptors you'd like to add for your mystery man?"

She was so angry, she stomped her foot. Actually stomped her foot. The last time she'd done that was when she'd refused to wear a corseted dress when Ryker first adopted her—when she was eleven. "I didn't have a choice! He knew where she was and the means to get there. How was I to believe you would help me save her when you couldn't even tell me where she was!"

"You could've talked to me first, explained the situation—"

"There wasn't any time! Lani was dying, Ceven. I did what I had to."

"And did you have to kill Ryker, too?"

She stared at him. His hair was a mess, his eyes wild. She was sure she looked the same. "I did what I had to," she repeated. And it scared her that she was seeing it that way. That killing a Nyte, *Ryker*, was just a means to end. No matter he had beaten her, manipulated her, and tortured Lani. She still took away his life and any chance he could've had for redemption, and she . . .

She didn't care.

"I don't even know who you are anymore, Eve." He looked hurt, and it ticked her off.

"I told you, I wasn't the same person. I told you that the girl you knew was gone. You chose to ignore that, to see who you wanted to see. That's not my fault."

He didn't argue, and his expression didn't change. Instead, his eyes traced her face, as if looking at her for the first time. "Do you not trust me because I'm a Nyte? Or because you no longer see me as a friend?"

She blinked. She never forgot who Ceven was, but . . . she didn't hate him for it. "So much has changed, Ceven. How was I supposed to know you were still the same boy that I crushed on—" The admission slipped from her, and her cheeks turned hot. She blurted out the rest. "The same boy who would help me braid my hair or rope me into playing tag in the halls. You could have later decided I was only a pampered pet." *Like the rest of the castle's inhabitants believed.*

He slid toward her in one smooth stride, and she angled her chin with his chest to keep his gaze. His hazel eyes looked browner in the dim room, hints of emerald slipping through like the first sprouts of spring rising from the dead underbrush.

"You never gave me a chance to show you I was always on your side."

Evangeline looked away, partly because her neck hurt, but mostly because she couldn't meet his eyes. Or face the fact that she was very aware of him suddenly. She wanted to stay angry, because exploring those other feelings . . . Well, honestly, what would be the harm in it now?

"Are you still on my side?" she whispered, looking at her feet.

His cool fingers coerced her chin up, and the last bits of her anger melted away.

"I don't think I could leave if I tried. And with how much trouble you seem to get yourself in, that doesn't bode well for me." He spoke the truth, but a spark of mischief entered his gaze. His lips twitched into a half smile.

Evangeline raised both brows. "Should we test that theory?"

Ceven chuckled. "I'd rather hear you talk about this crush you had on me."

Her earlier heat rushed back full-force. Ceven had already admitted his feelings for her the night after her training with him and Barto. A stolen moment in his suite that only happened days ago but felt like forever. And yet she still had a hard time admitting a crush she'd had on him when they were children. But the truth was she'd never gotten over it.

"We were kids . . ." she started lamely.

He continued to stare at her, and she knew he was getting a kick out of her squirming. She wouldn't let him get away with it. Before she could second-guess herself, she rose to her toes and melded her mouth to his.

Ceven stiffened, surprised, before he relaxed. She broke the kiss, but his fingers curled around her neck and pulled her back. His lips melted against hers. Hard and soft. Coaxing her. She wrapped her arms around his neck and deepened the kiss.

His wings unfurled and enfolded them, his feathers teasing her bare arms and the backs of her legs like light kisses. His arm snaked around her waist, and the other tangled in her hair, holding her to him. Excitement shivered down Evangeline's spine. The heat of Ceven's body touched her from her lips, to her hips, down to her feet, and yet she still wanted to get closer. She wanted more of him, yearned for it. . . .

He leaned back, his breath rough and unsteady. "Trying to distract me, I see." He tried to sound playful, but his words were a low rumble.

Evangeline knew her face was redder than a sunburn, but she gave him a lazy smile. Feigning a nonchalance she didn't have. "Why, I would never do such a thing."

His hand grazed her cheek, his thumb brushing her lips. "No one else gets under my skin as much as you do. You drive me crazy."

She wiggled her eyebrows at him. "Was that supposed to be a compliment?"

He laughed and kissed her nose, his eyes drawn to her lips. Her toes curled at the heated look, but he pulled back.

"I want you to know that you can trust me, Eve. I know we've had distance between us, but you have always been my best friend." He smirked, his eyes twinkling. "Well . . . most of the time."

She smacked his shoulder, and he gripped her wrist, sliding her closer to him again. Heat sizzled between them. This close, flecks of liquid gold danced in his eyes. Crushed leaves and spice encased her senses, and her hands curled into his chest. His nose nuzzled her neck, placing a kiss on the tender skin there, igniting the already intense flame inside her. She wanted to delve into that feeling, to feel his kiss again, when Ceven reared back. Something in his expression made her pause.

"What?" She touched the side of her neck where he was staring.

"Where did you get that Caster mark?"

Her brows furrowed, then smoothed, her teeth clenched. Raiythlen's mark. The one Avana had warned her about, that Raiythlen had used to track her down in the castle. "Where is it?" Evangeline reached for her neck, trying to pinpoint its location with Ceven's eyes.

His finger touched the space behind her ear. A place she wouldn't think to look, or easily see.

He scowled. "A present from your Caster *friend?*"

She scowled alongside him. "An unwanted one," she spat. "I knew he had placed one on me, but didn't know where. Avana said all I needed is some salt to rub it off."

His expression didn't change.

"What? I know that look. What else is on your mind?"

He shook his head. "I just . . . Why did you shut me out? Why don't you trust me?"

She frowned. There was a time when she would've done anything for Ceven, believed every word he said. Almost to the point it embarrassed her to think back on it. But then he left. For two years. She remembered what it was like to be a human alone in a Nyte's world again. Meanwhile, he lived free in Atiaca with Barto and the others. She had changed so much; why wouldn't she expect that of Ceven? How was she supposed to know the same man who left would be the same one to return? How would she know he wouldn't revert back to the tyrannical prince who had hated and insulted her before circumstance forced them into an unusual friendship?

"I'm trusting you again . . ." she admitted.

"But not fully?"

Evangeline huffed. *You say I don't trust you, but you don't trust me,* she didn't say. She didn't want to fight anymore. "You hate it when I go off on my own, and I hate it when you take it upon yourself to know what's right for me. It's hard to trust someone who still sees you as some child—"

"I definitely don't see you as a child, Eve."

"You act like it."

His hands caressed her back in slow circles, his fingers tracing the curve of her spine. He leaned down, and his lips curled into a sensuous smile. She flushed and pushed him back for some breathing room. Gods, the man was attractive. Dangerously so.

"I meant in how you treat me," she snapped.

"Oh?" He leaned down again, and she shoved him back.

"Blast it, Ceven, you know what I mean!"

"Maybe you can teach me to be better." He smiled, but then turned serious. "Nothing's perfect, but we can try."

Something sparked in his eyes, and Evangeline didn't miss the double meaning in them. Gods, she was burning up. Was this normal? To feel like her whole body was on fire? She thought a single kiss had been bad, but this . . .

Evangeline swallowed the feeling by diving into another kiss. She sensed the eagerness in him, his lips peeling open, as her mouth settled into his. His hand found the curve of her hip, his hand rubbing slowly up her back, but not demanding. He was soft, careful, tentative, but she didn't want that. She wanted passion.

She wanted him.

She pressed herself against him, and his breathing hitched.

His grip tightened on her waist. "Eve." Color darkened his cheeks, and his eyes smoldered. "Do you know what you're asking of me?"

Evangeline had no romantic experience in real life, but that didn't mean she was naïve in that field. She'd read her share of books, had heard the secret lover trysts in the gardens that weren't so secret. Channeling a scene from a particularly steamy novel, Evangeline gave a sultry smile and answered with the subtle shift of her hips. His eyes closed, his throat bobbing as he swallowed hard.

Ceven's calloused hand glided all the way down, from her neck to her thigh, the other sliding up her shirt, air brushing her warm skin before being replaced with his fingers. Bite-sized sparks tickled her skin. She pressed her hands to his chest, roaming up to cup his face before gripping his hair and tugging his attention back to her mouth.

Ceven grabbed her hips and lifted her. She gasped as she landed on the bed with a loud squeak.

"Show-off," she muttered, more out of embarrassment, as his body covered every inch of hers.

"Have you known me for anything else?" Ceven grinned, and she couldn't help but smile back.

He tugged at her shirt, peering at her for permission, before sliding it over her head. He unclasped the straps to her camisole as easily as if it were the clasps to his own combat attire then took off his own shirt and trousers. He paused, and she didn't move, both of them admiring each other.

Do I look like the girl you used to know? Are my breasts too small? Are my hips too bony? Evangeline covered her chest, her legs folding to shield herself from his gaze.

He placed a gentle kiss on her lips, pulling her hands away. "Don't you dare hide yourself from me. I want you, Eve. All of you."

A rush of warmth surged through her at his words, and she wove her fingers into his hair, but he didn't move.

"Tell me you want this. Tell me you want me."

She opened her mouth, but the words caught in her throat.

He lowered to his forearms. His face hovered close to hers, his skin warm and inviting against her bare skin. "What do you want, Evangeline?"

She licked her lips. "I want you," she whispered.

His mouth sought hers in a hungry kiss, and any lingering doubt burned away. Pleasure swelled inside her core as Ceven joined with her, and she couldn't help but think: *Why in the spitting blazes didn't I do this earlier?*

CHAPTER 18

❧ EVANGELINE ☙

Evangeline's arms and legs stayed locked with Ceven's, his wings folding around them, less for privacy and more because the bed was small. Too small. But she didn't want to move or break the silence, drinking in the moment. She felt revived. Warm. Safe. It was hard to imagine anything was wrong in the world as she lay in Ceven's arms.

Ceven ran his fingers through her blond hair, which was now a knotted mess. Completely his fault. She enjoyed strumming her hands over the palm-sized scar on his naked hip and up to the thick jagged one at his chest. The pink outline showing it was fresher than the others she'd explored on his naked body tonight.

His fingers brushed her hair, and she took his palm, kissing it. Her lips grazed the coolness of his ring, the gems twinkling at her even in the dark room. It was almost familiar. As if—

Red painted walls and marble floors enfolded Evangeline. A warm breeze touched her shoulders, her strapless dress brushing her knees. Funny how she felt free, like she could dance, run, and skip anywhere, but her own decision to do what was right had her trapped here. If she was right.

Will you be my queen?

Evangeline traced the fine lettering in the gold band in her palm. The kaleidoscopic gems encrusting it, dazzling and mesmerizing her with all their colors, reminded her of Jaden's eyes in the heat of battle. It was also heavy and distracting. The ring a bittersweet reminder of everything she had done, and what she was going to do. What was the point in doing the right thing if it felt so wrong?

Strong arms wrapped around her torso; whispers caressed her ear and hair. "My love, you're awake early."

Evangeline quickly put the ring back on and spun to see Jaden, with his dark hair tied back and eyes burning, true to the name Anali had given him, like jade in the morning sun. She swayed her hips and hid her feelings with a coy smile. His eyes darkened, and her gut tightened. *Please, don't look too closely at me. I don't want you to see the truth.*

"You're always up at dawn; I'd figured I might try it for myself. And get some things done," she murmured.

He sashayed closer to her, and as much as she wanted to step back, she didn't. That would make it too obvious. "Hmm . . . yes, being queen comes with its handful of responsibilities."

She twisted the ring on her finger. Its words burned into her flesh. Yes, she was the queen, and as a queen, she had to choose—her people, or the man she loved.

"Eve? Eve!"

Evangeline kept her eyes closed, but she chanted, "I'm fine, I'm fine." When she peeled them open, Ceven was hovering over her, his hands on her shoulders. She blinked up at him and smiled. He didn't smile back.

"What happened?"

A lump of guilt hit her stomach. Her secret was exposed. Another one she had kept from Ceven.

"It's nothing." She tried to roll away, but he held her tight.

"Really? We're going to go through this again? Now?"

She frowned, but he was right. She'd be a hypocrite if she shut him out now after everything. "I know, I know, but this . . . this is personal, Ceven."

For the longest time, she hadn't told anyone about this besides Ryker. After all, he had threatened to kill anyone who found out, but now . . . This was about admitting something she didn't fully understand herself. Avana had told her these were memories from a time before her, but it still made little sense to her. How could Evangeline have grown up here, a human in Peredia, but also somehow lived a life centuries ago? And with strangers she didn't know: Raiythlen and Avana's grandmother, Anali, and a man she was supposed to love, Jaden?

And what if Ceven didn't believe her? Or worse, thought she was crazy?

"This isn't the first time this has happened," he said, pulling her out of her panicked thoughts. "Remember when we were kids and played hide-and-seek from Tarry and Xilo?"

She nodded.

"Behind the mantel in the fireplace, we found that hidden tower?"

The memory rushed her. Long-haired Ceven, before he had grown two heads taller than her, giggled and ran ahead of her in the halls. They ignored the dirty looks and nasty remarks. Already being despised came with its perks. No matter what they did, Nytes and humans didn't like them anyway, so might as well do what they wanted, like climbing bookcases and hiding in fireplaces. It was pure accident they stumbled upon the hidden entrance into a part of the castle neither knew existed. They had climbed the winding steps, but when they reached the top . . .

"You started talking to yourself, your eyes looking at me, but not really. I kept calling your name, but you didn't hear me." Ceven's nose wrinkled.

It had been the second time in her life that she'd had a hallucination. And like all her visions, it wasn't a pleasant one. She had been facing a man with skin the color of almonds, eyes the color of the forest in summer. Jaden. He yelled at her while she cried, but before she could figure out about what, Ceven pulled her back to reality.

"It happened that night, too. When you were in my shower," he said in sudden realization. "When you screamed . . . It happened again then, didn't it? And when I rescued you from the dungeons, it was as if you were wrapped up in another world."

"Please . . . I don't want to talk about it. It . . . it makes me feel too vulnerable."

I don't want you to think I'm crazy.

His shoulders squared, and she readied herself for another argument, but the tension rolled out of him in a sigh. Propping himself on his arm, he lay beside her. He stared at her, then at the wall behind her. Thinking. "I won't press you about it, then. But just know, nobody's perfect." His lips twitched. "Not even me. I know—hard to believe."

Despite herself, she cracked a smile.

His eyes returned to the wall, his lashes falling halfway. "When I left . . . no, when the king forced me to leave Peredia, I felt worthless. Unwanted."

She brushed his hand, tracing the back of it with her thumb.

"I failed you. I didn't even have the power to stay by your side."

"Ceven, that's not your fault. I didn't expect you to always be there to protect me." Except she had. But now she realized she needed to rely on herself, because there could come a time when she was alone. Like she had been for two years. Like when she was lost in the west wing, surrounded by Wretched.

"I just feel like I'm constantly trying to prove myself. To everyone. That I'm not just a worthless bastard. That I could be a great king too, if given the chance. If my mother never had that affair. If her best friend had never betrayed her secret—" He paused, his teeth clenched. "I could've been respected."

Evangeline had always wondered how the queen's affair got out but assumed the king had caught them in the act. Not that someone close betrayed her. "But you already are respected. I respect you, and so does Barto, Xilo, Tarry . . ."

He sighed. "I know, it's just . . . I sometimes wish I could do more than I can."

Evangeline almost laughed at the irony. How she, a human, had wished she could be as strong as him, as any Nyte. To be an equal. "At least you're not human."

His eyes widened. "No, I didn't mean . . ." He turned away. "I know my struggles don't compare with yours, or Lani's. It wasn't fair of me to complain."

She squeezed his hand. "It's different, yes, but they're still real to you. They still bother you, as much as my own weakness bothers me. And you've tried to do so much for me and Lani. I know not being able to change anything is frustrating. Trust me. I know that feeling well."

His hand left hers and curled around her hip. Hair rose where he touched her naked skin. "It's why tomorrow I'll be leaving for the castle."

She froze, even as his fingers continued to move along her backside. "Do you have to?"

He sighed. "I want to figure out what the king is planning. No, I need to. I can't let him, or anyone, continue this . . . whatever is happening. I feel like I may be able to stop this—"

"Ceven, it's not up to you to save everyone—"

"But what would that make me if I turn a blind eye to it? If I did nothing? I could stop the king, maybe even my brother. I can save this city. This kingdom."

Evangeline pressed her lips. She wanted to say: *who cares?* All this kingdom had done was treat him like dirt. Both of them. He owed them nothing. Even as much as she wanted to save those humans, she only wanted to save her friend. It would be easier to just leave now and forget about everyone.

You're the kindest, most selfless person I have ever met.

Ceven's words sank to the pit of her belly. She couldn't tell him how she really felt. *Ceven, you're far more worthy of kindness and selflessness than I have ever been.*

"I wish you could stay here with me. That none of this was happening. That we were already in some small cabin far away from here, with that garden you promised me years ago," she finally said.

He tucked a strand of hair behind her ear. "Me too. And soon we will be."

But if he returned to the castle, she had a feeling it would never be.

CHAPTER 19

The next morning, Ceven, Barto, Tarry, and Rasha all collected their things to prepare to head back to the castle. Quan and Xilo would stay with Evangeline and Lani, waiting a few days until they could make plans to move them out of the city. In the meantime, Ceven planned to recruit several men from the army—rookies he trusted, he said—and have a talk with his brother to figure out more about what the king's goals were. If he didn't return in a few days, he told them not to wait for him and to stick to the plan.

Evangeline waited to hear said plan, but Ceven's lips stayed sealed on the matter and Barto gave him a nasty look, quipping with, "I'm sure the plan is secret from us Atiacans." Nobody commented on it.

Ceven fixed the collar of his navy coat and checked his belt for his swords and the two daggers hidden beneath his lapels. "I'll try to be back quickly," he said, his gloved hand cupping her cheek.

Evangeline picked off a loose thread from his shoulder, avoiding his eyes. His words from last night, about wanting to leave with her, settled in her chest. It was an odd feeling: being wanted and loved. Unlike the tumultuous relationship she had with Lani, or the cold one she had with Ryker. This one she felt she could lose at any moment. Or ruin it, like she had with Lani.

"Be safe." She hugged him and buried her head into his shoulder, soaking up all of him. It was possible it would be the last time she ever could.

They left, and the house turned quiet. Snow piled on the windowsill outside, but the fire Xilo started made the house toasty. Evangeline rolled up the sleeves of her oversized shirt.

Xilo checked on Lani, gave her something to drink to ease the pain, but she still wasn't looking good. Evangeline attempted to talk to her, but Lani was unresponsive. She didn't know if it was because of the pain, or if her friend hadn't forgiven her.

Evangeline stood in the bathing room, trying to peer at the Caster mark Ceven had spied. She thought of grabbing some salt from the kitchen and being done with it—if Avana hadn't lied to her about how to remove it—but if anyone would know where to locate a place, it would be Raiythlen.

She pressed on the mark, thinking loudly in her mind of the annoying, infuriating Caster with blue eyes she had once found pretty. Now, everything about the man ticked her off.

If only Ceven believed in me more . . . She frowned, wondering if neglecting to tell Ceven everything that had happened at the plaza was the right move. But knowing him, he would've had a fit and berated her for making such dangerous decisions. Mayhap even throwing her over his shoulder and marching off to the castle with her in tow. He was too protective and always felt she couldn't handle herself. It didn't help she had a horrible streak of proving him right in that arena—but blast it if she wasn't trying.

"Come out, come out, Caster," she whispered to herself in the mirror. She felt more and more foolish by the second. Did she seriously expect Raiythlen to magically pop up behind her? She shook her head. It was clear the mark was one-sided—that or Raiythlen never made it out of the west wing. That thought didn't sit well with her.

"Is there anything I can help with?" Evangeline asked Xilo later that afternoon. She had thoroughly waltzed the house, attempting to glean anything helpful from it, maybe maps of the city, or a list of inns in the area, but no luck.

Xilo's gaze was the same as always, indifferent but far more pleasant than Quan's. He sat on the armchair by the fire across from the bald-headed Rathan, whose head had turned away from her as she came down the stairs. Evangeline swallowed a retort. She was used to the behavior from most Nytes and had gotten good at reading body language, at knowing when one of them thought her lesser. The refusal to look at her or address her, the scrunch of their nose whenever she entered a room, or the occasional insult thrown at her. Most Nytes didn't bother acknowledging a human's presence, but Quan made a show of it, as if making sure she saw his hatred.

Evangeline pretended not to notice the Rathan as she glanced at Xilo. At first, she thought he was reading a book, but when she got closer, she saw it was a journal, judging by the hand scribbles.

"Not at this time," was all he said.

She bit her lip. Xilo had been around for most of her life, but she had never exchanged more than a handful if words with him. Did he hate her? Was he just good at disguising his emotions? "Are there any books here I could read?"

He told her about the study downstairs. It was nearly hidden behind a door, just a forearm's length bigger than her frame with her head brushing the top of it, squeezed in the crevice between the pantry and the back door. She'd assumed it was a closet and hadn't bothered with it in her initial exploration of the house. The air was cooler in the small, converted basement. She admired the shelves, the wood so dark it looked black. Odd bobbles and glass lined its spaces. She stood on her tiptoes to read the labels on the glass jars.

"Mugwort, rosemary, dandelion...." It was a list of herbs. At least she assumed so, only recognizing a couple from the ones Lani mentioned when talking about her work in the kitchens. Boring. The opposite side was more appealing, with colorful, both new and old, bindings. Xilo's son was an avid reader as well. However, her excitement died when most of the titles were on herbal properties. But it wasn't completely a lost cause: a few adventure stories grabbed her interest, and one on Caster magic. Something she'd never seen in the castle's library. She still didn't know if it was taboo or if the lack of knowledge was to fool the Aerians into thinking they were stronger than any Caster magic. Maybe both.

Evangeline would've preferred the couch upstairs but settled for the brown armchair at the desk, the arms frayed along the threading from use. It beat having to face Quan's scowls or Xilo's disinterest. Or Lani dying in front of her.

The book on Caster magic sat forgotten on the desk as the riveting story about a pirate, wielding scabbards and conquering the vast ocean, sucked her in. She imagined an expansive shimmering sea of blue and green, like the one Ceven told her about from his time in Atiaca. The two of them aboard a ship the size of this house, with the wind combing their hairs, blades at their sides and—

Squeak, squeak.

Evangeline yanked her feet off the ground and peered around the room. Her eyes narrowed at every dark corner, and she wrinkled her nose. What if it was Raiythlen's 'pet' with another message, like the one she'd received before the ball?

A palm-sized mouse skittered by the stairs, staring at her with black eyes. She whispered and cooed at it, but it didn't move. Maybe it only listened to its master.

She shrugged. "Go ahead, spy on me. Not like I'm doing anything interesting." But what if it was just a normal mouse? She felt childish and returned to her book.

Squeak, squeak.

She flopped the book on the desk with more force than was necessary and stomped over to the mouse. She snatched it up before it could scurry away.

"I'll put you outside, so you can stop chatting," she said. The mouse squirmed in response, its plump torso trapped in her hand, its tail wriggling against her pinkie.

I wonder how it'd taste.

Evangeline dropped the mouse. It landed with a squeal and disappeared back into whatever hole it came from while she blinked at her hand. What in the blazes was she thinking? She waited for the disgust to come, but all she could think about was sinking her teeth into the squirming mouse. Its blood rolling over her tongue and warming her belly.

A knock later, Xilo came in to find her standing in the middle of the room, still staring at her hand.

"Miss Evangeline?"

She looked up at him, and he frowned but didn't comment on her unusual behavior. Maybe he'd seen his share of it in his long life.

"I've prepared some food. Ceven advised me to keep you well fed."

Evangeline broke from her odd mouse fixation. "Advised, or ordered?" she countered. Ceven had been watching her eat, disappointment written on his face as he glanced at her unfinished food. It was just because so much had happened, she told herself. It wasn't as if she's had much of an appetite for the past few months anyway. *Except now for mice.* She extinguished the thought and followed the stoic Aerian upstairs, but not before tucking her Caster magic book beneath her arm.

CHAPTER 20

CEVEN

Ceven passed through the massive golden gates leading to the castle, past the ever-growing statue—the God of all Gods—each ridge in its expansive wings, which seemed to grow every year, glittering in the afternoon sun. He still couldn't get rid of that sinking feeling in his stomach. He flexed his muscles, expecting a beating or a scolding, even though Sehn and the king were deep in the castle's heart, somewhere in the main hall.

Guests from all over Peredia and a few from Atiaca and Sundise Mouche still lingered in the halls, their attire less regal than that displayed at the party of the century—but Peredians say that about every ball the castle hosted.

His crew followed behind him. Barto's green pants billowed, the cuffs tightened at his ankles. Like their Atiacan guests, he wore a shirt cropped short, revealing his pierced navel while

Rasha stuck with her armor, like Tarry. Ceven had never seen the woman wear anything but plated leather except on special occasions—like the ball or any festival involving the empress of Atiaca.

Aerians dressed in low-cut gowns and unbuttoned suits with ornately beaded corsets and jackets filled the halls. The beadwork was mediocre; the stones and gems used weren't rare finds, but designed for practical wear. Those designed for defensive measures against Caster magic sought a high price that even most Peredians shied away from. Or they felt secure enough in the kingdom that had held for hundreds of years.

The four of them stopped in front of Ceven's suite on the top floor. Two guards stood on either side of the carved mahogany, their spears straight and rigid, like Ceven's spine. Who were these men? When Ceven left to find Evangeline, he had placed two trusted soldiers to guard his suite. Where were they, and who had relieved them of their duty?

One guard sported a curly beard sprinkled with gray, the other brown flappy ears sagging on the sides of his face, blending in with his shoulder-length hair. Most Aerians were taller than any other species, but Ceven had been blessed—or cursed, depending how he looked at it—with an extra finger's length or two. He used this to his advantage, narrowing his eyes and uttering, "Where are Taryn and Ed?" He didn't waste time with politeness or formality. He wouldn't put it past his brother or King Calais to post spies at his door.

"Relieved of their duty, sir," curly-beard said.

"Obviously." His voice dripped in sarcasm. "Let me guess, Sehn assigned you."

The Rathans nodded.

Ceven and Tarry shared a look. They would have to keep their conversation quiet from eavesdropping ears and find out where his men went off to.

Tarry walked in first, and Ceven imagined his bodyguard's hand on his ax, his frostlite rings swirling like the last time they'd entered Ceven's suite like this. Not knowing who would be inside. But this time Tarry's ax remained sheathed and Ceven trusted the suite was empty—his bodyguard's instincts were better than his. Forty years in service to the king and even more before that as a mercenary, Tarry was a force to be reckoned with. Even with the remnants of his wound, which Xilo had to restitch from Barto's dagger, and torn wing, he still was lethal.

Barto, as far as Ceven knew, didn't tell Quan or Rasha about Xilo, Tarry, and Ceven's little "discussion" back at Eyvan's house. He was sure if Rasha knew, she wouldn't be as calm as she was now. Or maybe it was an illusion to give them a false sense of security. He was more wary of her than Barto. At least his friend would warn him before stabbing him in the back.

Unlike me, he thought with a frown.

"Well, nothing's changed," Barto said, breaking the silence. He tapped on a glass panel holding Vivian, a sword crafted in Beltore, a small town known for their mining of frostlite and other high-quality stones along the western side of the Frostsnare mountains.

Ceven frowned, staring at his friend's sharp claws. "Careful."

Barto rolled his eyes. "If the mere tap of my finger could shatter your precious trophy, I don't think we'd have a problem facing the Peredian army."

"We won't be facing anyone," Rasha said, her face still deceptively calm.

"I agree. This is between me and my family." Ceven grimaced. He didn't consider the king and Sehn his family. "I shouldn't have involved you as much as I have. I don't want to see you in any trouble." They may have different goals, but Barto was still his friend. A blasted good one at that, and Ceven wouldn't want to see him hurt. Or worse.

"Little late for that, don't you think?" Barto smirked and strolled past the white sofa to plop into the chair beside it. Rasha leaned against the purple wallpaper behind him.

Someone knocked on the door. Tarry put a hand on Ceven's shoulder and strode past to check. Down the hall of the suite, there was a mumble of words and footsteps before the door clicked shut once more.

Tarry re-entered. "A word, Your Highness."

Ceven glanced at Barto and Rasha. Barto's smile was gone, and a shielded pain clouded his eyes. Ceven ignored it and followed Tarry into his bedroom, shutting the white, paneled door behind him. They walked past his four-post bed and bookshelves, filled with more trophies than books, to close the curtains. The soft oil lamps fixated to the wall were the only light in the space.

Tarry pulled out a note from his pocket and handed it to him.

Ceven smiled. Sounded like Taryn, a rookie who acted like he owned the place. Even if they had become fast friends during his return to the country, any soldier would know better than to refer to Sehn or the king as anything other than His Highness or Your Majesty. Ceven recalled the soldiers back in the west wing and the thinly veiled disgust he'd experienced with those guards he met in secret by Eyvan's house. *But I guess that doesn't apply to me, does it?*

Tarry's voice was like distant thunder, low but ominous. "If we follow through with this, there's no turning back."

"You suggest we do something else?" Ceven didn't mean it but hated that Tarry assumed he hadn't already thought everything through. Multiple times.

"No. Barto's a good man, but his loyalty to the empress is a problem. Be prepared: I've intercepted a messenger bird meant for Rasha. She had sent for reinforcements."

Ceven's gut churned. "We'll need to move quick then. Send word to Xilo."

Tarry nodded, and they returned to the Sitting Chamber. Rasha and Barto stood by the foyer entrance.

"I think it's time for us to retire to our guest suite. It seems as if we have overstayed our welcome here." Rasha's dark brown eyes bore into Ceven's, while Barto kept his gaze averted.

"Very well." Ceven crossed his arms. There was no point in lying. "I plan to meet with my brother soon. From there, we can decide our next move. I'll have someone sent for you when I know more."

"Will you?" Rasha cocked her head.

Tarry and Ceven didn't respond, and Rasha curled her lip before turning on her heel.

Barto lifted his head and locked his gaze with Ceven's. "You've been a good friend to me these past two years. I know you're planning something, but I want you to know that I value our friendship. I won't betray your trust, Ceven. I just hope you have enough honor in you to do the same." Ceven looked away, and the click of the door told him Barto had left as well.

From his words, Barto might as well have already stabbed Ceven—in the heart.

Tarry put a hand on his shoulder. "Like I said, Barto's a good man. But I've met my fair share of 'good men.' Everyone has a tipping point. Be wise on this."

"I know, Tarry." He shrugged off his hand. The old Aerian was trying to help, but blast it, Ceven hated feeling unsure about himself. "For now, we just need to focus on getting information out of Sehn."

CHAPTER 21

Biting wind kicked up the ends of Evangeline's coat, forcing her shoulders forward to block the chill. She clenched the gold pieces in her coat's pocket with one hand and the palm-sized knife in the other as she passed darkened silhouettes in the night, their feet crunching snow into the bricked path. Her joints remained stiff, her hands fisted in case any Casters tried to snatch her. It wasn't the wisest decision, being out by herself in the middle of the night, but at least she was doing something. More than she could say about Xilo and Quan, who played more of the role of babysitters for her and Lani than companions with the same goal of escaping Castle Peak.

The night brought with it an additional layer of snow, about an arm's-length deep. Enough to break her fall from her and Lani's second-story window.

With her usual disguise in place, her cheeks smudged with soil, she had found the courage—or maybe it was desperation—to leap to the nearby tree branch that hung by her window. Of course, she had missed and plummeted to the ground instead, surprisingly landing on her behind with nothing but a slight pain up her spine. She was sure Xilo or Quan had heard her, but after a few heart-pounding moments, nobody came out to scold her, the house remaining as dark and quiet as the night that stretched before her.

Yellow light beamed behind fogged glass, a sign fixated to the storefront swaying in the wind that read, "Apothecary Solutions." Evangeline passed it, taking a right down the alleyway where she had pinned down that man.

"West of the plaza, about two blocks until you'll reach the inn. You'll know you're in the right spot when the wall is about four or five palms high from eye level and the sour smell of spilled drinks and urine will be strong enough to drive you away," the fourth human she had tracked down and asked had finally told her. The others she had asked either didn't know or had ignored her. Evangeline reached into her coat pocket to pull out a gold piece as a show of thanks, but the hooded human had already turned and continued walking, and Evangeline slid the piece back in her pocket. It was for the best. If tonight turned out to be a failure, she would still try her luck at the apothecary. Even if it was just a simple tonic to help her friend's pain.

The human hadn't been lying; a foul stench sent her nose reeling into the sleeve of her coat. Dim lighting leaked from the tall, narrow windows, taking up the expanse of the bricked path and illuminating questionable puddles that Evangeline was sure weren't melted snow. Shouting, laughing, and Gods-awful singing streamed from the two-story building and were loud enough to be heard a block away. Unlike the browns, grays, and dark blues she had passed, this one was a bold yellow, almost garish and unsettling, with purple painted flowers on some of the wood paneling. Odd. She had seen no other building like it.

She raised her head towards the hanging sign that sported quite a few scuffs and dents in the bronzed plate.

"The Flighted Inn. Finally." She buried her face into the collar of her coat, trying not to breathe as she entered.

If she had thought it was loud outside, inside was almost unbearable. In the few steps she had taken, she had narrowly missed a fist aimed for the Aerian behind her, and another reaching for a glass of brown, foaming liquid.

Evangeline tried not to let her nerves get the best of her, but it was hard when a suffocating heat, paired with strong body odor from the Nytes around her, pressed on her senses. Where the blazes would that man be? Had he tricked her? Or was she too early, or too late? After all, a day had passed since he had first told her to meet at the Flighted Inn past sundown.

Tables, fashioned like the king's mahogany one in the castle's royal dining room but half the size and twice as many, littered the tavern housing boisterous Nytes. A haze of smoke settled atop the heads of every patron, lingering towards the top of the low wooden ceiling. Either someone had sparingly placed lamps here, or the collective cigar smoke made everything more difficult to see.

She asked around, giving basic descriptors of the man with the four dots below his eyes, but they all either shrugged her off or cursed at her. At one point, a Nyte sloshed their drink onto the end of her coat—the foul liquid reeked—and it tempted her to turn around and give them a smack, but that would get her killed. She gritted her teeth, about to give up, when silence descended.

Evangeline turned and followed everyone's gaze to the Rathan that had entered from the beaten door. They peeled back their black hood to reveal a square jaw and hard-set eyes that were as dark as his coat. Thin, long ears flattened to the sides of his face, almost blending in with his shoulder-length brown hair, but it was the Rathan's unusual height and the jagged, long scar striking across his face that made her nails bite into her palms. And in that moment, she realized she didn't see a single human here, besides herself. Gods, what had she gotten herself into?

The mysterious Rathan waltzed toward the bar. Instead of sitting down at the cloth-covered stools by the counter, decorated with the same purple flowers as out front, he stepped behind it. Without hesitation, he picked up several glasses, filling them with that foamy liquid before plopping them on the counter with a bang.

"If you want your blasted drink, come and get it yourself," the man said without glancing up.

Several Nytes stormed the bar, snatching the drinks, the Rathan deftly replacing them with more glasses. It was amazing he could keep track of it all.

She frowned. There were no other humans here, including any human slaves or workers.

Evangeline swallowed and made her way to the bar after most of the Nytes had settled back down at their tables, the tavern notably quieter and more reserved than it was previously.

"Excuse me, my lord?" Her hands bunched the fabric of her coat.

The Rathan raised a brow at her, his dark eyes razing her up and down. "Do I look like a lord to you?"

Curse this man, this blasted place, and every puss-filled Nyte here. "Do you know a human man who looks like—"

He waved his hand. "Pipe it down, Pet. And by the Gods, wipe that dirt off your face. I almost mistook you for one of my customers."

Evangeline froze for a half-second before she remembered how to speak. "That's kind of the point here."

A faint smile dusted his face, making him quite handsome, if you discounted the scar rippling down to his jaw. "What you're looking for is the second-to-last door on your right, up the stairs."

"Stairs?" She turned but didn't see any.

"Outside."

Evangeline sighed in relief upon trading the muggy, hot tavern for the cold, brisk air, despite the stench. Rounding the corner, she expected to find stairs, but instead got a snow-covered alley. Had it all been a ruse to get her to leave the inn?

Footsteps fell behind her, and her heart sank. This was a trap, wasn't it?

But when she turned, she was greeted with the human man from the plaza, but he no longer sported the dots below his eye. He was shrouded in the same frayed coat and wearing a familiar scowl.

"Was hoping you wouldn't show." He curled his lip, stepping past her to the end of the alley. He stepped behind the large waste bin, swinging open a door she hadn't known existed. It didn't look like he would wait for her, so she scrambled after him, following him inside through the hidden door.

Carpeted stairs immediately greeted them. A faint glow coated the banister from the top of the stairwell, leading to a narrow but cozy hall, with its carpeted flooring and flower-embroidered tapestries. Not what she expected a secret meeting place to look like.

They entered through a side door, and Evangeline stopped

in her tracks. The room wasn't extraordinary by any means, with an interior that trickled in from the hallway. What made her reel back was the Aerian sitting at the square table shoved in the far corner, the reds, oranges, and pinks popping against the dark wood paneling behind him.

"I thought you were dead," Evangeline said.

Petri looked to have been in deep conversation with the Aerian woman across from him. The woman's wings shifted and it reminded Evangeline of a beach's shoreline—at least from what she had seen in her books—a bright blue merging with a faint beige, when Petri glanced up and smiled.

"And I hope to keep it that way. Glad to see you have changed your mind since we last met." He extended his hand to the rickety seat beside him, but Evangeline opted to lean against the wall opposite him and the other Nyte. It didn't feel far enough away, her standing only about five paces from the table they sat at. The room was as cozy as the hallway. And small. Too small, if anything went wrong.

"I didn't have a choice." She clenched the knife in her pocket. *The explosion, the smoke, it must've been tied to Petri's escape.* She frowned. *How did he get everyone to still believe him dead?*

The human shut the door behind them, bringing Evangeline's attention to a gray-eared Rathan woman sprawled on the green chaise in the opposite corner, chewing the nail on her thumb, and a human boy wrapped in an oversized coat next to her, perched on the arm rest.

"Ah, yes. You had a friend you were after." He frowned. "I . . . hope your journey had a happy ending. You made it out alive, at least."

She looked away, uncomfortable with how everyone's eyes were now settled on hers in the suffocating room. "We both made it out, but it doesn't matter, because it won't be long until she's dead."

"She was marked?" the Aerian woman asked. Evangeline looked at her and remained silent, letting her fill in the blanks.

Petri cleared his throat. "Well, let me introduce you to everyone. This here is Annabelle"—he gestured at the Aerian woman—"on the sofa is Rayne, and next to her is Kel. And you've already met Sebastian." He nodded at the man, who still wore the same scowl as he had outside. "Everyone, this is Evangeline."

"This is it?" Evangeline said before she thought better of it.

"Better than nothing." Rayne shrugged, but her eyes fixed on Evangeline through the tuft of brown hair.

"There are others inside the castle, but this is the extent of the party outside it, with a few exceptions," Petri said. "It wouldn't be safe to gather everyone in one place."

The floorboards looked as ancient as Peredia itself, but Sebastian's footsteps were silent as he approached her. She knew what he was grabbing before he took the dagger and aimed it at her throat. She forced herself to remain calm, which surprisingly wasn't hard. She had faced much worse.

"Now tell us why you're really here, Pet." His scowl turned into a smile. "I hope you are a spy, so I can slit your throat and be done with this nonsense."

Nobody stopped him, not that Evangeline expected anything from any of them. She didn't know them, and the last time she had met Petri, he had been at the end of her makeshift blade. Still, she found it ironic that the current threat to her in a room of mostly Nytes was a human from the castle. Then again, Petri and the others didn't need to flaunt a dagger to prove they could snap her neck.

"I told you already. I want to save my friend Lani. These blasted markings are eating away at her and nobody knows enough to save her." *Or cares, really*, Evangeline thought. Even Ceven. They all looked at Lani as if she were already dead. "I want to save her. I *will* save her."

"That's touching and all, but if you want information, you're going to need to give us more than that to trust you're not an insider." Sebastian's dagger drew closer, the edge resting against her skin. Evangeline was less afraid and more annoyed, wanting to snatch the dagger from his hand and chuck it across the room.

"We can trust her," a deep voice said.

Evangeline jerked, and she realized the voice had come from Kel, the small boy on the couch beside the Rathan. But that had not been a boy's voice.

He grinned, as if shocking people was his favorite pastime. "After all, she's already carried out part of our plan for us without realizing it."

Evangeline frowned, and judging by everyone else's expression, save Petri, she wasn't the only one confused. Sebastian even lowered his blade, narrowing his eyes at Kel.

"What do you mean?" she couldn't help but ask.

Kel cocked his head, the pale, shallow-cheeked boy staring at her with dark eyes that revealed much more than what he was showing. "To think the Pet killed her own master. Tell me, how did it feel when you murdered the king's esteemed advisor, Ryker Ardonis?"

CHAPTER 22

Evangeline froze at Kel's words. How did this man—boy—whatever he was, know when no one else had? And she could confirm no one else did, judging by the looks around the room. Rayne sat up, reevaluating her. Annabelle's smirk was slow and far more wicked than her previous gentle smiles and soft-spoken words. Sebastian's mouth hung open, as if in disbelief.

"If that had come from anyone else besides Kel, I'd call them a liar," Rayne said.

"I didn't kill Ryker," Evangeline lied. More to find out how this boy knew more than everyone else, where his reasoning came from.

Kel hopped off the couch, his curled black hair only reaching up to her chest. "You were the last person to see him,

considering the next time anyone saw the advisor, he'd been in a glamour." Kel winked. "I would know."

Well, that explained the difference between his voice and his outward appearance. "You're a Caster?" Granted, he didn't need to be a Caster to use a glamour, but it was a guess.

Kel's smile receded. "Partly."

"A halfing?" Evangeline blinked. It was rare for offspring to survive from two different species, and even harder to spot them, considering most looked normal on the outside, save for some that carried noticeable birth defects.

"And I like that title as much as you adore the nickname 'pet.'" Kel's face hardened. "Don't call me that ever again."

Sebastian sheathed his dagger, a smirk on his face. "So, you're the guiltiest one here."

Heat rushed Evangeline's cheeks, but she ignored it, pinning her stare on Petri. "You invited me here; now tell me how I can help Lani, or I'm out."

"Little late for that." Annabelle stood and stretched. Her wings brushed Sebastian's shoulder, and he shifted away, raising a brow at her. "But," she continued, "if you want to help your friend, you'll need to help us. The cause." She turned around and, from the brown bag at her feet, pulled out rolls of paper. "And you can start by stirring the pot."

Evangeline grabbed the stack of paper, unrolling one and skimming its contents. "Unrest in Castle Peak" and "Mysterious markings: the workings of a disease or dangerous Caster magic?"

"How will this help? Most people and Nytes already know about these markings and no one cares," she said.

"Only within the castle walls. Most outside its gates have heard nothing like this." Annabelle flicked back a lock of dark hair from her shoulder. "And whether it will prompt others to take action, it will create some turbulence and give the king and his royals something to focus on, away from the trouble we're about to cause."

It made sense when the Aerian put it that way, but Evangeline needed more concrete details. She said as much.

Petri nodded. "I'll tell you the gist of our plan. . . ."

To start, they would infiltrate the west wing, disguised as victims, whether by glamours or mimicking the markings with black ink, and sabotage the operation from the inside. Most humans were not fit to defend themselves, let alone move, so they would have to make several trips to get out as many people as they could. On the last trip, the plan was to demolish the rest of the west wing, triggering explosives all throughout the lower floors and the ground level, to make sure the entire place as inaccessible. This time permanently.

"But how would you get into the west wing in the first place?" Evangeline asked. "The place is crawling with Wretched and—" The beast Vane had become swarmed her mind, and her body reacted as if the monster were in front of her. Her heart raced, eyes wide, hands clenching the knife that would be nothing more than a paper cut to a Nyte like Vane. That spitting bastard.

Petri's calm voice brought her back to reality, and she noted a hint of sympathy in his eyes. She wondered if he knew about Vane, what he could become, before he sent her off to those holding cells. "I know of a few underground routes into the area. We would use those to come and go."

Evangeline's brows shoved together. Only the royal family and their trusted guards knew of those tunnels, from what Ceven told her. How would this Aerian know of them?

Before she could ask, Petri turned to Kel, who already suspected what he was going to say when he pulled out a palm-sized vial. It matched Evangeline's eyes, green with an occasional hue of blue, the only feature about herself she liked. Kel popped off the cork and swayed the glass vial back and forth in front of Rayne, who jumped off the couch at a speed that reminded Evangeline how quickly any of these Nytes could kill her if they wanted to.

"Cut that out," the Rathan growled.

Kel's grin grew, but he put the cork back on. At Evangeline's confused look and Petri's chagrined one, he sighed and explained how it was the closest thing they had to a cure, and also was everyone's ticket beyond the walls of the castle's city. One sniff was enough to knock someone dead—or close enough to it. It put them in a coma-like state, slowing down their heart rate where someone could easily mistake them for a corpse. This coma state also helped put a pause on the negative effects of the markings, based on experience, and could grant everyone more time to look for an actual cure. From there—with everyone resembling corpses—they would pile anyone who wanted to escape the city onto a wagon and cart them beyond the walls to the burial pit a few hundred paces away.

Evangeline had heard of the burial pit. Any excess dead were burned and then buried there, and she always knew when it was time for the next cart to roll out from the cries of humans as Nytes took their friends, sisters, brothers, mothers, and fathers away. Meanwhile, the Nytes had their loved ones put in the underground catacombs, built into the mountainside the castle rested on, each grave adorned with an altar filled with offerings. Evangeline sometimes imagined the mountain crumbling, burying with it both the castle and all its puss-filled Nytes, both dead and alive.

"Does this really hold off the effects of the markings? If Lani took this, could we save her?" She hated how desperate she sounded, but blast it if she wasn't at this point.

"From what we've seen, yes." Petri grimaced. "The other rooms outside this one hold a few people we saved before they got to the west wing. You can see them if you'd like proof. They're currently in this coma state and have lasted longer than those who chose not to inhale Kel's solution." He shook his head. "There's still a lot of work to be done, and there's no guarantee we'll be able to save everyone and stop this entire operation, but we have to try," Petri said.

You're right, there's no way any of this will work, Evangeline didn't say, because she wanted this to succeed. She wanted to save those people. She wanted to save Lani. "Why would you go through all of this? Why would any of you?"

Petri and Annabelle shared a look, small smiles with distant eyes. Kel's playful expression dropped completely, his face returning to the solemn appearance he had worn when she'd first entered. Rayne turned away, but not before balling her hands into fists. And Sebastian . . . well, his expression didn't change much at all.

"We all have our reasons," Annabelle murmured, lost in thought. "Whether it be for the sake of a loved one, themselves, or the sheer righteousness of it, all have brought us here. Much like yourself."

After that, they discussed points of entry into the west wing via the underground tunnels, and when and where to strike. Evangeline omitted the one she knew about within the barn that she, Ceven, and the others had all come from. It would be another bargaining chip in her pocket, in case they still didn't trust her or needed something more from her.

At one point, they took Evangeline to see the other rescued

humans in the extra rooms within the small hideout. Like Kel said, they looked dead, but occasionally, their chest would rise and fall, the faintest breath touching her finger when she placed it beneath their noses. The same inky tattoos covered their skin like Lani's, but they didn't seem to squirm or pulse with a deadly beat like Lani's did whenever she dared to touch them. Evangeline took a closer inspection of one of the girls with matted brown hair and sunken eyes. She gasped. It was Shani. The mother of the boy who had disappeared weeks ago, and whom Evangeline had threatened in the halls of the castle for information. Information she needed to save Lani's life because of that puss-filled Caster, Raiythlen.

Her hands curled into fists. It wasn't fair, none of it. How could Nytes like Vane and the king get away with this? All of this suffering they caused, and for what? More power? As if the power they already had wasn't enough?

Pain sprouted in her palms, her teeth mashed together, and something gripped her. The closest she could compare it to was a deep-seated rage, but it moved beneath her skin, through her veins, pulsing, pounding, and screaming at the skin behind her eyes. She thought of Vane, his muzzle dripping with saliva as his teeth snapped at her neck. Of King Calais's gray, cold eyes piercing down at her like she wasn't a living, breathing being. This time, the thought didn't paralyze her with fear, but sparked something darker. She wanted to kill Vane. She wanted to kill the king himself. Sink her teeth into their necks, rip out their throats, and—

A hand on her shoulder jerked her back to the present. Kel raised a brow, peering more closely at her than she liked. Evangeline swallowed and turned away, that dark rage rescinding and sinking into the pit of her stomach.

The night grew long, and Evangeline said she needed to return before anyone noticed. Nobody asked where she was staying, or her current circumstance, just nodded, and they all agreed to meet back up in a few days. Evangeline tucked the rolled paper into her coat and promised to uphold her end by posting these wherever she could. In return, Kel gave her a vial of their "temporary cure" and said when the time came, they would take her and Lani beyond the walls and to Helgard. Evangeline nodded, contemplating the offer. She still needed to see what Ceven's plans were, but it was something.

And it was better than nothing.

CHAPTER 23

Ceven stood in Sehn's suite. The hand he placed on the hilt of his sword quivered, and his pulse quickened with a familiar fear. Instead of his brother, as Ceven had planned, King Calais lay in the center of the luxurious suite. It was larger than Ceven's and adorned in dark hues of reds, browns, and gold, matching the darker nature of its owner and current occupant.

The king sat on the sofa facing the grand fireplace made of black marble, a contrast to the one in Ceven's, his arms and wings spread out across its red velvet upholstery. All the curtains in the suite remained closed, the only light coming from the fire, which cast dancing shadows along the walls. King Calais didn't turn at Ceven's arrival, nor was he dressed in his usual exuberant attire—vibrant robes overtop a tailored suit and polished boots. Instead, he looked unusually normal in a plain, cotton top and riding trousers. He still wore an excessive amount of jewelry, however, with rings adorning multiple fingers and chains roping down his exposed chest.

"Your Majesty," Tarry said, bowing at the back of the king's head. Ceven kicked himself for not speaking first and letting Calais's unexpected presence rattle him. He hated how this man had the power to make his gut turn inside out, his legs feel like they were on board a ship. Like he'd woken up from a wicked night of drinking only to find all his weapons and armor stolen and a knife at his throat. No, that night was preferable to what he was feeling now.

Ceven strode farther in, with Tarry at his side. He squared his shoulders and kept his chin high but avoided meeting the king's eyes. "Didn't expect to see you here. Where's Sehn?"

From his peripheral, Calais smiled, and Ceven recognized the condescending expression without turning to look at him. "I was curious when you would return to the castle. And if it would be Sehn whom you'd meet with first." The king cocked his head at the blazing fire. "But I'm more curious about what you have to say to a brother whom you've always loathed."

Ceven's stance wavered, and he cursed himself for keeping his hand on his sword. He folded his arms instead and forced himself to meet his father's eyes. "Perhaps you should ask him yourself."

"You've been avoiding me. I've left you to your own devices, but now it seems you're hiding things from me." Calais flicked his hand in Tarry's direction, only Ceven noted the brief hesitation in the Royal Guard before they locked eyes. Tarry bowed and left.

"I've done what you've asked of me since returning here. I've kept my nose out of the kingdom's affairs, entertained those Aerian women you insisted I court with—even attended the ball with one of them. If I'm not going against any of your direct orders, I don't see what the issue is with how I spend my free time." Ceven kept his voice firm. Anything less and he risked the king seeing right through him. Seeing the truth.

"My advisor has gone missing. You wouldn't have anything to do with that, would you, my bastard son?" Without shifting his head, Calais's gray gaze flicked toward him, freezing Ceven in place.

Ceven ignored the usual jab and forced his brows to furrow. "Lord Ryker is missing?"

The king laughed mirthlessly before standing. Ceven couldn't help himself; he took a step back, but the king turned and whipped open the heavy maroon drapes blocking the glass doors to the balcony. Ceven's suite didn't have one, not that he would've used it like most Aeriens did anyway—as another entrance to come and go as they pleased.

The rays from the rising sun reflected off the ripples in the king's gold wings as he fully stretched them. It was odd to see such regal wings paired with attire similar to Ceven's. In the light, dark veins coursed through Calais's body, his skin paler than Ceven last remembered. He beckoned Ceven forward, and despite himself, Ceven obeyed, standing a couple of paces away.

"Run your sword through me."

Ceven blinked, his mouth ajar. "Have you lost your mind?"

"Oh, don't try to act noble now. I know you've thought about it countless times. It was written all over your face."

When Ceven made no move to stab him, King Calais snatched him by the front of his shirt and yanked him forward—over the balcony.

"Put me down!" Ceven spat. His feet dangled in the air, and he flapped his wings furiously, knowing they wouldn't work, even now with the risk of dropping from one of the highest points in Castle Peak. The freezing air whipped at his hair and clothes, and he gripped the king's arms for dear life.

"You've always been too soft–hearted, boy. You're nothing like this family," he sneered as he kept a firm grip on the front of Ceven's shirt. "You still can't fly, can you?"

Ceven's eyes fixed on a landing not too far below him, the blue-and-white scaled roofing angled in such a way that he could land with his feet or latch on with his hands if needed. "You spitting know I can't!" Ceven's teeth were clenched. He had dealt with that humiliating fact his whole life, but it had been bearable when he'd been in Atiaca, surrounded by Rathans and welcomed as a foreign prince. Then he had returned to Peredia and was reminded of what he really was. An unwanted, bastard prince whose beauty served as nothing more than a trophy for how useless both his wings and himself were to this kingdom.

"Prove to me you're worthy. Use that anger and hurt me."

"Why are you doing this? What's the point!" Dots danced in his vision, and he remembered all the times Sehn had held him to the floor, pounding his fists at him, demanding he fight back. But he hadn't; instead he had cried out for his mother, cried out for anyone to help him. He felt just as helpless now as he had back then.

The king loosened his grip, and Ceven hated the sound that slipped from his throat. "From this height, even a Nyte would die instantly as soon as they hit the ground. You've seen me do worse things. Do you really think I won't follow through?"

Ceven knew he would. He wore a similar expression to the time he had forced Ceven to fight him until he could no longer move. He had only been fourteen at the time, and the king still mercilessly attacked him, even when he had already broken Ceven's arm in three different places.

Drawing on that anger, Ceven snatched his sword and rammed the blade into his father's stomach.

The tip missed as the king leaped backwards, using his wings for momentum before dropping Ceven. He landed on his feet, on the balcony floor.

"Finally, you've learned to fight back."

Ceven's whole body shook, his teeth clenched and his heart slamming against his ribs. "Do that again and I'll kill you."

The king took a step toward him, and Ceven raised his blade higher. He had never held a weapon against his father willingly before. As a kid, he hadn't had the guts, but now . . . he wouldn't hesitate to strike the final blow.

"The strong outlive the weak. And you, Ceven, had always been weak. Never fit enough to rule this kingdom and always cowering in your brother's and my shadow." Ceven's grip tightened on his sword, and the king's eyes narrowed. "If you decide to go against me and this kingdom, you won't stand a chance."

Ceven's knuckles stretched thin and appeared white before he exhaled through his nose and sheathed his sword. "I'm leaving." Ceven turned on his heel.

"Ryker . . . he had been working with someone else. And I fear the biggest threat to this kingdom is yet to come."

Ceven wanted to keep walking but paused in the archway to the foyer. "And why should I care? You said yourself I'll never be fit to rule this kingdom, anyway." He tried to deliver the words with the same careful control as his father but failed.

"Because it has to do with Evangeline. You'd do best to kill that girl now while you have the chance. Before it's too late and she dooms us all."

I'd sooner kill you, Father, he didn't say as he strode off, an unsettling feeling weighing on his chest, pressing against his still-racing heart.

CHAPTER 24

The following day, Evangeline went about the house reading, stopping for cooked beans and rice Xilo had set out for her. She insisted she could cook for herself, that she wasn't a pampered pet, despite what everyone called her, but Xilo continued to make her meals. She later realized it was to ensure she was eating at Ceven's request, and that upset her more. If he had been there, she would've eagerly given him a piece of her mind. As it was, she was riddled with thoughts of the king and Sehn finding out the truth and beheading Ceven, or locking him up in the dungeons. Gods, she wished he had never gone back, especially now that she knew about Petri and the others. That there was another solution to all this.

Last night, after leaving the tavern, she had put up a couple posters before returning to the house, but she still had eight more. She made a plan to leave again tonight and the following nights leading up to their next meeting, to make sure she had planted the papers as far and wide as she was able. She had also given Lani Kel's potion, murmuring "this will help" and "I hope you're feeling better," though she knew they were empty words. Still, Lani smiled, squeezing Evangeline's hand despite their previous conversation. Evangeline turned away as tears gathered. Shortly after, Lani had fallen into a deep sleep, her face more relaxed than Evangeline had seen in a long time.

After finishing the afternoon meal that Xilo had prepared and insisted she eat, Evangeline washed her bowl and others in the sink. It was odd, doing things like washing up after herself, let alone other Nytes—willingly. Last time, she didn't have a choice. Whilst drying her hands on the embroidered cloth, a thought came to her, one that had been at the back of her mind, but she hadn't had the chance to ask.

She found Xilo with his purple wings furled at his sides, his eyes narrowed on the twin needles in his hands, weaving a green thread into the half-started blanket.

"I didn't know you . . . knitted." She kept her tone neutral. It wasn't every day she saw a Royal Guard doing something so . . . mundane.

He nodded and kept silent.

Evangeline bit her lip but decided to just blurt out the words. "Where is your son?" She'd assumed he would be here, or at least have returned by now. But he hadn't, and Xilo hadn't mentioned anything about him.

Xilo paused for a moment, as if feeling for the right words. "Eyvan is in Sundise Mouche at the moment."

Her brows rose. "Wow, for what? I didn't think any Peredian would want to go there." Not that it was illegal or anything now, but with all the distrust and tension existing between the two countries still, it seemed dangerous. Treaty or not.

Xilo continued to weave the needle and thread with an adept speed. She searched for the smallest tic in his jaw or a crease of his brow, but she found nothing that would imply she was annoying him. Or maybe nothing fazed him anymore. The old Aerian, like Tarry, had always possessed an eerie calm. She envied that about them.

"Their modern technology and magic have always fascinated him," he said. "Ever since he met a Caster at one of the Peredian balls. Like him, she also practiced medicine. From then on it was hard to dissuade him." His lips puckered briefly.

"You didn't want him to go?"

He set down the needles and looked at her. It was odd, having his full attention, and it reminded her of Ryker. "It's not that at all. I'm glad he's found something he's passionate about." But there wasn't any sway to his words.

Evangeline wondered if the mother was still around, but since Xilo didn't mention her name, she felt as if she had her answer.

For the rest of the evening, she curled up in the leather chair by the fire downstairs and read the book on Caster magic she had found, hoping to find a cure within its worn binding. It reminded her when she would sit in her chair in the castle's library and read for hours, the only time she could escape being a human living within a Nyte's world and could be someone other than "Ryker's Pet."

Although she found nothing that could cure Lani, a slip of paper shoved towards the back of the book piqued her interest. The handwriting was crisp but hastily written. *Saliver: a small green plant, found near riverbeds in warmer climates, highly poisonous if taken in large quantities. Easily mistaken for Vetiver, or swamp weeds, and . . .* She skimmed, a little disappointed that it wasn't something more important, until . . . *a common practice amongst Atiacans. In small amounts, over a prolonged period, it can counteract the magical properties in Caster blood, making the user immune to direct magical influences on their person.*

Immune to Caster magic . . . Evangeline smiled. She imagined Avana's shocked look if, when she had blasted Evangeline with her sleep powder back at Ryker's suite, instead of sleeping, Evangeline had decked her in the face instead. It would be what she deserved.

When the only light in the house came from the fire and an oil lamp overhanging the table in the kitchen, Evangeline stretched from her spot, her limbs aching from staying the same position for a while. She covered her mouth as she yawned. Maybe some sleep would help before she left again tonight.

"Going to bed?" Xilo said from the kitchen. She hadn't even noticed him sitting at the table until now. She nodded, about to head up the stairs, when her eyes shot to the stack of papers beside him. Her heart sank.

Xilo unfolded the rolled parchment, reading the cursive ink, dotted with different hues of red and blue, to make it stand out more on the creamed paper. Evangeline had to admit the penmanship was remarkably done, especially for so many posters having been made.

She folded her arms. "When did you find out?" He hadn't given her the slightest inkling that he knew anything about her nightly excursion from their earlier conversation.

"The moment you left." His eyes flicked to her folded arms. Beneath the long-sleeved sweater were cuts and scrapes from where she had fallen from the tree last night.

Evangeline couldn't even muster the strength to be upset. Had she really expected to fool Xilo? An Aerian who had been with the Royal Guard for decades and had equal time to hone his instincts and skills? "Does Quan know too?"

Xilo nodded, his eyes still perusing the paper's contents. Whether he agreed or disagreed with the cause, he didn't show it. "If it hadn't been for him, you would have had a far rougher night." He glanced up at her. "A single human girl out in the city in the middle of the night. You should know better."

She frowned. Quan had protected her? *But of course,* she thought, *he needs to present me to his empress, and it would help if I'm in one piece.* "I've been out plenty on my own. Day and night."

"On castle grounds, not here."

She neglected to tell him the many times she had snuck into the city on her own at night. Well, maybe not many, and it wasn't always at night, but enough to where she didn't need to be scolded by him. Was this what Ceven felt like with these two older Aerians growing up?

"It's dangerous day or night for a human living in Peredia." She dared him to argue with that statement. He didn't. "Why didn't you stop me, then?"

Xilo rolled the paper back up and gently set it on the table. "Information."

Her skin broke out in bumps, her heart racing. Was he going to rat them out? Get the Royal Guard involved in this? She shook her head. *Get a grip, Eve. He's currently committing treason by hiding me and Lani here. He doesn't have time to deal with a rebellion, let alone care what happens.*

Xilo handed back her stack of rolled paper, and she took it. "Get some sleep, Evangeline, and please try to stay inside for the remainder of our time here."

For the next couple of days, Evangeline had tried her hardest not to stay inside. And every attempt she made to leave the house, her Nyte guards caught her in a heartbeat. Whether it was from her window, or the window in the other bedroom, day or night, Quan or Xilo were always there to greet her. The former Nyte a lot more disgruntled and aggravated than the latter. She even tried to sleep in the basement, pretending she had already gone upstairs for the night before attempting to leave out the back door. Xilo had stopped her before she even turned the knob.

Her patience was running as thin as the two Nytes that watched her, but whenever she confronted them on the matter of going outside, even suggesting that they come along and watch from afar, the answer was no. She was not to leave the house until further orders. And the fact she couldn't do anything about it irked her. Who knew how long Kel's potion would last? Would Petri and the others still be at the same location if she didn't show up on the third day? What if they decided she'd betrayed them and told the king about her treason, or her whereabouts?

She wanted to scream in frustration.

Yanking open the bathing room door, she glared at herself in the mirror. She felt for Raiythlen's mark on her neck and pressed down. *I don't know if this works, but I swear to the Gods you better be alive, you puss-filled Caster. As much as I hate your previous uninvited visits, I could sure use one of those right about now. I hate to admit it, but I need your help.*

No response.

"Stupid, blasted, puss-filled Caster. What good is your mark if you can't even communicate?" She refused to think he had perished in the west wing. There was no way. "Fine, if you don't want to answer, I'm removing your blasted thing. See how you like that!"

She knew she was being ridiculous as she dug her hand into the bag of salt she'd dragged upstairs from the kitchen. She slapped and rubbed the side of her neck, staring at her own scowl in the mirror. Avana had said salt would remove it, and Evangeline hoped the woman hadn't also been lying about that.

Her neck tingled, and a moment later, she couldn't see any marking.

It was the dead of night when Evangeline rolled over, the thick comforter wrapped around her feet. Tree branches rustled outside the window, chipping away at the glass at alternating intervals, but that wasn't what woke her. It was the sound of nails scratching over something.

And it was at the end of their bed.

Her eyes shot open. Slivers of moonlight scattered across the dark floorboards and threaded rug to the violet wallpaper—outlining the shadow in the room's corner.

Evangeline bolted upright but held back a scream when she recognized the familiar smirk. Raiythlen leaned back in the chair, hands behind his head and his black knee-high boots resting on the edge of the four-post bed. As if he had an invitation to be here—then again, wasn't this what she wanted?

"How . . .?" She shook her head. "I shouldn't be surprised."

He raised his brows and removed his hands from his head. "What? Didn't miss me?" His nail scraped along a metal pendant at his neck.

She glanced at Lani and looked pointedly at him. He curled his finger at her, commanding her to come closer. Like a dog. She snarled at him, and it didn't improve her case.

"Unless you want me to wake up Lani, I'd suggest you come here."

And I'd suggest taking your puss-filled self back to the blasted west wing, she didn't say, because she cared about Lani more than her petty words. And, inconveniently, she needed his help.

Evangeline got out of bed, and heat rose in her cheeks. Her oversized t-shirt was enough to cover the essentials, but not much. She wrapped her arms around her torso as if that would restore her dignity.

To the Caster's credit, he didn't remark on her state of dress but reached for her hand. A silver ring sat on his finger with a serpent curling around the band, its tail ending in a sharp point. He pricked his index finger with it, and Evangeline shivered at the touch of his blood inking her skin.

The dark liquid made her mouth water as the smell of iron and fire teased her nose. Her eyes widened, and she swallowed, forcing her attention back to the symbol darkening and branding her forearm. She recognized it. It would fade away in an hour.

It's about time you showed up. I was thinking you'd died, she said in her mind. It was still as uncomfortable as all the other times she'd done this with him.

He smirked. *So, you did miss me.* His eyes flicked to her neck. *When you removed your mark, I lost track of you. I thought the worst may have happened, or my sister had caught you. I'm lucky it was only your foolishness and that you were still in the same place as where you removed it.*

So, he hadn't heard her through the mark; it only served as a way of tracking her. At least in the end, she got him here one way or another. *You shouldn't have marked me without my permission.*

He ignored her comment and turned to the bed. *I'm glad Lani is okay.* His expression was devoid of sarcasm, but she still didn't trust it.

She's not. We saved her, but whatever they did to her, she's not doing well. She frowned, debating telling him, then figured he probably already knew. He always knew. *I've met with others who want to put a stop to this. One of them gave me something to help Lani. They might be able to save her and the rest of the humans in the west wing.*

Looks like you've been a busy girl. His lips thinned. *Whatever they gave you, it's only temporary. I can sense the magic is still draining her.*

There has to be a way to stop it. She hugged herself tighter. The heat from downstairs didn't quite make it to the second floor. *Isn't there something you can do? Some kind of magic?*

He raised his brow. *I'm not an all-powerful god that can heal with the tip of a finger.* He wriggled said fingers for the full effect. *To counteract Caster magic, it requires knowing what the original spell is, the strength of it and length, and then using a trial-and-error method of figuring out what potion or spell can cancel it.*

She wasn't liking the sound of that. *So, you're saying there isn't anything you can do?*

He held up his hands. *I just don't want you to get your hopes up. I have a few potions I use to ward against offensive spells, but it's designed for me and my body.* He narrowed his eyes at Lani. *I don't know how it will affect your friend, or if it would have any effect on this type of magic. I don't even know the full extent of it, just what it does at the surface level.* He looked up and met her eyes. *Lani will die from this.*

Evangeline turned around, blinking. She hated how her first reaction was to cry, even more so now because this man had to witness it. He brushed her arm, but she jerked away.

With her back still turned, she said, *I want to try everything. She can't die. I won't forgive myself if she dies.*

Why? It's not as if you did this.

She spun around, hoping he didn't notice the wet gleam in her eyes. *Didn't I? She wouldn't have been a target if it hadn't been for me.*

She would've been a target, regardless. Life isn't fair, Eve. Sometimes things happen out of your control.

It's Evangeline, she reminded him. He raised an eyebrow as if to say, "Are we really going there again?" *And it wasn't random. Lani said Ryker went after her because of me.*

We've established he's a manipulative ass. Good thing you killed him.

Her nails bit into her palms. *You made me.*

No, I gave you the tools. You're the one who pulled the trigger, so to speak.

Her lip curled. *You're no better than Ryker.*

His face darkened, and she remembered his knife at her throat, the blood trickling down her neck. She hadn't known if he was going to kill her or not. She still wasn't sure.

It's time to grow up. Take responsibility for your life and actions. You're a smart woman, one who can make her own decisions, unless I misjudged you?

She scowled at him. He was baiting her, and she wouldn't give him the satisfaction. *I can, which is why when you threatened Lani's life, put a dagger to my throat, and told me you could kill me and her whenever you wanted, I played my cards the best way I knew how. To save Lani and me.* He still terrified her, just like the king terrified her, and Vane and the Wretched. But she couldn't let it control her. Not when it wasn't getting her anywhere. *Don't talk down to me.*

In one graceful move, he stood. He wasn't as tall as Ceven, her eyes level with his, but she straightened and met his gaze. He was an arm's length away from her.

I wasn't talking down to you. He took a step until they were a finger apart. He bent his head slightly, a black ringlet dancing across his slanted eyes.

She stepped back, not caring if he took that as a win. She hated being close to him. Seeing his cocky smile up close and personal.

He didn't follow her, and the smirk was wiped from his face. She dared even think he looked . . . apologetic?

Look, we got off on the wrong foot, but I think we'd actually make suitable partners. Together, we can gather a lot more intel, he eventually said.

Her jaw dropped. *That has to be a joke. A poor one.*

You have potential.

She held back a snort. *You know partners don't lie to each other, or trick each other into murder.*

He looked at Lani, then back at Evangeline. *If you hadn't killed Ryker, I wouldn't have been able to impersonate him and gather information on where Lani was. If we hadn't worked together, your friend would still be missing, or worse. Do you regret that?*

"There are other ways," she mumbled under her breath.

To prove that I mean what I say, I'll let you in on a secret. He waited, and she gave him the obligatory "well?" look. *The Council sent me here.*

That's not a secret. I figured that out on my own. Evangeline hadn't exactly figured it out, but she had made a guess after Avana told her she had worked for the Council herself. It wasn't too far off to believe her brother also worked for them.

But not the reason they sent me here. He smiled. *My original mission was to capture you.*

She stared at him. *What?* His words tumbled in her brain, and the longer she thought on it, the more cogs clicked into place. All the times Raiythlen offered to take her and Lani back to Sundise Mouche, when he promised her safety and freedom away from Peredia. It really was all for his gain.

Before she could combat his statement, he continued, *But everything's changed, and that's why I'm offering a genuine partnership—based on mutual gain. The Council has betrayed me, its own people. The treaty was all a ruse. Sehn was never alive to sign it to begin with—*

She waved her hands. Too many things were buzzing by her. *Wait, what? What are you talking about? What mutual gain? How did they betray you?*

The bed creaked, and Lani moaned.

"Eve? Everything okay?" Lani whispered.

Raiythlen had disappeared, leaving Evangeline to stare at where he'd just been standing.

Evangeline turned and smiled. "Yeah, yeah, just . . . couldn't sleep. Might get some fresh air." Her smile wavered. Kel's potion didn't last long at all; maybe Lani required a stronger dose. Evangeline needed to see the glamoured boy sooner rather than later, but first she needed to figure out how the blazes she was going to leave without her "guards" noticing.

"You're going to catch a cold like that. Come back to bed."

Evangeline had no intention of going back to bed, not until she finished her conversation with Raiythlen—if he hadn't already left her. But she humored Lani for a bit, sitting on the edge of the bed and looking down at her friend's haggard face.

Lani squinted at her before her wrinkled hand rubbed Evangeline's arm back and forth. "If you don't get some sleep, you'll regret it tomorrow."

"I'll be fine."

Her friend made a disapproving noise. "If you don't get up before dawn, I won't save any sweet rolls for you."

Evangeline frowned. "Lani, you're not in the castle anymore. We're at Eyvan's house. I've told you this."

Lani opened her eyes, but they were glazed over, staring past Evangeline. She didn't respond for a bit, then closed her eyes. "Come to bed, my sweet. It will all be okay. Mama Delani was lying; I'll save you as many sweet rolls as you like." She then hummed a familiar lullaby Evangeline hadn't heard since she was eleven.

My sweet. Her heart squeezed. Lani hadn't called her that since Ryker had adopted her and the divide between the two of them had begun.

Lani's cheek was warm when Evangeline placed a kiss on it, pulling the blankets tighter around her. It wasn't fair. She didn't deserve this.

Hoping Raiythlen was still nearby, she snagged on a pair of pants and threw another shirt over her baggy one for extra warmth. Her and the Caster's conversation was far from over.

CHAPTER 25

EVANGELINE

Evangeline snuck down the stairs into the living room and found Quan on the couch. Awake.

"Going somewhere?" He took a swig out of a fist-sized leather canister in his hand. He hissed, his face crumpling like a piece of paper.

"Drinking your sorrows away? Wouldn't have taken you for that kind of man," she said, hoping the loose button-down, tied and tucked into her sagging pants, didn't detract from her intimidating stance. Oh, who was she kidding? She looked like she could only break a stick.

To no surprise, he scowled. "I don't drink."

"Could've fooled me."

"Answer the question."

She was tempted to just give him an inappropriate hand

gesture and move along, but she didn't need him hoisting her back up the stairs.

"I'm going to sit on the porch. I need some fresh air . . . away from Lani." That wasn't a total lie. "Is that a problem?"

Judging by his face, it was, but he didn't move from the couch. Xilo's coat hung by the back door, and she slipped it on. If his coat was here, it meant he was sleeping upstairs. Or pretending to, at least.

"If you try to run, you won't get far."

She rolled her eyes. "I spitting know that, Quan. Thanks for stating the obvious." She cast another look at his leather decanter. He said it wasn't alcohol, and knowing anyone from Barto's group, they wouldn't take something that would inhibit their fighting skills, not with the current tense atmosphere. Saliver, supposedly, was common practice within the Atiacan empire. It wouldn't be too much of a stretch, would it?

"Is that a flask of concentrated saliver?" she asked.

His slitted pupils widened a fraction before pinching together. He didn't reply, but it was answer enough for her. Interesting.

Without waiting for a proper response, she left out the back.

Xilo's coat was large and lined with thick white fur. It didn't erase the cold, but it helped keep it at bay. The painted green floorboards looked like they would break if she stayed in one place for too long. She brushed off snow and dirt from the chair that looked less sturdy than the floor, but she took her chances anyways and sat in it.

Can you hear me?

Evangeline jumped and played it off by snuggling into the coat. *Yes.* Her breath billowed out in hot steam in front of her. She took a few more breaths, watching the puffs of clouds vanish.

Good thing you're sitting, because what I'm about to tell you . . . well . . . you're going to be tempted to call me a liar, but it's the truth.

Just tell me already.

His Highness, Prince Sehn LuRogue, is dead. Has been dead for years now. The man you've seen and talked to wasn't him but Aimee Hysander—one of our beloved Council members.

Disbelief struck her, and Raiythlen was right; she was tempted to call him a liar. The idea was too . . . impossible. *You're lying, and why not? You've done it to me before.* But then an image of Sehn, his high cheekbones, blood-red wings, and stormy gray eyes like his father, came to mind. The uncharacteristic smile he'd given her at dinner all those nights ago. The feel of his cold fingers on her cheek as he tucked a white, blossoming flower in her hair from the main hall's garden before parting with her, his chilling words echoing in her head as he left.

"There are monsters lurking in every dark corner," he had told her. The realization of it all was a sharp blow to her gut. Had Sehn—the Council—known about the Wretched and what was happening in the west wing all along?

Evangeline remembered the soreness of the saddle biting into her legs and the taste of snow at the back of her throat as she crashed onto the ground, surrounded by Casters in the middle of the Olaaga forest. That ambush, the Caster in Ryker's suite, and the one that had attacked her at the plaza, had they all been sent here by the Council? Did they want her for her marking as well?

Raiythlen pretended as if she hadn't spoken. *The only way this could get any worse is if my sister was involved, but thankfully, I don't think Avana is aware. At least if she was, maybe we'd be on the same side again. She hates the Council more than anything.*

A memory of her and Avana's conversation spoken in the middle of the night, far from the castle and its city walls, drifted into her mind. Avana mentioned she had worked for the Council and Evangeline got the impression there was a good reason she no longer did. *I don't understand. If Sehn is dead and this . . . Caster is taking his place, why sign a treaty? Why feign an alliance when a real one could be had?*

He didn't reply right away, and the howling wind added to the dark atmosphere and her growing dread. If a Caster—no, a Council Member—was pretending to be Sehn . . . what did that mean for Ceven? She had to tell him.

Power. Curiosity. Control. All of the above. We've always been the strongest country until this . . . disease started happening. Then Peredia proved to be a problem, and my guess is that the Council wanted in on it. But our Council works for the people. If they wanted to make such a political move, they needed to be sneaky—to hide from their own country what they were really doing. Even I didn't know, and still wouldn't know, if I had never taken the mission to track you down, which I only did to stop my sister from doing the very same thing our own Council is doing.

Evangeline shook her head. This was why she hated politics.

And it gets worse, he continued. *Humans have no rights here, unlike in Sundise Mouche. I haven't found any proof, but my theory is that they're going to ship humans to Sundise Mouche from here and secretly continue the process of what's happening in the west wing. That way, the Council doesn't alert the public to what they're doing, and they get access to this power at the same time.*

All her fantasies of maybe traveling to Sundise Mouche in the future melted away. She would never find out if ships really flew in the air, or if pictures danced across flat surfaces. *Nowhere is safe, it seems.* At least for a human.

All of this because of your mark, he said. *This magic. This is why*

it shouldn't exist, why I burned all of Anali's journals. It corrupts people, promises things that aren't going to end well.

You said it opens a link between people's souls. She'd always wondered what her tattoo meant, and now that the answers were unfolding before her, she wished she could forget. Or better yet, that she had no part in this. *Why am I not affected?*

That, I don't know.

Evangeline told him Avana's theory: that she had been sent forward in time, that these hallucinations she was experiencing were memories. If it was true, maybe she could figure out more about her mark and who she was by triggering these hallucinations. To see why she was sent forward in time in the first place. If it somehow tied to what was happening in the present.

Raiythlen had the same reaction Evangeline did when Avana had first told her. He laughed, the sound rumbling through their connection. Evangeline clutched her coat tighter and pursed her lips. This must be how Avana felt.

Then explain why I remember your grandmother, who died long before they brought me to Peredia. How I ended up with a mark on my hand that dates back centuries ago, she retorted.

He didn't, because he couldn't.

I knew Anali and her team of people had done multiple experiments back in their day, he admitted. *They earned quite the reputation. Maybe you were a product of one of them.* She imagined him shrugging, as if this entire conversation wasn't as crazy as it was. *In that time, many humans worked with Caster magic and technology to enhance themselves. As for time travel, I've never heard of anything like that. I don't even know where she got that idea.*

Evangeline confessed to their travels to the ruin where she was found, the odd Shadow Door, and the journal stored in the blood-locked safe. Raiythlen went silent.

For a long time.

You still there? she had to ask.

I don't know what information is in that journal, but let's hope it doesn't damn us any more than we are now.

Another roil of wind snapped through. *I'm freezing; are there any more bombs you'd like to drop on me?*

She imagined him smirking. *Not at this time. And you never gave me an honest answer.*

On what?

On whether you'd like to be my partner.

It was her turn to laugh. *Not even a little.*

Even if I gave you the means to escape Xilo and Quan?

She shut her mouth. *It's the least you could do after what you put me through. What I'm still dealing with, without your help.*

She expected him to make her an offer. Of whisking her away to a safe place like he did in the past—though now she knew it was for ulterior motives. But he surprised her. Again.

I am sorry about that. I'd offer to get you and Lani out of here, but you're safer with your Aerian prince and his lackies. It seems I was just a backup plan for the Council. Now, I'm a loose end. He sighed through their connection. *I need to go deal with that—and have a pleasant chat with my sister. Maybe she won't try to kill me this time.*

Well, try not to die, I guess. Her lips twitched. *What about helping me escape?*

Don't worry, I've already left a few things for you in the bedside table upstairs.

She shook her head. It was no surprise he'd already thought of everything ahead of time.

Take care of yourself and Lani, he continued. *I'll be back to find you. When I can.*

Raiythlen left, and Evangeline rolled up her sleeve. The Caster symbol was already fading. She remembered the mark she had removed and wondered how the Caster was going to track her down again . . . unless he neglected to tell her she had another mark somewhere she hadn't found yet. Knowing Raiythlen, she did, the bastard. He seemed to always have a plan, and even then, a backup plan. She scowled, though she was grateful for the information and finally some means to get back to Petri and the others.

Crunch, crunch, crunch!

Her head jerked up. Maybe it was Raiythlen coming back to tell her something? But he wouldn't have made a sound.

Her heart sank when two tall figures emerged in the distance. Evangeline ducked to the floor, but it was too late. They saw her.

And were heading straight towards her.

CHAPTER 26

It took longer for Ceven to track down his brother than he would've liked. The oldest prince of Peredia had an odd schedule of meetings and trips to Gods-know-where that Ceven regarded with a hint of suspicion. But that didn't bother him as much as King Calais's parting words.

You'd do best to kill that girl now while you have the chance. Before it's too late and she dooms us all.

He cursed himself for letting it get under his skin. He knew the king had a tendency to say things to unnerve others, throwing them off their guard. It was a common tactic he employed in every conversation to gain the upper hand. And yet, there was always some truth to it.

Tarry had trailed beside Ceven in silence after the encounter. He didn't pry, thankfully. Ceven knew opening that discussion would only raise his bodyguard's suspicions of Evangeline further. Besides, more important things were at hand. Like finding his blasted brother.

Ceven hadn't reached out or spoken to Barto since, but he assumed he and Rasha were staying busy. Tarry had intercepted another messenger bird sent their way, but this time it involved correspondence with the king. He was sure Rasha planned on telling this information to the king sooner rather than later, if she hadn't already. After all, Castle Peak was a fortress, and it would be the only way to get their soldiers inside unless they wanted to start a war. Ceven didn't know how long it would take for their soldiers to travel here. A week at best, by horseback, if that was their means of transportation. But depending on when they had sent the note, they may have even less time.

He and Tarry had been gathering potential allies where they could in the meantime, whether it be through soldiers of lower rank in the army that Ceven had trained, or those who had looked up to and respected Tarry and Xilo. It was always good to know who had their backs, in case things turned sour.

This morning, they caught wind of Sehn's return, something about a meeting with the nobles and territory that could be overturned to them in exchange for financial gain. Ceven didn't care as he stormed the halls towards the circle room that his brother had fastened into his new study. The Old Council had it used centuries ago, when they ruled, as a meeting spot for important guests and collaborative planning. It was odd that Sehn would want to use the space now when he had never showed interest before. He wasn't even king yet, and he was already making changes.

Two Royal Guards stood on either side of the twin doors. Ceven recognized the yellow-feathered one. Troy. Ceven rolled back his shoulders and straightened his spine, even puffing out his feathers a bit. This Aerian was the same one that had stood by and watched as Vane tortured Evangeline.

Troy nodded in respect alongside his broad-shouldered Aerian partner but didn't meet Ceven's eyes.

Ceven entered the room, with Tarry close behind him. It was less toasty than his own suite and smelled of peppermint. Sehn stood up from the circular table that crowded the space, its dark wood etched with an image of a time before King Calais, and his father before him. Four figures stood hand-in-hand. An Aerian, a Caster, a Rathan, and a human. Around them was an artful representation of the castle and its people encircling them. Everyone wore a crown.

The image wasn't familiar. Ceven had only been in this room once, when he'd stumbled upon one of his father's meetings. The king had smiled at him, patting his head, as his guests frowned in impatience. It was before they branded him a bastard, when the king still loved him and Ceven had wanted nothing more than to make him proud. When he had foolishly believed he would amount to something more in the kingdom.

Now all of that belonged to Sehn.

His brother smiled and waved his arm, offering them seats around the table. Ceven wondered why the king would have kept such a controversial table within the kingdom as he sat in the chair fashioned out of dark wood and purple velvet, across from Sehn. Tarry propped against the wall behind him. Ceven had expected more guards inside, but there were none he could see. It was just Sehn, a cold fireplace, and a freshly brewed cup of tea on the table.

"You're back," Sehn said, a hint of surprise in his tone. "But since you always carry a scowl in my presence, I can't be sure if dear Evangeline is well or not. Or if Delani survived."

Ceven's gaze narrowed. He had never mentioned Lani's name to Sehn, or why Evangeline was in the west wing. "I didn't die, if that is what you were hoping for. And I find it interesting that you knew where and exactly why she'd be there. Anything else you'd like to share with me?" Ceven trained his features to match Tarry's. Impassive and detached.

Irritation flashed across Sehn's face as he took a seat. He had revealed something he shouldn't have. "Of course I'm glad you all returned safely." He flicked back his hair, cool casualness back in his figure.

Ceven rolled his neck, easing his tension and the desire to leap across this table and throttle a man he wished he couldn't call brother. "What is your plan?"

Sehn leaned back in his chair, looking like the epitome of leisure. And why wouldn't he be? None of this affected him. He couldn't care less about Evangeline, and as the heir to the throne, he could take his time doing whatever the blazes he pleased.

"I have many, but I'm sure there is one in particular you'd like to know more about," he said.

Ceven was going to deck him in his smug face.

As if time wasn't of the essence, Sehn straightened, taking a sip of his tea. He offered Ceven some.

"You know I don't like it." And last Ceven remembered that his brother didn't either, but he was always good at molding into new environments. It didn't surprise Ceven that his brother had gained new characteristics from his time in Sundise Mouche. "Get to the blasted point, Sehn."

He frowned and muttered, "Still lacking in manners." He glanced at Tarry. "If you would give us some privacy."

"He stays." Ceven knew whatever plan his brother had in mind, it was going to involve Tarry and Xilo anyway.

"This only affects you. And as it is very personal, I'd suggest some privacy. The fewer eyes and ears, the better advantage we have."

Ceven folded his arms, gripping the brown cotton of his shirt. He hadn't bothered to dress for this occasion, and since returning from Eyvan's home, he rarely did now for anyone's sake, much less Sehn or the king. "If you're suggesting Tarry is going to betray me, you're wrong. He stays." There had been a time when he believed Tarry and Xilo would obey only the king—as the Royal Guard code called for. But his bodyguards had kept his secrets, had even helped him go against the king's direct orders. Maybe it was because of their unique background: they hadn't been born into the Guard and trained since birth, like other Aerians. They had to earn it, fight for it. Ceven was proud to have them at his side.

Sehn looked at Tarry. "Leave us." His tone and posture changed. Like he was king.

Tarry didn't move, and Ceven's lips twitched at Sehn's lost expression, even if it lasted as briefly as a flicker of flame. Then his spitting smile was back.

"I wonder if you'd still disobey my order if I were king." Sehn waved his hand as if they were discussing different teas. "I guess in time we'll test that loyalty, but for now, I'll concede." The leather chair crinkled as he leaned closer, his hands folded on the table. "I have many ways to go about this, but in the end, our mutual enemy will be removed and we will both come out on top."

Mutual enemy, as if the king had tried to have Sehn killed, belittled, or thrown out of the kingdom like he had Ceven. Still, none of it would have mattered, at least not enough to murder King Calais—until Evangeline got involved.

"Will we?" Ceven raised his brows.

"We've made a pact, brother. Neither of us can back out now." He raised his arm, showing the dark tattoo, a line in the shape of a sword cutting through a circle, matching Ceven's on his upper arm. The mark of their blood promise. The promise that Ceven would help Sehn kill the king and, in return, Evangeline was to be acquitted of her previous crimes and was not to be injured in any way. Then the two of them would be free to leave Castle Peak.

The unwavering bold lines may show proof that they were both bound to their oath to one another, but Ceven was sure his brother would think of a way to weasel himself out of it. Or use it to his advantage. Ceven would have to be smarter than his brother, which admittedly was a challenge. Ceven preferred to negotiate with swords; he'd always hated politics.

"I have set up the stage, so to speak. There will be an execution, and this time, King Calais will be the executioner."

Ceven frowned. Executions were rarer nowadays since the Red Wash, when the king had hundreds of humans slaughtered, let alone one that got King Calais's attention. He rarely bothered with the beheadings, hangings, or torches, letting others do his dirty work. "Why would he bother doing it himself?"

Sehn smothered his smile into his porcelain cup. The glass cup clinked against its saucer. "Because this isn't any normal execution. It will be one of great magnitude. It will shake the core of this kingdom."

"Because we will execute the king himself during this?" Ceven hated having to ask, but he hated even more the lack of straightforwardness his brother possessed.

"Of course." Sehn's smile didn't waver, and Ceven was sure his face had to hurt. "During this time, I will have an inside man. One close enough to the king. They will strike when he is vulnerable and least expects it. From there, I'll create a distraction, and then I want you to finish the job."

Ceven met Tarry's gaze. The Aerian hadn't moved once. He was good at that—having people forget his presence until it was too late. "What if this fails?"

"I have other back-up plans. Trust me, no matter what happens, Evangeline will be safe and the king will be dead."

"I don't trust you, which is why I'm asking."

Sehn raised his arm again, showing the mark. "You don't have to trust me. If Evangeline becomes injured in any way, this mark will melt into my skin and I will lose my arm. Just as if you fail to kill the king, you will lose yours in return."

Ceven gripped his arm, as if it were already falling off. Sehn had made him aware of the consequences and he didn't like it—but at the time he had little choice.

"But to keep you in the loop, I have placed valuable people in the castle loyal to me. During this execution, they will be ready to attack if all else fails."

"Is that one of your back-up plans? What's the other?"

Sehn raised his marked arm again, and if he did it one more time, Ceven would rip it off himself. "Allow me some secrets, brother. Besides, it matters not to you, since you will still benefit."

He didn't like the sound of that, but a knock on the door interrupted any further discussion. Sehn stood and Ceven followed, his hand on the hilt of his sword.

A Caster woman with short dark horns curling around her black hair waltzed in. Her navy dress wrapped around her lithe form, showing off swirling Caster tattoos marking her legs and arms.

"Welcome, Avana," Sehn bowed, and she curtsied before taking a seat beside him. She was half his size, even with her heels.

Ceven didn't have to look at Tarry to sense his discomfort. It matched Ceven's feelings, the unease and suspicion nestling into his chest as he retook his seat. It didn't help that this was the same woman who had traveled beyond the walls with Evangeline—and who had betrayed her to Ryker and had her thrown into the dungeons.

"Why is she here?" If he had it his way, he'd make sure they barred her from the city, or maybe threw her into the dungeons. If only to get a taste of what she had done to Evangeline.

A small smile teased her painted lips, as if to calm him. "Good evening, Prince Ceven. I mean you no ill-will. I will keep everything we discuss private."

"Too bad you didn't keep the same promise to Evangeline."

Satisfaction roared in his gut at her bewildered expression. Good, he wanted to knock her off her guard.

She cleared her throat. Maybe it was because she couldn't breathe properly with her collared dress buttoned to her neck, like Sehn's silk blouse. "And I'm sure she neglected to tell you the full story, the important part about what Ryker had already known. That I had no choice but to play along, for both of our sakes."

"Everyone has a choice," Ceven growled.

Sehn raised his hand. "Enough, I didn't bring you here to argue. Avana, if you would."

Her fingers tapped the table. Rings adorned both hands. If he were closer, he'd be able to tell if they were real or fake. "As you may not know, I'm not the only Caster here. We have found another, one I'm embarrassed to say is my brother."

Ceven stared, and then it sank in. The Caster that Evangeline was working with—it had to be one and the same.

She continued, "Unfortunately, he was not here on as amiable terms as I was. In fact, he was here to assassinate the king, of his own volition. I guess he didn't agree with the treaty between our countries." Her eyes slid to Sehn, who nodded in encouragement. "And I have it on the Council's word that they did not sanction this and respect Peredia's decision to eliminate him on grounds for treason, and hope all will be forgiven for a prospering and everlasting treaty."

Sehn then turned to Ceven, and repeated the statement, as if Ceven were too slow to understand, "The execution will be the beheading of Raiythlen Quincara, the Council's former spy and now a wanted traitor to both of our countries."

CHAPTER 27

⌒ EVANGELINE ⌒

Evangeline's gaze narrowed on the two Aerians approaching the house. They weren't dressed in all black as she'd originally thought. They certainly weren't dressed as guards. Their shirts were tucked into dark leather pants, and their full-length soil-colored coats flapped in the wind that had beaten away a few of their feathers—a mix of orange, white, and red dancing in the sky. They were either young or both had a birth defect, because their wings were on the smaller side. She guessed on the former.

Evangeline didn't need to warn Xilo about their intruders when the purple-winged Aerian came from around the house, his footsteps gliding across the snow. He kept quiet, not even acknowledging Evangeline's presence, and waved his hand at the two Aerians. They paused and marched back the way they had come, with Xilo on their trail.

Evangeline didn't wait for an invitation. These Aerians had to be involved in how Ceven planned for her and Lani to escape.

Close to the house, a small shack stood with parts of the foundation caving in. She stepped over crumbling planks of wood resembling stalls, and the second-story loft looked sturdy enough to hold only a wicker basket. Like the building they had crawled out of after the west wing, this was an old barn house.

The two strangers flicked their wings, shaking off the snow. Vibrant orange feathers caught her eye, the tips melting into red. Similar to Petri's, except his reminded her of when the sun was almost set, the darkness of night softening its rays, whereas these wings were akin to its initial descent. The Aerian's friend's, in contrast, were starkly white, but equally beautiful.

But still not as beautiful as Ceven's, she thought with a tinge of yearning.

Evangeline slid in next to Xilo, arms folded. Partly from the cold, but mostly to appear more intimidating than she knew she looked.

"I was wondering where my coat went," Xilo said, narrowing on the fur-lined coat that brushed past her knees. The other two Aerians pulled back their hoods, and they were younger than she'd thought. Maybe her age or even younger.

"You weren't using it." Her own boldness surprised her. It was getting easier talking back to Nytes, or maybe she just didn't care anymore. Probably the latter. "What's going on?"

The Aerian with the fiery wings grinned at her, his sloppy smile matching his messy blond hair. "A human with some spitfire, that's a quick way to meet your end, miss."

His friend didn't smile, and with his black hair tied into a neat braid behind his back, he reminded her a bit of Xilo if he were decades younger. He also stood half a head taller than Sir Sunset, but Xilo still had a good hand's-length over both.

Young Xilo smacked his friend on the shoulder. "Pipe down, fool. This is Ceven's girl you're talking to."

Xilo didn't react, but she was starting to pick up on his subtle body language. His hand, sliding into his belt loop, was equivalent to impatience. She also thought she heard him sigh but couldn't be sure. "Evangeline, meet Taryn," Sir Sunset waved. "And Ed." The other gave a half-bow.

Two more Nytes that didn't seem to mind her humanity, or at least didn't sneer or spit at her—or maybe, as Ed had said, it was only because she was "Ceven's girl."

"They're here to help you and Lani leave the city," Xilo said, his eyes scanning their surroundings. It made her aware of where they were—and the fact that Quan wasn't here or a part of this conversation.

"How?" Evangeline swayed from foot to foot. It was freezing.

Taryn thrust his hands on his hips, a cockiness that could've been hers, maybe, if she'd been born Aerian. "We got everything geared up. I did a fantastic job of persuading the gatekeepers to let us slip some horses and supplies through."

Ed snorted. "You nearly gave the whole spitting plan away. If it wasn't for me convincing them it was a trade shipment to the nearby army brigade to the north, we'd be dead human." He shot her a look. "No offense."

She was offended but shrugged it off. "I've heard worse."

"If Ceven doesn't return by the morrow," Xilo said, "we will leave that night. The tunnels are already cleared out, courtesy of someone in the ranks who owed Tarry and me a favor. They will provide us cover, and when we get to the other side, Taryn and Ed will be waiting with others to take you two to a trusted friend in the mountains."

Evangeline rolled the plan over in her head. It sounded solid, except . . . "But we still don't have a cure for Lani. And what would happen to Ceven?"

"This friend is resourceful and has seen her fair share of the world. If anyone would be able to help Lani, it would be her. As for Ceven, either he found it more important to stay where he is, or it's too dangerous to return here."

Evangeline didn't feel reassured in the slightest, not when Kel had already produced results and seemed closer to a cure than this stranger, who may never have even seen these markings. Not to mention she hated the thought of Ceven staying inside the castle. Especially now that she knew Sehn's real identity. She had to tell Xilo, but she thought it wiser to wait until they didn't have company. "I don't like the idea of leaving Ceven behind."

"You should focus on saving yourself and Lani. He's more capable than you think."

That wasn't what she was worried about. It would be like her Aerian friend to take it upon himself to save others besides her. It was a worthy trait, one she admired and saw a bit of herself in. But she saved that for her friends, for people who mattered, not strangers who'd done nothing but scorn her.

You're the kindest, most selfless person I have ever met.

She wasn't. Everything she'd done had been to help herself.

"And Quan?" she asked.

Xilo shifted, the only sign of his unease. And that was just her guess; the man was the most closed book ever. "We will take care of him when the time comes."

Alarm rang in her head. "You're not going to kill him, are you?"

"I hope not; I actually like the Rathan," Taryn informed the group. "Just a shame he's playing for the opposite team."

"We're all on the same side, just currently have differences in opinions." Ed gave her a look, almost retracting all his earlier friendliness. "Just hope a war doesn't happen over one human girl. No offense."

Evangeline returned the look and said, "Offense taken. Nobody's forcing you to do this." Actually, she didn't know that for certain, but she wouldn't stand there and have him accuse her of something she had no control over. It wasn't a crime for her and Lani to want to live normal lives.

Ed frowned but said nothing.

"We're going to discuss in further detail, if you'd like to join, but we've told you everything you need to know." Xilo peered down at her. It was clear he was dismissing her, and her stubbornness wanted to stay just to prove that she could, but she was cold and tired, and Raiythlen's words still weighed on her.

"I can take a hint." She grimaced, then glanced at Xilo. "I also have something important to discuss with you. Later." Xilo's brow pinched for a moment before he nodded. With that, she turned and marched back to the much-warmer house, all the while thinking—should she follow through with Ceven and Xilo's plan? Or take her chances with Petri and his crew?

CHAPTER 28

CEVEN

Tarry and Ceven returned to the suite. The same guards still held post outside his doors; during the discussion with his brother he'd forgotten to gripe about his new spies. He didn't bother looking at them, as if it were their fault for following orders, and stormed inside, peeling off his jacket and tossing it onto the back of the couch.

Tarry said nothing—thank the Gods, Ceven didn't want a lecture right now—as he plopped onto the sofa, not caring that his boots were getting dirt and whatever else on the white fabric. Everything in this room wasn't his choice anyway, but he kept it because his mother had designed it for him.

The crackling of the fire was his current serenity.

"Why do I feel Sehn is hiding something?" He rubbed his nose and sighed. "What am I missing?"

It was more to himself, but Tarry responded, sitting next to the fire. "Executions of assassins don't come often, but to have the king involve himself . . . either he is neglecting to tell us who this Caster really is, or there is another step to this that has yet to reveal itself." Ceven felt the old man's eyes on him. "Either way, I will make sure you come out of this alive. I'll protect you no matter what happens."

"As long as you survive as well." Ceven didn't like that he had almost lost him to one man—no, some beast. He didn't like the odds if the king went against Tarry for siding with him. "I mean no disrespect, but I'd understand if you wanted to step away from this. Where this is going, there's no guarantee the king won't have you killed or thrown in the dungeons, or—"

"Uttering those words is still meaning me disrespect. Xilo and I came here in search of a greater purpose outside of our past."

Ceven remembered the time Xilo had admitted it to him during one of their excursions in the Atiacan jungle. *We had left behind the Gods and Goddesses long ago when we slaughtered innocents. Still, we searched for something to cleanse us. We found our religion in serving in the Royal Guard. In serving something greater than just the next meal or a bit of coin.*

"We thought it was serving the kingdom. But during the Red Wash . . . watching its king slaughter more innocents, we realized we had never left our sins behind. Had only traded them to be the weapons of another sinner." Tarry was quiet, and Ceven didn't dare interrupt. Tarry's confessions of his past life, of the inner workings of his mind, were rare. Like an absodian jewel. "You have grown into someone worthy of serving, Ceven LuRogue. Even if your path hasn't been laid out yet, my faith is that you will do the right thing. Because of you."

The weight of those words toppled him, a heavy breath knocked from his lungs. "Well, damn. No pressure, right?"

Tarry smiled, another rarity. He was just full of them tonight. "No pressure."

Ceven lay in his four-post bed, wide awake when he should be sleeping. He was drowning in the purple comforter, so he kicked the whole thing off. Still, it beat sleeping on that small mattress at Xilo's son's place. Then again . . . He rolled over, wishing he could gaze at a green-eyed, rosy-cheeked girl whose hair was always a mess. His hand rubbed the silken sheets where she could've easily lain. If he were with her, he'd gladly take the cramped mattress and scratchy sheets any day. But he had to focus on Sehn's plan, on saving his own behind in the meantime. He wanted to get back to her as soon as possible, but it helped to know Xilo was with her. Even if Ceven wasn't able to make it back, Xilo would get her away from here safely.

He left the door to his bedroom open, and Tarry stood across the suite. His dark metal armor shimmered in the dying firelight. Ceven didn't know how the man could stand for hours on end. It was the only part during his training with the Royal Guard Ceven hadn't been able to master.

Sighing, he decided lying on his back was his best bet before closing his eyes.

Ceven was on his back, disoriented. The world tilted and blurred, but he could make out Sehn. And the king. They were laughing and pointing at him. He tried to shout back, but a cloth covered his mouth. No, wait, it was a snake. He tried to snatch it off, but his limbs were too heavy to lift, and the sounds of hissing and laughter grew louder and louder.

"I have an inside man." Sehn's tongue slid out, but it was forked. "You'd never guess who!" A black serpent wrapped around his arm, the head bowing closer to his face. Ceven tried to yell again. It was no use; his body had turned to stone.

"An execution of this magnitude." Sehn laughed and laughed. "Surely the king would involve himself in that!"

The king bent down, his frosted face sneering at Ceven. "Of course, I would love nothing more than to behead you myself!"

Tarry was next to Ceven when he shot up in bed. His body dripped sweat, despite having slept with no blanket the entire night. Light slithered in from the curtains, but it didn't ease his frantic heart.

"What happened?"

Ceven shook his head. "A dream, but . . ." It hit him. What Sehn meant to do. He hopped out of bed, throwing on his shirt from last night. It didn't matter; he didn't have time to change his clothes. "We have to go. I know what he's planning—"

Someone pounded on the door to his suite.

Tarry snapped his head at him. Ceven hooked his sword, sliding a dagger into the band of his boot, another into the hidden pocket of his cotton trousers. Not that it mattered. When the Royal Guard came in here, he couldn't fight back. Not with just himself and Tarry, injured or not.

Tarry was ahead of him, axes drawn, when nine armed Royal Guards stormed into the suite. It was overkill, but Ceven was flattered. To think, Sehn thought it took nine trained Royal Guards to take him and Tarry into custody.

"I'm the inside man Sehn was talking about. The Caster isn't the only one planned to be executed," he hastily whispered to Tarry.

A familiar face stood at the front of the Guard. It was Troy. "Under the authority of the king, you, Ceven LuRogue, are under arrest for the murder of Ryker Ardonis."

PART 3

HEADS WILL ROLL

CHAPTER 29

CEVEN

Troy and the eight other Royal Guards barricaded Ceven on all sides. The carpeted rugs muffled their boots, but the shifting of all that metal was hard not to hear. Then again, they weren't the assassins and spies of the kingdom that Ceven knew the king employed by the dozens. These men didn't need stealth on their side to destroy their enemies.

Tarry stayed behind, even if every muscle in him said otherwise. The man nursed an injured wing and had almost died from the wound in his side that hadn't healed yet, but still he had raised his sword at the small army of Royal Guards without hesitation. It wasn't the unsheathing of nine blades at his throat that made him stand down, but Ceven's repeated suggestion of not getting himself killed, so that he could help him later.

As expected, they deprived Ceven of his thin blade made of Atiacan steel with the practical leather hilt. He had wanted the one with the gold-encrusted hilt, emboldened with sapphire and emerald, when they passed the blacksmith stand at the bazaar in Kazuumar, capital city of Atiaca, but for practicality he had gone for the leather one.

They also took a parrying dagger from him, as well as the knife in his boot. One more rested in the hidden pocket of his pants. It made him not feel *so* insecure, but still wouldn't help him much against nine trained Aerians that have devoted their lives to protecting the king.

Ceven stretched his neck, the joint groaning in pain from the crappy cot he slept on down in the holding room. "Kirk, I thought I recognized you," he said to the Aerian next to Troy. His wings were a similar color, a Gods-awful yellow, but his long, fiery-red beard gave him away. "Still haven't trimmed the beard yet. Surprised someone hasn't chopped it off in battle."

Kirk grunted, which was as much of a response as he was going to get. Ceven remembered the older Aerian being a lot more amiable during his years of training with him and a few other Royal Guards. Ceven scanned the surrounding heads and wings. Some familiar faces. "And Leon, I thought you hated working with swords." His gaze dropped to the twin blades hooked to his sides. "Guess people change in a couple of years."

Leon didn't even give him a grunt like Kirk. Ceven knew they wouldn't side with him over a direct order of the king, not like Tarry and Xilo. But it didn't hurt to remind them he used to be their ally. Had trained beside them for years.

This morning, instead of meeting in the king's suite or Sehn's new study in the circle room, they entered the throne room. Ceven had gotten used to the polished white marble speckled with black, the wide sweeping windows that speared to the tops of the massive ceiling. The room was the same size as the castle's famous glass room but used far less frequently. It may have been a place of significant decision-making back when the former king had been alive, whom Ceven had once thought to be his grandfather. Now, it was a waste of space, only serving for the occasional execution "of the utmost magnitude" and meetings when Calais wanted to show off the castle to newcomers.

Calais lounged on top of the raised platform with purple rugs spilling down its stairs like expensive wine down the cheeks of intoxicated nobles. One gold, embroidered pant leg crossed the other, the beige fabric a fine compliment to the pale blue jacket that was fastened by one gold piece. At that point, it would make more sense to have the whole thing open. Then everyone would get a much better view of all the gold chains that hung from his neck. Ceven may have a fine appreciation for jewelry, but he preferred it to be protected behind glass. If he wore every piece he found worthy, he would be useless in combat—and laughed off the field by Barto and other Atiacans. He wondered if Barto and the others had heard the news of his capture?

"Didn't expect us to meet again so soon." Ceven forced a smile. Sea watery hells, all the old Aerian had to do was look at him to make Ceven feel he was that twelve-year-old boy again, facing his father's hatred for the first time.

"Silence, traitor." Calais uncrossed his legs, looming closer. Maybe his eyesight was failing him and he needed a better glimpse.

Traitor today. *Not bastard son, or snake, or worthless waste of space*, he thought with enough snark that Barto would be proud. The only redeemable thing about his situation was that he could focus on the gold-encrusted throne instead of his false father.

"Sehn told me of your despicable deeds. Your interference in the west wing and harboring a prime suspect." For once, Calais didn't sneer at him. Maybe he was bored with this already, eager to remove Ceven from his sight.

"Harboring a suspect?"

"Silence!" His roar shook the ground. Or maybe that was what it felt like to Ceven. Never once had King Calais raised his voice at him when he was a kid. But now, ever since Calais had found out no familial ties bound them, Ceven was used to nothing but scorn and shouting from him while he gave Sehn the soft criticism and proud compliments. "Don't act stupid. You may not be my son, but I've raised you as one with the finest tutors. This was a poor move on your part. To think you would give up what little opportunity you had to be something greater, to make me proud. And you squandered it on a *human*." The word left his mouth like he'd tasted spoiled milk.

"Let's be real, *Father*, you'd never be proud of me."

To his surprise, King Calais didn't slap him or kick him in the ribs right there. Maybe he really was done with him.

"I always knew she would be the death of you. Like mother, like son. Siding with the weak makes you weak." He stared off, beyond Ceven and the surrounding Royal Guards that hadn't moved from their blockade around him. As if he'd attack the king. Well, they wouldn't be too off the mark. "Tell me, was she worth it? Worth killing Ryker over?"

Ceven had learned to hide his expression when he was around nobles. And especially the king and Sehn. So, he tampered down the confusion that tried to raise his brows and concentrated on being like the statues around the castle. Like Tarry and Xilo.

Sehn had laid Ryker's death at Ceven's door, but if Evangeline was involved, it made sense for the king to think it had been Ceven who killed his advisor to protect Evangeline, whom they both knew had beaten and mistreated her. It made it seem as if Ceven had finally reached a breaking point with all of it. That was much more plausible than a human killing a Nyte.

"I'd do it again," Ceven lied with a smile. Either way, he was going to be sent to the dungeons. At least he could clear Evangeline's name. By now they should be about ready to leave Castle Peak, and with this turn of events, they would be safe from the king's attempt at a vengeful retaliation.

Calais shook his head and pursed his lips in disappointment. He was as good an actor as Sehn was, who had turned manipulating the masses into an art form. It was obvious where he got it from.

"I should've known, the day I found out your mother's secret, that you'd be a burden on this kingdom, on this family. Like him, you're a despicable, conniving liar whose only real strength was hiding behind others."

Ceven frowned. *He knows who my real father is?*

"A pathetic passerby who was easily discarded, no real value than for a brief pleasurable blip in time," he continued.

Ceven debated holding his tongue, but blast it. If he was going down, might as well make a show of it. "But pleasurable enough that Beatrix chose him over you."

King Calais had no self-control this time as he hurled a fist at Ceven. Ceven ducked but couldn't escape the roundhouse kick to his ribs. He sucked in air, which catapulted painfully off each rib inside his chest.

"I loved her. . . . I loved her so much," the king whispered, more to himself.

To Calais's credit, Ceven knew it was true. Everyone did. The king had never taken any mistresses during his marriage with Queen Beatrix. He had doted on her, expanded the main hall's garden for her since she loved it so much. It was no secret that the merciless king had been besotted with the beautiful Aerian. But the feeling wasn't mutual. That public fact humiliated him and destroyed the love he'd once had for his wife.

"Every day I look at you, it's a reminder of her betrayal. Of her *filthy, disgusting betrayal!*" Red stained his pale cheeks, and Ceven blinked, making sure he was seeing right. King Calais never showed this kind of emotion. His anger Ceven was familiar with, usually veiled behind a cold mask and callous words, like their meeting in Sehn's suite. The king's temper was arguably the only thing the two had in common, but this . . . Ceven had felt the same way when he found out Evangeline was working with another.

The king leaned down, the single button straining at the movement. His icy fingers fastened to Ceven's jaw, jerking his head up to meet his eyes. His voice lowered to whisper, even though it was pointless in the grand room, where even the crinkle of a shirt echoed. "Everyone believed I kept you alive, by my side, because of my love for her." His thick white eyebrows faltered, his pink lips taking in a shaky breath. The cold facade dropped, and for the first time since Ceven had turned twelve, he saw the man he used to call father. "But my love for that woman died the day she spurned me. It was my love for you, Ceven, that kept me from turning you away." The same disappointment shone in his eyes. Maybe it had never been feigned. "But like your mother, you chose another over what could be. This time you have decided your own path, and I won't feel guilty about reminding you of your consequences."

For one delirious moment, Ceven was compelled to claim his innocence in the face of this admission. A man he had loved had just dangled something he thought he didn't care about in front him. Love and respect from the one Aerian he least expected. It swayed back and forth precariously in front of him like a prized jewel hooked on a gold chain.

The doors opened, and Sehn walked in. The chain pulled up, and Ceven had missed his chance to snag the jewel.

The king released him, and Ceven rubbed his jaw. Sehn walked past them, his long navy jacket brushing the floor. The buttoned collar looked to be choking him from how tightly it was clipped at his neck. It was a shame it wasn't.

"Sehn, what are you doing here?" The king revered the oldest prince with the love and respect Ceven could've had. Ceven was still reeling from the Calais's words.

Sehn smiled, not even acknowledging Ceven. "I came to make sure you were okay. If this man is devious enough to trick our once-esteemed advisor, and kill him for it, I had reason to believe he might have done the same to you."

The familiar cruel expression was back on the king's face. "How kind of you to care about my well-being. I may be old, Sehn, but I'm not a fool."

Sehn's smile grew, like a cat with a mouse trapped in its claws. The king had held this kingdom with a fierce rule for almost a century now, but it was clear where the real power now lay. And Sehn was far more cunning and underhanded than even Calais had been in his youth. He was so thirsty for power he couldn't even wait for the king to die before taking the throne. And it was obvious his deathbed was near. Ceven would've never been able to avoid his father's swings in the past.

An unexpected thought bobbed to the surface. *Is killing Calais the right thing to do?*

Sehn spared him a glance. If it could be called that. Ceven wished they were alone, so he could show off the new moves he'd learned fighting with the empress's brigade in Atiaca. He'd knock Sehn down a peg or two.

His brother flicked his wrist at him and the guards. "Have him taken back to the dungeons. The traitor can rot in the dark before the king's merciful ax will end his suffering." Traitor. As if he wasn't referring to his own flesh and blood.

The Royal Guard remained where they were. The king laughed, and Sehn's chin raised a fraction higher.

"You're not king yet, my boy." King Calais waved his hand. "Yes, move him to the holding cell with the other one. Double the guard. I've trained this one well and wouldn't want him to get the upper hand."

Kirk and an unfamiliar face grabbed Ceven's upper arms. They hadn't touched him on the way here, but maybe they wanted to make a show of their loyalty by man-handling him in front of the king. Ceven swallowed his pride and let them haul him to his feet and out of the room. He thought back to when he'd stood in Sehn's suite, the king sitting there so calmly compared to today's encounter. He wondered if Calais had already decided then that Ceven was involved in Ryker's murder, and if he knew how today's events would unfold.

Maybe the king had been there to warn him, to bait him into leaving the kingdom before Calais would be forced to kill him by his own hand.

Ceven furrowed his brows. *And maybe he already suspects Evangeline is the real murderer, and that's what he meant by "kill her now."* But why mention Ryker had been working with another and that she would doom everyone? Why would the king be so afraid of one human girl?

Blast it all, Ceven was suddenly unsure of everything: if killing the king was the right move, who Evangeline really was, and if Sehn's goals truly aligned with his.

And whether he wanted to ruin his brother's entire plan.

CHAPTER 30

Now do you see how Ceven's in danger?" Evangeline leaned against the concrete wall of the basement office, twirling her finger tirelessly around a strand of her hair. The smell of parchment and dried herbs filled the tight space, which felt even smaller with Xilo standing in the middle of it. "Sehn, who's not Sehn, might kill him, or have other plans we don't know about."

"Did this Caster tell you this?" Even when Xilo whispered, it carried with it a sense of his sternness.

Evangeline dropped her hand, flinching as the piece of her hair came down with it. "It doesn't matter where I got the information; just know that I'm telling the truth."

He said nothing, but his eyes spoke volumes.

She shook her head. It made sense that he wouldn't believe something as crazy as this. After all, she had trouble believing it herself, but they didn't have time to question it. Not when it could be true and put Ceven at risk. She said as much.

"My concern right now is getting you and Miss Delani to safety."

"I want Lani to be safe, but I'm not leaving Ceven." She threw up her hands. "He doesn't even know about any of this!"

He pointed above him, and she pursed her lips. The door had opened moments ago, indicating the Rathan had returned from surveying the borders. After her and Xilo's excursion last night, Quan had been suspicious, taking more patrols, trying to sniff out the plan Ceven had hatched from the start.

"I'll make sure word gets to him," Xilo said, but it didn't sound convincing. "But it's too dangerous for you to return to the castle."

He doesn't believe me. She wanted to howl in frustration. "Never mind."

She went to storm past him when he stepped in her path. She craned her neck up to look at him and cursed at how tall Aerians were.

"Need I remind you, you will not leave this house until given further orders." He took in her expression. "Ceven wishes for your safety. If you take matters into your own hands, he will do everything in his power to protect you. Even at the cost of his own life." His eyes bore into hers. "I won't have that happen."

Uneasiness settled over her skin. She had never felt uncomfortable around Xilo—awkward, yes, but never in danger. This time, she couldn't be too sure.

Evangeline held the pendant Raiythlen had left for her, the same metallic necklace that had hung around his neck when he'd appeared in her and Lani's room. The symbol etched into the silver plate reminded her of a keyhole enclosed in a circle. She didn't know what it meant in the Castanian language. Beside it, in the drawer closest to her side of the bed and farthest from Lani's sleeping figure, was a palm-sized vial, a pouch of dust, and a note containing instructions. How thoughtful of him.

Despite Xilo's veiled threat from earlier, she planned to do exactly what he said not to do—take matters into her own hands. If Xilo wouldn't believe her or help Ceven, she would just have to convince Petri and the others. With them, she had the means to help Lani *and* get back to Ceven. Even if it meant having to face the west wing again. Or Vane. Or the king himself.

The pendant shook, and she realized it was herself that was shaking. She took a deep breath and tied it around her neck, a thick black cord going through the metal pendant. It hung just below the collar of her navy blouse—the darkest color she could find in Eyvan's drawers—tied and tucked tightly into brown slacks. Throwing on her floor-length coat and dusting her face with soil, she was ready to make her escape.

The remaining rolled posters Annabelle had given her lay in the room across from theirs, the one with the twin beds that Xilo chose as his temporary sleeping quarters tonight. It was too risky to bring them back with her.

From her pocket, she pulled out Quan's leather flask and took a sip. The saliver solution stole her breath, the liquid burning like fire down her throat and making her want to immediately hurl, but she gripped her nose and held back. It didn't hurt any less the first time, but she handled it a lot better this time around, after the Rathan had given her his flask. A surprising gift, if it could be called that.

Quan had given it to her after a small fight they'd had earlier that day. Still reeling in disappointment after her and Xilo's previous conversation, Evangeline had brought her Caster book downstairs again and sat at the kitchen table. The sun had just slid across the dusty floorboards when Quan showed up, cotton-threaded shirt tucked into tight brown leather breeches. The same outfit he'd been wearing since they got here, yet the Rathan didn't smell. It was a talent.

"How much saliver do you take every day?" she had asked.

He didn't respond, not that she expected anything else, but his hand reached for his left pocket, where it stayed. It was her guess that was where he currently kept his flask.

"How long until it creates an immunity?" she continued, this time more to herself.

The bald Rathan had looked down and noticed the book in front of her for the first time. "I thought it was illegal for humans to know how to read in Peredia," he said instead.

Evangeline didn't point out that she had been doing just that since they've arrived here, but it proved how little he cared about her.

"It's illegal to know how to write too. Should I show you my best cursive?"

He growled, and she smiled. Her cursive was as horrendous as her grasp on the Castanian language.

"I don't know how you made it alive this long." He gave her a leering glance. "Then again, being buddy with a prince probably gave you a few extra lives."

Evangeline was proud of herself for her temper not sparking. Then again, this wasn't anything new. He was only reiterating what humans and Nytes had thought about her ever since she became friends with the prince. "And while you're at it, you could even say I charmed the king's advisor. Why, I must be such a charming, lovable person to have made my way into the Aerian court." She threw up her hands. "To be scorned by everyone and beaten nearly twice as much!" She guessed her temper wasn't *that* much in check.

"If you're so agreeable, I've yet to see it."

She raised a brow. He clearly missed her sarcasm. Maybe it was only reserved for intelligent people. "Look, I'm just trying to survive. Is that so horrible?"

Quan went quiet for a moment, an unreadable look on his face. He stunned her when he took a seat across from her on the rickety chair. "I don't know who's more stubborn, you or Rasha." He sighed. "Saliver is a common practice in all territories of Atiaca, thanks to Empress Zelene. I drink it every few days, taking a hearty swig." He did a once-over. "I don't know if a human could handle it."

She frowned; she would be the judge of that. "How does it work? Does it hurt?" The look he gave made her feel foolish. "Well, it is poison, isn't it?" she defended.

"Of course it hurts. It feels like claws tearing down the inside of my stomach every blasted time I drink it. The first time my bowels turned to water, and for the first sun lapse, nausea is your enemy." He rubbed his chin before pulling out his flask and waving it in front of her. "How about this: You survive a swig, you can have the whole thing."

Evangeline smirked. She couldn't back down from a challenge like that.

The rest of the day her insides betrayed her, and all the while Quan laughed, but blast it if in the end he didn't hand her that flask with—maybe, just maybe—a hint of respect in his eyes.

And now it'd save her from any unwanted Casters that came out to pursue her tonight. Or at least give her the element of surprise when their magic didn't work.

The air prickled like needles against her flushed cheeks as she stared out the window and down at the snow-covered ground.

A pinch will soften your landing and silence it, Raiythlen's note had read. Reaching into the brown, palm-sized pouch, she pinched a bit of the white and pink speckled dust. It caught in the flashes of moonlight that sifted through an overcast sky, almost like grounded hail twinkling in the air as it fell.

The spot at the bottom of the two-story drop morphed, the snow rescinding, overtaken by an almost gelatin-looking pink slime. She glanced back at Lani, still fast asleep. Even from beneath the patterned quilt, her skin pulsed and oozed a darkness that hadn't left her since the west wing, the black lines wringing the life from her friend, pulling back at her skin and leeching the color from her hair.

"I'll be back," Evangeline whispered, her hand clenching the windowsill. "I'm going to get help. I'm going to save you."

Lani's chest heaved with a sigh, but Evangeline knew she was talking to herself. Convincing herself that this would work.

She stepped onto the ledge, gently shutting the window behind her. *Here goes nothing,* she thought as she jumped.

Icy wind scratched at her face, knocking back her hood as she plummeted to the ground. She kicked out her feet, her arms scrambling for purchase a split-second before her behind landed on something soft. The pink gelatin cushioned her fall, but she didn't have time to be amazed as she jerked her head around, expecting Quan or Xilo to come after her any moment.

In her pocket, she found the vial of Raiythlen's blood and popped off the top. The smell of cinnamon assaulted her before the overwhelming scent of fire took over. It made her eyes widen and her belly lurch, but most of all, it made her mouth water.

Her eyes remained fixed on the dark liquid as it swirled around the glass. To say it tempted her to down its contents was an understatement. Some instinct came from deep inside her where the darkness slept, curling around her gut, its tendrils lurching up her throat, choking her with desire.

You'll get used to it. I couldn't keep it down the first time either. The familiar voice, from a memory past, echoed in her head. One she now knew was Jaden's, his low but smooth tone unmistakable and strangely alluring.

It tastes disgusting, she responded, despite not remembering this incident at all.

It does . . . but it gets easier. Trust me.

She recalled experiencing the same hallucination in Ryker's suite, after they had dinner with the king, and before she knew Avana would betray her. Before she knew Sehn was Council member Aimee.

The sound of a door shutting jerked her attention to her left, towards the rear of the house. Somehow, Quan or Xilo had heard her.

"Pull yourself together, Eve." Without thinking or bringing the vial too close, she dribbled a drop onto the pendant at her throat and watched in awe as her body peeled away from existence. Based on Raiythlen's note, this wouldn't last long, so she scrambled to her feet, not waiting to come face-to-face with one of her Nytes, and stormed towards the tavern.

Blurred lights flared in the distance from the busier district of the city, farther in, away from the towering walls. Late-night figures shuffled along the cobbled pathways that had been cleared of snow. Pathways Evangeline followed, despite the foot traffic and occasional wagon and even rarer carriage holding the wealthier Nytes of the city. She may be invisible, but she didn't want Quan and Xilo to follow her tracks in the snow, and merging with the general populace helped hide her scent more than walking alone. She blended in with the muted brick buildings and dark alleyways. Not once did anyone give her a passing glance or a frown. The familiar stench invaded her along with the smell of smoke, as if someone had just thrown a bucket on a blazing bonfire.

When the screams hit her, her blood turned to ice.

No . . .

Evangeline took off in a sprint. Her shoulders and arms collided with Nytes and humans scrambling past her in the opposite direction as she squeezed through the crowd. The trail of smoke wafted above the two-story brick buildings that enclosed her on both sides, leading her farther until its source blazed brighter than all the streetlamps in the city combined. She shielded her face from the abrupt wave of heat that pelted her as she turned the corner and stood open-mouthed at the fire-ravaged tavern.

The fire had been burning for some time, the painted wood breaking away bit by bit to reveal a black and tarnished inside. Evangeline tried to see if anyone was still alive in the flames, searching for a familiar face—or praying not to.

The heat swatted at her exposed skin as she delved as close as possible without getting attacked by the loose flames. "No!" She choked back a sob, noticing the shriveled corpses flickering between waves of yellows, oranges, and reds. The black, unmistakable symbols appeared even darker, as if it were cling-ing to life while its hosts burned. These people, these innocent humans . . . Shani. They were all dead.

"*You!*"

Evangeline whipped around in time for someone to slam into her, taking them both to the rubble-filled ground. Pieces of glass and wood bit into her back, and she gasped as a soot-cov-ered face appeared above her.

"*You did this!*" Sebastian screamed at her.

She shook her head. "I didn't do anything! I don't know what happened!" Her invisibility had faded that quickly? She tried to ask where the others were when the air left her throat, Sebastian's fingers pressing into her neck.

"I told them not to trust you. I told them! And look where it got us," he shouted as she pried at his fingers, kicking her legs. "But you won't kill us that easily. We're just like vermin—but worse. We'll always come crawling back, bigger and stronger." His grip grew tighter and tighter. "But you won't be."

She thrashed harder against his grip, her nails biting into his skin, leaving trails of blood, but the look in Sebastian's eyes was crazed. Bloodthirsty. Just like the Nytes that day during Petri's hanging, he wouldn't stop until there was death.

Heavy footsteps fell across the cobblestone and broken de-bris behind her. Sebastian glanced up, his eyes widening before a metal-plated hand socketed him right in the gut. Smoke-filled air rushed back into her lungs. Needles pricked her throat as she coughed and massaged her neck. Her eyes watered as she turned, hoping to see Xilo, or even Quan, but instead met unfamiliar eyes and a brand of stars enclosing a pair of wings emblazoned on the Aerian's plated chest.

They were surrounded by the Royal Guard.

"Search the place. We don't want any more escaping," said the Aerian in front of her, his voice as cold and unforgiving as she expected from a Royal Guard. A few nodded and walked off, two guards remaining by her and Sebastian, alongside the Aerian who had spoken.

Panic gripped her, even more so than when Sebastian had his hands around her throat. She couldn't be caught. She wouldn't.

Sebastian got back up from where he was hunched over and shoved a finger at her. "It's her! She's the one you want! She murdered her own father, the king's advisor!"

The glow of the fire reflected off the guards' metal armor and their drawn blades, shifting closer around her. Eyes fell on her, and Evangeline's mind whizzed for a plan. *Run, escape, run, escape!*

"Kill her! Kill her! *Kill her!*" Sebastian cheered as he stumbled toward her. His eyes were still wide, but gone was the fear, replaced with the same crazed look as before. As if he had nothing left to lose.

Everything after that happened so fast.

A hand reached for her, and she yelled, "No!" as she pushed to her feet, shoving Sebastian back and fumbling for Raiythlen's vial. She clasped it as Sebastian let loose an ear-piercing scream. The Royal Guard's sword was now stained scarlet—and running right through the middle of the former human rebel. Time seemed to freeze as his eyes glared at her, right before shutting entirely.

"Grab her!" a guard yelled.

With shaking hands, she dumped the remaining contents of Raiythlen's blood on her pendant. The dark liquid decorated the front of her navy shirt and brown coat, some spilling onto the cobblestoned road. It made drops in comparison to the river that flowed from Sebastian's stomach.

"Where did she go?"

"Was that Caster magic?"

"Find her!"

The shouts and roars of the Royal Guards faded behind her as she lurched away from the toppling tavern and Sebastian's dead body. She pummeled through alleys, shoving unsuspecting Nytes and humans out of her way, the familiar pulse of adrenaline taking hold of her limbs. Her mouth tasted of salt and copper from where her tears met her lips. And as she ran, all she could see were Sebastian's eyes glaring at her, accusing her as his life flowed away from him.

CHAPTER 31

Hands caught Evangeline's shoulders when she burst through the front door of Eyvan's house. Fiery heat still brushed her cheeks, smoke settling into the worn fabric of her coat, suffocating her.

From the darkened house, Xilo's tall figure loomed above her, dagger in hand. His face was rigid, without emotion. Evangeline's eyes widened, and she tried to step back, but his grip was unshakable.

"Xilo! Stop! It's me!" she blurted, still sucking air back into her lungs from sprinting all the way back here.

His face went lax for a second before he regained his composure, but his eyes weren't meeting hers, then she realized out loud—"You can't see me." Raiythlen's magic still clung to her just as strongly as the smoke did, and she had used the rest of the vial on the pendant. She removed the necklace, letting it drop to the ground at her feet. The spell fell away from her.

"I could've killed you." Xilo's expression didn't shift, but something fierce shone in his eyes. "What were you thinking?"

Voices blared behind them. Metal and the pounding of footsteps stampeding just beyond the simple wooden door that separated her from the Royal Guards that still combed the streets. Looking for her.

Without wasting any time, she told Xilo everything.

Her lips wavered as she recounted the burned bodies and how she had escaped. "I'm sorry, I didn't know this would happen. I only wanted to help—"

He cut her off. "Go get Delani. Bottom drawer on the right, you'll find the supplies you'll need. I'll arrange for us to leave tonight." Dressed in dark brown leather, with knitted metal sliding over the joints of it, Xilo already looked prepared. Had he heard the commotion before she got there and planned ahead?

She nodded at first, then thought about Ceven. About Council member Aimee. "Once Lani is safe, I'm coming back with you to help Ceven."

He didn't reply, instead turning on his heel, heading toward the back door. Evangeline had a sinking feeling he wasn't agreeing with her but didn't want to waste time arguing.

"Wait! I need a sword." Her eyes flicked to the one strapped to his back, alongside the daggers that hung at his waist, with more probably tied to his thighs and arms, even his boots.

"You don't need one, I'll protect—"

"I want a blasted sword!" Like blazes was she going to be left without a weapon, and she had practiced with a sword. Then again, the way Raiythlen's daggers had felt in her hands, the ease it took for her to wield them in mere moments versus the weeks it took for her to grip a sword correctly . . . "No—I want a dagger."

Xilo shook his head but removed one of the sheathed daggers at his waist. He tossed it to her and she caught it, the blade the size of her forearm, the hilt black and silver. She slid it into the waistband of her trousers, tightening the straps before heading upstairs.

Lani was awake when Evangeline stormed into the room. Her back curved like the shape of the moon peering through the curtains. Shouts of the guards echoed in the distance outside the window, and she wondered if that had woken her friend.

"What's going on?" Lani asked as Evangeline rummaged through the drawer Xilo had told her the supplies would be in.

"We're leaving the city. Tonight." She pulled out piles of folded clothing—a lot smaller than what she had been wearing from Eyvan's wardrobe. She glanced over her shoulder. "Are you going to be okay to walk?"

She swatted her hand, a familiar Lani gesture. "Of course. If it meant leaving here, I'd walk over spitting glass."

Evangeline's brows knitted. Lani didn't seem delusional, which was a good sign—for now. "Well, it's a good thing you'll have a brand-new pair of boots to wear so you won't have to worry about that." Evangeline plopped the boots and clothes on the bed. She assumed Taryn and Ed hadn't shown up empty-handed earlier in the week. She quickly changed, glad to have clothes that fit her. Her sheathed dagger hugged more snuggly against her waist, shoved in the band of her black trousers, which hung close to her calves, with her flask tucked into its pocket. The white blouse molded to her skin, and the thought that it matched Lani's deathly pallor had her frowning.

Her friend wore a similar outfit, with more room around the torso, fitting into thick cotton breaches. The velvet green looked a lot better on her than the black uniform she always wore back at the castle. The extra-sturdy coat and fur-lined boots completed the look and provided more warmth than Evangeline could've if they stuck to their original escape plan. She thought about the supplies she had shoved into that tree along the outskirts of the castle city just weeks ago. Were they still there?

"Did you start trouble again?" Lani said.

Evangeline helped lace up her friend's boots as Sebastian's face appeared in her mind. Eyes as red as the blood that poured from his gut glared at her as the heat of the blazing tavern seared her skin. She squinted against its reflection off the plated Aerians surrounding her, their sharpened swords inching closer to her face. Her breath caught in her throat when laughter came from the flames, claws crunching across glass and wreckage as Vane's dripping muzzle came into view, his slitted eyes narrowing on her. "Welcome back, Pet," he growled through blood-stained fangs.

"I'll do anything to save my friends," she bit out, but she didn't know if it was in response to Lani or to herself.

A discreet, rounded pouch, big enough to fit several hardcover books, had been stored away in the drawer along with bits of bread and cheese covered in wax. The dinner they had tonight, before she left, had been heartier—salted beef and steamed potatoes—but she didn't know when their next meal would come, or if she would meet her death well before that happened.

"I can't believe . . . I can't believe we're leaving." The hope in her friend's voice pulled Evangeline away from any thought of failure. She couldn't. Not with Lani and Ceven's livelihood on the line. Lani always said Evangeline was the optimistic one,

Lani the pessimist. The world wouldn't be right if Evangeline changed now.

"I'm glad . . . I mean . . . I wish none of this had happened, but I'm glad . . ." Blast it, she didn't mean to cry. Why did her body have to betray her? "I'm glad you're still here," she whispered.

Lani smiled, the first one in weeks. Her arms were as thin and frail as Evangeline's now when they wrapped around her, but she squeezed with strength. Evangeline wasn't the only one crying.

"I'm sorry," Lani said. "For how I've treated you, those awful things I said."

"It's fine."

"No." She hugged her tighter. "You were right to try to leave this place. You never gave up. Maybe the Gods do exist"—Lani pulled away to look at her face—"and they blessed me with you."

Evangeline said nothing. Her words wrapped in a heavy ball in her throat.

Xilo came upstairs and told them to wait by the window, that Taryn or Ed would flash a light in the distance toward the dilapidated barn house they had met at the previous night. When the two of them gave the signal, they would meet them there and take the tunnels running beneath the castle and its city, trekking the few miles from here to the city's walls.

She asked where Quan was and felt a pang of guilt when Xilo said he'd left to look for her. She wondered why Xilo hadn't done the same until she realized they needed someone to remain here, in case she returned to the house. Which she had, along with a score of guards.

They didn't wait long. Yellow cut through the snowy night, casting shadows on the bedroom floor.

It was time.

They bundled themselves into their coats, and Evangeline smiled in bliss as the fur hugged her skin. Xilo didn't have a coat, but the thick black armor looked durable enough. And his Aerian blood ran hotter than a human. At least that's what Ceven told her, and sleeping next to him had proved that his body was better than any fire.

Gods, she missed him.

The three of them headed outside. Two Aerians and a Rathan in similar black mesh armor greeted them. Evangeline reared back, her hand snapping out as if her branch-thin arm could protect Lani from even a swarm of gnats.

Xilo nodded at them, they in return. No introductions were necessary, and Evangeline assumed that they were along for the ride. They trudged through the field of snow, the white mass reaching the tips of her knee-high boots. When they reached the dilapidated shack, Taryn and Ed stood waiting. They moved wood planks and debris to show a hole in the floor big enough for one Aerian to squeeze through at a time, if their wings were fully tucked. Even then, it was a tight fit.

No one said a word. Nothing but the roar of the wind howled in Evangeline's ears, the press of cold fluttering up her coat. Thank Gods, her boots and gloves were fur-lined.

Ed went first, the lean, white-feathered mass behind him pressing into his form easier than the other two Aerians who followed. Next were Evangeline and Lani. Evangeline went first, her feet dipping into blackness. It ate up her legs as she grabbed at the sides of the hole, feeling the makeshift ladder carved into the wall. Below, someone pulled out an oil lamp, the flames flickering off rock walls that hugged close but wide enough to fit two Aerians with their wings tucked, side by side.

She helped Lani down. Her friend was taking all of this better than she thought until she gripped her hand. The woman almost snapped Evangeline's wrist with the force of her squeeze.

Evangeline slid an arm around her shoulders and pulled her closer. At least with Lani here, she was more focused on protecting her than the pounding of her own fear. The hollers of the guards ebbed and flowed. Getting closer, and making her heart race and everyone freeze, until it would fade once again into the rustling wind.

Taryn and Xilo landed behind them. Overhead, they sealed the hole again, but the last Nyte that had been with them was missing. A slight breeze wafted through the tunnel, their boots clattering against the ground in rhythmic clumps. Rocks were crushed or skittered out of the way. Xilo murmured directions, keeping pace by Evangeline. Two Nytes were behind them and two Nytes ahead, each with their own lamp to light up their surrounding area. Not that there was much to see besides rock.

She was glad to have the tall, purple-winged Royal Guard next to her. Like Tarry, Xilo always intimidated her, but she had to admit he had treated her with more respect than she expected and was helping her and Lani. Even if it was under Ceven's orders, she would forever be grateful to him.

"You had planned to leave tonight anyway, didn't you?" After walking for several minutes in silence, Evangeline whispered the conclusion she'd come to. "You were already armed and ready to go when I returned to the house. And there's no way you would have been able to get word to everyone here so quickly." Not to mention everything happened a lot more smoothly than she'd expect for a last-minute operation.

"Yes," was all Xilo said, focused on the heads of the Nytes walking ahead of them.

"Why didn't you say anything?"

He didn't reply right away. "There was a chance you'd try to escape, to contact those rebels instead. I was right, but you had already left before I could bring you back." It went without saying that he would've gone to any means to make sure she and Lani made it out of the city, even if it meant catching her unawares and dragging her out by force. "I'm sorry," he finished, genuine sorrow tugging at his expression. She didn't know if he was apologizing for not telling her the truth, or if it was about Petri and the others, or both.

Evangeline felt Lani's eyes on her, filled with questions, when the rhythm of steps shifted—No, it was another's that disturbed it. Others were down here.

In one quick motion, the group froze, the lanterns shut off, drowning them in darkness. Lani's hand tightened on Evangeline's bicep even more than she thought possible for the old woman; her breath came in haggard gasps. Evangeline squeezed back to reassure her. Of what, Evangeline didn't know. Maybe it was to calm herself as well.

The shuffle stopped. Nobody moved.

Small *whooshes* broke the silence. Xilo lunged in front of her and Lani as something clattered off the walls and the Royal Guard's armor. Ed and the other Aerian in front shot off down the tunnel. Xilo nodded at Taryn, and he moved next to them as Xilo followed in pursuit. Evangeline gripped her friend tighter and pulled out the dagger at her waist. She remembered Quan's insult, that she reminded him of Rasha. In that moment, Evangeline wanted nothing more than to be her, or any Nyte. All over again, she was reminded of her shortcomings, and she was back in the west wing, but this time she didn't have a magicked weapon to guide her swings.

But as quickly as it started, it was over. The clambering of metal faded, and silence descended. Xilo and the others returned with what she hoped was victory based on their expressions—well, Ed's expression, as Xilo's remained as impassive as ever.

"I apologize," Xilo said to her, as if it was his fault. "We had checked this route to make sure it was safe, but it seems a few slipped through. But no alarm has been rung. We still have secrecy on our side."

"Until they wake up with a pounding headache." Taryn smirked. "We'd best get the fiery blazes out of here."

Evangeline was glad they were on her side. It touched her that these Nytes cared enough to help them. Either they weren't as bad as they led her to believe, or Ceven was a far better prince than he gave himself credit for.

The tunnel wasn't as long as the one connecting the castle to Eyvan's house. Xilo mentioned they had passed beneath the wall. She didn't know how he knew, and for one claustrophobic moment, the walls slid closer to her, threatening to tumble down on her from the weight of the thick heavy stone that layered to form the sturdy, thick walls of the castle city. Then there was light. Dull and faint, but brighter than the glow of their lanterns. Either the entrance beyond the wall wasn't covered, or someone was waiting for them at the end of it.

Xilo found his place next to her again. She had sheathed her dagger after the fight but continued to clutch it until Xilo reached for her hand, guiding her as the tunnel curved up, forcing her to lean forward and gain better footing on the incline. She kept her arm as firm as any walking stick for Lani as they climbed. Ed and the other Aerian passed them, wind rushing through and shaking their lanterns.

Evangeline grinned. They made it. They were here, beyond the wall. She thought she heard Lani mumble something, or maybe it was a laugh, but she could have imagined it.

The night felt cool and crisp, the snow just as thick, if not thicker, than behind the walls. Bare branches swayed like shadowy hands in the night, and she remembered the last time she was in this forest—when she encountered something that shouldn't have existed.

Evangeline shoved away those thoughts and clung to the feeling of freedom. *But we're not out of the woods yet.* She chuckled at her own pun.

Then Lani collapsed.

One blink, she was upright, hand gripping Evangeline's. The next, she plunged into the bank of snow, eyes closed. Not moving.

"*Lani!*" Evangeline fell to her knees, a rattled gasp clawing at her lungs. *No, no, no!*

Xilo's fingers dug into her shoulder, and Evangeline craned up to look at the Aerian. The usually stoic Royal Guard was far from calm. His chest heaved, hot breath escaping him at a rate that told her something was wrong—and it wasn't Lani.

Her gaze jerked to Taryn, Ed, and the others when six figures burst from the thick snow around them.

It was an ambush.

Evangeline didn't have time to process what was happening as each black-clad figure moved with blinding speed, hooking their limbs around the Nytes in a deathly embrace. Powdered snow danced from the eruption, and Evangeline's scream was swallowed by the shouts of violence.

Xilo shielded Evangeline and Lani with his body as their Aerian entourage clattered to the ground in a matter of seconds. They didn't even have time to draw their weapons.

Black figures surrounded them. Half their faces were shrouded in masks, the uncovered half revealing slanted, unblinking eyes that stared at Xilo and Evangeline. With skintight leather armor, masks, and different-colored horns adorning each figure in various sizes and shapes . . . was this the same group that had ambushed her in the woods with Avana? The same group that infiltrated Ryker's suite those nights ago and had attacked her in the plaza?

Hooves stampeded, and the familiar clinking and clattering of a carriage emerged in the distance. Lanterns, attached to the front of the sleek cabin, dangled like the last leaves of autumn from the corners as it pulled up in front of them. The six figures moved. Three stood on both sides of Xilo, Evangeline, and Lani, the bodies of their fallen troupe scattered in the snow. Orange and red feathers splattered the white-blanketed ground. Taryn hadn't even known what hit him.

The gold-trimmed door to the carriage opened, and a slender form stepped out. Squeaky new boots sank into the ground, and burgundy feathers dragged behind them, like a trail of blood in the snow. Prince Sehn LuRogue—no, Council member Aimee Hysander—stood before them and smiled.

CHAPTER 32

Hello, Evangeline," the Sehn lookalike said.

Evangeline scrutinized every feather, every strand of their hair down to the fitted emerald shirt that was fastened by black buttons tucked into black slacks. Their coat hung open behind their arms, their hands shoved into their pockets.

She whipped to Xilo and back to the fake Sehn, then at Lani. Nobody moved.

"How . . .?" she stammered. No, all their plans, everything . . . it couldn't end now. Her grip tightened on Lani's shoulders. Her skin was cold to the touch. Evangeline had risked her life for Lani, fought against Wretched, against Vane, only for it to come to this? She needed to get her friend out of here, somewhere warm. She wouldn't let this Caster take her.

Fake Sehn took a step toward them, but Xilo blocked them.

They cocked their head with Sehn's gray-eyed gaze aimed at Xilo. "It's a little late to change your mind now, Sir Leander."

Evangeline stared at Lani's wrinkled face. *It matches the color of the snow.* She blinked, then glanced at the two Nytes. One by one, the pieces clicked in place. The surrounding figures had all been strategically placed, taking out everyone—except Xilo. They knew where they would be and when. She may not have excelled in strategy during the times she played chess against Ceven and Ryker, but it would take a fool to not figure out Xilo had betrayed them.

Xilo held Aimee's gaze, then dropped it. He moved aside, and Evangeline felt as if she had just lost her enchanted dagger in a dungeon full of monsters.

"I thought so." They smiled.

Xilo didn't even bother to look at her. To own up to the fact that he had just betrayed her. Betrayed all of them.

But for what?

Sehn—no, Council member Aimee—held out their hand. It was hard to see the intimidating Aerian as anything other than the older brother that had treated her with disdain and scorn in the past. Raiythlen could be wrong—or lying—but this felt too big for even him to lie about.

Without thinking, Evangeline pulled out Xilo's dagger, the blade coming between her and their outstretched palm. Lani didn't move or say anything, and Evangeline's arm tightened around her friend's coat, rubbing her pale, white cheek. So cold.

"I won't let you take her." The blade shook in her hand, but she ignored it and cast her gaze to Xilo. Pleading. "Please, help Lani. She's tired. She needs a warm place to rest up."

Aimee glanced down at Lani and frowned. Evangeline clutched her friend tighter.

"Yes . . . we can get her somewhere warmer," they said. "Once she is . . . well again, may I then have your undivided attention?" A small smile. "I'd also ask for your support as well, but I'm jumping ahead of myself."

Aimee's words sounded muffled as Evangeline continued to look at Xilo. His eyes were cast away, transfixed on something in the distance. Or maybe on nothing at all.

You were right to try to leave this place . . . Maybe the Gods do exist and they blessed me with you, Lani had said.

Lani. Oh *Gods,* Lani.

Evangeline dropped her dagger and dug her head into her friend's chest, clenching the sleeves of her coat. She hiccupped on a sob. Her lips wobbled, and she swallowed and swallowed and swallowed, but it wasn't dissolving the heaviness in her throat. What did any of it matter anymore? Any chance for escape was ripped out from under her, and now—

Her friend was dead.

And the worst part: Evangeline had seen it coming. Somewhere in the back of her mind, she knew Lani would never leave this place alive.

"I risked *everything* to save her..." Her voice trembled alongside the trees. Her face was wet, but not from the falling snow. "Why did this have to happen?"

I can't fix this.

"I am deeply sorry, Evangeline."

The world became blurry as she furiously wiped the tears away. She pursed her lips, as if she could force her emotions at bay, and pinned the glamoured Caster with a hateful glare. "Shut your *spitting* mouth," Evangeline snarled at the future king of Peredia.

Aimee didn't appear upset. In fact, their brows furrowed

more, their expression the epitome of sympathy. Lies. "I know what it's like to lose a loved one, but sitting here, clinging to her corpse, won't save those who are still alive."

Evangeline's glare didn't waver. Lani was dead because of this filthy Nyte. All because of these filthy, puss-filled *Nytes.*

Something festered in the pit of her stomach, the familiar sense of darkness and dread she had danced with before. It crawled up her throat, blotting her eyes, seeping into her mind. *Welcome, old friend,* it seemed to whisper to her, before caressing her arms and legs, tugging and pulling with fiery pinchers, adding to the uncontrolled fire that was spreading, and spreading, and spreading . . . She wanted to kill them. Kill them all. *Kill them all!*

The air tasted of metal being forged in a blazing fire, and Evangeline realized it came from the surrounding Casters. She inhaled and also picked up the faint smell of sweat and fear. It didn't come from Xilo but the Casters, all standing by the fallen soldiers, weapons held steadily in their hands even whilst their hearts pounded inside their chests.

And underneath it all, she could taste the spilled blood at the back of her throat.

Evangeline felt her lips curl, even though she didn't remember smiling. She raised her gaze slowly to Aimee and purred in satisfaction at the startled expression they wore, even if it vanished just as quickly as snow on hot pavement.

"You're all the same, starving for power when you're already on top of the world. Using any means necessary. It's that hunger that will bring you to your knees." Evangeline's smile widened. "I would know." Her voice had lowered to a near-rumble, like a sharpened knife wrapped in velvet. She didn't recognize it, nor understand what she was saying, but the darkness inside her had full grip of her body, pumping images, words, and thoughts that weren't her own, at a speed she couldn't comprehend. Except for the rage and hunger. *Gods,* the hunger.

Fake Sehn's face wrinkled, the porcelain skin folding between their groomed brows down to the chiseled jaw and full lips that pressed in a thin line before it all smoothed out. "Interesting . . ."

A rustle behind her—no, above her—was hushed against the soft whistle of wind. The other Casters hadn't moved, their daggers still drawn, pointed at her and Xilo, who also hadn't moved or turned to look at her. Aimee remained still, so still, as if waiting for something.

Evangeline sensed the shift in air as soon as the Caster, perched from the trees above, landed behind her. *There can be no hesitation; you must strike to kill. Anything less and you'll be the one killed,* Jade's words echoed in her mind. Dagger in hand, she whirled around faster than she herself thought possible and met darkly painted eyes, the shape of almonds, widening for a fraction before Evangeline shoved the dagger into their heart. It went in easier than expected, even with their thick leather armor and glowing runes that died on impact along with their master, who fell into the snow as soon as she retracted the blade.

The area erupted into motion.

The surrounding Casters had dashed in opposite directions, while Aimee backed away, their face inscrutable. Black-clad figures rushed her while others darted in and out of the woods at a speed Evangeline could easily follow with her eyes. In fact, when two Casters lunged at her, she could move away in time, watching them grab aimlessly at the space she had just been in. Their leather boots trampled Lani's hand, her pale body still lying in the snow.

"Get away from her!" Evangeline whipped out her dagger, watching their meager attempt to match it with their own steel, barely dodging in time before Evangeline could land a blow. Drops of blood stained the snow where she had nicked one of the Caster's shoulders. Another whoosh of air came from her left, and she twisted her body around, dagger angled in one hand, the other fisted and close to her side. Purple fire exploded out of the corner of her vision, tumbling atop the snow and aimed towards her as if a trail of smoke powder was lit, leading right to her. She jerked away and hissed when hands made of blue, pink, and red wisps of smoke grabbed her legs with the strength of a hundred Aerians.

The tip of a sword shaved the space inches from her nose, right before she bent backwards in time, her dagger lashing out and slicing the underarm of the attacker in front of her.

"I want her alive!" Aimee yelled, paces away. A distant thought wondered why the Council member didn't join in the fight, but she remembered Xilo was here and jerked her head to see the Royal Guard held fast with the same smoke-made hands, sword and dagger out, his face more alive than she'd ever seen it. And he was staring right at her.

Take it. Take it. Take it all and leave nothing. The darkness chanted inside her, focusing her attention back to the Casters creeping in around her. She turned her blade inward and brought it down on the smoke hands. It went right through them, nicking her calf and drawing a crimson line down the back of it. The hands remained steadfast until the dribbles of blood had them smoking and drawing back with an inhuman screech. Evangeline didn't have time to wonder how when pain blossomed in her lower right part of her back. Forcing her entire herself into the motion, she whipped around. She aimed her dagger at the exposed neck of the Caster, who raised their sword—one painted red with her blood—when purple flames blinded her. The sharp needles of heat ripping and eating at her skin came seconds after, and Evangeline hissed as fire engulfed her, touching only her.

In a pain-induced haze, Evangeline watched as the Casters retreated, weapons still drawn, watching her warily as she thrashed and moaned against the fire eating her skin. *Think through the pain. If you can't think clearly, you've already lost the battle.* Evangeline followed Jaden's voice, imagining herself grasping his hand as he led her out of the blazing inferno. *Make them pay, Eve. Take it. Take it. Take it all and leave nothing.* A Caster lingered closer than the rest, their eyes wide as they took her in. Evangeline saw her chance and leaped. The dagger fell from her hands as she sank her fingers into their neck and the cowl of their hood, ripping at black hair. The end of their dagger entered her stomach, but Evangeline ignored the pain as instinct took over, darkness swirling at the edges of her vision, narrowing on the pulse of their neck.

"I'll take it." She snarled to herself and sank her teeth into their neck.

CHAPTER 33

Anali, why am I treated so differently from the other children?" Evangeline pointed at the window, where a cluster of young kids played outside. "Why can't I play, too?" She was told she was the same age as them, yet Anali never allowed her to do the same things. She was always stuck inside this house with its plain walls and plain rooms, empty of life. "It's our temporary home," Anali had once told her. "This won't last forever."

The Caster woman looked down at Evangeline and patted her head gently. "Because you are my special little girl."

Evangeline frowned. "You always say that."

Anali leaned down until they were the same height. "Evangeline, sometimes people fear things they don't understand. Fear changes people, makes them do hurtful things. I don't want you to get hurt."

Evangeline's chest ached, and she felt she knew all too well what Anali meant by that. She would always be different. "Do you fear me, Anali?"

Anali smiled. "There are scarier things in this world, my dear."

"Evangeline, come here. I have someone I'd like you to meet."

Evangeline lingered in the doorway. Anali had opened the windows in the house, a warm breeze carrying through its empty halls. A rare occasion, since the curtains were usually drawn, the house dark and foreboding.

"Don't be shy. He won't hurt you." Anali put out her hand, beckoning her forward.

Evangeline hesitantly stepped forward. The young boy, perched next to Anali on the brown chaise, gazed at her with haunting green eyes. Evangeline glanced down. He had the same marking on his hand, like her.

"Evangeline, I'd like you to meet Jaden, your new friend. He's just like you." Anali patted the spot next to her.

Evangeline came over and sat beside Anali and the strange boy.

"I'm afraid I won't always be here to keep you two safe." Anali reached out and took both of their hands in hers. They were marred, Evangeline knew, from the various experiments she was always doing, cooped up in the forbidden room at the back of the house for long periods of time. She had never confessed to Anali that she heard all of her crazy mumblings, knowing her "gifts" weren't normal. "I need you two to promise me you'll look out for each other and protect each other."

Evangeline reached up to cup Anali's face. "Anali, why are you crying?"

She smiled despite her black bangs covering the clouded expression she wore, creases forming around her eyes. "Promise me you'll always stay by each other's side. This world is too cruel to endure alone."

Jaden and Evangeline looked at each other. For the first time in a long time, she felt herself smiling. She had finally found someone she could play with, and she wouldn't have to feel so alone.

They spoke together. "I promise."

Evangeline woke with a gasp, bringing in treacherous winter air that needled down her warm throat. Darkness and bare trees surrounded her, snow clinging to her fur coat and leather boots, as if she had been lying on the ground for some time. For one delirious moment, she couldn't remember where she was or what had happened. Then it all came back to her. Lani, Council member Aimee and the Casters, Xilo's betrayal, and her . . . she . . .

From the glow of the stars, she held up her hands as if they weren't her own. The brown gloves were ripped and covered in dark splatters that she knew were blood. The rest of her attire didn't fare better, dark scarlet staining in drops along the brown-and-white fur of her coat's collar, down to the larger, darker splotches that would have blended in with dark trousers and boots if she hadn't smelled it. It still clung to her nose, all her senses stirring that . . . *thing* inside her. But it didn't awaken, leaving her blissfully with her own thoughts.

Her lips felt crusted over, and she swiped at them, her sleeve coming back with dried blood. Her eyes stretched into saucers, remembering the feel of her teeth piercing that Caster's neck, the warmth of it as it drizzled down her throat. She turned and vomited. Its red contents made her hurl more until her insides felt empty and her body was shaking.

Rising to her feet, she tried to gather some sense of direction. She couldn't have wandered that far from the city. What in the fiery blazes had happened to her? Had she gone insane and blacked out? Pressing her knuckles to her temple, she tried to remember, but all she got was the overwhelming rage and that awful hunger. Did she kill those Casters? Aimee? That seemed unlikely, but then again, the way she had moved, the dizzying speed at which she kept up with the Casters and their magic . . .

No human could have been able to do that.

The thought left her feeling more alone than when she had faced Lani's dead, white face. *Lani . . .*

Evangeline marched toward the city's lights, the monstrously tall walls looming higher than the trees running next to it. Even in the dark, Castle Peak's protection against the surrounding wilderness stood out like Barto's atrociously yellow pants the first time she'd seen him. The massive gray-and-white speckled stones layered together, defending the castle and its city for centuries. It looked the same as it had back then when she and Jaden . . . She shook her head at the odd thought, focusing on the perimeter and any signs of disturbance across the snow-covered grounds. She had to get back to Lani and give her a proper burial. She refused to let her wither away, abandoned out in the woods.

Tears burned her eyes, her throat scratchy, but she fixed her gaze ahead. She recognized the familiar lay of the land, the pockets of snow where a fight had broken out.

And the grotesque amount of blood darkening the ground.

Evangeline turned away at the sight, searching for Lani, or even Taryn and Ed, or any of the other Nytes. Aside from the obvious signs of battle, there was no evidence of any bodies. She was surprised the guards hadn't stumbled upon this, or hadn't spotted the scene from atop the spearing towers lining the city's perimeter. Then again, if Aimee was involved, there was no telling what they did to keep their encounter private.

A branch sticking out of the ground caught her eye. It was two hand-lengths wide and came up to her waist. It looked sturdy, far sturdier than the surrounding bare twigs that swayed in the gentle wind. Tied to it was a scrap of cloth, plain dark material double-knotted around it, and etched into the material was a name.

Delani Thorp.

Evangeline sank to her knees in front of it, touching the carved name as if it were Lani herself. Who had taken the time to bury her? It couldn't have been Aimee or the other Casters, right? Her hands brushed the snow beneath the marker before she bowed her head, the occasional gust of wind covering her muffled cries.

Pinks and oranges streaked the sky, the sounds of people stirring awake and the clicking of wagons and horse hooves on stone carrying from beyond the walls. Evangeline knew she was close to its entrance, the massive iron enforced gates that stretched as tall as the walls. Or at least she should be after trekking for what felt like an hour now. Sore didn't begin to cover what she felt like. It was as if she had been swept up in a turbulent current, her bones smashing into every boulder on

the way down the river before being dropped off a waterfall. Not that she'd ever seen one aside from the small streams of water that ran through the city's cobblestone pathways before plunging into the sewers below.

The familiar line of guards, their silver-plated armor dull in the wall's shadow, stood on either side of the closed gates. Five on each side, with three sets of pairs to patrol the walls at all times. She knew because she had memorized their patterns before making her escape the first time she'd left the castle city. Swords hung at their sides, and a mixture of wings, tails, and both floppy and pointed furred ears were her best indicator at telling them apart. When she took another step, the floppy-eared Rathan's eyes darted her way before a flurry of swords reached for her.

Evangeline tossed back her hood, knowing she looked ghastly. She'd been crying for the remainder of the night, most likely leaving her eyes rimmed red with a permanent hollow expression. She'd tried to wipe the blood from her mouth the best she could, if only to be rid of the smell of blood so close to her nose, bringing back the nausea in waves, but she was still coated in it. And while a terrifying thread of doubt told her she may not be human—something she *really* didn't want to dwell on—on the outside, she was. And she was without a Nyte escort, beyond the walls.

As the guards came closer, a myriad of hushed voices rushed her.

"Is that a human? I can't tell."

"She's covered in blood."

"What in the Gods—"

From between their outstretched weapons, a Nyte shoved forward, white-furred ears shooting up from the sides of his helmet.

"Halt!" he shouted in a brusque tone, the steel tip of his sword inches from her throat. "Tell me why I shouldn't kill you on the spot, human. It is against Peredian law to be without a Nyte escort beyond your district."

Evangeline's hands were steady as she raised them in a sign of surrender. Her heart didn't beat faster, nor did her body itch to run as far as she could in the opposite direction. It was as if all emotion had been drained. She carefully removed the glove from her marked hand, showcasing it to the guards. "His Highness, Prince Sehn, has requested my presence, and I seem to have gotten quite lost." A smile teased her lips, suddenly finding the situation humorous. "And maybe, sir, I'm not entirely human. You ever think of that?"

CHAPTER 34

Ceven's Royal Guard entourage moved him to cell block seven, on level two. Or at least, that was his guess. Like last night, they blindfolded him and dragged him down here. He attempted to count his steps, to smell and listen to his surroundings, but admittedly he was getting rusty. Hanging with Barto, Quan, and Rasha the past two years had made him lazy. He had relied on them and his two shadows to be his eyes and ears around him, while he focused on slicing anyone that crossed their path. At least he had convinced Kirk and the other Royal Guard to stop man-handling him once they left the throne room, but maybe that was because they placed cuffs and chains around his wrists, made from tazmite.

The rock was an accidental discovery in the Ka'taz territory before it became part of the Atiacan empire. The rock was smooth and only bendable at temperatures Ceven couldn't currently manifest if he wanted to break free of these chains. No one has been able to shatter the rock by normal means, and he didn't expect to suddenly conjure that strength now.

The cell door swung open into an empty, cramped room. At least they gave him a bed and a pot so he wouldn't have to relieve himself in the corner, like the other cell, though it smelled as if the previous tenants had.

Someone—probably Troy—shoved him into the room. The door slammed shut, and the only light was the small slit in the metal-framed door. Then it slid shut.

Ceven sighed loudly. "And here I was, hoping for a luxurious holding cell, complete with some tea and biscuits." It was more to himself, to push the growing unease in the pit of his stomach, than to the guards outside his door. All ten of them. Even if Tarry did storm the cells with those they had swayed to their side, it wouldn't be enough soldiers to get him out of this mess.

Someone chuckled, but the placement was wrong. It came from the other side of the wall, instead of the metal door.

"They must've put you in the wrong room, mate, because I'm living in the lap of luxury in here." The words were muffled, but Ceven could make out the gist of what they were saying. The walls were built thick enough to prevent him from punching his way out and insulated to reduce the heightened hearing Rathans had, but not completely soundproof. He could still tell they had an accent, but he couldn't place it. It could've been a dialect from a region of Atiaca he hadn't been to, or an odd mix of western Peredian and street slang.

Ceven smiled; at least he wasn't the only one with a sense of humor down here. Then it vanished. "Well, ain't that a shame. I'm surprised the king would place a Caster traitor in such high regard."

"Caster? Nah, mate, Rathan. From the tropics. I got the hair to prove it and damned fleas too. They haven't cleaned up down here in a while."

Ceven paused. It made sense there were others down here. Assassins and traitors, sure, but also petty thieves and cheaters. All Nytes—humans were immediately killed. Now it clicked in place why Sehn had suggested they put him in the holding cell and not deeper below where they held the more treacherous criminals. Whatever plan his brother had in store, having Ceven closer to the exit worked better for him. Ceven just hoped it also worked better for himself.

"I thought you had a funny accent." Ceven attempted to rub his wrists. No luck. He wouldn't be comfortable until the blasted cuffs were off. "Never been to the tropics, only the Capital. I can imagine the mosquitos are even worse over there."

"Annoying little buggers, they are." There was movement, and Ceven guessed he was sitting on the ground. "And you? I'm only good with two dialects—rich or poor. I'd say with your tongue, you were raised a lot more comfortably than meself."

Ceven almost laughed at the irony. "Well, you're not wrong. I was only half kidding about the tea and biscuits."

The Rathan laughed. It was a gruff, maybe even muffled one. Ceven scrunched his nose at the ground but took the risk and sat against the wall. He wondered if the Rathan was leaning against the same one.

"I'm surprised they got a richin in here. You must have done something real bad. So, what was it? Murder your wife? Cheat another noble out of his money? That's what they got me for. Should've known better than to try my hand against a noble. Even when they lose fair and square, they still want to call everyone else a cheat."

Ceven leaned his head back. He couldn't even make out the lines on the stone walls around him. Maybe the Rathan had better luck at being able to see his cell. And maybe that was a disadvantage in itself—to see how pathetic and hopeless escape was. Ceven knew how they were designed. He had sent his fair share of men down here too, when he had spent most of his time with the guard, avoiding his father and brother and the pointless "princely" duties that were more to keep him in line than any real responsibility.

"No cheating, just wrong place at the wrong time." Wasn't exactly a lie. If he'd caught on to Sehn's plan earlier, he wouldn't be in this predicament. But just like when they were kids, Sehn was always one step ahead of him.

Ceven loosened a breath as he recalled his brother sitting on top of him, his hand forcing down his inept wing. Pain had rioted down the arm of it, twisting down his spine as he struggled to get him off, but he hadn't been strong enough.

You think you deserve to be king? His brother had laughed. Cold, manipulative, and everything that embodied what the king wanted. *You can't even save yourself, let alone this kingdom.* The same words the king had said to him. Ceven curled his hands into fists.

"A bummer. At least we have each other now. Almost romantic." The Rathan pulled him from his thoughts.

Ceven snorted. "Well, if we escape, I'll show you what a proper date looks like."

The Rathan laughed, but this time it was clear, not as gruff. "And I'll wear my best dress." Rocks crackled and crumbled. He was leaning against the same wall. "You know, for a richin, you're not too bad of a guy."

"And for a poor, cheating Rathan from the tropics, you're not too bad yourself." The gruff laugh was back, more muted.

Ceven wanted to ask if his eyesight was better than his, but the guards were right outside and he didn't want to raise any alarms. Hopefully, this guy was smarter than he had made himself out to be. "At least they were nice enough to give me a pot and flimsy bed here. Though a bit more space would be nice. Almost hit my head on the blasted ceiling."

He got the hint. "You must be pretty tall. I got plenty of headroom here. I also got a pot and a bed from what I can see. And a few writings someone left behind on the wall. 'The mighty Gods of the skies, fall down on me, and end this misery,' to which someone replied, 'A noose works better.' Well, they ain't wrong."

So, the Rathan could see a lot better than Ceven could. It was something, even if it didn't get him out of this cell. Ceven rattled his chains. "I might try my hand at some drawing if they didn't cuff my spitting wrists. Have an itch on my back that's been driving me sky-high since."

"Same. Can't even use my toes to scratch my underside."

They chained his feet too? Ceven pursed his lips. Either this guy really ticked off whatever royal placed him down here, or he was more dangerous than he let on.

They passed a few more subtle descriptors. Ceven concluded that there were no cracks in the wall, or at least the foundation was sturdy enough that the metal cot in the room would be no use in carving a hole in the wall or ground. If his cell buddy didn't point out any weaknesses in his own cell, there would unlikely be any in Ceven's. Unless Sehn planted something in here on purpose, but he didn't think that was likely. Ceven couldn't see his hands in front of him, and there was nothing in the room when he had first swept it over before being shut in.

Ceven gritted his teeth and cursed.

Time passed gruelingly slow. Ceven exchanged a few more words with his cell partner, but they both had fallen quiet. There was only so much to say when someone was trapped down in darkness with nothing but their impending death weighing on them. Though Ceven was less concerned about escaping than he was his brother's plan and the fate of the kingdom. The more he thought about killing his former father, the more knots wound tight in his belly. Calais's words in the throne room had hit him harder than any blow or insult. What would have things been like if his circumstances were different?

Blue-green eyes framed by wheat-colored hair popped into his mind. If the king had never shunned him, would he have ever befriended Evangeline? He knew the answer, as much as he'd like to believe otherwise. His younger self was no less a tyrant, a selfish monster than the other Nytes that lived in this city. He once had accepted a human's place in their society without a doubt, gleaning from the privilege of it, without batting an eye. It was when he was forced to live on the outskirts of the people who once revered him that he saw the other side to things.

He was disgusted it had taken so much for him to become a decent man.

Unlike Barto, whose heart had always been open and without judgment. A sharp pang in his chest had him crinkling his hands into fists. Gods, he hated being so unsure of himself. He snorted. And to think he once wanted to be a captain, king, some kind of leader, when he couldn't even make the right decisions in his own life.

There was movement, but it was distant. Ceven came alive, stretching his neck. He opted to rest on the floor rather than the mattress that most likely had some form of disease. Or maybe fleas, like his cell mate said. A pair of shoes padded down the hall, a slight squeak that told him they were new. It was either an additional guard that hadn't broken in his armor, a noble, or—

"Leave, and be back when the sun strikes the roof," came Sehn's muffled voice outside his cell door.

Ceven wondered if the Royal Guard would listen to him, since they hadn't listened twice now, in front of Ceven. This time they did, or he assumed they did, when more footsteps than he could count rumbled outside his door and down the hall. Interesting . . .

Metal shaved against the rough stone as his cell door opened. Sehn took up the space of the narrow frame. He still looked like he was being suffocated by his—now gold—coat.

"Come to join me?" Ceven rattled his chains.

Sehn bent next to him. "Hold out your wrists." Ceven didn't like his tone, but seeing the set of keys in his hand, he complied.

The cuffs fell to the floor with a caustic clang. Ceven rubbed his wrists and itched his back like he had never itched it before. His freedom was short-lived, though, when his brother offered him another set of cuffs.

"They're not made from tazmite. When the time comes, you'll be able to break these," he whispered, so low that if Ceven wasn't next to him, he wouldn't have heard.

"Would've been nice to have known that *I* was the inside man," Ceven said in equal volume, but with twice the venom. "Is there anything else you've neglected to tell me?"

Sehn smirked. "If you'd known, you wouldn't have complied as obediently as you have. Tell me, brother, would you have not run back to Evangeline?"

Ceven matched his smirk. "Who knows? A little too late to find that out now. But I can tell you, if you try to pull another fast one, I won't be as *obedient*."

Sehn didn't look concerned. And why would he be? Ceven had let him play him for a fool. He would have to rectify that. When he wasn't in chains, in a cell, bound by a blood promise.

His brother handed him a dagger, one Ceven slipped into his right boot. He still had the other one sewn into his trousers. "Once you're in the throne room, next to the king, break these chains and stab him in the throat. I'll create a distraction. Timing is everything here."

"It sure is, since it'll be my head on the ground and not yours, if this fails," he growled. "Why are you so eager to kill your father? He'll be dead soon enough. Are you that hungry for power, Sehn?"

"He used to be your father, too," he said, but there was no love. No former respect for the parent that had raised them. They both had turned out so differently. "The guards will be away awhile longer, and Avana will be here shortly. I want you to listen and tell me everything she and Raiythlen say." Sehn handed him a silver cylinder, with one side bigger than the other and about a hand's length long. Ceven'd seen nothing like it. "Press that against the wall with your ear to it and you'll be able to hear what they're saying."

Sehn stood, never answering Ceven's question and leaving him more confused. Why would Avana be down here? And who was Raiythlen?

The cell door closed, and Ceven was blind again. Even on the darkest nights when he lay out on the patchy grasslands by Barto's village, he could still make out the sloppy smile and slightly crooked nose of his friend an arm's length away from him on the grass mat. Nothing like this lonely, dark hole. Was this what Evangeline felt when Ryker left her alone in a cell? He wished he had gotten to her sooner and that they had left that night. If only she had stayed by his side . . .

The clicking of heels echoed not long after Sehn's absence. It had to be Avana.

Instead of pausing outside his door, she clicked past it, to his Rathan buddy beside him. Was he the Raiythlen his brother mentioned? The Rathan never did tell him his name.

Testing out the odd listening device, Ceven pressed his ear against the smaller silver end, the bigger, rounded end pressed firmly against the wall. His cell mate's door groaned open as if he was in the same room, the Rathan's chains chattering.

"How nice of you to walk all the way here, just for me." Ceven would have smiled at the good taste of attitude this man had if it wasn't for the change in his voice. It wasn't as deep now, nor gruff.

And he spoke Castanian with perfect ease.

"Shut up. You're lucky I haven't killed you yet." It was the opposite of the calm, controlled woman he'd seen in Sehn's study.

"Lucky me," Raiythlen murmured. "What do you want, Avana? Clearly you don't believe a single word I say to you, so if you're here to ask questions, it's a little late for that."

Something sizzled, and the hair on Ceven's arms prickled.

"Perhaps, but the promise of pain sometimes makes the truth come out a lot easier. And I know your weak spots, brother."

Ceven jerked. Brother? Not only was this man lying about being Atiacan, he wasn't even a Rathan, but a cursed Caster. *The* Caster.

"Ah, yes, rather than face the facts, you'd still believe in your own spun illusions. Torturing me will still get you the same answers. The same ones you don't want to hear."

"Shut up!" A powerful slap of a whip slammed into the ground, and the floor vibrated. Raiythlen's hiss told Ceven that whatever Avana did, it hit its mark.

"What are your plans with Evangeline? What does the Council want with her now?" Her voice was closer and so was the sizzling. Ceven didn't like to hear anyone in pain—but this man deserved it for dragging Evangeline to the west wing. For putting her in danger.

"I already told you, woman," he growled. "I was here to capture her alive. When I found out the Council's *real* plans, everything changed."

"Lies."

Ceven didn't hear a reply, but a moment later, Raiythlen's howls crawled down his spine.

"You're lucky . . . I'm cuffed." His voice went ragged.

She laughed, but it was hollow. "As if you could beat me. You've failed, what, twice now?"

"I bloody told you . . . I wasn't there to fight you, but of course—!" Another bone-chilling yell pounded the wall behind Ceven. "If you're so confident," he gasped, "then why did you involve Sehn? Why didn't you . . . just capture me yourself?"

"Why dirty my hands when I can have others do it for me?" She and Sehn were identical in that sense. Ceven's lip curled.

Raiythlen snorted, a feat given his current predicament. "And that's why the Council liked me more . . . I got stuff done . . . you always danced around everything."

"I played my part well enough to get me *here* and you *there*."

Raiythlen chuckled as if he were sharing an inside joke.

"What? Working for the very same Council you despise? You're a fool, sister. You've always allowed your passions to control you too deeply. It's why the Council didn't believe you about Evangeline, about her mark. Why they thought you were crazy—"

He yelled. This one louder. Then he yelled again, and again. A low whimper. Then silence.

"They're the *fools*!" Her voice quivered, and Ceven imagined the woman shaking with fury. "I'm not crazy. Anali wasn't crazy, and Evangeline is *proof*! How dare they belittle us, what our family did for our country! If they'd listened to me, if you'd listen to me, if everyone would've *believed* me, Mom and Dad would still be alive . . ."

Raiythlen didn't respond. Ceven didn't think he could after that last battle, but he surprised him. "Congratulations, Avana. We all believe you now . . . and soon you'll see just what that got you . . ."

Ceven imagined if he were in Raiythlen's shoes, Sehn would've acted much the same way as Avana was now. Avana's words rang with no mercy as she said, "I'll be able to see it, but you won't."

"You won't kill me . . . you can't . . ."

"On the contrary, I'm going to make sure of it. Remember, I know all your tricks. I've been watching you for years, waiting for this moment. Nothing is going to save you this time, brother." The low sizzling hum came to a halt, slithering back to its owner. "And I'll find that familiar of yours. My raven has been having an increased fondness for mice as of late." The door opened. "You shouldn't have crossed me, Rai." The words were soft as the door shut and her heels clicked away.

Something slid against the wall, and Ceven was sure Raiythlen had just slumped to the floor.

CHAPTER 35

The carriage was warm. The hot coals in the iron brazier had fogged up the glass windows. Evangeline had only been in a carriage twice. Once when she was brought to the city as a child, and again when Ryker dragged her back to the ruins where she was found. But both times, never had she sat on velvet upholstery or had expensive glass fixtures dangling on either side of her head. Or been cuffed to the walls with chains made of tazmite, like an Aerian or Rathan prisoner.

Council member Aimee mirrored her, minus the hand-cuffs—unless she counted the tight gold cufflinks that matched the trim of their waistcoat and brought out the cream tunic and slacks, nothing at all like what she'd last seen them wear—with one leg crossed casually. But their gaze was anything but casual.

To Evangeline's extreme good fortune—or misfortune depending on how she looked at it—the false Prince had conveniently appeared behind her when she confronted the guards at the city's gates. The shock and confusion on the Nytes' faces would have been priceless if it had been any other day. And she didn't know if it was because they doubted she truly was human, with her being covered in blood and lacking the proper fear a sane human would have after being caught beyond the walls, or if it was the disguised prince's sudden appearance. The false prince and their carriage had appeared—almost magically—from the Olaaga woods behind Evangeline, supposedly returning from a "brief retreat for solitude." Or so they had told the guards. Evangeline saw the questions and doubt forming in their faces as Aimee yanked her inside the carriage, letting the six Royal Guards that surrounded the carriage on horseback ease their doubts and allow them entry into the city.

Aimee's intense stare continued to sear into Evangeline's skin, despite their attempt at light conversation. Evangeline ignored them. Her gaze was as cold as the snow-covered rooftops that whizzed by.

With a heavy sigh, Aimee leaned back. "For one mere girl, you sure have cost me a lot." Unlike their earlier attempt at politeness, this time impatience seeped through. Perhaps even a hint of anger. "I've been searching all night for you. Then you show up, seeking *me* out, and now you ignore me. The audacity."

Why? Evangeline didn't ask. If they had been searching for her, she obviously meant something to them. And the fact she was still alive meant they needed her to be coherent. She stored that bit of important information away for later.

"Now I'm sure those damned guards will cause a stir with rumors and gossip about my whereabouts and why I was in the company of a hu—a girl covered in blood and rags for clothes."

Another sigh. "And of course you don't care. You haven't the slightest idea the gravity of the situation."

That this may ruin your cover? That the real Prince Sehn is far, far from Peredia? Evangeline remained silent and kept her gaze out the window.

Aimee didn't attempt another conversation, and the silence stretched the entire ride. Only the occasional rattle of her chains whenever they hit a bump on the path broke the silence. In between, the soft whistle of wind and the stampede of hooves filled the quiet until they stopped in front of the castle gates. Evangeline peered out the window as the two guards waved them through. As a joke, she attempted to wave back, but her bindings held her too tightly, resulting in her fingers twitching. She had walked up the winding hundred-plus stairs every single day to get to the castle gates. Now, she sat in the future king's carriage. If the two guards recognized her, they didn't show it.

"Now, no bolting away. Or else it'll look suspicious," Aimee said as the door opened and a blast of cold air invaded the toasty carriage.

"I obviously don't plan on it," she said for the first time since stumbling upon the false prince again. If she were going to run, she would've had a better chance standing in the woods, before she entered the wagon with a deadly Caster.

Aimee left the chains on her but kept them hidden under an additional coat they threw on top of her before leaving the carriage. As if the disguised Council member didn't trust her, they settled their arm behind her back and dragged her closer, her head brushing their shoulder. It reminded Evangeline of how tall she was, knowing most humans came up to the chests of most Aerians, and even then, they were mostly male. Curiosity struck her. Was the real Council member this tall? Or was this part of the illusion?

They climbed cleanly-cut stone steps, passed the God of all Gods statue—Evangeline gave it a disdainful glare—and entered the castle.

Evangeline was grateful to lean on someone, even if it was Aimee. Here, she felt vulnerable. Humans and Nytes stared at her. Some stopped dead in their tracks, others dropped whatever they were holding—mostly trays, except one girl who dropped a bucket of sudsy water. It sloshed over the sides and sprinkled Evangeline's leather boots and riding breeches—another oddity to be stared at. Not only was she a human out of uniform, but lacking the proper corseted dress for women of the Aerian court. Though she wasn't a part of that court anymore (she wasn't really to begin with) now that Ryker was dead.

It was no surprise Nytes and humans fought to get a better glimpse. The infamous Evangeline, the first human to be adopted into court, being escorted by Prince Sehn himself. That piece of gossip would trickle to every wall of the castle—alongside Ryker's murder.

She had no choice but to continue to walking. Each step, almost mechanical. Her gaze fixed straight ahead, as if the gears in her neck had rusted over. She wanted to crawl back into that carriage and have the driver send it straight off this mountain.

As they passed humans in their long black-sleeved and purple apron uniforms and Nytes complete in floor-length gowns with low-scooped necklines and frock coats held together by a few buttons, Evangeline assessed the fake prince. Like Sehn, their crimson wings were large, so large that they dragged on the floor behind them. Each feather shifted and danced of its own accord, ready to take flight at a moment's notice. If they were fake, they didn't look like it. Their long mahogany hair was swept half-up, half-down, with a gold ornate pin matching the gold assembly of chains hanging against their shirt, which was unfashionably buttoned up all the way. When Evangeline had first seen "Sehn," she'd assumed his stay in Sundise Mouche had affected his new style, but now it made better sense, because it hadn't been him at all. It seemed Council member Aimee didn't have a taste for the court's fashion.

They took several flights of black marble staircases, glass chandeliers dangling precariously above them from the high arched ceilings. Vases of white lilacs dusted the air with a light and refreshing aroma, contrasting against the purple and gold floor runners spanning the length of the hallways. They were in the castle's main hall, where Evangeline had spent a good chunk of her life. She didn't miss it one bit.

They weren't on the top floor of the castle, which meant they weren't going to Sehn's suite, but somewhere else. They entered a room at the end of the far wall with two Royal Guards standing in front of it. "Guest room," Aimee informed her.

The room, as expected, was half the size of a royal suite, but not lacking in Peredian taste. With soft pastel walls and marble flooring, it fit the mold of the castle's decor. A large canopy bed was settled in the middle of the room, furnished with a purple satin comforter and an array of dress pillows. The fireplace, which was half the size of a horse, was on the opposite wall, accented by a dark purple loveseat and one chair. The heat of it hit her all the way from the entryway.

Her gaze lingered on the balcony. From this side of the castle, she could see the garden that stretched the main hall's length. It was where she'd ran into Sehn, or who she had thought was the young prince. To think a Council member had been playing them all this time . . .

A slim human girl with nut-colored skin came in and bowed. Never once did she look up. Aimee asked for refreshments and then some food as an afterthought, while glancing at Evangeline with an unreadable expression. The Caster sat on the loveseat, the shadows from the flames dancing across their skin. Evangeline had yet to see any flaws, any imperfections in the disguise. Was this really a Council member?

"Please, sit." They patted the spot next to them.

Evangeline pointedly rattled her chained hands.

"Your legs aren't chained." They gave her a look that second-guessed that decision. "And after that remarkable display you put on earlier, I have to be cautious, dear. Now, sit."

It was no matter she defended herself beyond those walls, that she had let that . . . thing inside her take over and attack those Casters. That for a moment in time she hadn't been herself or . . . human. But standing here, chained, cold, and crusted over with blood, she felt anything but powerful. Despite that, Evangeline still fantasized about fighting her way out of the room, like she had in the woods. Destroying Aimee and saving Ceven from Gods-know-where, both of them fighting their way out before escaping through the city's gates on horseback, as if they were in some sort of adventure novel. But this was reality. And she was as trapped as she'd always been. Stuck inside this blasted castle.

But at least this time it had been her decision.

Evangeline sat next to the Nyte, albeit as far away as she could get on the loveseat. Aimee's stare sent her skin crawling, and it was more unnerving than the passing looks of those in the halls.

"It's remarkable. You look absolutely ordinary, but you're far from that. A true mystery," Aimee said.

"Did I kill that Caster?" That had been on her mind for some time now. Evangeline didn't know why the idea bothered her so much. They'd attacked her first.

Aimee went quiet for a moment. "Do you not remember?"

Evangeline wanted to squirm, to break these blasted chains. "If I did, I wouldn't be asking." As if she were back in Ryker's suite with the former advisor, she waited for a slap or some kind of blow for her retort. Instead, the Caster raised a brow.

"You snapped her neck and massacred the rest of my team," they said. Evangeline jerked, cold needles prickling up her spine and neck. She had remembered none of it. Aimee continued, "It's strange how some of our spells didn't affect you. Was it because of you, or perhaps something else?" The question seemed to be directed more at themselves.

Evangeline did remember how the smoke hands had withered when she'd sliced her leg. Had it been because of the saliver running in her blood? "Where's Prince Ceven?"

"Ah, yes, the young prince. That's the real reason you came back, isn't it? I'm sure it wasn't to chat with me." Evangeline didn't deny it, though that wasn't the entire reason she'd returned to this dreadful place. It was a risk to use Prince Sehn as a way back inside the castle, but she knew her limits. Even if the weak, movable boulder within the wall still existed, there was no way she'd make it through the city and into the castle without someone recognizing her and the guards dragging her off straight towards the king. Or possibly being murdered outright.

Aimee leaned back and placed an arm along the back of the couch, their hand resting behind Evangeline's head. The Caster's thigh brushed hers. "Do tell, what is your relationship with my brother?"

"He is my prince, Your Highness," Evangeline said carefully, gauging their reaction.

"My dear, there's no need to be so formal. After the night we've had, I'd say we're beyond formalities." Their gaze never strayed. "Much like you and Ceven," they added coyly.

Evangeline balled her hands into fists. Even if this wasn't Sehn, they were just as good at playing mind games. She'd prefer to face the Council's brutality than this flimsy falsehood of friendship.

"Tell me where he is," she demanded.

Aimee's face hardened, but before they responded, a girl rolled in a cart of food. Her eyes focused on the ground as she placed silver platters on the knee-height table in front of them.

"Do you require anything else, Your Highness?" Even her voice was small, delicate.

The disguised prince flashed a charming smile. "No, my sweet. I will see you tonight."

The girl blushed and bowed before leaving.

Evangeline stared at the food in awe of the pure gluttony of it. There was more than enough here to feed several human families. And it looked a lot more appetizing than Xilo's beans and toast. An ache formed in her chest.

Lani was dead. Xilo had betrayed her. And worst of all, she was more than crazy. She truly was a monster.

Suddenly, the corners of her lips twitched, and laughter bubbled in her throat. Life was just one big joke. Almost unreal.

Aimee waved their hand. "I'm sure you're hungry, please eat. Unless there are other things that would satisfy your appetite."

The memory of that Caster's blood filling her mouth was enough to make her stomach cramp in anticipation while she felt ill, but Evangeline didn't want to give this Caster the pleasure of rattling her. She picked at the honeyed hams and whipped potatoes that should've made her drool but didn't stir any hunger in her. There were even pieces of peppermint chocolate and sweet rolls glazed in icing and cinnamon—her favorite—and still she had no desire to eat any of it.

Aimee shifted, their arm on the back of the couch now resting against Evangeline's nape, her braided hair brushed over the side of her shoulder. The feel of them on her exposed nape made her skin break out in bumps as Ranson's snapped neck sliced her thoughts, then the Caster's as she'd sunk her teeth into their flesh as if she had bitten into a sweet roll. She gagged on a slice of ham and set the uneaten half back on the table. Her stomach recoiled, and all the food before her seemed a waste now, as she couldn't bear to touch it.

There was a scrape, like claws on marble. It came from under the bed, then rounded the corner and—

Evangeline bolted onto the couch. "A wolf!"

The wolf in question didn't move but sat on its hind-legs, its pink tongue licking its white-and-gray muzzle. Aimee looked amused, their fingers brushing back the wolf's fur. "No need to be frightened. He's harmless."

Evangeline sank back down but kept her eyes on the wolf. It looked like the same one that had chased her outside of Lani's slave quarters. And if that was the case, it was far from harmless.

When Evangeline settled back on the couch, Aimee's wings curled around them, forcing her closer. She stiffened and caved her shoulders in.

The Caster mistook her stiffness. "He acts more like a dog than a wolf. Isn't that right, Fastah?" they cooed to it. The wolf snuggled into their hand, urging to be petted.

It hit her. This was Aimee's familiar, the same one that had been following her around.

Raiythlen's words, from when Ryker had thrown her in the dungeons, echoed in her brain. *There have been footsteps outside Lani's window, fresh prints, nearly every night. But when I try to catch them, they are just out of my grasp, as if they know that I am watching you as well.* How long has Aimee been stalking her? Evangeline scratched her skin as it crawled, leaving raised flesh in its path.

Aimee's eyes slid back to study her as Evangeline stared at their familiar with growing horror.

"Something you'd like to share?" They cocked their head, their fingers leaving Fastah to curl beneath their chin.

Evangeline wished her wit was as fast as the beat of her heart. Blast it. She said, "Have Casters always been employed under the oldest prince?" Referring to the black-clad Casters that had taken down the Aerian soldiers.

Their gaze narrowed, and Evangeline straightened.

Yes, I know your secret. What are you going to do about it?

That same darkness unraveled inside her gut, stretching its claws, but she tamped it down, imagining the chains she wore binding it as well. She didn't want to lose control here. She didn't want to lose her mind.

"I was wondering how long you would hold this charade." Aimee moved—fast. Fingers gripped Evangeline's chin, and the silvery lines of their fake eyes—or they could've been real, for all she knew—were a finger's width away from hers. Her squeak was trapped in her throat, but their touch was gentle. "I think you know full well who I really am. But at least now we can be completely open with each other."

Evangeline jerked out of their grasp. She would've fled from the couch as well—if Aimee's fake wings didn't trap her in.

"I don't care who you are. I want to know where Ceven is."

The Caster's face dripped with interest. "So bold, you are." Their lips curved into a seductive smile. "What if I told you that Raiythlen needed your help as well?"

Evangeline wasn't surprised that Aimee knew of his presence here. Raiythlen had insinuated as much. "Where is he?"

They didn't move, and Evangeline was starting to think this Caster didn't know the definition of personal space. Still, she met their gaze straight-on as they said, "In the dungeons." Then, as if divulging a juicy secret, they whispered, "And tomorrow, he will face a public execution by your king."

Her mouth peeled open. He got caught? She'd thought the Caster assassin was infallible, untouchable. That the king would kill him tomorrow in front of the entire city was inconceivable.

"And?" Evangeline forced a nonchalance she didn't possess. Inside, she was a storm of emotion. She owed Raiythlen nothing. He may have helped her find Lani, but he had also poisoned her friend and threatened their lives. He had tricked her into murdering her foster father.

Aimee tapped their chin. "No remorse for your Caster friend? Even if he and Prince Ceven are taking the fall for the murder of Ryker Ardonis? If they're reaping the consequences of your actions?"

Evangeline's jaw slackened. "What?"

Their brows rose as if surprised. "Oh? Did you think everyone had forgotten about poor old Ryker? That his murder would go unnoticed? Someone had to pay the price, Evangeline." Aimee moved away, grabbing the glass teapot on the table. The smell of ginger was strong.

Everything around Evangeline dimmed—the sounds of the fireplace crackling, Aimee sipping from their glass, the red and orange hues of the oil lamps. Everything faded away as Ceven's dead face, his eyes upturned, his skin cold, blared at her mind's eye. Just like Ranson's face. Like the woman who died in her hallucination and the Caster whose neck she had ripped open.

Like Lani's cold corpse.

The laughter bubbled up again, tickling her throat. It wanted to burst free, but Evangeline squelched it. She closed her eyes, and for a moment she was far away from here. Back in the garden with Ceven before any of this happened. Sunlight kissed her cheeks, her hair. Water trickled somewhere deeper within, and nothing but the smell of jasmine and Ceven's wood and spice surrounded her.

When Evangeline opened her eyes, Aimee was sipping their tea, their other hand petting Fastah. They didn't press her to answer, and Evangeline was glad their gaze was fixated on something else.

"Raiythlen . . . he used to work for you. Do you not care that he will die as well?" Was that her voice? It was too calm and collected and . . . distant. It sounded like a stranger to her.

They took another sip before setting the cup on the table. Fastah whimpered when they removed their hand. "Of course I care. I've known him since he was eight. Like his parents, he turned out to be an excellent agent. I will mourn for him as I do all of my members who sacrifice their lives every day for our country." The glimpse of a scowl slipped through. "Including those you killed beyond the wall."

"You attacked me first."

"If you had stopped and listened, you would've realized I was there to help. Then you became . . . unstable. I had to protect myself and the others."

"If you really are here to help, then stop this," she said, this Council member's words spurring the embers in her belly. They were acting like Raiythlen was already dead. "He doesn't have to die." *Ceven doesn't have to die.* They both heard those unspoken words.

Aimee stood, flipping their coat behind them. "But he does. When he decided to put his own endeavors above the Council, he terminated his contract. He knew what he was getting himself into. He's no longer that eight-year-old boy, but a man now."

"And Ceven? Did he not fit into your plans, either?"

The Caster faced the fire. "On the contrary, he's vital to my plan. And so are you."

The weight of Aimee's words was ruined when they turned, the large red wings knocking over the cup of tea and platter of ham and potatoes. They hurled a curse as Fastah eagerly chowed down on the spilled food. Light brown liquid seeped into the porcelain platter of sweet rolls, and a chill ran down Evangeline's spine as the liquid dripped onto the floor, staining the carpet. Like it had when Ryker clawed at his throat, gasping for air right before he collapsed and died.

"I hate these bloody wings." They shoved the wolf out of the way, trying to salvage the food. When they realized it was pointless, they threw up their hands and let Fastah resume their lucky meal.

Evangeline didn't move. She couldn't, and it wasn't because of the chains still sagging down her wrists and arms. It was as if she'd been glued together and moving would cause her to shatter. "I don't think you brought me here just to tell me that my friend is about to be slaughtered. What do you want from me?"

"And I don't think you came back just to see Ceven," Aimee said a bit impatiently. They sat back down with a sigh and grabbed a cloth from the table. The blue cotton linen soaked up the steaming tea, but Evangeline knew from experience that a towel worked much better. And faster. "While you've proved to be much more . . . unpredictable than I would have liked, I believe our goals align quite well." They waited for a response, but Evangeline remained silent. They shrugged. "I want you to eliminate Calais LuRogue."

Evangeline went still, not because she hadn't expected Aimee's answer, but because of the sudden hot, putrid rage that knifed her gut. It had almost been enough for the darkness to break the mental chains she had put on it. The Aerian who had started it all. Who oversaw and employed others for the enslavement and torture of hundreds of humans for his own benefit. Who had watched this dark magic eat and corrode away at their skin and not feel a thing as people like her precious friend, Lani, died slowly and painfully.

Aimee hadn't been wrong. Even if it was foolish, Evangeline hadn't returned just to warn Ceven, but to seek revenge. She didn't know how, nor did she have a plan, but one way or another, she would make them pay for the atrocities they'd committed.

Make them suffer, Eve. Like they've made us suffer, Jaden whispered in her ear from a memory past.

After some time, and when some sense returned to her, she said, "And just how do you expect me to accomplish that?" She took in their expression. "I don't know what happened out in those woods. I . . . I had lost my mind. I'm not doing that again." Not if Ceven and other innocent people were going to be close by. "Not to mention the king is always surrounded by the Royal Guard. I'd never get close enough."

Aimee tossed the sopping cloth on the other side of the table, where it landed with a wet slap. When they looked at her, Evangeline flinched. There was nothing gentle in their features. "So you think the king deserves to live?"

Evangeline was at a loss, confused by the sudden change in them. But before she could answer, there was a soft brush of velvet as they slid closer. Gone was the charming smile, the curious glint in those gray eyes. This time it was menacing, calculating. "Do you not hate him?"

Evangeline didn't trust this one bit. Like if she answered wrong, she was going to be killed right there. She channeled her anger, using it to burn away the cold hole in her chest. "I do, but to kill the king—"

The Caster lunged at her.

Gold and beige blurred before Aimee gripped the loveseat on both sides of her face. "Are you telling me you're okay with the king murdering hundreds of humans during the Red Wash? Painting these halls with their blood? Whipping, beating, and torturing your kind for his gain?"

Evangeline stopped breathing. The world went silent. She was both entranced and terrified by the fire in Aimee's eyes. "No," she whispered.

"For treating you and Delani like vermin, picking the next rodent to carve his blade into, to mar their backs like he and Ryker did your friend? To laugh and revel in her pain every time they carved another symbol into her skin, knowing it was sucking the life out of her."

The darkness stretched and yawned against its mental chains. "Stop it."

"Or maybe you're okay with the king chopping off Ceven's head? Watching him get drunk off his own power and status as his blade cuts through your lover's neck—"

It rattled and yanked harder, itching, screaming to be let out. "Stop."

"—slicing and splitting him open as his head pops off, leaving a bloody trail across the throne room—"

She wanted to kill him, kill this Caster, kill all of them. "Stop!"

"—his eyes staring blankly at you while you stand there and do nothing. Ceven, Lani, Raiythlen, all of them dead because of—"

"Stop it!" Evangeline screamed at both Aimee and herself. The darkness seeped through its chains, creeping up her limbs and throat with a burning fire laced with an insatiable hunger. She couldn't let it escape. Not now. Not ever. She clenched her eyes shut, imagining Ceven's eyes lighting up in the sun, his face crinkling into a smile as he looked at her. The way he tossed his head back, his brown hair teasing his handsome face as he laughed. She imagined Lani's warm embrace and the smell of dough and sugar clinging to her apron after a long day in the kitchens. The happiness Evangeline felt when Lani would sneak her sweet rolls.

When she opened her eyes, the first thing she saw was Aimee's smile, and the blood dripping down their index finger, a rune prepped on the skin of their forearm.

"So, you can control it after all. Interesting . . ."

Quiet, angry tears streamed down Evangeline's face. She shuddered from the air that she couldn't seem to get into her lungs. She *hated* this Caster for making her cry. They pulled out a silk cloth from their trouser pocket. Evangeline heaved as Aimee dried her face, the silk soft against her skin. A warm hand tucked a stray blond hair behind her ear.

"Poor Evangeline. Life has always been so unfair to you. But here's your chance to save your friend and yourself." They smiled. "And seek revenge for Lani."

Evangeline bared her teeth, but she nodded. If only to get them out of her face.

Aimee tilted her chin up, and Evangeline read the words from their lips as they spoke them. "Then let us prepare for the final act."

CHAPTER 36

Night had fallen, patches of moonlight hitting the creamy marble floor of the guest suite. Aimee advised Evangeline to get some sleep, as if she could with two guards by the door, watching her. The sheets were silky against her skin. The bed sank in perfectly to conform to her body. It was like sleeping in the clouds, but it was a temporary comfort. A temporary distraction from the hell that had been her life these past weeks.

And tomorrow would be the most pivotal moment in all of it.

Let us prepare for the final act. She didn't know what Aimee had meant by that, but it wouldn't be easy. The Royal Guard surrounded the king at all times, and they were not the same caliber as normal guards. What possibly could she do against them?

She glanced down at her hands, remembering the way she had gripped those daggers, how powerful she had felt. Just what in blazes had happened? *Was* happening? The familiar pulse of darkness still stirred beneath its mental chains. This time, it seemed it was here to stay for good, but she didn't want to lose herself like that again, to be . . . to be a monster.

Even if it's to fight other monsters? The question probed her.

Aimee informed her that the execution would be held tomorrow at dusk. Evangeline had asked to see Ceven, to make sure he was alive, but unsurprisingly, the Caster refused. Aimee assured her he wasn't going anywhere, that he and Raiythlen were being held in the upper floors of the dungeons. And the time to save them would be at the execution itself.

Most public executions involving destruction of property, slander against the king, and murder were often held outside in the plaza beyond the gates to the castle so all humans and Nytes could attend. However, on rare occasions, traitors or those that had committed treason against the crown were executed in the throne room by the king personally. With so many Nytes and people, it would be easier to create a temporary diversion, and with Aimee's aid, Evangeline would have the opening she needed to kill the king. As if it would be that easy.

If we work together, there's a chance everyone will win. You, me, and Ceven, Aimee had said.

What do you win? she had asked, not bothering to point out that if this failed, they would kill only her and Ceven. It made her wonder where Barto was, if he knew his best friend was going to be executed. If he even had the power to stop it or wanted to, after Ceven's betrayal.

Why, the throne, of course, they had said. Which didn't tell her anything. Did this Council member want the throne for power? Resources? Information? Was it to stop the king's plan to go to war with Sundise Mouche? If that was who he planned to go to war with? Not that it mattered to Evangeline. Either she'd be far away from this place when it was all over—or dead.

But the idea of death was getting more and more comfortable, snuggling and taking up residence inside her brain like an uninvited guest. Of course, Evangeline wanted to live, but it was getting harder to survive. Like she was in the middle of a swordfight, but where everyone else had steel scabbards, daggers, and swords, she had a stick. She'd always had that blasted stick, waving it around like it was something more than it was. Or maybe now it was less a stick and more like sharp teeth that—

Evangeline rolled over, silk sliding against her bare legs. Aimee had only given her a knee-length nightgown to sleep in. Maybe it was from their own personal wardrobe. If it was, the Caster was a lot shorter and more petite than their Sehn-disguise. Evangeline would've preferred to sleep in her black leather pants and long-sleeved shirt—for the added protection and mobility. She felt like she was back in Ryker's suite again, being watched, forced to dress like the Aerian court she despised, with no hope of escape. If only Aimee wasn't her best bet at rescuing Ceven and getting her revenge, she'd sooner find a way to escape this suffocating bedroom with its marble floors, glass chandeliers, and silk sheets.

In a fit of fury, she kicked off the sheets and sat up. As if she were connected to a string, the two guards shifted. The silver metal mesh slid against itself as the brown-haired Rathan reached for the hilt of his sword, the pink-winged Aerian grabbing for his spear.

"Oh, calm down. I'm just going to the bathing room," she growled, daring them to strike her. She was tired enough and angry enough that she could handle a few blows if they chose. It wouldn't hurt any less than the slaps Ryker gave her, or Vane's punch to her jaw, or the feel of his blade.

They relaxed, but she didn't miss their glares. Even if they didn't strike her, they definitely wanted to. How often did a human talk back to a Nyte, and a guard at that? Never.

She twisted the knob on the oil lamps, and the flame flickered against the blue and white tile of the bathing room. She shut the door and locked it. There weren't any windows or any other exits, so it wasn't like she could leave. She just wanted privacy—and to cool down.

Turning on the facet, she splashed cold water onto her wrists, then on her neck and forehead. She was burning up. It would be just her luck if she caught a fever. And this time Lani wasn't here to care for her.

Evangeline clenched her teeth against the surge of emotion that blasted her chest and threatened to crumble her legs. Gods, they had been so close. She could've saved her . . .

Squeezing her eyes shut, she focused on calming her breaths. *I'll make it through this. I have to. I'll save Ceven, even Raiythlen. And then we'll all finally escape this place.*

Her lips trembled, and an annoying buzz grew in her temples. No matter what lies she told herself, her body didn't believe her. And in her heart, she didn't believe it either. No matter what Aimee's plan was, she couldn't kill a king. Killing Ryker was an accident. Knowingly killing the king who always stood so high above her . . . A constant looming threat to her and Delani, who had orchestrated the lives that she and her friends had suffered . . . How could she kill a man she always imagined being untouchable? And if she somehow did, if she lost control of herself again like she had in the woods, what would that mean for her? Immediate death? A trip to Vane's torture room? He'd surely love to open her insides to see how a human could bare fangs.

Enough, Eve. You can't think like that. It won't do you any good. She peeked at the door a moment before squatting down and pulling a leather flask from between the folds of cloths in the white wooden cabinet at her waist. She had stashed Quan's saliver out of her coat pocket and somewhere safe before Aimee noticed. She thought about the magical hands that had shied away from her blood when she cut herself and the purple fire that had engulfed her. It didn't protect against all magic, but it was far better than nothing. She closed her eyes and swallowed a breath of air before taking a small swig. And she immediately spat it out.

"Oh, Gods . . . it tastes like the back end of a stable boy's boot." She'd forgotten how blazing *awful* this stuff was. Her face scrunched together, and her stomach rebelled at the idea of making another attempt. But she had to. She refused to be defenseless.

The second time she didn't breathe as the liquid hit the back of her throat, burning and clawing its way down, where it settled in a nauseating puddle in her stomach. How did Quan drink this every day? She struggled not to breathe lest she vomit back up as she stored the flask away.

As she leaned down, her head spun—but it wasn't from the saliver. The buzzing got louder in her skull, and she squinted at the blue speckled sink. Her face flickered and frowned back at her in the glass bowl. Then it blurred, and she knew what was happening before everything faded.

She was in a large room. Concrete all around her. Bright white lights shined overhead.

"Kill him."

Evangeline tested the weight of her sword before moving with immaculate precision. Her speed and agility were unmatched. She was fast. She was efficient. She was deadly.

Her blade came down hard, pausing right before the artery pulsing in the red-headed Aerian. The Aerian stared at her, ice-blue eyes betraying his own fear of dying.

She tossed the blade, and it landed next to her with a clang. "No."

Evangeline was struck behind her knees. Sharp pain vibrated up, and she crumpled to the ground. A purple-horned Caster stood over her and struck her four more times with his metal baton before barking at her to get back up. Her limbs screamed, but she ignored the pain as she got back on her feet.

"You will kill him. That's an order."

"No."

The next blow fractured her ribs. She coughed up blood.

"Kill him."

Evangeline shook her head and prepared herself for the next blow, but a loud grunt interrupted them. Her blue-eyed Aerian slumped to the ground, his life spilling out of him. The black-haired man next to the body removed Evangeline's blade from his torso and wiped it clean on the corpse.

"That was not your target, soldier," the Caster barked.

"The end goal is all that matters. Am I wrong, sir?" he said without the slightest inflection in his tone.

The Caster snorted. "Return to your cells," was all he said before he walked away.

The black-haired man lifted Evangeline off her feet. She gasped in pain.

"That was unnecessary, Jaden," she ground out behind clenched teeth. "That Aerian was innocent."

"If he was truly innocent, he wouldn't be dead," he said. She knew better than to argue with him.

Jaden carried her back to her room. It was small, dark, and cold. A stone cage fitted for an animal, like herself. Jaden said nothing, just held her in his lap. Evangeline closed her eyes, imagining the pain away.

Eventually, his voice broke the silence. "Could you kill me, Eve?"

Her eyes flew open to meet his. He was serious.

"Could you kill me?" he repeated.

Evangeline blew out a sharp breath. "Shut up, Jaden. I don't have the patience right now."

"Would you kill me if you knew I was willing to destroy the world for you?" He leaned down, his hair brushing her face. "Would you kill me then?"

Evangeline looked up at him. She brushed back his hair, tucking it behind his ear. "I'd rather stand by your side and watch it burn."

A bitter smell drew Evangeline's eyes open. She found herself in bed and not on the bathing room floor, where she last remembered being. A gold ornate tray was set on the table next to her, filled with eggs, breads, and cheeses that did nothing to stir her stomach. A steaming mug sat beside it.

"Breakfast and tea. Today is going to be a big day. You should eat and get all of your energy," Aimee said, dressed in a high-collared gold shirt tucked black slacks embroidered with gems. Their long brown hair was held back by a matching clip.

Evangeline sat up and ran a hand through her own hair. It was a nest of knots. At least the guards from last night weren't there to stare at her disheveled appearance. She wondered as she wrapped her fingers around the cup if they had been the ones to drag her back to bed. The scent of mint wafted towards her, and . . . orange? She didn't care, grateful for its warmth as her hands curled around the glass, drinking the steam and smell in.

The Caster sat on the edge of the bed. Evangeline caught a whiff of vanilla and daisies, but beneath it she could now recognize the familiar smell of magic: metal and fire.

"Did you sleep well?" Their fingers twined around their own steaming cup.

Evangeline had squeezed two hours of sleep in. "No."

They cocked their head, ignoring her irritated tone. "Well, that's unfortunate. Maybe—"

"Just tell me the plan for today."

Aimee raised a brow, their lips pressing into a thin line. "You have about the same manners as Ceven." They got up from the bed, setting their empty cup on the tray next to Evangeline. Evangeline wondered if the same human girl from yesterday had brought it. If she had visited this Caster in Sehn's suite when they had left last night.

"Well, first, we need to make you presentable," they said.

Before Evangeline could ask, or have a chance to fully wake up, several humans were called in. Each had a specific task of changing Evangeline into a beauty that rivaled even the late queen's. Evangeline had been to several executions before. The royals treated it as an event, dressed in the finest attire, and this one wasn't just any execution, but a prince's. One of only two princes of Peredia. It would be an event that would be talked about for years to follow. She just hoped it wouldn't end with anyone's death.

Well, except the king's, she thought as her insides puffed and rattled against their chains.

She wondered what was going through Ceven's mind right now, if he was scared or angry. If he was thinking about her. A pang of sadness shot through her chest. He didn't even know Xilo had betrayed him, that she was still here. He'd be furious if he knew what she was about to do. And she was still going to do it anyway.

They scrubbed Evangeline down so hard that red streaks appeared in deformed patches on her pale skin where it had been rubbed raw. She wanted to smack the girl who had continued to yank out the knots in her hair while another grabbed her arm to put paint on her nails. She had to remind herself that it wasn't their fault; they were just following orders. Orders that would get them killed or punished if they refused.

Still, when the brown-haired girl yanked out the fourth knot in her hair, she wanted to turn and snarl at her.

Aimee returned—what felt like hours later—with another tray of food. Apparently, it was now noon. Evangeline's long blond hair had been curled and swept up in an elegant bun. Several golden pins stuck out, but Evangeline patted them back in. Her face had been powdered, drawn on, and pinched. The only thing left was her dress.

After Aimee set down the gold tray of small, square sandwiches, the same slim girl from last night came in with a mass of silk and velvet. Evangeline's gaze fixed on the girl's calloused hands and bandages wrapping her fingers, then at the dress. She bit down on her cheek, her newly painted nails digging into the sides of her nightgown. The Caster took the dress, casting the girl a smile that had her face darkening before she left the room.

They turned that smile on Evangeline, lifting the dress in all its beautiful glory. It was a deep gold, trimmed with burgundy lace and ribbons. The skirt was thick and rich, the sleeves cutting off at the elbows with spare material hanging loosely, to give the wearer a majestic and graceful appearance.

"It's gorgeous," Evangeline couldn't help but say. And had likely been made by a girl only a few years younger than herself, forced to work on the layered Aerian attire, probably all night, to be ready for the upcoming event—Evangeline had had a similar task when she was seven. Fortunately, she wasn't good at the needle and was then moved to work in cleaning the Aerian suites after that for a few short years.

She looked around to make sure they were alone. "How do you expect me to kill anyone in that?"

"Don't fret, my dear. Killing the king will all happen in a matter of seconds."

It didn't answer her question, and she didn't like the look of satisfaction Aimee was attempting to conceal by turning away from her. Evangeline didn't know what compelled her to do what she did. If impatience had finally eaten away her insides and all logic, or if she was coming to despise this Council member more and more. Or maybe it wasn't her moving at all, as she carefully reached for the knife under her covers. One she'd squirreled away from dinner last night.

Aimee didn't turn around, even as Evangeline pressed the knife to their throat. "I'm sick of your games. Tell me what the blasted plan is, or I'll make my own."

Gone was the smile, but the rest of Aimee's expression was hidden under a curtain of hair. "Tell me: were you always this bold with Ryker? Or did you kill him when he tried to beat it out of you?" Evangeline's eyes widened as the knife in her hand burned her skin, the gold cutlery steaming and melting in her hand. She dropped it at the same time Aimee whipped around and snatched her throat.

Evangeline snarled and dug her nails into Aimee's wrist, which stay fixed on her neck, but paused when she met their face. Gone were Sehn's silver eyes, full lips, and square jaw. In its place, a scar mangled the left side of their cheek, tugging up the corner of their thin lips with slanted eyes that peered at her with violet irises and a look that screamed death.

"Don't tell me you're this foolish, Evangeline," they spat. "You may be an abomination, a powerful spawn of the unnatural, but I can disintegrate you in the blink of an eye. I didn't become who I am from mere words and placations." Dots danced in Evangeline's vision as their hold tightened. "And I'm *far* from forgiving you for killing my people. Watching them die as you lost control like some beast."

The only place you're going is in a cage, like the beast you are, Ryker had yelled at her, but he hadn't been the only one to say that, even if she couldn't recall where she had heard it before. She shook.

The dots danced faster in her eyes until they blurred and she lost all thought. Aimee released her, and Evangeline stumbled back, reaching for the bed to balance herself. This Caster's words unnerved her to the core, stirring something inside her that had been festering since the rest of her kind had branded her an outsider for having an odd marking and no memory. For eventually being the first human adopted into the Aerian court. She smirked. "So, tell me, why don't you kill me then?"

In a blink, Sehn's features took shape, wiping away the scar and violet eyes. A calm expression took over, as if nothing had ever happened. They answered with a smile, telling her all she needed to know. Aimee wanted to kill her. That much was clear, but the Council's mission included having her alive. Whatever plan Aimee hatched here today, it didn't include Evangeline leaving with Ceven to ride off into their happy ending afterwards.

There was a knock on the door, and the high-pitched, scratchy voice filled her with dread.

Aimee raised her brow, as if this were her true act of revenge. "Speaking of abominations . . ." Evangeline's next breath was labored as the Caster opened the door and Vane Jarr strode into the suite.

CHAPTER 37

Time passed, and Ceven's "friend" still remained silent despite his shouts. Either the Caster was ignoring him, or whatever Avana had done did a number on him. The guards had returned in a shuffle. The entire horde of them.

He moved, his back aching. He refused to lie down on the ground, not wanting to expose any more of his body than was already necessary to the dirty cell floor. Still wasn't as bad as standing in tazmite shackles for hours. His punishment for not mastering his parry with a dagger, his least favorite weapon. It was Kirk's idea, the sadist. Ceven hadn't seen any other Royal Guard subjected to the shackles. Then again, when he trained with them, he was the only rookie at the time. And they had constantly reminded him of that fact.

Ceven pressed his ear against the sound device he had used earlier, the metal cylinder cold against his skin as he flattened it to the wall, listening. Something rustled. The first sound of movement since the return of the guards some time ago.

"Awake yet?" he asked in Castanian, the words unfamiliar in his mouth. It wasn't his preferred language, or even his preferred second, but it was unlikely the guards understood it outside a handful of words, speaking mostly Peredian and different dialects of Atiacan.

There was a groan, clanking of chains, then a low, "Barely, friend," in Castanian. At least he didn't bother with the accent this time.

Ceven's nose scrunched. "Have a friendly chat with your sister, *Caster*?"

He didn't laugh. "Certainly have had better conversations. At least she left all my limbs intact." There was another moan, and chains slid against the stone floor. Ceven hated the pang of pity he felt.

"I'm surprised. From the sounds of it, I would've thought she cut off at least something." Ceven finished flexing his right hand, the joints cracking with a satisfying pop when he growled, "Why didn't you just tell me the truth from the beginning?"

The Caster snorted. "Because then you wouldn't have been as nice."

"I could've put aside some differences." It was a lie. He knew himself too well for that. "But now that's all in the past. You've just proven to me how untrustworthy and conniving you really are."

"You're too kind." He sighed. "So yes, as I'm sure you've heard, I'm a Caster. While we're at it, I'll introduce myself. Raiythlen Quincara, at your service." When Ceven didn't respond, he continued, "Well, no need to introduce yourself. I already know all about you, Your Highness. Though not much of one anymore."

Ceven's lips curled.

"What else do you know about me?" Raiythlen asked, as if Ceven were the spy snooping around in other people's business.

"I know you left Evangeline, a human, alone to fend for herself in the Wretched-infested west wing. That you tricked her into—" He'd almost forgotten about the guards outside the door, but regardless of whether it was in Castanian or not, he wasn't that foolish. "You know what you did. I'd sooner have your sister come back and finish the job than consider you a 'friend.'"

The Caster didn't reply right away, and Ceven pressed his ear tighter into the listening device to make sure he was still alive.

"That's fair," he said eventually. "I won't lie and say I didn't use her to my advantage. But I never intended to kill her, or have her get killed. The risk was there, but I always had a plan to ensure sure she'd make it out alive."

"But not necessarily uninjured. Not that it matters to you. Nothing and nobody matters to you." Ceven licked his lips, his gut boiling. "I hate people like you. No morals, using others for their gain, not caring who they step on. You'd fit right in here."

"Since you've already decided on my character, I'm assuming there's no chance you'd want to scratch my back?"

Ceven's brows knitted together. "What?"

"I've had this itch on my lower side for some time now. Who cares about food and water when a good ole nail or even punch would do?"

There was a message here that he was struggling to understand. Scratch his back. Did he mean to work with him? Maybe, but he said lower side . . . a nail or a punch would do . . .

Ceven rolled to his knees, sliding the metal cylinder into his pocket while his cuffed hands rubbed the wall. He couldn't see, but he could feel. "Ask the guards. Maybe some would be sympathetic to your plight. Or not."

Raiythlen switched back to Peredian and said in a singsong voice, "Oh, guards! Would you please, oh please, scratch my back?"

Ceven rolled his eyes but concentrated on the sound of his voice, on where he was on the other side of the wall. He said lower back. Lower . . . lower . . . There. A crack.

"Nobody? You know, the last dungeon cell I was in, they were a lot more welcoming than here," he continued, and Ceven scratched the wall. It chipped away with ease, but it was going to take him forever to claw at it. He was going to have to knock it in.

Ceven started coughing, hoping the Caster would take the hint.

He did, but not in the way Ceven expected. "You know, before I became a spy, I used to be one hell of an opera singer. Everyone would come to see me." Ceven raised a brow, but when the Caster belted out a tune, it ratcheted painfully in his ears. One guard couldn't take it either, eliciting a not-so-gentle pounding on the door. Ceven didn't waste any time and rammed his fist into the weakened spot.

The wall crumbled but was still intact. The guard had stopped pounding.

"Oh, come on, you just have no taste. I heard there weren't even any theaters in Peredia. How do you guys keep yourself entertained? Maybe you'll like this one better." Another off-pitch tune rang out, and Ceven curled his fingers even tighter and prepped his fist.

The door to Raiythlen's cell clunked open.

"Did you like—"

There was a loud slap, and Ceven winced for him. The guard said nothing, not that he had to. Raiythlen still mumbled a "guess not" as the footsteps retreated to the door. Ceven waited for it to come, and when the door slammed, so did Ceven's fist into the wall.

It crumbled, and a small gap tore open.

He leaned down but couldn't see how big a hole it made. The edges of the opening were sharp and jutted to the touch. He guessed it was about a hand's-length wide and two hand's-lengths tall. He sensed a shift in the air and guessed Raiythlen had leaned down as well and, for all he knew, could be staring at him through the hole.

And he probably was when his words came straight through the opening, in a low whisper but clear and unmuffled, as if he had pressed his face against it. "Glad you're not as much of an idiot as the rest of your family," he said, switching back to Castanian.

Ceven didn't like that he couldn't see this man, but maybe it was the same for him. Judging by the rattling, they'd cuffed his arms and legs separate from one another so he couldn't draw blood. They were also most likely carved from frostlite. While Peredians used the sensitive rock to detect magic, Ceven knew from his training with the guard that in large enough quantities and with close enough distance, it could affect a Caster's ability to wield magic. Making it too unpredictable for even the Caster to risk it.

"Is this your plan? Maybe you have some pen and paper on you and we can pass notes back and forth like we're in a tutoring session," Ceven retorted in a low voice. "How'd you know the wall was weak there?"

He imagined the Caster smirking by the tone of his voice.

"My sister was never great at wielding a whip. I know someone that would put her flimsy attempts to shame." He paused. "As for my actual plan, it first starts with you breaking these cuffs. You can with your Aerian strength."

He could, but did he want to? Freeing him wouldn't guarantee anything, except letting the Caster that had put Evangeline and himself into their current situation go.

"And then what?" he drawled. "You go gallivanting around with your magic, free, while I sit here waiting to be executed?"

"How flattering of you to think I could take on ten of your Royal Guards. Maybe if I had proper traps placed and the advantage of surprise . . . but no. I'm not escaping here any more than you are. But I can trick my sister and buy you some time to leave or . . . do whatever it is you need to do before the axe hits."

Ceven scratched his chin, and his nails scraped against rough hairs. He needed another good shave, not that anyone cared about their looks before being executed. "What kind of tricks?"

"I have a few spells up my sleeve, but there's a good chance she'll dump me in salt water before the execution, or inject me with a drug to make me lose my own inhibitions."

Ceven snorted. "From what I heard earlier, that seems unlikely. It sounds like she wants you to suffer."

Raiythlen hummed in agreement. "Either way, she'll have a plan to counteract any magic I'll have at my disposal."

"That's not much of a plan."

"For me? No, but it's better than sitting here, cuffed and useless. At least this way there's a chance she'll miss a spell or get cocky. And if that fails, I have one last thing up my sleeve to knock her off her game, gain some leverage. For you, I can create a distraction, buy you enough time to escape."

Ceven didn't need to escape, even if the idea ate at him. He didn't want to willingly walk into his own execution, even if it was for him to get close enough to murder the king, but leaving now, as things were . . . he would be hunted, and he wouldn't make it very far past the castle walls, let alone the city's. Not when he was at such a disadvantage. "I don't need a distraction; I need information."

"That I can give as well. Depending on what you want to know, I'll answer half now and the rest when you break these chains."

It seemed fair. After all, it was true what he'd said. There was no way either of them were escaping, so why not try to even the odds, even if it was more in Ceven's favor?

"I want to know exactly why you're here and what your mission is." He'd heard a little between the scuffle with Avana. It concerned Evangeline and something about their family history. He wanted to know more, and what the hell that meant for Peredia, and all those marked humans in the west wing.

"Well, I'm not sure how much you overheard, but the Council sent me here. But like I tried to tell Avana, all of that changed when I found out . . . something."

Ceven felt his skin fold between his brows. Frowning and scowling were becoming common ever since he'd returned to Peredia. Atiaca was much more carefree. "How very ominous," he mocked. "But that doesn't tell me anything."

"I discovered Ryker was working with the king and Sehn, along with other Nytes in the west wing. The missing humans, these markings they have, it's connected to the magic, to the work my grandmother used to do. To what is on Evangeline's hand."

Ceven mulled over his words. They'd already figured out that much, except for the part about it being connected to Avana and this Caster, Raiythlen. "Does Evangeline know?"

"Yes."

He shouldn't be angry, but he was. She'd admitted that her and Lani's lives were in danger, and yet his hands still curled into clenched fists. His lips thinned. "How is she involved in all this? And what does your Council want with her?"

"Break these chains first, prince."

Ceven nodded, even if he couldn't see it. It was only fair. With his bound hands he reached as quietly as he could into the crack. "It's going to be too loud." And he didn't want to alert the guards any more.

"Then it's your turn to make some noise," Raiythlen said.

"But I'm not as good of a singer," he volleyed back.

The Caster chuckled and quickly smothered the laugh with a cough. Ceven turned around, his eyes focusing on what could have been the cot.

He got up and hooked his foot on the corner of the flimsy bed. As expected, the frame screeched against the ground. At the same time, his door opened.

The fiery beard greeted him before he met Kirk's pale blue eyes.

"Just doing some spring cleaning," Ceven said, the Peredian language flowing more easily from his mouth than the tangled words of Castanian. When Kirk didn't respond, Ceven gave him a mocking salute. Well, as good as one with both of his hands cuffed together.

Kirk smiled but then remembered himself. "Your Highness, if you would please keep it down. Any sudden movements and noises give us reason to think you're up to no good."

"I'm just trying to rip a leg off this bed. No trouble here."

He raised a furry red brow, but the look he gave Ceven was far from stupid. Ceven returned it, hoping he owed him enough to let him get away with this.

"It's not as if I'm going to escape here, Kirk," he whispered, and it was enough for the burly man to give him a sad nod and shut the door.

Ceven dragged the bed closer. "Put out your cuffs," he whispered in Castanian again. Ceven felt for the metal around his cellmate's hands and, using his foot, he dragged the bedframe across the ground, cringing at the noise, and squeezed against the metal that felt flimsy beneath his fingers. Definitely wasn't tazmite.

It cracked.

Ceven stopped moving the bed at the same time the metal cuffs fell free. Something scraped the ground, and there was the softest hint of shuffling as Raiythlen went to work doing Gods-know-what.

"I've done my part. Now finish yours."

"One second," he whispered, but it was faint. What was he doing? "Son of a—"

Ceven leaned, trying to peek through the hole, as if he would be able to magically see now. With a Caster next to him, who knows?

"What?" he said.

There was a scoff, an empty laugh. "Well, I guess the Aerians aren't complete fools. I don't know what these cells are made of, but the salt concentration is too high for any of my offensive magic to be effective."

"Thought you said you wouldn't try to escape," he drawled.

"It was still worth a shot. Here's hoping Avana isn't as thorough on her death promise." The last part he muttered to himself. He leaned back down next to Ceven. "If you let me put a symbol on you, we can talk a lot more easily. Wouldn't have to strain your voice whispering."

"No."

"I'm not going to kill you, prince. It's just a—"

"I said no. Now tell me, what does the Council want with Evangeline? What does her mark mean?"

"At least you have the demanding part of being a royal down. Her mark means 'life' in Castanian, and if you haven't found out already, it opens a link between two people's sources. Or souls, as you Peredians call it. I don't know how, but someone here figured out a way to activate it, if you will."

"I speak Castanian—"

"Obviously."

"—*And* know both scripts, modern Castanian and old symbolia. I've never seen that symbol in my entire life." If this Caster thought he could pull a fast one on him, he would be sorely mistaken.

"Congratulations"—it sounded anything but congratulatory—"except you wouldn't have. It's not in any official set of characters you'd find in a book. It's a written dialect that took slang of its time period and engineered it to be a language used by my grandmother and her group of scholars. Which is why this doesn't make any sense to me. Everyone from that period should be dead. The only remnants of that language are found in—well, that doesn't matter. I burned them anyway. But the point is, no one should have been able to decipher it, let alone use that language to their advantage."

Ceven frowned. He wasn't a slow learner, but Caster magic always eluded him. It had seemed complicated and unpredictable whenever Ryker tried to explain it to the king in their meetings, or to Ceven in their tutoring sessions. Using his sword and strength were anything but that. "Can't you just somehow . . . deactivate it?"

He sighed, the same one Ryker would give when Ceven or Evangeline failed to learn a simple lesson. Raiythlen even said as much. "I don't know what they taught you in your tutoring sessions. Probably nothing accurate if it's Peredians teaching about Sundise Mouche." He paused, as if waiting for Ceven to argue. He didn't. He was aware of the biases, or at least he was when he visited Atiaca for the first time and saw that their history didn't line up.

Raiythlen continued, "Language and intent are the key to unlocking our magic. And our blood, obviously, but that's more of the catalyst. Do you cook?"

It was an odd question. "Not really, but I know enough to make something palatable."

"That's fair, considering you were a pampered prince for most of your life—"

"You know nothing about me."

"—but to the point, think of magic like cooking. You can change out some ingredients and roughly get the same outcome. But, unlike cooking, following someone else's recipe won't get you the same meal as theirs. Because your ingredients will always be different from other Casters, because of who you are as a person. Sure, you'll have a base line, a simple recipe to start with, but the only way for you to figure out what works for you is through trial and error.

"And before you ask me why the magic lesson, it's because the mark on Evangeline's arm is an unfinished recipe, created by my grandmother. The only way to finish the product she started—or change it—is to know the intent behind it, the language, and have a Caster whose blood and intent are similar to the one who created it. Three *very* specific ingredients. But not impossible, as we've seen."

Ceven absorbed this information. "But it sounds impossible. How would the king, or Ryker, know anything about this, let alone have the tools to do it?"

He imagined the Caster shrugging by the slide of fabric. "It's what I'm trying to figure out, prince. And why the Council sent me to kidnap Evangeline. They think she knows more than she's letting on, though I've told them she's as naïve about magic as any other Peredian."

"Not all are naïve, Caster," he bit out.

"So you say, but I've yet to be proven otherwise. Anyways, even if she doesn't know anything, her blood might. Or her bones or muscles. Who knows what tests the Council would do to discover the truth."

Ceven was finding this man less charming and more irritating. "How could you just willingly kidnap an innocent, knowing what they would do to her?"

"I didn't know she was innocent. In fact, I still don't think she is, but she's not dangerous like I once thought. And I don't work for them anymore, clearly."

Raiythlen had mentioned he'd traded sides because he discovered something, but he'd never told Ceven what. Ceven opened his mouth to ask when there was a scuffle—no, a stampede of footsteps. He wished there were a window, something to tell him the time. All he knew was that the execution would be held during the day, but he had no way of knowing if the sun was even out.

Raiythlen's door swung open first, then his. Sehn, along with at least twenty other Royal Guards—more than a bit excessive—greeted him.

Sehn swept out his arm, his fingers almost brushing the floor, in a bow. The gems embroidered into his black slacks twinkled in the light from the fixed oil lamps on the wall. It was the first time his brother had ever bowed to him. But Ceven was going to make sure it wouldn't be his last.

His brother smiled. That sharp, infuriating smile. "The stage is all set, brother. Now, off to your execution."

CHAPTER 38

Evangeline's heart ratcheted against her ribcage. Vane walked beside her like a hungry wolf prowling the main hallways. Her hands and legs shook, her mind filled with images of herself tripping over her dress, smearing her makeup, or ripping the precious fabric. Doing something that would give Vane the excuse to slap her, cut her, or break a bone in the hand he currently squeezed. Tightly.

When Vane had first entered the guest room, Evangeline's legs had turned to liquid. If she hadn't clutched the bed for support, she would've collapsed to the floor. Before Evangeline could lock eyes with the Rathan—who now looked like his former brown-haired, beady-eyed self, versus a beast—Aimee stepped between them.

Officer Jarr, a pleasure, they had said with a controlled tone that told everyone in the room who was in charge. *I'm glad you decided to follow through. Obey me in this, and I will grant you free rein for whatever . . . activities you wish to pursue.* When fake-Sehn turned to Evangeline, she saw the real Caster underneath for the second time. A glimpse of their expression. Cold and unfeeling, like someone who'd killed and manipulated anyone and anything to get to where they stood. This Council member knew what Vane did to Evangeline, knew the terror he incited in her, and they were using it to their advantage.

Now, Vane Jarr was her escort to the execution.

To ensure you don't change your mind, dear, Aimee had said, as if Evangeline needed another incentive to not watch the king remove her friend's head from his shoulders. As if running away in a castle swarming with Nytes on her tail would ever end in her favor. No, this was a reminder for Evangeline to keep her head down and her mouth shut. About everything.

So now, here she was, flush against the Rathan that made her knuckles bleed white from how hard she clenched them and her stomach settle in her throat, as they skated through the influx of people. On any normal day, everyone, Nyte and human alike, would be scrambling to get away from Vane, but the halls were more crowded than it had been for the princes' banquet. Hot, sticky bodies cramped the castle, wall to wall, and if Evangeline thought about it for too long, she was going to hyperventilate.

More than several turned their way as Vane and the two guards escorting them elbowed through the crowd. Nytes glared at them until they caught sight of Peredia's most notorious torturer—the last stop for misbehaving humans or unlucky Nytes who thought to betray the crown—and turned away. A few Nytes brushed by, close enough to give her a handful of pinches to her arms and waist. She hissed in pain as Vane wrenched her through the sweaty mass. Over the pounding footsteps, distant music, and clattering trays of humans passing by with hot meals for the after-event—only Peredians would have an appetite after watching someone be hacked in two—whispers pricked Evangeline's ears.

"They haven't even buried Ryker yet and she's already found a new master," someone snickered.

"Look at the pretty *pet*, all dressed up," others chimed in.

"She'll play for anyone, it seems. Even *Vane*."

An Aerian woman snagged her arm, scratching it deep enough for red lines to puff up from where the nails tore into her skin. Vane yanked Evangeline to his side as the two guards shoved the Aerian lady away. Evangeline *hated* execution days. As unavoidable as the death of some poor soul, so was the plague of bloodthirstiness that possessed every Nyte (and even some humans) during these events. Evangeline didn't know what frightened her more: the mass of bloodthirsty Nytes, or Vane, whose growl rang in her ears as his nails drew blood where he gripped her forearm. She kept waiting for him to turn back into that beast and rip out of his gray coat and matching slacks. No chain dangled from him like other Peredians, but the stark, swirling Castanian symbols were blatant on his chest, matching the parallel markings roving across his shaven head. He didn't even bother trying to hide it.

The guards did their job of protecting them from the masses. Evangeline could hardly hear herself think, her arm burning from where that woman had attacked her and Vane's grip. Her heart pounded so hard she struggled to breathe. She was used to the contemptuous looks, the snide remarks, but being next to Vane with no hope of safety in sight, she felt like a glass doll being fought over by spoiled children.

"Where is Sehn?" Evangeline worked up the courage to ask. It was the only thing she had said to Vane since she'd laid eyes on him in the guest room.

She yelped when his grip tightened. "It's His Highness, you ill-mannered pet." Then he smiled, his two incisors longer than usual—or maybe she imagined that. "Why? Not enjoying my company?"

His breath smacked into her cheek. Garlic wafted up her nostrils. She was going to vomit, and not just from the sheer terror gripping her insides.

"Listen up, pet. His Highness put me in charge, so if you disobey me, or do anything to compromise our situation, I will slit you open in front of the entire city. You understand?"

Evangeline was still reeling from his breath, the loud murmur of people, and the sweat and blood she tasted in the air. He jostled her, and her neck snapped back. "Yes, my lord." It was a whisper, but she couldn't be sure with everything and everyone ringing in her ears.

He continued, "When we enter the throne room, we will sit near the front with the rest of the royal family." His lip curled, and he muttered, "Useless, empty-headed sacks of flesh." Razor blades cascaded down her spine at the menace in it. "Next to the cousins and wives and any other fool who scrambled to claim a royal title, we'll be closest to the king and away from the masses. In the middle of the service, right before the ax falls, you will do as you're told."

Before the execution, Aimee still hadn't given Evangeline much of a plan, except a weapon to use prior to leaving the guest suite. It was small, the size of her palm, but heavier than it looked, made of black metal. *A gun,* something in her mind told her. It was the same weapon those humans had used on

Anali, Evangeline, and Jaden in her hallucination—memory—the night before she left for the west wing. Aimee had showed her how to hold it, gripping the curved handle while a single digit wrapped around the lever attached to it.

When you are ready, and only when you are absolutely ready, you will aim this at the king and pull this trigger. Make sure you're close enough, and you may have to fire more than once to ensure the deed is done.

To show her, they had cocked the gun and pulled the trigger, releasing something too fast for her to follow with her eyes, before the lamp next to her shattered. Aimee then handed it to her, the weight of it like five hardback novels in her palm. The only thing coursing through her mind was how in spitting blazes was she going to do this.

Think of it like an automated bow and arrow, the Caster had said. *But you won't need to worry too much about your aim. I've magicked one of the king's necklaces. All bullets in that gun will go for it like a magnet.*

Evangeline stared at the dangerously innocuous weapon. It looked harmless, but she knew anything Caster-made was far from that. It was also loud. Obvious. She swallowed the lump in her throat. Aimee didn't care if everyone knew she was the king's killer, making it nearly impossible for her to hope for any means of escape after this ordeal.

And when they hear this . . . Evangeline had glared at Aimee. *They'll know it was me who killed the king.*

They didn't deny it; in fact, they smiled. *Sacrifices need to be made, my dear. Your life, or Ceven's?*

Did the Council agree to this? Aimee didn't respond, and Evangeline wondered if the Caster was going to have her killed after all, despite the Council's wishes to keep her alive. Or at least that was what she concluded.

Evangeline inhaled the swirling mix of perfume and sweat, drawing her back to the present. She had strapped the gun to her thigh with a firm leather band, the metal cool against her skin. Aimee had picked this dress purposely, the drapes of fabric layered to hide the gap for Evangeline to swiftly pull out her weapon. Despite everything, a part of her still hoped for a happy ending. One where she and Ceven survived and lived in that cottage far, far away. Like Lani always said, she was a fool. At least if she died—more like *when* she died—Evangeline would get to see her friend again. Tears threatened to fall from her eyes, and she blinked rapidly, ignoring the pain, the fear, and the blasted unfairness of it all.

No, she wouldn't be a spitting sacrifice, and neither was Ceven. She would get her vengeance *and* make it out of here alive with her friend. Even if it meant losing herself, she'd sooner release that darkness inside than go out without a fight.

Vane dragged her to the narrow, arched doors leading to the throne room, where two humans struggled to hold open the thick wood amongst the sea of gowns and frilly frocks. Evangeline had been to the throne room twice in her entire life. These executions were rare, and she'd been told by Ryker that the throne room had long been abandoned for any other purpose, since King Calais had abolished the need for tithes to the crown that had occurred in past reigns. King Calais was the first to provide a fair tax to all Nytes in Peredia, as Ryker always praised him for. Evangeline had sat there, her head bowed, thinking it didn't matter because she was still a human with no rights.

Aside from the last execution Ryker had forced her to attend—an assassin that had almost killed the king, a scar hidden underneath the king's long hair and high collared robes being proof of that—her earliest memory was when she'd first been brought to the castle. Nobody knew her actual age, and she guessed she could have been four in human years, when a couple of Nytes from the neighboring town brought her forth in front of the king and queen. All she could remember was feeling so small in the large room. She had reached out to touch the throne, mesmerized by its beauty, before being slapped so hard it threw her off her feet. She felt the sting of it for days to come. It was her first encounter with the king. Her fingers curled inward; her teeth clenched tight. She wished she could make him suffer like he had Lani, but she would have to be content with a bullet through his heart instead.

They stopped, and Vane yanked on her hair hard enough to bring tears to her eyes.

"Stand up straight and keep your eyes on the prize. This won't work if you're cowering," he barked.

Evangeline forced her hands to her sides rather than massaging where Vane had pulled on her hair. Despite everything, she still felt pathetically human. Helpless, despite the weapon strapped to her side and the darkness buzzing in her gut.

The throne room was as big as she remembered it. An enormously large, elongated room, if you could even call it one at this point. Pristine white marble covered the floor and walls. Large sculpted columns aligned in a row, parallel to each other, from the entryway down to the two golden thrones sitting atop the raised platform. The windows stretched as tall as the high ceilings, each adorned with a mosaic piece representing a story of Peredia's history. Some showed Aerian's faces, others blood and war, the red crystal glass shining like fire from the fading sunlight dripping in. But the most disconcerting thing to Evangeline was the synchronization of hundreds of faces turning to stare at them. The pleasant buzz of conversations swarming the room died at the sight of them.

Evangeline's throat convulsed, and she swore it echoed in the large room.

Vane waved and cast a wicked smile at the crowd, who turned away, scared to draw his attention, but their eyes still lingered sideways on her. More callous whispers greeted her. Ceven may be taking the fall for Ryker's murder, but everyone suspected she was to blame. That she had forced the prince to do her bidding. It was funny how they cursed her for being a weak human yet believed her to have the power to bring a prince to his knees.

Then again, now she had the power to bring a king to his knees as well.

If Evangeline had been holding on to Vane's arm like the other Nyte couples here, the slickness of her palms would've had difficulty finding purchase on his crisp coat. At least his tight grip kept her from falling to the floor.

She couldn't do this. It was too much. She didn't want to die.

Deep breaths, she told herself, squaring her shoulders. *You can do this. You* will *do this. For Ceven. Even for Raiythlen, the blasted bastard.*

Rows of wood benches with velvet cushions bordered the large floor runner that Vane and Evangeline walked down, getting closer and closer to the thrones—but only one would be occupied. This close, Evangeline was almost blinded by the sheer perfection of it. Made of solid gold, the throne sat tall and imposing. The arms and the legs were bejeweled with priceless stones that shone brightly, as if they were polished daily. The top of the throne had two small wings engraved, in symbolism of the Aerians that had taken over Peredia centuries ago.

Vane led her to the second-to-front row. The place was full of Nytes and almost as many guards, who stood along the back walls of the room. The Royal Guard clustered around the front, closest to the throne. Evangeline didn't see a familiar pair of deep purple or blue-and-gray wings. Not that she expected either of them to be here. Xilo was probably long gone, and Tarry surely fought back to protect Ceven. She just hoped the old Aerian wasn't killed for it, or worse, already dead.

In front of the thrones was an ax, the blade ten times the size of her head with a hilt encrusted with expensive jewels, impractical for battle. It was the king's executioner weapon, reminding Evangeline that this wasn't just any occasion; it was a public slaughtering. Prince Ceven and Raiythlen's executions.

"These are my favorite events," Vane whispered in her ear, and Evangeline jolted out of her seat. Doubt clouded her thoughts. She wrung her hands, sweat oozing from her pores, beads of it running down her skin and cooling like the tip of Vane's blades slicing across her chest, hands, and arms. How could she kill the king when she couldn't even stop herself from shaking?

"I can't do this." She squeezed the words out over the boulder in her throat.

"Yes, you can. And you will." Vane released her, and her arm prickled painfully where the blood flowed back. But his next words froze her blood in place. "Because if you don't, you'll be next in line to be executed."

CHAPTER 39

Two long hours of sitting, itching and sweating in the crowded throne room weighed on Evangeline's chest like a thick smog. More bodies than she's ever seen packed into the rows of benches, others fighting just to find a place to stand. From between flurries of reds and blues and frills, between wings and ears and tails, a crowd still hovered outside the doors to the room before they clicked shut. She didn't see any sign of Barto, Rasha, or Quan here or in the crowd outside the doors. Were they not allowed in? Did they leave the city when they found out what was happening?

Gossip and news always spread at an alarming rate throughout the castle and city, but it was almost absurd and disgusting the amount of people lining up to watch two Nytes be killed.

When Evangeline was sure she was going to pass out—either from nerves or the heat, maybe both—the doors to the throne room swung open once more. The silence that followed told Evangeline it had to be the king, even if she couldn't see over the towering heads of Nytes.

It had begun.

Everyone stood up in reverence to the king's glory. Evangeline was so shaken that Vane had to haul her onto her feet.

King Calais walked gracefully to take his rightful place on the throne. He wore many layers of clothes in a show of class. A thick white fur coat settled on top of a purple silk jacket that outlined his black vest. Like the other Peredians in the room, he wore a multitude of gold chains around his neck. His white, slender fingers were adorned with multiple bands of jewels as they gripped the arms of his throne. His silver gaze swept the room, demanding for his presence to be known. Evangeline's entire body froze when his eyes loomed in her general direction. And paused on her.

For the second time since she'd ever known the king, he smiled at her, and her throat plummeted to her stomach.

"You may sit," he boomed, his eyes leaving hers. The crowd sat. The king began his speech, his voice rumbling like a stampede of hooves on cobblestone. "Today, I present to you…"

A shift in the crowd had Evangeline's eyes moving. And her heart stuttered at the sight. Four Royal Guards accompanied Ceven with fake-Sehn at the lead. Her friend looked more polished than previous criminals she'd seen executed. His hair was dark, from a shower maybe, and slicked back. His firm jaw was clean-shaven, and he stared straight at the king with a stubborn defiance. He was in a dark purple satin robe, to symbolize his royalty, on top of a dark silk, collared shirt, outlined in gold threading that matched his trousers. His wings had been cut and groomed to shimmer. If it weren't for his hands being cuffed in front of his body, she never would've guessed it was his execution she was attending.

He looked more like a prince while walking to his own funeral than he ever had.

". . . charged with the murder of our esteemed advisor, Ryker Ardonis, the former prince, Ceven LuRogue, will face his punishment: the executioner's ax."

Nobody said a word, but if they did, Evangeline wasn't sure if she'd be able to hear it over the rushing in her skull.

Her fingers touched the gun at her side between the folds of her dress. Watching the two Royal Guards drag Ceven in front of the throne and force him to his knees, his head leveled with the ax . . . She wouldn't let Ceven die for her mistakes. Even if her bullets missed, she'd fight to protect him. Or die trying.

Fake-Sehn bowed before the king, their squeaking boots echoing in the silent throne room. Nytes shifted out of the way as their false prince stood next to her. The smell of metal and fire was stronger than ever; Aimee's perfume of vanilla and daises was not enough to cover the overwhelming scent of magic. Surely others had to notice, but everyone's attention had turned back to the king. Evangeline tightened her grip on her gun.

The king didn't bother to look at Ceven as they forced him to sit on his knees. A yellow-winged Royal Guard, whom she recognized as Troy, pressed his hand against Ceven's back while another with a long red beard held down his shoulders. "And for this momentous day, we will also be eliminating another threat to our kingdom. A traitor charged with assault, thievery, and conspiring to murder your king. As punishment, this traitor will also seek death by the executioner's ax." King Calais raised his hands. "Bring forth the Caster, Raiythlen Quincara!"

A rejoicing cheer shook the crowd. It was so loud, Evangeline had to stop herself from covering her ears. It seemed everyone was scared to cheer for their former prince's death, but not a Caster's.

The doors to the throne room opened, and everyone turned to see the criminal dragged down the hall in chains. Raiythlen looked much more the part than Ceven.

He was dressed in all white, as Evangeline expected. It was a tradition that had been put in place long before King Calais was throned, so that the blood was more vibrantly displayed when the head was severed. Ceven's rare case must have been an exception, an act of respect that seemed out of place and ironic to Evangeline.

Raiythlen's hair was unkempt, waves of its curls falling over his face, a face that had seen the back sides of a few hands, bruises and cuts littering his temple and cheeks. His hands were chained behind his back, a connecting chain wrapping around his neck and to his feet, where another metal band was in place to keep his feet close together. Judging by the number of cuffs and restrictive bands, it looked as if the king was more scared of Raiythlen than Ceven. Then again, like herself, Peredians didn't truly understand magic, as much as they pretended otherwise.

The shock of seeing Raiythlen, his head down, his body slumped in on itself, made Evangeline's gut twist. With him looking so helpless, it almost felt wrong. Even if he had gotten all of them into this mess.

A Royal Guard tagged him on both sides, holding a chain that was attached to his neck, pulling him forward towards the king. They didn't give Raiythlen any mercy as they yanked on his restraints harshly, dragging him off his feet.

The guards halted before the throne with Raiythlen in tow. As if this were another day, the king stared at them, his face apathetic.

"The criminal, Your Majesty." They bowed.

The king motioned with his hand, and an older Aerian woman slowly approached the throne, her movement hindered by a limp. She wore a simple purple robe and leaned heavily on a golden cane. Her wrinkled hand reached into her pocket to pull out a small book. Licking one singular finger, she opened the book to a specific page and began chanting.

She had begun her prayer, preparing Raiythlen's soul to ascend with the God of all Gods.

Evangeline's mind was racing. Aimee had said to strike right before the king beheaded Ceven, and for some foolish reason, she'd believed Ceven would go first. That she would make her move before anybody was killed. She's been to more executions than she cared to admit—mostly in the city's plaza. She hated them, but she had become numb to it. Just kept her head down, pretending the screams and cries were a woman in labor, or someone getting their wounds tended to . . . not the screams of the dying.

But could she do the same knowing it was Raiythlen? Sure, she'd wanted to kill the Caster a hundred times over, but now that it was happening . . . she wasn't sure anymore.

The lady's voice droned on, and Evangeline glanced at Aimee. They looked ever the confident and cool part. No sign of remorse for their previous agent. No regret at watching Raiythlen's head roll from his shoulders. But maybe they were going to change their mind? Give Evangeline some sign to strike now? Aimee couldn't seriously sit by and watch King Calais decapitate Raiythlen.

The prayer ended. The chains attached to Raiythlen rattled caustically as the guards shoved him to his knees in front of the king, next to Ceven. They didn't look at each other, the Royal Guard at both of their necks, forcing their heads down. But standing this close, Evangeline noticed Ceven's mouth twitch. Her chest swelled. Did he have a plan? How?

Heels clicked behind her, and Evangeline, along with other heads, turned. Her blood boiled at the sight of the slim Caster woman weaving through the crowd.

Avana, like every other Nyte attending, dressed in silks and heavy fabrics. Unlike her usual slim, simple dresses, today the tight bodice gave her petite form curves, the neckline scooped low, threaded with silver ribbon. Unlike the rest of the female Aerians in the room, her blue hoop skirt was short in the front, showing off several Castanian runes that slithered down her toned legs into the silver heels. It was a bold statement, reminding everyone she was a Caster, despite the horns that curled around her face. For all Evangeline knew, the trailing skirt behind her housed several knives, the clip in her hair magicked with some sort of spell.

And all Evangeline had was a gun that she could barely wield and an unknown, wild animal caged inside her.

Avana's heels clicked up the platform to stand before the king, the traitors, and the surrounding Royal Guard. She gave a graceful curtsy. The king's eyes narrowed, but he conceded a nod. Evangeline thought she saw Raiythlen tense up.

"I stand before you"—she swept her hand out at the crowd—"to formally apologize for the actions of this Caster, whom I'm ashamed to call brother." There was a collective gasp.

"But it was your idea—" Raiythlen squeaked out before the Royal Guard knocked his skull, his head swinging down.

Avana turned to look at her brother. It was an expression Evangeline hadn't seen on Avana before. It was ruthless. Terrifying. It reminded her of Aimee when they'd revealed their scarred face and the hatred they had toward Evangeline.

"To show my loyalty to the king and atone for the misdeeds of my blood, I will perform this execution myself."

Raiythlen didn't react, not that he could, being held down physically and wrapped in chains. Ceven didn't move either.

"But first." She bent down and picked up the tin bucket beside the king. Evangeline had thought it was to collect the heads, but she heard the slosh of water inside it. Avana dumped the contents over Raiythlen. He flinched, but that was all he did as the water soaked his white uniform, the cotton molding to his chest, droplets falling from his black curls.

The king said nothing. He'd expected this, but Evangeline didn't, nor did the crowd, judging by the whispers and—

"What did she do?"

"How bizarre."

"Some Caster tradition?"

The murmurs rose until the king raised his hand. Everyone hushed.

Avana set the bucket down, a smile on her painted lips. A crimson red. *How fitting*, Evangeline thought as her lip curled.

"I was ensuring that this traitor had no additional tricks up his sleeve." Avana bent down again, but it was to grip Raiythlen's chin. She jerked it side to side, then—none too gently—yanked down the collar of his shirt, then lifted it up before examining his legs and back. "Just to make sure there are no Caster symbols I missed."

Evangeline blinked. *Finding the Caster's mark and rubbing a little salt on it should do the trick.* Avana's words from the ball echoed in her ears. The bucket had been filled with salt water. She jerked to Raiythlen and wondered if he was feeling the same horror she felt. But it was probably worse.

Avana stepped away from Raiythlen and reached for the ax. The ax, whose head was more than half the size of Avana's length, was sheathed in the bejeweled case next to the king with a handle made of pure gold. Ryker had told Evangeline it had been passed down for generations. She wondered if the afterlife was real, if Ryker was smiling at her current situation.

If he were still alive, none of this would've happened.

Seeing Avana next to the ax was almost comical. There was no way she could lift that. Not when the thing was almost the same height as her, even with her heels. The crowd felt the same, judging by the snickers and blatant words of disbelief. Avana proved everyone wrong when she lifted the heavy ax with ease, but Evangeline was more enthralled by the glow on her legs as the swirling runes lit up in blue. Avana was using magic to wield the ax, and she was doing it on purpose. To prove that she was just as powerful as an Aerian and to incite further fear that rippled in the crowd. Or maybe earn the king's respect, since she no longer had Ryker as a partner.

Evangeline's lips curled into an unpleasant smile. If Avana was putting on this performance, she had to be feeling quite vulnerable. Good.

"Any last words?" Avana asked her brother.

Raiythlen managed to look condescending as he gazed up at her, the barest hint of a smile grazing his lips. He whispered something, but Evangeline didn't hear it.

Pink dusted Avana's cheeks, but her eyes remained focused, her temperament controlled, exacting. Avana gripped the ax, sliding its sharp edge against the back of Raiythlen's neck, to draw out the fear and suspense for not only the crowd, but the victim.

Evangeline stared at Raiythlen. He had to have a plan. He had to. It was Raiythlen; he always had a plan, but the look on his face told her he wasn't all that powerful, that even he had his limits. And he was going to die because of it.

Avana raised the ax higher, the metal glinting in the rays shining through the patterned glass windows. Raiythlen titled his head, and Evangeline stilled. He did have a plan.

He shouted at Avana, something in Castanian. Evangeline didn't know if it was a spell or if he was trying to convince her not to kill him. Avana paused, lowering the ax and leaning closer to her brother. Evangeline thought maybe it had worked, but judging by Avana's face, it didn't. That was his ace card, his trick up his sleeve. Whatever he said, it didn't work, and the fear on his face spoke volumes.

Avana raised the ax again, her dress kicking back from the movement, her legs glowing. If she wanted respect, or fear, in that moment she got it. She looked like a force to be reckoned with.

The tip dangled high in the air, and in that fraction of a moment, Evangeline came to the shattering realization—if she didn't do something this instant, Raiythlen was going to die.

The weight of the moment built up before propelling her to action, beyond her coherent control. She didn't think, she just had to do something, anything, to stop this.

Evangeline stood so fast that even Aimee jumped next to her in surprise. "Stop!"

Avana's stare shot to her at the same moment the ax swung down, missing its mark. The heavy blade cut into Raiythlen's arm instead, lodging itself halfway into his bicep, nearly slicing it off. Raiythlen roared in pain, blood spurting from his arm, rivers of crimson liquid staining the white cotton like a morbid explosion of color.

Evangeline covered her mouth at the same time the crowd turned to stare at her in utter horror. Hundreds of eyes settled on hers, but Ceven's shocked one was the only one that stole her attention.

"You fool!" Aimee snapped at her at the same time metal clanged. Ceven had broke free of his cuffs, his fist already flying at Troy, who had been holding him down. Aimee cursed and raised her hand, her index finger crossing her palm.

The stained-glass windows along the border of the room shattered, and black-clad Casters flooded in.

The throne room erupted into chaos.

CHAPTER 40

The king shouted something, but it was swallowed by the roar of the crowd, screaming and rushing for the doors. Aimee snagged Evangeline's arm, but she jerked away, elbowing, ducking, and shoving through the sudden press of bodies. She had to get to Raiythlen and Ceven.

Her hand strained for the gun strapped to her thigh, as it was her only protection against guards who clashed their swords with Casters. The king had withdrawn his own sword, along with the Royal Guard that pressed around him and Aimee. Ceven had wrestled a blade from a guard, but he was surrounded, and the odds weren't in his favor. Nor were they in Raiythlen's, who had crumpled to the ground, bleeding out, staining the marble. Avana was nowhere to be seen.

Evangeline pulled the gun from its holster and aimed at the guards surrounding Ceven. She fired.

The small device kicked back with more power than she'd thought. The sound ricocheted in her ears, but who she shot wasn't the target she aimed at. Red blossomed from the chest of the red-bearded Royal Guard who was standing in front of the king, and she remembered what Aimee had said. *I've magicked one of the king's necklaces. All bullets in that gun will go for it like a magnet.*

Even if she wanted to help Ceven, her attacks would only target the king.

Suddenly, everything dimmed. A cold fog sifted through the room, blinding her and everyone in it. Pure, unadulterated fear gripped her as she struggled to see the outlines of people around her. Of blades swinging out and punches being thrown. Screams and howls of pain blocked her from hearing where anyone was. Her senses were thrown into chaos.

Someone rammed into her side, and Evangeline fell to the ground. She struggled to get up, the thick material of her dress hanging on her like a death trap. She rolled over, fumbling for the weapon that slid out of her grasp. Cold metal brushed her hands, and she squeezed the gun, yanking it to her chest as something struck the ground beside her. She jerked, her eyes wide at the blade of a spear that penetrated the marble right beside her head.

Release it, she thought to herself, her hands shaking, her eyes darting at the madness around her. *I have to release the darkness or I'll die.* While crunching close to the ground, avoiding swings and cracks where marble split and ran with blood, she reached inside herself. The darkness lay in the pit of her gut. She mentally unchained it and waited.

Nothing happened.

Evangeline gasped when something jabbed her shoulder, her dress lacerated and blood welling up in its place. *I'm going to die! Come out, come out now, you blasted, puss-filled thing!* she called to it, but it didn't stir, didn't even so much as acknowledge anything that was happening.

Her hair flew backwards with a rush of wind. The fog cleared briefly for her to catch Ceven, who had whipped back his wings, a sword aimed at the king. His blade met with two Royal Guards' swords as four others ushered the king away. Blood pooled on the floor by the throne, but Raiythlen was no longer there.

Evangeline held up her gun, her finger sliding over the trigger like Aimee had showed her. This time, she didn't bother aiming, scooting closer, keeping to the ground. If she were close enough, it didn't matter if the bullet went awry, as long as it hit one of the Royal Guards that had his sword aimed at Ceven.

Ceven's sword clashed with Troy's when a blade sliced Ceven's left side. He spun and, with the hilt of his blade, came down on the guard's skull. They crumpled. Ceven then wrenched the blade from the knocked down guard's hands in time to parry another blow from Troy, leaving him vulnerable to the two other metal-plated guards that rushed him and sliced his legs, the purple fabric ripping open.

Evangeline kept low to the ground, crawling closer. Someone stepped on her, their boot pressing into her back, but she ignored the sharp pain as she peeked between shifting legs, the barrel of the gun facing the cloister of guards.

Now!

She pulled the trigger, and the weapon knocked back, the bullet exploding from the barrel with contained force. It struck Troy's wing, blood dripping, staining the yellow feathers.

The Royal Guard roared in pain, eyes darting to find the culprit. He caught sight of her, but so did Ceven, who shouted something, but she couldn't hear over the clashing of metal and screams. It was probably to tell her to run. *If only he'd take his own advice!*

The yellow-winged Aerian started her way as other metal-plated Nytes swarmed Ceven. Evangeline turned and ran, the curtain of fog enclosing her once more. This time, she clenched the gun to her chest, keeping as low as she could as everything moved around her.

"Foolish girl!" Aimee yelled in Sehn's deep—now furious—voice before they wrenched her forearm, jerking her forward to meet their face. "Kill him now!"

Specks of spit flew onto her cheeks as Aimee shoved a finger into the fog. Like Evangeline could *see* anything. She didn't reply, struggling to escape the Caster's hold, needing to get out of this mess, so she could see. So she could breathe. So she could survive.

Aimee shrieked, releasing her. The leather-bound hilt of a small knife stuck out of the Caster's shoulder. *Xilo!* Evangeline whipped her head with Aimee's, but it was Quan who came out of the darkness. His brown, leather armor—the same as he had worn when she'd first met him weeks ago—was already splattered in blood.

He swung the body-length spear at her, twirling the sharpened ends. Aimee hissed and jumped back, the fog dissipating a little around them. Quan didn't look at her but uttered the words, "Go."

Evangeline didn't have time to say thanks when he slashed out his spear again to meet with a small parrying sword Aimee had on hand. Evangeline fumbled towards the door, her dress like a bag of stones she lugged behind her.

White-hot pain shot up her leg as something struck it from behind. She turned to see the uncoiling of a whip from the darkness. It unfurled again, and she yelped when it lashed her side. The silks of her dress didn't stand a chance, splitting apart like her skin, which oozed red.

Vane emerged from the fog, whip in hand. "Hello, Pet."

CHAPTER 41

CEVEN

Ceven didn't hesitate. He couldn't, not with so much on the line. The instant he'd heard Evangeline's voice call out from the crowd, he'd felt a blade sink into his heart. No. She couldn't be here. Not now. But he didn't have time to question his actions or plan. Nor did he have a choice, not with Sehn's bloody mark on his arm.

Avana's shock was notable, and it translated into the blade that almost chopped off the Caster's arm instead of his head. Ceven's muscles tensed at Raiythlen's yowl, imagining the pain, but then he focused on Troy behind him. His sword hung on the belt on his left leg that Ceven knew he favored.

He had to act now.

Ceven ripped free of his cuffs, whirling and punching Troy's weak leg while pulling out his sword, all before his chains hit the floor. Sinking to the ground, Ceven aimed his blade for Troy's heart as shattering glass reverberated on all sides of him. All hell broke loose.

Troy and a few other guards closed in on him, while others left to protect the king. Ceven had prepared himself for killing Calais, for cutting him straight down the middle before he could regret it, but Evangeline changed everything. Now, his priority was to get her out of here. The king could wait.

But that was proving to be harder than he'd thought when more guards surrounded him. Tarry was locked up somewhere, and if Evangeline were here, something had happened to Xilo and their plan. Ceven had betrayed Barto. If he, Rasha, or Quan were still in the kingdom, they weren't coming to his aid. No, he was alone.

A loud shot boomed next to him, and he whipped around in time to see Kirk's neck explode in red. Ceven didn't have time to grieve the loss of a former comrade when he planted a kick at the guard behind him, shattering his kneecap while blocking a blow to his unprotected left side. His sword broke in two. *Sea Watery hells, this is bad*—pain needled up his side as a blade pierced his body.

"I'm going to *spitting* kill you," Ceven hissed, knocking the hilt of his broken sword into the guard's skull. As he fell, Ceven yanked the spear from his hand in time to block two incoming sword strikes, but he wasn't quick enough, and they cut into his legs. Fiery heat licked up his limbs, pulsing in time with his side.

Boom! Another shot. This time closer.

Troy yelled, yellow feathers changing scarlet. Where were those shots coming from? Ceven turned to the crowd at the same time Troy did. There. On the ground, where Evangeline was gripping . . . was that a Caster weapon? She aimed the barrel at Troy, and it didn't take long for the Royal Guard to put two and two together. He marched toward her.

This woman . . . she was going to get herself killed! "RUN!" he shouted, blocking another blow to his side. His wounds stung, but he'd had worse, and he wouldn't bleed out like that poor Caster bastard. Where did he go?

Another blade stabbed past his ear, cutting the top of it and a chunk of hair. He needed to focus or he was going to die. At least Evangeline had listened to him. If only he could've stopped Troy, but he was surrounded.

He felt a pang in his chest, not from a blade but from the hatred he felt at himself. For betraying Barto, letting Evangeline get hurt, letting his brother fool him into this blasted mess, for not being the strong, in-control leader he always wanted to be. Instead, here he was, a bastard prince with no one to help him because he had turned them all away. Because he had failed to make the right decisions.

And now he was alone. Alone and losing.

CHAPTER 42

The whip lashed out again, smacking into the ground by Evangeline's bare feet, having kicked off her heels to run faster. She grabbed a handful of her ripped dress and tore it further, giving her legs room to move. The next time the whip snapped, her legs were free to jump away, but the tip sliced her shoulder. She yelped.

"Not nearly as entertaining as your friend was. She screamed on the first hit!" Vane laughed, his irises swallowed by black orbs. Her nightmares, her worst fears, came to life. Again.

Evangeline gripped the gun and fired. And fired again, and again, and again. The *booms* were nowhere near as caustic as the screams of agony around her. The bullets didn't listen to her, dodging left and right, trying to find their actual target. King Calais, not Vane.

The gun clicked, but nothing more came out of it. *No, no, no, no . . .* Vane approached her, and she chucked the useless hunk of metal to the side, eyes searching the ground. She snatched up a dagger, but what in blazes was one dagger going to do against this beast? *Run! Run! Run!*

Her legs pedaled air. She didn't care that she couldn't see, that she could be slit open with a blade or a claw, or trip over the many bodies on the floor. She would've preferred that to—

Vane yanked her hair, and she sprawled backwards, her small blade skittering from her hand. Vane's hungry gaze stared at her from above. "I can't wait to hear your screams again."

"S-Sehn! Can't hurt me!" She fumbled for the words, ice needles swimming down her throat and pricking her insides.

His gray jacket bulged, brown hair crawling through the ripped seams. His tattoos glowed like Avana's had, but these were purple, illuminating the surrounding smog. "You failed." He licked his lips. "And now it's time for me to clean up the mess."

She scrambled to get away, but he snatched her throat and choked off her air. She struggled to breathe as he smacked her skull on the marble floor. The world spun. *No!* Evangeline gritted her teeth, forcing herself to stay coherent as she plunged deep inside herself and raged against the darkness, trying to rattle it awake, but her hands slipped through it every time. Like it was blackened smog, intangible and unresponsive to her panicked pleas and internal screaming.

"And this time, there's no one to stop me." Vane's face shifted; his teeth elongated. The beast was back, his dripping muzzle next to her face. Evangeline cried out, searching for a familiar face around her in the gripping fog. *Ceven, Raiythlen, even Avana, please, help me. Help me. Someone help me!*

Vane lifted her again by the throat, and her cheek exploded in pain when he slammed it against the floor again. "Come on, scream! Fight!"

His fingers were gone, and she soared through the air before colliding with a wall. Her back splintered in agony as she rolled over, curling in on herself. Despite the chaos, only his boots crunching glass into marble rang in her ears. Closer, until he loomed over her. She gasped when his fist pummeled her stomach. Then her chest and her face. She couldn't breathe, she couldn't move, everything hurt. His laughter surrounded her, and a hollowness sprouted in her heart. This was it. Nobody was coming to save her. Would she get to see Lani again?

The blows stopped, but Evangeline wasn't saved. He gripped the front of her dress and jerked her forward. "How pathetic. Just like your friend, like every other human. Fight back, pet," he mocked her. "Why don't you fight back?" He slapped her, but it was nothing compared to the aching throughout her whole body. "Your friend wasn't a fighter either, crying and pleading for her life as I broke every single bone in her right hand. Then . . .when she thought it was over, I moved to her left!" He laughed, but Evangeline's world was spinning, whirling. He continued to speak, but she had already lost her grip on this reality.

Evangeline spat out blood, her hands around the hilt of a spear lodged in the dirt. Jaden was staring down at her, a chain wrapped between his fists and the bands of his arms.

"You're slow, you're not accepting yourself. Feel your body, your power, what you can do." Jaden bent and whipped the chain out. She abandoned the spear, tumbling away, and quickly settled on her feet to draw the two daggers from her belt. Although the captain forced them to learn every weapon, she was most confident with her daggers. Jaden's metal links strained and struck the ground where she'd been. The land cracked. A hole was left in its path.

Jaden twirled the chain again, and Evangeline lunged. He dropped the chain and pulled the sword from his back. Taken off-guard, she wasn't quick enough to dodge the blade cutting into her side. She hissed in pain, but Jaden was ruthless, striking a fist at her face. She dodged, sliding backwards. He kept her on the defensive.

"Stop, no more." She held up her hands.

He didn't; instead, he recoiled the chain before lashing it out again. It hit her shoulder, and she yelped.

"On the battlefield, there is no mercy. They won't stop, Eve. So I won't."

She rolled as another lash of the chains echoed in her ears. She clenched her daggers. Jaden had been to war. Forced to go to war. Meanwhile, she had been deemed weak. Not strong enough. She hated she wasn't able to be by his side, but she hated being forced to kill even more.

He tossed the chain and charged her, sword drawn. She reacted in time to parry the blow with both daggers. This close, the fury in his eyes was unmistakable. The impatience. It pissed her off.

She surged forward, forcing him back, and his sword to fell to the side. Not losing momentum, she launched her boot into his stomach. He stumbled back. "I'm not weak," she growled.

"Then prove it." He charged again.

She blocked his attack but wasn't paying attention and felt the blow of his fist in her ribs. She crumpled.

Jaden was the best fighter out of all of them. He was a force to be reckoned with. She had never defeated him, never desired to. But she wanted to rise to his challenge. To prove to him she was strong, that she could beat him. But to do that, she needed to find his weakness.

Knocked to the ground, she swiped at his feet with her leg, but he dodged. He was precise and calculating in his moves. He rarely played defensively, but he didn't need to, since his offense was aggressive enough. And his hits always landed.

But he had a weakness. Her.

He raised his blade again, but this time, she let it hit her. She was used to the pain by now, the beatings from both their captain and the other soldiers. It was Jaden's expression that told her how bad it was. He had expected her to dodge, and the glimmer of doubt, of panic, rose in his eyes. She grabbed it and ran with it.

She fell to her knees, gripping her side. The pain was dull, an annoyance, but she played her part well. "I can't, Jaden . . . it hurts too much . . . I don't want to hurt you."

"Eve . . ." His grip on his sword became lax, and his doubt deepened.

He leaned forward—either to help her or scold her, she didn't know or care—when she jumped to her feet. The tip of her dagger touched his throat, a steady stream of blood trickling down the powerful muscles of his neck. He blinked in surprise, and pride swelled inside her.

She smiled wickedly. "I win."

Clashing metal, shouts, screams, and Vane's rambling rushed back at her. So did the pain in her face, her chest . . . spitting blazes, it hurt *everywhere.*

". . . and when I break your ribs, maybe I'll take the time to shatter both kneecaps and . . ." Vane was looking at her, but not really. His expression was almost glazed, as if he were more enraptured by his own fantasy than what was happening. Evangeline coughed, feeling as if her ribs were already broken. But she wasn't dead.

You're slow, you're not accepting yourself. Feel your body, your power, what you can do.

She wasn't as powerful as Vane, not in her current state. But he had a weakness, she realized. One she could use to her own advantage. The first touch of hope flickered in her chest, and it gave her the courage to ignore the pain, the frozen shackles of fear.

Her eyes flicked to his belt, the array of knives he carried with him all the time. She only needed one. Preparing for the pain, she sat up and rammed her shoulder into Vane's chest. He was taken aback, but then growled, his claws sinking into her skull. But she got close enough to pull out one of his knives.

"Is that all you got?" she taunted and hoped she sounded convincing. On the inside, she screamed, her instincts telling her to run.

Well, look where running got her.

She got the reaction she was looking for. He snarled and backhanded her. She whimpered, tucking the knife firmly into her hand, and cowered, shielding her weapon with her body.

He pulled back her head. "Or maybe I'll just take a chunk out of you now . . ." His teeth entered her neck.

Her vocals stretched, a scream burning up her throat. With all her might, she threw herself away from his grip, but only managed to tear her skin.

Do it, do it now!

"Please, no," she sobbed in earnest, as her sweaty palm squeezed the knife. She had one chance; she had to make it count.

He grinned, and her blood stained his teeth. He said something, but she couldn't hear as she focused on his neck, the outline of muscle buried in fur. He leaned forward again, and without thinking, without doubting, just letting all her might, her power, her focus into this one move, she pushed the knife into the furred folds of his neck.

His eyes widened, the black rescinding to show brown once more. Blood spurted from his neck, and he reached to pull it out. The wound was already closing back up. In a panic, Evangeline shoved him back onto the marble floor. Her slick hands pushed the knife back into his neck as he struggled to breathe, to understand what was happening.

His weakness was his own hubris. And now a pathetic human like herself was going to kill him for it.

"I want you to suffer just like you made us suffer. Like you made Lani suffer." Her voice sounded like she had been screaming for hours, rough and strained. "You won't be able to hurt anyone anymore."

Like she'd always fantasized, the knife slid into his neck with ease. Images flashed before her. War. Blood. The woman whose neck gaped open at her. Evangeline embraced all of it, forcing the knife deeper . . . and deeper . . .

Vane gurgled, and his eyes rolled back. She realized he'd been clawing at her arms, but her grip remained firm. *Powerful*, she thought with a surge of warmth.

"It's not so much fun, is it? Being on the other end of the knife," she spat. "I hope the God of all Gods flies you up as high as he can, just to let you plummet to your death. Over and over again. For all eternity."

Red-veined eyes came back and locked on hers, a mix of hatred and disbelief swimming in their depths. Vane's lips curled back, mouthing the words, "I'll see you there," before he went limp, his hands falling to his side. Hair growing back into his skin. The beast fell away, back to the lean, shaggy Rathan it had been before. He looked truly pathetic, almost harmless, after all of his stolen power fell away. Power he stole from the lives of humans. From Lani.

Evangeline removed her hold on the knife. She was covered in blood. Vane's blood. Her lips stung as she smiled, then laughed. Vane was right about one thing: she would see him again. On the path she was heading down, she would never see Lani in the afterlife. Not for a monster like herself.

"Who's the weak one now?" she said to Vane's corpse.

CHAPTER 43

Ceven's side hurt more than he'd originally thought, and with the next block, he tried to sidle back, to give himself an opportunity to leave and find Evangeline. But everywhere he turned, he was cornered by armored Nytes. He got lucky with his blows and Evangeline injuring Troy, whom he still couldn't see in the crowds. And that made him nervous.

Steel pierced his shoulder, and he jerked. He forced a steady breath and kept a firm grip on his sword. It was hard to prepare for the next attack when he couldn't hear them over the noise and there were too many bodies to watch.

I'm done for.

Another blow to the back of his leg made him fall, but he lifted his blade in time to stop the guard's sword from cutting his skull open. This was bad. He needed to get back on his feet.

Another stab. He rolled, but the purple sleeve of his coat slit completely open, blood seeping in its place.

Something slammed into the two Royal Guards in front of him, the three behind him distracted by something else moving in the fog. Ceven didn't waste time and shoved to his feet, sword out. He shook his matted hair out of his eyes, which widened at a familiar face.

"Barto?" he said in disbelief, but his friend didn't have time to respond as he kept low to the ground, using his claws to cut the guards' legs between their mesh of armor as they howled in pain. He was quick, thorough, and everything Ceven needed right now.

Rasha was behind them, two swords out. Her body was a flood of acrobatic precision. Her braids danced with her lithe form, sashaying back and forth to the beat of metal. He couldn't believe it. Why were they here? Why were they helping him?

"What are you doing? This is treason! This could cause a war!" Ceven used Rasha's distraction to his advantage, stabbing the guard from behind. He hated such dirty tactics, but right now he needed to stay alive. He needed to make it out of this.

"Already looks like war," Barto shouted back. "Shut up and accept our help. I still plan to kick your ass after this!"

He shook his head and shoved a sandy-haired guard who had been about to impale Barto's right leg. Ceven yanked Barto to his feet. While gripping his friend's arms, he twirled, and the knives attached to the bottoms of Barto's boots sliced everyone close by.

"Watch where you're aiming!" Rasha yelled, ducking in time to miss Barto's boots of death.

His friend landed on his feet with his back touching Ceven's. It reminded him of their time in the humid Atiacan jungle, standing side by side, surrounded by bandits.

Barto smiled, sharing the same memory. "This takes me back."

Ceven tried to smile, but it came out like a twitch as a weight of emotion bowed down on him. Barto had come back for him. After everything Ceven had done, Barto had come back, defied the king, risked a war, and was currently committing murder for his sake.

"You can kick my ass from here to Atiaca when we make it out of this. I was a fool." Ceven stepped out and feigned a left hit at the guard before striking right. He was close, but the guard blocked at the last second.

"I tried to tell you that, but you were never a good listener." Barto lashed out in a sequence of kicks and punches. It was a flurry of motion, and the guard was slow to block with his large spear, giving Barto the advantage.

"Well, with you talking my ear off all the time, I had to learn to be selective." Barto's hand fell on Ceven's shoulder before he leaped over him, striking the guard from above. Ceven sliced his legs at the same time. The guard tried to get out of reach but wasn't quick enough, blocking Ceven's blow but getting a fistful of Rathan claws to the face.

"We got this, prince. Now, go find your princess," Barto yelled.

Ceven didn't bother arguing. He knew Barto and Rasha could hold their own now that most of the guards had either fled to protect Sehn and the king or had been felled by his sword. Ceven went to sheath his borrowed blade and cursed when he realized he didn't have his belt on him. He awkwardly tucked it into the waistband of his pants and jumped into the fog.

Pockets of clean air were scattered around, made from the flap of wings or the wave of motion as guards and Casters fought one another, other Nytes running and screaming. Two black-clad Casters jumped out in front of him with daggers, their hoods reaching only to his chest. Ceven withdrew his blade, but the Casters looked at him and ran back into the fog. He frowned but didn't complain, trying to find a blond-haired girl amongst the calamity.

He found her sitting on top of . . . was that Vane? Blood covered her hands and dress, her face bruised and broken. Ceven snarled at nobody. Sehn had promised she wouldn't be injured, that she would be protected. Of course, his brother had lied; Ceven just wondered, what else did he lie about? What was the true meaning of this mark on his arm? Ceven was going to kill him and whoever had hurt Eve.

But when he ran towards her, flames licked at his brain. Searing hot pain flashed across his skull, and he collapsed, gripping his head.

Kill the king. Kill the king. Kill the king.

His arm flared in response, and he tore off the ripped fabric. Beside the cuts and slashes the Royal Guards had given him lay Sehn's blood promise. And it was glowing.

Kill the king. Kill the king. Kill the king.

He took another step toward Evangeline, and his legs buckled. "Kill the king . . . I have to kill the king," he roared, fighting his own mind. At least Ceven didn't have to wait long to find out the truth. Only lose his arm . . . His brother had conned him into losing his spitting mind.

Ceven gritted his teeth, but when he looked up, the fog had crept closer—no, it was a different color. Blacker, thicker. In the distance, something illuminated red. The king.

King Calais, now surrounded by only three Royal Guards, made for the double doors. Wait, he was aiming for the framed painting of King Peredia I. And behind it was surely the entrance to the tunnels.

Kill the king! Kill the king! Kill the king!

Ceven clenched his sword tighter. He strained his senses, focusing on the glowing red figure. Like a Rathan who's picked up a scent, he leaped into the black fog, eyes on his prize.

Others framed him on either side, black-clad Casters running next to him. He gripped his sword tighter, but they didn't engage with him. Instead, they sprinted ahead. There were three . . . no, four . . . maybe seven attack the king's guards. They were small, a lot shorter than the Aerians, but like Avana, they glowed and zoomed at a pace faster than any Rathan he'd seen.

The king withdrew his sword, the thick blade the length of one of his great, golden wings that fanned out. It dissipated the surrounding fog. The floor was littered with bodies, soldiers, and innocents alike. Corpses sprawled out to the point you couldn't see the marble. In the distance, remaining Nytes fought, but the shouts and banging had lessened. Ceven needed to kill the king now, before the chaos settled.

He went to launch himself at his former father when a gust of air smacked his face. King Calais landed in front of him, his long golden wings sweeping the floor. The first few buttons to his vest had come undone, his pale chest peeking through. No tattoos. Ceven thought it odd that he subjected his soldiers to the dark magic invading this city and its castle but refused to do it to himself.

King Calais's eyes glowed, but his expression still betrayed nothing as he settled on Ceven. "Ceven, my son."

Ceven raised his sword. "I haven't heard you call me that in six years."

The king extended his leg, one foot following the other, walking closer. Ceven's muscles tensed. Calais stopped when they stood a head apart. Their eyes locked, neither backing down.

Ceven's chest heaved, his arm burned, every inch of his body screaming to hit the king as hard as he possibly could. "I loved you. I could've still loved you."

The king cracked, the smallest sliver of a laugh taking reign. "Don't claim something you know never would've been true. Even if you were my true son, you and I are as different as night and day. Sooner or later, you would have come to hate me."

King Calais held up his sword, but it shook. His purple robe slid back, showing the frail, veiny arm of an old man. Ceven had once looked up to the king as someone all-powerful. He'd stared at paintings of him on the battlefield, heard the stories of him felling the rebel attacks from Atiaca before it became its current empire. Ceven had created this illusion of this mighty foe he could never tackle. He was so caught up in it he didn't even realize the king was far past his prime, that he hadn't been strong or powerful for a long time. But instead of feeling smug, all Ceven felt was pity.

"It doesn't matter, because you never bothered to try. I could have been a great son to you. Better than Sehn." Ceven tried to hold on to his anger, but it wavered. The only thing holding the sword to his former father's throat was the burning in his arm and head.

Kill the king! Kill the king! Kill the king!

"Don't pretend otherwise," Calais said. "You always were a weak-hearted boy. Sehn possessed more leadership than you ever did."

Ceven knew he shouldn't listen to his words, that anything

he said held no merit. Not when this man claimed to hate him all his life. Still, the words hurt him. Ceven could've been a great leader, a great king, but nobody ever believed he could. He was starting to think it, too.

"But if believing in a fairy tale will make it all better for you to kill me, it would only be fitting for the son whose father lived in frivolous fantasies instead of reality."

Ceven jerked. That was the second time the king had ever mentioned his real father.

The king laughed. "Then again, maybe I'm the hypocrite, for wanting to start a war because of a broken heart. Maybe all this time, I was the weak one. Because I loved your mother so much."

"Who is he? My real father?" Hot rage filled him, controlled him, pulsed in time with his blood rune, but he fought it. He didn't want to kill the king. It felt wrong to murder a man who could barely lift his own sword. Then the rest of Calais's words hit him. *Go to war because of a broken heart . . .* "Mother . . . the man she had an affair with . . . he was Mouchian? You're going to war because of that?" It was a guess; for all Ceven knew, he could've been Atiacan, but the king's bitter smile confirmed it. The treaty had been a ruse after all.

"We never would've been powerful enough to go against Sundise Mouche as we were. We needed an edge, one that Ryker had provided us, and an in, which Sehn brought about." He looked around, but his face showed no emotion. "But it seems they had known all along. It's a shame they struck first before we could rise to our full potential." Calais's eyes pinched in thought.

One that hinged on the deaths of hundreds of humans. Ceven shook his head. "That would've been suicide. So many would have died, and for what? That all happened years ago!"

The king fixed his cold stare on Ceven. "If you truly loved that girl, you wouldn't have asked me that."

Ceven opened his mouth, but he couldn't find the words.

"You came here to kill me. So stop wasting your breath." The king tossed his blade to the side and rushed him at a speed Ceven thought him no longer capable of. He grabbed Ceven's sword, his bony white knuckles clenching tightly against the blade. Ceven jerked back on the sword's hilt, but King Calais yanked it forward, thrusting a fist into his gut. Ceven coughed, the wind rattling violently back into his lungs.

"You remind me so much of her. I can't stand it." Calais swung another fist at him.

Ceven dodged the punch this time, expecting it. "When did you find out? And why didn't you tell me? Why keep me around if you were only going to hate me?" Ceven tried to remain in control of his emotions, but his father's words sparked a fit of fire within him. "You know what? I'm glad you're not my real father. An empty shell of a man who would never know what humility and compassion were, even if they smacked him in the face."

King Calais lunged. Ceven raised his sword in defense, but Calais knocked it aside. He grabbed Ceven by the front of his shirt, his face a breath away. "Don't speak to me of things you know nothing about. Everything I've ever done has always been for this family," he snarled. "All you've done is throw my dead wife back in my face, disobey me every chance you got, raising scandals by being with that blasted human. You never understood why I did what I did. You'd never understand!"

The king gripped Ceven's limp blade, pressing it against his own heart. Ceven saw red, felt red, was red.

KILL THE KING! KILL THE KING! KILL THE KING!

"No, I never will, because you never gave me the chance," Ceven ground out, fighting the instinct to shove the blade. Calais was taunting him, like he always did. He didn't really want to die . . . right?

The king turned his head, and Ceven followed his gaze. Sehn approached them, his purple robe flaring out, the bottom coated in red from the corpses he stepped across. He held a dagger in his hand, slick with blood, and a circle of crimson highlighted his shoulder, but Ceven didn't know if it was his own or someone else's.

Ceven's gut clenched as the king looked at Sehn with utter respect and adoration. If only he knew his own death was orchestrated by the very son he loved so much . . .

"Sehn, my boy." The king left Ceven's side, striding to his brother. There was a slight limp in his walk, as if he had been hit a few times in the chaos. "I'm glad you're okay; I was so worried—"

Sehn shoved his dagger into the king's heart.

King Calais's eyes flew open, surprise loosening his lips before he looked down at his chest. He coughed, falling to one knee. He gripped his heart, and when he coughed again, blood dribbled from his mouth. Calais looked up at Sehn, trying to speak, but he choked on his words.

"No!" Ceven ran to his side, holding the king's chest, as if he could somehow stop the flow of blood. After everything . . . everything the king had done . . . grief still gripped him.

The king didn't respond, the light fading from his eyes. He sagged, but Ceven caught him, lowering him gently to the floor. King Calais was dead.

"How could you!" Sehn yelled.

Ceven blinked and whipped around. His brother pointed a finger at him, shouting at the top of his lungs. The fog was gone, and the guards and few civilians, cowering in the corners, turned to them. Sehn sank to the ground, holding the king's dead hand. "Father, no." His brows furrowed, and tears stained his cheeks. "How could this have happened?" He then looked at Ceven.

And smiled.

No, the puss-filled Aerian was going to—

Sehn's words carried across the entire throne room. "Kill him, for the murder of our king!"

CHAPTER 44

Evangeline's legs shook as she got back on her feet. Wiping blood on her torn and haggard dress, she frisked Vane's body, palming a dagger with a curved blade the size of her hand and two knives. She crammed the knives into the holster still strapped to her thigh. It didn't fit perfectly, but it was enough for them not to fall out as she escaped through the double doors and into the main hall.

Nytes in shredded dresses and coats splattered with blood rushed alongside her, scattering like roaches throughout the castle. Guards followed in the opposite direction into the throne room. Evangeline ducked into the crowd, trying to see past the bold blue, green, and yellow silks and fabrics. She didn't have a plan or any idea of where to go, just some place where a sword wouldn't impale her, or where a horde of confused Nytes wouldn't stampede her to death. Her whole body ached,

and if it weren't for the adrenaline keeping her on her feet, she would've passed out somewhere from the beating her body had just taken.

Something caught her eye—pale blue wings fading into beige at the tips next to a gray-eared Rathan that had her hair pulled back into a tight ponytail, revealing freckles on her face that Evangeline hadn't noticed the first time they'd met. It was, without a doubt, Annabelle and Rayne. Were Petri and the others still alive?

Another stampede of guards shook the floor—no, it wasn't the guards that streamed in past her and the throne room doors, but an explosion that shook the castle. For a split moment, Evangeline was a little girl bracing herself against the paneled wall. The edge of a framed painting dug into her back as Nytes rushed by her, much like she was now, watching metal-plated guards, ripped dresses, and unraveled tunics race by, explosions and panic filling and expanding the castle's arched hallways.

Did Petri and the others succeed? Despite all odds, were they able to infiltrate the west wing and rescue those humans?

There are others inside the castle, Petri had said. He'd neglected to tell her just how many allies they had.

Sweat-slicked fingers grabbed her wrist, pulling her from her thoughts. Evangeline whipped around to find Avana. The Caster's arms and legs were no longer glowing, but her eyes did, the sky-blue irises popping off against the widened whites. "Evangeline, come with me. I can get you to safety!"

Evangeline yanked back her wrist. "Let me go!"

Avana's expression was feverish. "Quickly, now!" Her grip tightened, and pain hummed in rhythm with the rest of Evangeline's body. Avana didn't wait for a response and pulled her forward, rubbing Evangeline's arm with her bloody finger. She shouted in Castanian, and the symbol solidified into a black rune, sinking into Evangeline's skin—before it oozed off in a black blob. Like in the woods, beyond the walls, the magic withdrew from her skin as if she were slicked with oil and Avana's magic made of water.

"What . . . how?" Avana blinked in shock while Evangeline burned with rage. The woman had been about to take her away by force.

"I. Said. Let. Go!" Evangeline curled her fingers into a fist and decked Avana in the face. She stumbled back, and her nose spurted with blood, but Evangeline didn't care, already merging into the crowd.

"Eve!" She spun. Quan stood a few paces away, elbowing his way through the crowd. His leather armor was darkened with more blood, and he had traded his spear for a sword. Evangeline ran toward him, but a sharp blow from someone's elbow knocked her back. She jerked and met Rayne's brown gaze, her eyes swimming with hate. "Filthy traitor."

You traitor! How could you do this to me? To us? To your kingdom!

Evangeline shook her head, but she didn't know if it was at Rayne or at the voice inside her head. "No, I didn't—" she started, but Rayne had already vanished into the crowd.

Quan appeared in Rayne's place, his eyes round and alert, and more serious than she'd ever seen him—if that were possible. "Barto and Rasha should be with Ceven. We need to go!" he shouted.

"Go where?" The place had turned into a war zone. Caster assassins were everywhere, and it felt like the entire Peredian military had stormed the castle. And now she had an angry Caster after her. *I killed Vane and Ryker. Let's add another Nyte to that list.* Evangeline shook her head. She'd seen where arrogance had gotten Vane. And for all her previous luck, she was still a human in a swarm of bloodthirsty Nytes . . . but was she?

She remembered looking at her hands, the strength they had to hold down Vane in his beast form. The pain from his blows that were already subsiding, just as when she had been in those woods, alive with power and slicked with blood.

If she were human, she would've already been dead.

Quan peered over her, shoving her to the side as a herd of Nytes flooded the hall, tripping over one another. Someone screamed, and Evangeline covered her mouth as a Rathan boy in a once-polished suit got completely trampled.

"Get on my back! It'll be faster and more efficient!" Quan hollered, and Evangeline didn't waste any time. She wrapped her legs around his waist, her arms circling his neck. She wasn't heavy, but the way he shot off down the hall almost made her feel like a sack of feathers. Her head even snapped back. He veered through the mass with ease, jumping left. Right. An elbow to someone's side and a punch to their shoulder, knocking them out of the way. Evangeline tamped down the guilt at watching the Nytes and humans stumble to the ground. She didn't turn around to see if they got crushed, too.

Her hair came out of its coifed up-do and whipped past her face as they sprinted down a side hall. Guards stepped into their path. Quan reared, turning around. They entered back into the crowd, and Evangeline spotted Avana. She was chasing them.

"Go, go, go!" Evangeline screamed.

He growled. "What the blazes do you think I'm doing, woman?"

Quan veered down another hall before coming to an abrupt halt. In front of them stood other Rathans, all in the same brown leather armor as Quan. Other Atiacan soldiers were here too?

"This way!" The woman with short black hair and white furred ears in the front waved at them. Quan followed, and as they ran, the other Rathans fell into formation, two in front and two behind. Guards blocked their way, but the Atiacan soldiers were quick to distract them, pulling them off their tail as Quan continued to pound through the halls. They made it to the east wing, past the kitchens that still smelled of food even though nobody entered in or out those double doors. It seemed everyone in the castle was hiding away. Or had fled.

Evangeline recognized where they were going. "We're headed toward the dungeons?" Her fingers and legs cramped from squeezing the bald-headed Rathan, but she wasn't about to let go or tell him to slow down.

"Ceven will be sure to head there when Barto tells him what happened."

"What happened?" He dropped her to the floor. Her world spun for a moment.

"The hallways are too narrow. Come on." He grabbed her hand and tugged her into the stairwell. Her insides clenched, and her feet dragged. Images of being stranded in the dark, of losing her mind, of manacles and whips haunted her.

She stopped. He huffed and turned. "What?" he said, none too gently.

"Why are we going here?" she demanded.

"Tarry and Xilo got captured for fighting against the Royal Guard," he conceded. "Now, will you come before more guards show up?"

She followed, taking his hand and forcing his momentum to keep her from freezing to the spot. It was an odd sensation to have adrenaline burning through her body, but the cold pockets of fear tickling her spine.

"Xilo is here? How?" She didn't bother asking how Quan felt about that, her and Xilo leaving behind his back, or why he was even helping her now. *Wait a second . . .* She stopped and snatched her hand out of Quan's hold. "This is a trap, isn't it?

You're going to lock me up!" Gods, she was a fool! How could she have let him—

"Eve!" Ceven's voice called from down the hall. Barto and Rasha stood by him with other Atiacan soldiers and . . . was that Taryn and Ed?

Quan gave her a pointed look and sprinted down the hall, leaving her in the dust. She followed behind a few strides later but froze. Guards were on the floor, their faces ripped open. Mutilated. Evangeline gagged and turned away.

Ceven snagged her waist and pulled her into a tight hug. *Gods,* it felt so good to be in his arms. "Eve . . . Oh, Eve . . ." His fingers caressed her face. Her bruised and bloodied face. Not that he fared much better, blood and nasty gashes lining his temple, arms, and sides. Unlike his Atiacan friends, he didn't have any armor on him. His purple shirt hung in shreds off his arms and chest like the torn tapestries in the west wing.

Something rattled, and she turned around. Barto snatched a pair of keys from the guard's corpse.

"Is this the cell?" Rasha stared at the metal door, and the brown-leathered soldiers around them nodded.

Barto banged on the door. "Hello, this is your personal rescue team. Any chance Xilo or Tarry are home?"

Nobody laughed. How could the Rathan could have a sense of humor right now?

"We're here," Tarry's unmistakable deep voice replied, but something was off.

Barto unlocked and opened the door while everyone unsheathed their blades. Tarry's forearm pressed Xilo's throat to the wall.

"What's the meaning of this?" Ceven released Evangeline, gripping his own sword.

"He betrayed you, Your Highness." Tarry didn't flinch or falter. Xilo had his hands raised in surrender. He wasn't fighting against Tarry's hold at all.

"Not much of a prince now," Rasha stated at the same time Ceven asked how.

Tarry yanked his arm back to allow Xilo to speak, but didn't release his hold. "Tell them. Tell them what you told me."

Xilo kept his head down, a sight that hurt Evangeline despite everything. "I'm sorry, Ceven. They had my son. They had Eyvan. I—" His shoulders sagged. "There's no excuse for my actions. I only ask that you grant me a quick death."

Evangeline had wondered why Eyvan's house had felt more abandoned than if he had left for a routine trip out of the city. Had Xilo lied to her when he said his son was in Sundise Mouche, or had he not been telling her the full truth? But why was Eyvan captured in the first place?

Ceven's expression hardened. "I'm disappointed, Xilo."

Tarry raised something—a sizeable chunk of stone, after closer inspection. Evangeline gaped at Ceven, then Tarry. They couldn't kill him.

Xilo glanced up, his eyes cold, as if he were already dead. "I don't deserve to live."

Ceven raised his hand, and Tarry paused. "I won't kill you." Evangeline sighed in relief. "But I'll impart my last orders."

Xilo bowed his head. "Whatever you wish, Your Highness."

"You will stay here for three days. You will tell no one of this, of our plan." Ceven took a breath. "Goodbye, Xilo."

Tarry stared at his partner, but Evangeline couldn't read his expression. Her heart stung. After all this, how could they just leave him behind? Ceven had known him his whole life. Xilo had betrayed them, yes, but it was because they had his son. How could they condemn him to stay behind? He'd be captured and tortured. Killed.

Ceven's hand returned to her waist, but Evangeline slid away from him. "How could you guys do this? Don't you have any mercy? Forgiveness?" she said.

Everyone sheathed their swords and moved into a line. One of the Rathan guards handed Tarry a pair of axes as he shuffled out of the cell. "He is being merciful. Anyone else would have run a blade through him," the old Aerian said.

Rasha nodded. "Your charge comes first. No matter the cost, it's what you pledged your life for."

Ceven reached for her again. "Come on, Eve." With his back turned to everyone else, the truth shimmered in his eyes. The pain, hurt, and regret. Then it was gone.

Evangeline let Ceven gently tug her down the hall. She looked over her shoulder. Xilo had walked out of the cell and stood there staring at their turned backs, his figure appearing smaller and smaller as they walked away. His lips were moving, and Evangeline glanced at Ceven and the others, but she was the only one watching.

She read his lips and flinched before whipping around. Her heart hammered away in her chest, but she masked her alarm with a pouted lip and scrunched brows that trembled, bordering between sadness and mortification which she only partly faked.

Tell him the truth, tell him the truth, tell him the truth, Xilo had been mouthing repeatedly—aimed directly at her.

CHAPTER 45

They left the dungeons, taking a series of hallways. They slipped between secret passages and the underground tunnels, avoiding the hysterical crowd that died down in volume. All that was left were bodies on the floor that Evangeline avoided looking at. They passed by several soldiers and guards who took out their swords, but one look at Ceven, Tarry, Ed, and Taryn had them sheathing their weapons, saluting them before passing. Others weren't as accepting, but they quickly cut them down, several of Barto's soldiers dispatching and distracting the Peredian soldiers to let them run away.

They continued down a narrow set of steps in the east wing, leading into a cavernous basement. Evangeline gaped at the metal doors, almost equivalent to the city's gates in size. This wasn't a basement, but an underground fortress.

In front of the doors stood more soldiers. Both Peredian and Atiacan, if she were judging by their armor.

"Glad to see that you rookies made it," Taryn bellowed, clasping the Rathans on the back. Like Ed, he was in silver-plated armor with the winged crest on the breastplate.

"Rookies," Ed snorted. "You're more wet behind the ears than any of us, Tar."

Ceven walked up to the doors. The soldiers straightened and saluted him. It was bizarre to witness such respect after all those years of the nobles snuffing their noses at him. Maybe after all his training and years of sweat, Ceven had earned his place in this kingdom. Or at least with these soldiers.

A metal box with number pads was fixated on the wall beside the massive doors. It reminded Evangeline of the machinery back in the ruins she and Avana had explored. Ceven pressed his hand to the screen, and the doors opened with a thunderous roar. Evangeline jumped back, and Quan smirked at her, but she remained fixated on the large room in front of her. Bright lights flickered on overhead to illuminate the large, concrete fortress. She'd thought she was beyond surprises at this point, but she was wrong.

"What is *that?*" she exclaimed at several hefty machines that reminded her of a bird about to take flight.

"They're airships. Machines built for flight." Ceven's face hadn't changed since they'd left Xilo behind. Like a closed book, all his thoughts were kept behind a mask of indifference. "This is Peredia's largest shipping warehouse. Everything of importance is sent here through a complex system of underground tunnels."

The room they were in was vast, with ceilings high enough to encompass not just one, but several airships, amongst other things. Evangeline recognized some machines from her readings in the library and discussions with Raiythlen. Crates filled with guns and other large machines she assumed were used to transport people and objects, based on her present knowledge. The room was too large, however, to even see its entire contents.

"It's going to be a long ride, and bumpy," Barto chimed.

Evangeline didn't understand. Were they going to take an airship? How would they get out of the basement? How did they get it in here to begin with?

Ceven led her past the airships to an opening in the side of a round metal container, taking up the expanse of the room. Inside was a smaller metal pod set upon two steel rails.

"This is our ticket to Atiaca," Ceven told her bewildered expression. He waved several people over. He asked for a med kit and helping hands. "Like Barto said, it'll be a long trip, but we should be safe." His hands grazed her cheek, and she winced. "And we'll get you patched up and some sleep. We have a lot of catching up to do."

"As long as you fix yourself up too." She pointed at the side he favored and kept trying to hide from her. He looked just as bad as she did.

Barto hopped inside the metal cylinder, placing himself at the front. He tampered with several buttons before pulling a lever. A loud hiss came from the machine, which Evangeline prayed was a good sign. It had no windows, no seats, and felt as if it lacked proper ventilation. Were they really going to ride in this? Then again, what choice did they have?

Ceven helped her into the container, and she tried to squash down the feelings of being trapped. Rasha and Quan squeezed in beside her, then Tarry. Even with his blue-and-gray wings folded, she felt the air tighten. This truly was going to be a long trip.

Still on the platform, Ceven faced Taryn, Ed, and the other Peredian soldiers. They all had their fists over their chest.

"You are the true king of Peredia," Ed said, and others nodded.

Ceven put a hand in front of him and bowed. Like a king to his subjects. "I'll be back. I swear it on the queen's grave." Evangeline raised her brows at him. They did have a lot to catch up on.

Taryn grinned. "We'll keep the place warm and ready for your safe return."

Ceven was last to step into the metal pod. The door slid shut behind him, and he propped himself beside her on the floor. With everyone sitting cross-legged—except Quan and Barto and the Rathan woman who sat beside her, a med kit opened on the floor—the pod was still a tight squeeze. A single light shone painfully bright above them. Even if she tried to sleep through this trip, it would be near impossible with a makeshift sun blinding her. Then again, her body craved to do nothing but sink into oblivion—regardless of her surroundings.

The ground rumbled as the vehicle departed the station.

The Rathan woman, with soft brown eyes and dark hair curling around a kind face, carefully rubbed Evangeline's cheek. She tried not to wince as Barto spoke over the vibrations. "It'll be a long journey to Atiaca, but trust me, you're going to love it, Eve. It's nothing like this dreary place."

Evangeline gave him a half-hearted smile but winced again when the woman grazed over the fresh skin that had healed from Vane's bite. She clenched her eyes shut, remembering his teeth sinking into bone, but now an almost numb, stinging pain took its place. Ceven rubbed her back, and she loosened a breath. For a moment, everything was okay. Ceven was here. Alive. They both were alive. Even if the pod they were in came crashing down, they'd made it this far, alive and together. She leaned against him, grateful for the comfort, his warmth. She was finally leaving Peredia. After all these years of dreaming about it, it was now happening. She felt selfish, and yet she still wished Lani were here with her.

I made it, Lani. Can you see me from where you are? Evangeline looked up as if she could peer through the bolted metal mesh to wherever her friend was now. *So much has happened. I wish you were here with me; I miss you so much.* Evangeline's smile wobbled. *I love you, Lani. I hope you have finally found the peace of mind you have been searching for.*

Evangeline let the soft vibrations of the vehicle relax her. This past month had been enough excitement for her for the rest of her days. She didn't want to dwell on the fact that she had left Raiythlen, not knowing if he was alive or dead. That Sehn—Council member Aimee—was now king, and what that meant for the future. If Petri and the others had successfully saved those humans or if the rebellion for human rights was another war lying in wait after today.

But a dark part inside of her uncoiled, the one who had embraced the war, the violence, the blood. Who had sunk their teeth into that Caster's neck and relished its taste. Who had celebrated Vane's death, whispered, *who cares, they're not your problem.*

Evangeline shoved down the unsettling thought and closed her eyes.

The pod hummed, swaying slightly, her head bobbing against Ceven's shoulder and the cool metal wall at her back. The closet-sized pod smelled of cleaning alcohol, but at least it covered the stench of blood. Nothing but the rustling and occasional hiss as everyone's wounds were cleaned, bandaged, and stitched took over the silence.

"A new country, a new culture, new faces. A little scary, but exciting, huh?" said Barto, breaking the short-lived silence.

"I think I can handle it," Evangeline muttered.

"But I don't think *I'll* handle it if you talk this entire trip," Rasha snapped at Barto, whose furred ears flicked back. Evangeline couldn't help but laugh—she'd been thinking the same thing. Ceven chuckled, and soon everyone joined in, breaking free of what had just happened.

If only for a little while.

EPILOGUE

A V A N A

Avana's pointed nails scraped her temples. She peered over her desk in her room in the tower. Shouts and screams still echoed outside her door, which she had marked with runes and traps. Nobody was getting in.

Her grandmother's journals lay open on the black, elegant desk. Its surface was immaculately clean, every paper, book, and writing utensil filed neatly in their corresponding place. She skimmed the yellowed pages and Anali's rough sketches again—for the hundredth time.

Her nails dug deeper into her temples. The Quincara legacy—her grandmother's legacy—everything Avana had been searching for was now in danger. No matter how many times she stared at Anali's journals, they wouldn't give her the answers she needed. But now Ryker was dead, along with all of his knowledge, and Evangeline had been taken away. Avana's raven scouted the castle grounds, but she couldn't find her. Much like Raiythlen, who had disappeared. Hopefully, he bled out somewhere.

His poisoned tongue had tricked her in the past. Had convinced her to hand over the journals to him, believing he was helping her, their family, in pursuing Anali's legacy. He knew how much it meant to her, the years she'd spent studying it. Instead, he had betrayed her *and* their parents by burning them.

And like those journals, he had permanently burned the bridge between them.

All she had left was this journal and Evangeline. And now she didn't even have that. Everything she had worked for was slipping through her fingers. She was going to be stuck, yet again, at a dead end. And she didn't want to wait—potentially years—for some stroke of luck like this to happen again.

She turned another page when she felt it. An electric current. A shift in the air. It couldn't be . . .

Avana whipped around, an incantation leaving her lips. Light like a feather, swift as a bird. Her arms and legs vibrated with magic, the runes beneath her breast and lower stomach coming to life. She had already used these spells a few times today. She estimated about an hour left before the symbols disintegrated. Maybe less. She'd only used this spell a handful of times and didn't know its full effect.

A familiar pressure soaked up the room. No way . . . But there was no mistaking the sensation of a nearby Shadow Door. One that previously hadn't been in her small tower room. The space by her single-sized bed shimmered, and her fingers unwound the bun from her hair, the beaded hairpins sharp at the end. The tips, dipped in a concentrated toxin, would kill any opponent, either in seconds or minutes, depending on the type of Nyte and their body mass.

A tall, exotic man stepped out from the distorted space, and Avana propped her clips, ready to aim at the intruder's throat. Emerald eyes squinted as they met hers, but what made her hands shake and her stance falter was the symbol on his right hand.

"Avana Quincara, granddaughter to Anali. I believe it's time we met."

Her breath caught. It wasn't often that she lost her calm, but ever since stepping foot in Peredia, her logical, calculated life had been a series of dark corners and abrupt turns.

"Who . . .?" She swallowed and straightened but never lowered the beaded clips. "Who are you? What do you want?" His eyes crinkled into a smile, but she was more focused on the circular symbol encased in old Castanian on his right hand. The same as Evangeline's.

"You may call me Jaden." Something ancient layered with an unknown depth of wisdom poured from his words, his posture—his very existence. Would he be the one to finally bring her what she had been searching for all these years?

Jaden cocked his head. "As for what I want, that depends on you. Do you want to help me save the world?"

GLOSSARY

Aerian(s)- A humanoid winged creature with extraordinary strength.

Rathan(s)- A humanoid creature that shares a likeness with a specific type of animal. Possess a greater agility and sense of smell.

Caster(s)- A humanoid creature with horns and the ability to perform magic through their blood.

Halfling(s)- A creature born from two different species.

Nyte(s)- Umbrella term for all superhuman species: Aerians, Rathans, Casters, and Wretched.

Castanian- Primary language spoke in Sundise Mouche and by most Casters.

Atiacan(s)- Primary language spoke in Atiaca. Also refers to a citizen of Atiaca, or anything of Atiacan decent.

Peredian(s)- Primary language spoke in Peredia. Also refers to a citizen of Peredia, or anything of Peredian decent.

Frostlite- A mineral found in the Frostsnare mountains. Reacts to Caster magic.

Saliver- A plant found near riverbeds in the warmer parts of Atiaca. It's ingested to counteract Caster magic.

LEARN MORE ABOUT THE AUTHOR

WWW.ALEXANDRIACAINLOCKE.COM

Twitter: @WriterAlexLC

Facebook: @AlexandriaCainlockeBooks

Patreon: Patreon.com/AlexandriaCainlocke

ACKNOWLEDGEMENTS

For starters, this book went a heck of a lot smoother than Kingdom of Nyte, but it certainly had its ups and downs along the way. I was absolutely blown away by all the love and support from friends, family, and new readers for my debut novel, Kingdom of Nyte, and how excited people are for the next installment. No matter how many rewrites, revisions, or total redoes I've gone through during the writing process, there's always that fear that others won't enjoy the story as much as I do, but I couldn't have been more wrong.

I wanted to again thank my amazing editor Alexandra Ott for polishing and making this story shine. With her crazy attention to detail and professional feedback, this book has really grown and improved from its earlier drafts. So happy I got to work with you again for the second book in this series.

To everyone at Enchanted Ink Publishing who helped bring this series to life so far, through the beautiful cover and interior designs, thank you all so much! I always had a vision for this series in my head, but you all really took that to a level I could never have even imagined.

To my family, whose words of encouragement and constant love have been my saving grace more times than I can count. Don't know what I'd do without you all.

To my friends who occasionally pull me out of the house to see the light of day and lift my spirits up, my life would be a lot emptier without you all. Thanks again for all your support, and to Kat for buying enough of my books to start her own bookstore.

And to Matt, thank you for always being there and listening to my incoherent ramblings. I'm glad to have you by my side.

ALEXANDRIA CAINLOCKE is a toss-up between artist, musician, writer, and avid gamer. Coffee is her number one life source and second love to her amazing friends and family. The sunshine state of Florida is where she was born and still resides.

9 781735 270449